Sierra Fall

By Martha O'Sullivan

ISBN: 978-1-7367667-4-3

Sierra Fall by Martha O'Sullivan

Cover and Formatting by coversbykaren.com

To never giving up

ABOUT THE AUTHOR

Martha O'Sullivan has loved reading romance novels for as long as she can remember. Writing her own books is the realization of a lifelong dream. She is a graduate of Illinois State University where she wrote for *The Daily Vidette* and was a member of Zeta Tau Alpha. She is also a former Acquisitions Editor at MacMillan Computer Publishing. Martha writes contemporary romances with male/female couples and happy endings. Her *Chances Trilogy—Second Chance, Chance Encounter and Last Chance*—and fourth novel *Christmas in Tahoe*, are available in print and digital formats at online retailers everywhere. A native Chicagoan, she lives her own happy ending in Florida with her husband and daughters.

Please visit marthaosullivan.com to learn more.

CONTENTS

PROLOGUE

The news had been a shock to say the least, but the gossamer, cocoon-like brume that followed had been a bittersweet blessing, a double-edged sword. A seductive, insidious blanket that swaddled Mackenzie Bishop and held her tight, then cruelly and indiscriminately released her with no respect for time or place. And as that fog lifted, reality set in.

She was a widow.

She'd gotten word in the middle of the night and had initially convinced herself it was just a bad dream. So much so that she forced herself to go back to sleep so she could wake up again to prove it. But when she did Kenzie found herself trapped in a nightmare that would become her new normal. And the worst was yet to come.

Telling the kids.

Emma had rushed over, seeing the lights burning in the kitchen in the wee hours of the morning, knowing something was wrong. Knowing it had to be bad, so bad that Kenzie, frozen in the inertia of disbelief, hadn't called her. Knowing it could just as easily be her standing half-dressed and shell-shocked in her kitchen, falling into Kenzie's arms as gut-wrenching sobs consumed her.

Kenzie couldn't think straight, let alone put a sentence together, so Emma sprung into action. She called Kenzie's mother, less than two hours way in Palm

Springs. Jay and Sheryl Scott made it to Twentynine Palms before the sun came up. And more importantly, before the kids woke up.

She went through the motions on autopilot—the service, the luncheon, the Honors Ceremony. Whenever reality tried to rear its ugly head, Kenzie traded it for denial. Matt was deployed. One of those missions where he was out of touch for weeks at a time. If something happened, she'd know.

But she did know.

A routine training exercise had taken Matt away from them forever. It was ludicrous, really. He was only two states away, not flighting on some foreign battlefield. He was coming home in time for the Spring Fling at school next weekend.

But he didn't.

CHAPTER ONE

"I've got it," Kenzie told her mother, grabbing the laundry basket filled with pool toys and shoving it into the back of her SUV.

Sheryl Scott sent her daughter a pointed look over the rim of her sunglasses. "I'm just as capable of loading the trunk of a car today as I was last week."

"I know," Kenzie replied, shutting the tailgate. "But there's no sense in pushing it." She'd heard from friends with older parents what a difference there was between your sixties and your seventies. "I don't want you to strain your back."

"My back is fine, same as it was before my birthday," Sheryl maintained, tipping her head toward the storage unit. "That's the last of it, right?"

"Yeah."

"All right, let's turn in the paperwork and get over to the house. It won't take the movers long to unload. I'll start making up the beds in case you guys want to sleep there tonight."

Nodding, Kenzie agreed with a hug. "Thanks, Mom."

"Of course."

Sheryl started to pull away, but Kenzie wasn't ready to let go. She tightened her grip on her mother. "I mean for everything. I couldn't have made it through the last year without you." Technically, the last fourteen months, three weeks, four days and ten hours, Kenzie inwardly amended.

Sheryl gave her daughter one last squeeze before easing back. Tears were brimming in her whiskey-colored eyes now. "You might be forty, but you're still my little girl. I'd give anything for there to be nothing for you to thank me for."

Kenzie swallowed hard. Her parents had loved Matt like a son. "Me, too."

On a sad smile, Sheryl cradled Kenzie's face in her hands. "Everything is going to be all right. Remember there are no endings, only new beginnings. And today is another new beginning. A fresh start, a new home. Where you and the kids will make new memories to walk along side the old ones."

Kenzie bit back the lump growing in her throat. "I know."

"I didn't think I could be any prouder of you than I was, but you keep raising the bar."

That forced a smile out of Kenzie. "Prouder than you are of McGovern?" she asked, speaking of her brother.

"Absolutely. But I'll deny it if you repeat that."

"Why? You tell him the same thing."

"True," Sheryl admitted around a laugh. Then she dropped her hands to her daughter's shoulders. "Ready?"

"Yeah," Kenzie replied on a sigh, taking in the empty storage unit that had held most of her worldly belongings for the past year. "I'm ready."

"Then let's get a move on it. Dad can pick up the kids after school and bring them to the house. They haven't seen their new rooms painted yet. Then he can take them out for ice cream or something while we dig in. I'm in no hurry for you to move out, but it's probably best to get them settled over the weekend. That way they'll have the last few weeks of school in the new house, maybe meet some kids in the neighborhood before summer break sends everyone their separate ways."

Kenzie looked back to her mother in stunned reverence. The thought of meeting kids in the new neighborhood before school got out would never have occurred to her. "Mom, you think of everything."

"Once a teacher, always a teacher," Sheryl said, sliding her hands down Kenzie's arms and giving hers a supportive squeeze before letting go.

They drove up to the rental office and relinquished the storage unit. When they arrived at the new house twenty minutes later the movers were just starting to unload. Jay Scott greeted them with a big smile and a hearty wave.

"Perfect timing. They just finished prepping the inside. I took their lunch orders—they want burgers. I'll handle that while you guys manage things here. I'll bring something back for us too."

"Thanks, Dad. You're the best."

"Wish I could do more, but it's not worth the lecture I'd get about my heart." Jay sent his wife a measured look from under raised eyebrows.

"Not to mention the one you'd get from the cardiologist," Sheryl replied cheekily.

"That too. I'll be back in an hour or so. Text me if you think of anything you need while I'm out."

Jay took his leave and the women went inside. While Sheryl spoke with the movers, Kenzie stood in the foyer of her new home and took stock. The house was exactly what she'd been looking for and she'd jumped on it right away. The market in Reno was hot and she'd lost two houses to higher bidders. She'd offered over asking for this listing and as luck would have it, just enough to tip the scales in her favor.

She'd loved the feel of this neighborhood right away. Lots of young families, a community pool down the street and close to shopping and restaurants but not so close that traffic was an issue. And most importantly, it was in the same school district as her parents' neighborhood so the kids wouldn't have to change schools again. Fate, her mother had said. But since fate had not been kind to Kenzie lately, she preferred to stick with luck. Luck, she decided with a wistful smile, had proven to be much more providential.

She'd met Matt at a wedding neither one of them were invited to. Kenzie was in San Diego visiting a college friend and her flight home had been cancelled. Unable to get out until the following night, she went back to Jory's apartment. Jory was attending her cousin's wedding later that day and insisted Kenzie be her plus-one. Kenzie initially resisted—she didn't have a dress, she wouldn't know anyone, she'd gotten up at the crack of dawn for her flight and would be fine calling it an early night. But Jory wouldn't take no for answer. She had a closet full of dresses to lend her, Kenzie knew Jory's family from school visits and it was an afternoon wedding with a reception immediately following. They'd be home by nine. So Kenzie, fresh out of excuses, acquiesced.

Matt, stationed at Camp Pendleton at the time, was at the wedding as the date of a friend's girlfriend's sister. She and her boyfriend had just broken up and she didn't want to go to the wedding alone. Matt, off duty and at loose ends for the weekend, had no reason not to accept the invitation. To say he and his date didn't hit it off would be a gross understatement. She'd gotten drunk and spent most of the reception crying in the bathroom. Bored, Matt struck up a conversation with one of the bartenders. He'd noticed Kenzie from across the room, but assumed she was with a date. When she showed up at the bar alone, Matt wasted no time introducing himself. They ended up talking for the rest of the night. He called her the next morning and asked her to dinner before her flight home.

Kenzie knew that night there was something different about him, about how she felt around him. It was unlike anything she'd experienced before. Their first kiss was a kiss good-bye at the airport. But the flutter in her stomach, the stirring in her chest, told her it wouldn't be their last. And that kiss ended up being her last first kiss. She visited him two weeks later and knew the moment she was in his arms again that he was the one. He would be her husband, her children's father, her soulmate, the love of her life. And later Matt would tell her it was the same for him. They married the following year ahead of his first overseas assignment.

They saw the world together through two overseas tours and the travel opportunities they provided. But other than those early years and a stint in North Carolina, they'd been fortunate enough to be stationed in California for the majority of their marriage, including when both kids were born. Not too far from Kenzie's native Reno and even closer to Palm Springs where her parents spent the winter. Matt was from a multigenerational military family and had lived all over the world, but considered Southern California home. He'd lost both his parents in recent years and his younger brother, also a Marine, was stationed in Virginia. Once Kenzie had gotten her wits about her that fateful day, Mick had been her first call. She'd wanted to get to him before the grapevine did.

"Kenz, the movers need to know where you want the couches." Sheryl's voice drew Kenzie out of her reminiscence. "I'm assuming one against the wall and one floating between the kitchen and family room?"

Kenzie shook off the reverie. "Yeah, but they aren't interchangeable. One is more worn than the other. I'll be right there." She wiped a tear from the corner of her eye and took an emboldening breath. If she could get through the last fourteen months, surely she could figure out which couch went where. And everything that came after that.

*****

Brennen Banks killed people for a living. And as is often true of things we love, he was good at it. But the best part about it, aside from the inordinate amount of money he made doing it, was that nobody knew. It was his little secret. Well, his mother knew. But she wasn't going to tell anybody. She liked her swanky condo with the sporty two-seater parked in the garage. All courtesy of her favorite son and only child, the greatest thriller writer who never was.

Some people would deem him a sellout, but Bren considered himself an entrepreneur, a visionary, a pragmatist. Someone who knew when to fold 'em. Someone who'd accepted that the time had come to throw in the towel and reconcile fantasy with reality. Someone who was smart enough to surrender a lifelong dream and instead live vicariously through that of someone else.

Handsomely.

Bren had loved sports growing up. It had been an outlet for his boundless energy, a channel for his unrelenting competitiveness and had served as a coping mechanism for not having a father in his life. He'd been a natural at baseball since the first time a bat was put in his hand, could snatch a football out of the air with his eyes closed and make an alley-oop look like a cakewalk. But unlike most of his teammates, his passion for reading was just as voracious as his passion to win. And from an early age, Bren had seen no reason why he couldn't combine the two things he loved most into a career.

But he learned the hard way that does not a professional writer make. He'd held his own as the sports editor of his high school newspaper and yearbook, managing editor of his college paper and as an intern at a prestigious L.A. publication for two college summers. But as much as he loved sports and writing about them, Bren wanted to write thrillers. He'd read everything from Encyclopedia Brown to Jason Bourne to Jack Ryan. He'd seen every James Bond movie at least ten times. He'd even created a character of his own, the ideal combination of every protagonist he'd ever read about and had written a series about him and his right-hand man. A larger than life do-gooder and his loyal wingman who, against all odds, manage to leave the world a better place than they'd found it. He'd sell millions of copies, sign over his movie rights and live happily ever after writing his next novel from his yacht with his beautiful wife and two perfect children.

Or not.

Instead, Bren found himself rejected time and time again. He'd been told he had talent, ingenuity, potential. But it just wasn't what Joe Publisher or Jane Agent was looking for right now. Not to mention the litany of challenges facing the publishing industry in recent decades. The self-publishing revolution, the onslaught of digital piracy and the contraction of traditional sales channels had left Bren teetering on the edge of a brave new world without a parachute. And deeply in debt.

Those student loans weren't going to pay themselves off.

So he'd had little choice but to take freelance work. What started as copy editing evolved into reworking storylines, creating subplots and layering characters before he knew it. And that had not gone unnoticed by the literary agency representing an aging thriller writer who shall remain nameless.

Otherwise Bren would have to do what he did best.

And since he'd been doing that for the last ten hours, Bren decided it was time for a beer. He was on track to beat the deadline for his latest project and was thinking about taking a staycation after it was done. Spring had come early to the Sierra and thanks to a record-breaking snowpack, everything from skiing to rafting to kayaking was his for the taking. It would be shoulder season until Memorial Day so the locals would have the basin to themselves. And Bren intended to take full advantage of it.

He could live anywhere in the world but chose to live here among the soaring pines and pristine waters of Lake Tahoe. He loved the seasons, the way the lake bore patient witness to them, never freezing, never warming, always stalwart and undaunted. He loved how the snowcapped peaks stood in perfect relief to the blinding blue sky in winter, the way the meadows came alive with the lushness of spring, the wall-to-wall sunshine of summer and the colorful reckoning of fall.

But his mother not so much, which is why he'd set her up in a retirement community in Scottsdale where she could want for nothing. In his mind it was the least he could do. She'd raised him alone, rarely thinking of herself, while never ceasing to remind him that he was the best thing that had ever happened to her, her life's greatest gift. However unexpectedly that gift had been bestowed.

Bren knew little to nothing about his father and suspected that was by design. He'd had moments of childhood curiosity and confusion, followed by others of resentment and anger. His mother had always answered his questions honestly, thoughtfully and succinctly. She and his father had dated for several months during which time she'd discovered she was pregnant. He was not interested in being a father and had offered financial assistance to put the matter to rest. She, however, was interested in being a mother and in so doing ended their relationship. She'd listed father as unknown on Bren's birth certificate and to his knowledge had never heard from him again. She'd made her peace with that and over time Bren had as well. He'd gotten the impression that his father had been older, perhaps even married with a family. His mother had been a second grade teacher and his grandmother had taken care of him until he was old enough to go to school himself.

They'd had adventures every summer, spending a few days in Tahoe, a day or two in San Francisco, sometimes driving up the coast from Sacramento to Crescent City or down to San Diego. Mom was a trooper, coordinating their trips around Giants games whenever she could, scheduling ballpark tours when she couldn't and taking him camping in Big Sur one summer and Yosemite the next. But something about Tahoe stayed with him, became a part of his soul, wove itself into the fabric of his being. By his second visit Bren promised himself a place here someday. Where he could wake up in the morning to the sun rising from behind the rugged mountain peaks and wind down at night to the alpenglow setting the basin on fire. And that promise was second only to the one he'd made to always take care of his mother. Bren had made good on both of those promises and then some. But the one thing he hadn't counted on was finding himself alone.

He'd always assumed he'd get married, have a family. Not to any woman in particular and without much thought to a timeline but eventually, someday.

He hadn't given it much thought again until lately, but something about turning forty last year had brought it top of mind. Sometimes when he grabbed a beer to watch the sunset Bren wondered what it would be like to have someone to share it with. Someone to run dinner ideas by, someone to ask about their day and relay the highlights of his, someone to plan a vacation or a holiday celebration with. Maybe even someone to watch play baseball or help with homework. A partner, a family. The family he'd never had despite how hard his mother had tried to check all the boxes—mother, father, sibling. There was always something missing and that something eluded him still. He couldn't help but wonder if it always would.

When Bren was out here on the deck he felt like he was on top of the world. And in some ways he was, nestled high in the hills among the towering conifers and leafy aspens. The evening was warm and clear and he could almost make out the tortuous paths of the ski runs on the mountainsides across the lake. The snow was melting more each day, revealing the high desert terrain and craggy switchbacks for which the Sierra Nevada is known. Soon the lake would be punctuated with boats and jet skis from sunrise to sunset, but for now it was still except for the crashing of the waves in the evening wind. Of course Bren couldn't hear the waves from his mid-mountain elevation but their euphonious symphony played in his head at will, forever ingrained in his memory.

Bren remembered his first visit to Tahoe all those years ago like it was yesterday. They'd pulled over just past the fork in the road where the lake first comes into view, peeking through the gaps in the trees. He'd dropped his mother's hand and ran to the water's edge, then looked back at her. She'd nodded in silent permission and within an instant the cool water covered his shoes and spit spindrift on his ankles. The sun's rays bounced off the sharp crests of the waves like millions of tiny diamonds glittering under a cobalt blue haze. And that was it. He was hooked.

It had taken him a couple of decades, but Bren owned his own piece of Tahoe now. Where the crimson sun burst through the charcoal dim of the mountains in the morning. Where the air carried the sweet scent of pine straw and was so fresh and crisp it snapped. Where the star-studded night sky guarded the lake and cradled the basin as he slept. Where he had the privilege to live.

Alone, Bren reminded himself and took a deep pull from the bottle. But alone or not, he had to eat. He'd scarfed down some leftover pizza around noon, all that his refrigerator had to offer. It would probably do him good to get out a little. He hadn't been to town in a few days. He rubbed his hand under his chin. Or shaved. Or checked the mail. He could have a couple of beers and a decent meal, then hit the grocery store on his way home.

Standing, Bren took in the view one more time. The top of the sun was barely visible now, its dwindling light painting the sky in soft pinks and vibrant oranges. If he timed it right, his drive down the mountain would be alight with stars. And that, Bren decided finishing the last of his beer, made secretly killing people for a living all that much more worth it. Even if he had to do it alone.

CHAPTER TWO

Kenzie loved the house. The rooms were bright and airy, her furniture fit perfectly and the few things she needed would come in time. She'd had the interior painted before they moved in and had spent the last two days setting up the kids' rooms. Katie had chosen a warm pink for hers and they'd picked out a new comforter and curtains to complement it. Typical of a nine-year-old boy, Mattie couldn't care less about how his room was decorated. Since she anticipated living here for the foreseeable future, Kenzie had gone with a sage green that would take him into adolescence. For the remainder of the house she'd gone with neutral hues, allowing the furnishings to do the heavy lifting.

The kids hadn't seen some of their things in almost a year and Kenzie was excited for them to see their new rooms unpacked and organized. They'd stayed with her parents last night, leaving her alone in the house. She couldn't remember the last time she'd spent the night alone. Definitely before Katie was born almost twelve years ago. She'd been too exhausted last night to think much about it, but now it gave her pause. Next year Katie would be in middle school, where sleepovers were a rite of passage. And Mattie was already talking about baseball camp. So she'd better get used to spending the night alone.

She also needed to think about getting a job. She'd gotten her degree from USC in Marketing and had worked for a healthcare company before marrying Matt and moving abroad. Katie had come along before she knew it and Mattie two years later. She'd been a stay-at-home mom since Katie was born. In addition to the military death benefit, they'd carried private life insurance for Matt and had owned their home in Twentynine Palms, on which Kenzie made a good profit when she sold it last summer. That, along with living with her parents for the last year, had provided a substantial down payment and a respectable nest egg. But she needed steady income for the long-term and had been considering getting her teaching certificate. That way she would have the same schedule as the kids and be available to take them to after-school activities and be home for dinner and homework every night.

She fluffed the throw pillows she'd arranged on Katie's bed and moved on to Mattie's room. She gave herself a moment to take it in; it wouldn't be this neat and clean for long. But that was what a house was for, to be lived in. To eat and sleep and play in, to laugh and cry in. And, as her mother said, to make new memories in. That was what Matt would have wanted and what Kenzie intended to do. She'd come this far and there wasn't any more room for half-measures now than there had been fourteen months, three weeks, six days and, she glanced at her watch, fifteen hours ago.

Kenzie walked down the hallway to her room. She'd unpacked a bit in her bathroom, wiping out drawers and starting to organize her cosmetics and supplies, but there were still boxes everywhere. It had occurred to her last night that although this wasn't the first time she'd settled them into a house by herself, it was the first time she was moving into one without Matt. There was no one else to keep in mind when choosing a side of the bed or a section of the closet or a drawer in the bathroom. Not that Matt had given much thought to those things, but it seemed odd not to have someone else to consider. And everything in the bedroom and bathroom was hers. One more thing she'd have to get used to.

Sounds of entry pulled Kenzie our of her musings. She made it to the kitchen seconds before her parents and the kids burst in from the garage.

"Mom! Look! We got pizza for dinner *and* doughnuts for breakfast!" Mattie exclaimed. "It's a special occasion because it's our first school day in our new house!"

"Wow! That was awfully nice of Grandma and Grandpa." She gave his sandy brown hair a loving tousle.

"And Grandpa and Mattie went mini-golfing while Grandma and I got manicures!" Katie chimed in, proudly displaying her shiny pink nails.

"So pretty!" Kenzie complimented, giving Katie a side hug.

"Grandma said next time all three of us will get manicures. We'll have a girls' day."

"Sounds fun." She looked at her mother. "Thanks, Mom."

"Sure."

"Kenz, where do you want the pizzas?" Jay wanted to know.

"Just there on the island is fine, Dad. Put the doughnuts in the pantry, though. Out of sight, out of mind."

"Got it." So saying, Jay obliged.

"It looks great in here, honey," Sheryl commended. "You've made a lot of progress."

"Thanks. I was up early, back at it," Kenzie replied, turning to her children. "You guys ready to see your rooms?"

"Yeah!"

"All right, let's have a look and then we'll eat."

"Don't worry, we picked up wine too," Sheryl told Kenzie under her breath as they walked out of the kitchen.

"Thank God."

The kids loved their rooms, especially Katie. Mattie was more excited about seeing his baseball trophies again. Then they ate pizza off paper plates out on the deck. The night was balmy and the backyard was bursting with buds and blooms. Kenzie had decided to continue the lawn service the previous owner used and Sheryl had volunteered to help with the gardening.

"Let's see what comes up and go from there," Sheryl suggested.

Kenzie nodded in agreement. It was just the two of them finishing their wine at the deck table. Jay was playing catch with Mattie out front and Katie had gone inside to pick out her outfit for tomorrow. "Thanks again for keeping the kids overnight and entertaining them today."

"Thank you for letting us. We'll have to get used to it being just the two of us again. We're going to miss you guys."

"We'll only be fifteen minutes away. My first apartment after college was farther away from your house."

"I know. But I was used to you being gone then. It's been nice this last year, being able to see you and the kids every day, be a part of your routine. I'll treasure that time always."

Kenzie laid a grateful hand on her mother's arm. "Mom, I can't thank you enough. I don't know how I—"

"Then stop trying so hard," Sheryl gently admonished, cutting her off. "I won't say it was my pleasure because under the circumstances it wasn't. But Dad and I were glad to be there for you, glad to help. And we always will, until our last breath," she finished through a watery smile.

Choking back tears, Kenzie returned the smile.

"Besides, the kids keep me young. And unless McGovern and Laurel get on the stick, your two might be all I get."

"They've only been married for two years. And Laurel's book just came out. Maybe now with the launch behind them they'll start thinking about it."

"I hope so. I know Veronica is anxious too," Sheryl added, referring to Laurel's mother. "But they're still trying to strike a balance between living here and in L.A."

"I told him we'd take care of Boot when they go to Maui."

"That's nice of you."

"It's more self-serving than anything," Kenzie replied with a shrug. "It buys me time before making good on my promise to get a dog since we have our own house again. And we get to stay at their place in Incline. The kids will love it up at the lake. It's a win-win."

"I'll say. It gets me out of dog sitting duties. Even at his ripe old age, Boot can be a bundle of energy."

"Yellow Labs are usually calmer than their chocolate or black counterparts, but leave it to my brother to find the exception."

"Been researching?"

"A bit. But Labs are rarely up for adoption. I'm trying to go that route."

"Speaking of going, we'd better head out," Sheryl said, standing and throwing the plates and napkins into the empty pizza box. "You guys have school tomorrow and Dad has a meeting first thing."

Kenzie stood and corked the wine bottle. "At the club?"

Sheryl nodded. "He's training the summer staff. He's looking forward to playing golf again and I'm looking forward to him working part-time again. It's good for each of us to have a little me time. Talk about a win-win."

Kenzie walked her parents out and got the kids showered and into bed. Afterward she had every intention of working in the kitchen. She wanted to unpack a few more boxes and needed to make lunches for tomorrow. But instead, she found herself standing at the kitchen sink staring out the window. The night held clear and quiet and a scattering of stars spanned the sky. She'd had the window open to the spring day and now she could hear the rustlings of wildlife and the melodious call of an owl. She'd forgotten what a miraculous time of year spring was. The air was so fragrant and fresh, the world so full of life and growth. It'd been years since she'd experienced all four seasons.

In the first days and weeks after Matt's death, Kenzie had trouble sleeping. She'd been bone-tired, but just couldn't settle. It wasn't that she wasn't used to sleeping alone; Matt was often gone more than he was home. But it was as if her body, as much as her mind, knew this was different. Matt wasn't deployed or out-of-town. He was gone forever.

She'd been told insomnia was normal, a natural reaction to grief and the stress and shock she'd experienced. Her doctor had prescribed a sleep aid but she never took it. She wanted to be alert in case the kids needed her in the night. She'd tried a couple glasses of wine to take the edge off, but that hadn't helped. And when she did manage to drift off, she'd have the same horrible dream over and over again. She'd wake up startled, her breathing labored, her skin clammy.

But it was more like déjà vu than dream because it had actually happened.

The night before Matt left they'd fought. They didn't fight often, but when they did it was usually a doozy. And this one was no exception. Kenzie knew better than to start something the night before a mission, even if it was just training. Soldiers were taught to treat training exercises as life-or-death situations or there was no point to them. But this trip had been unexpected. Matt was supposed to be home for a year, maybe even two. And by then he would have his twenty years in and could retire.

Kenzie knew Matt was getting restless with the base assignment, but that wasn't the root of the problem. Retirement was the last thing on his mind. Matt wanted to be a colonel like his father. But Kenzie was tired. Tired of the deployments, resentful of the idea of moving again, exhausted from the never-ending worry of what could happen next. And they had to start thinking long-term. High school was just around the corner for Katie and Mattie needed get established with a baseball team.

But the service was in Matt's blood. He'd grown up all over the world and saw nothing wrong with that. In fact, he thought it made for a more well-rounded childhood. But the world was not what it used to be and Kenzie didn't want to live overseas again. She also didn't want Matt to be gone for months at a time. The only way to ensure that neither happened was for him to declare a target separation date and start the preretirement process, something he refused to do. So when this training assignment came from out of the blue, Kenzie used it as an example of the uncertainty with which they lived. And Matt reminded her that she'd known what she was getting into. He wasn't going to be home every night for dinner like her father had been. And she'd countered with the fact that she'd been supportive all these years, but they'd never agreed he'd be career military. To which he'd pointed out that he'd never said he'd only do twenty. And she'd maintained that they'd also never agreed he'd do forty like his father. The moment the words left her mouth Kenzie regretted them. Matt's father hadn't been gone for long at that point.

The conversation ended there and resulted in Matt sleeping on the couch. Kenzie set her alarm for five as not to miss him in the morning. When she got out to the kitchen, he handed her a cup of coffee and told her he loved her with a kiss on the cheek. She returned the sentiment and he walked out the door. That was the last time she saw him. Except, of course, in her recurring dream.

She'd taken advantage of the grief counseling offered to military spouses and it had been somewhat helpful. The counselor had pointed out that the last thing they'd said to each other was I love you. Kenzie tried to remember that and eventually sleep started to come easier. Whenever that dream started to play in her mind, she tried to replace it with that morning and their last words to each other. But she still felt guilty. She'd never told anyone but Emma about the fight that last night. Emma understood; she was in a similar situation with her husband. But the difference was John was still alive.

Kenzie still thought about Matt every day, just not every second of every day. In fact, sometimes she saw him more in her dreams than in her mind's eye. And that made her feel guilty in an entirely different way. She couldn't imagine being with another man, being touched by someone else. She and Matt had had an active sex life and Kenzie felt guilty about missing that too. This was the longest she'd gone without having sex since she started having sex in college. She'd been with two men before Matt, but the intimacy she and Matt shared had been different, so visceral and innate. And, like finding your soulmate, that kind of sexual connection only happens once in a lifetime. So she'd might as well get used to living without that too.

CHAPTER THREE

The last weeks of school were a whirlwind. Homework was minimal, but there was a fifth grade field trip for Katie and a baseball tournament for Mattie. Kenzie woke up each morning raring to go and often stayed up late checking off her to-do list. She wanted to feel settled in the house so she could relax and enjoy the summer with the kids.

Spring had come early to the valley but it didn't stick around for long. The days grew long and hot, ushering in all things summer. Katie met some new friends at the pool and Mattie made the AAA Little League team. Between the kids and the house, Kenzie could hardly catch her breath. But she loved it.

June folded into July and the next thing she knew it was time to head up to the lake. Baseball was on hiatus and everyone was looking forward to a change of scenery. Kenzie grew nostalgic as she drove up the mountain to Incline Village. She'd spent many summers here when she was growing up and was excited to share Tahoe with her children. She'd brought them here once or twice over the years, but not recently and never for any length of time. Her brother and sister-in-law would be gone for almost a month, so they'd have plenty of time to experience Tahoe as locals.

"Look guys, there's the lake!" Kenzie said as they rounded the curve on Lakeshore Boulevard. This had been her favorite part of the drive when she was a girl.

"It's so blue!" Katie exclaimed.

"I know! What do you think, Mattie?"

"It's okay, I guess. How come there's snow on the other side but not here?"

"That's a good question," Kenzie replied. "It's because we can see the top of the mountains on the other side of the lake. There's snow on the peaks on this side too, up higher."

He thought about that for a moment. "Then can we go up higher on this side? Boot likes snow."

"Maybe."

"I'm sick of snow," Katie protested. "I want to go to the beach."

"We'll do that too."

"The beach is boring," Mattie groaned.

There wasn't time for further debate because they turned into to her brother's subdivision and headed up into the hills. The quiet, well-kept neighborhood was made up of mid-century and half-timber homes built on generous, wooded lots. Boot greeted them enthusiastically at the door and ran around in the front yard while they unloaded the car. Kenzie had already decided, despite her sister-in-law's insistence to the contrary, that she and Katie would share the guest room and Mattie would take the third bedroom with the twin bed. No way was Kenzie sleeping in her brother's bed.

Once they got settled, Kenzie fulfilled her promise of the beach for Katie. Then they grabbed Boot, picked up subs for dinner and headed to the dog park. The park paralleled the lake and was surrounded by a split-rail fence reinforced with clear panels to prevent escapes without obstructing the view. The evening was clear and temperate, the breeze woodsy and sweet. It took her back thirty years to summer days when she didn't have a care in the world. What a wonderful gift her parents had given her with those memories. As she watched the kids play fetch with Boot, she pledged to do the same for them. Lost in thought, Kenzie jumped when she heard a voice behind her.

"I'm sorry. I didn't mean to startle you. I was just wondering if the anyone was sitting here?"

Kenzie looked up at the man attached to the voice, standing at the far end of the picnic table. He had dark, smiling eyes under expressive brows and a tentative expression on his square, angular face. He was wearing a San Francisco Giants baseball cap and carrying a small pizza box and a water bottle.

"What? Oh, no," Kenzie stammered. "Please, be my guest." She gestured with open palm.

"Thanks," he said, swinging his long, denim-clad legs over the bench and sitting down. "It's crowded tonight, even with the Fourth behind us."

"I'll have to take your word on that," she returned with a smile.

"On vacation?" he asked, opening the water bottle and taking a swig.

"Sort of. Dog sitting."

"Got it," he said with a nod. His wavy, nut-brown hair matched his eyes and was peppered with touches of gray at the temples. Kenzie wondered how it would feel to run her fingers through it. She sucked in a breath. What the hell was wrong with her? Mortified, she turned her attention back to the kids.

"Wow. That kid has an arm."

Kenzie glanced down the table, then followed the man's line of sight to Mattie. "So I'm told."

He swallowed a bite of pizza and wiping his mouth with a napkin, turned to her. "Is that your son?"

"It is," she told him proudly.

"Can he hit?"

"Yes, but he'd rather be fielding."

"Let me guess. He pulls a little to the left."

Kenzie felt her jaw drop. "How'd you know that?"

"For starters, he's right-handed," the man replied, his stare settling on Mattie again. "He's light on his feet, agile as a cat." He found her gaze again. "Shortstop?"

"Defensive," she affirmed.

"For now. Give him a couple of years. You could have a Cal Ripken Jr. or a Derek Jeter on your hands."

"They are some of his favorite players."

"He keeps good company. I was a big Will Clark fan myself. Even after he went to Texas."

"That makes sense," Kenzie said, nodding to his hat.

He seemed to have forgotten he was wearing one. "Oh, right. Giants fan?"

Kenzie shrugged. "My dad and brother didn't really give me another choice."

"Good training for a future baseball mom," he remarked with a grin.

"True." God, he had the cutest dimples. And could his jawline be any more chiseled? Her eyes clung to his for a long moment. They were a deep chocolate brown dappled with flecks of gold and had a smokiness about them. They danced a little as they held hers. Kenzie felt her pulse begin to race. She was taking an overdue breath when the kids and Boot appeared. She hadn't even heard them come up.

"Mom, the ball went over the fence," Mattie stated. "Can I go get it?'

"Ah, sure. Go together. You'll have to go out the front and walk around. Boot can stay with me." Kenzie watched them run off, petting the dog's head as he sat panting beside her. "I think you need some water, big guy." She reached into her bag and pulled out a collapsable bowl and a water bottle. She filled it and set it on the ground. Boot lapped some up, then shook before moseying over to the end of the picnic table and cozying up to her tablemate.

"Hey, Boot. I thought that was you, buddy."

Kenzie looked on as the man used his large, dexterous hands to give Boot a rubdown. Appalled to find herself envious, she cleared her throat. "You know Boot?"

"Oh, yeah. We're old friends. Where's Gov tonight?"

Kenzie wasn't sure how much to tell him or how well he knew her brother, but she went with her gut. "He's on his honeymoon."

"Well, it's about time."

"I'll say. But my brother isn't one to stand on ceremony. No pun intended."

"Gov's your brother?" he astonished, meeting her gaze again.

Nodding, she gave him a knowing smile.

"No way! He and I have a mutual friend."

"Let me guess. Mac."

"How'd you know?"

"Because Mac knows everybody around here, thus so does Gov."

"True. They seem pretty tight. In a friend/uncle/big brother kind of way."

"That's a good way to put it."

"So you're Gov's sister."

"That I am."

"I honestly don't see any resemblance."

"Thank you," she said with laugh. "Actually, I favor our father other than in the height department. McGovern got all of that."

"McGovern. That's funny." Standing, he walked over to her and offered his hand. "I'm Bren. Nice to meet you."

"Mackenzie." She stood and took his hand as Boot joined them. "Nice to meet you too, Bren." His handshake was firm and confident, but not overbearing. And her hand fit his like a glove. She swallowed hard. "McGovern was my mother's maiden name."

He didn't respond at first, just kept those rich, soulful eyes glued to hers. Finally, he nodded saying,

"Right. I just never think of him as anything other than Gov."

"I don't think he does much anymore either."

"How's your sister?" Bren asked, releasing her hand.

"My sister?"

"Gov had a sister who lost her husband in an accident of some sort. How's she doing?"

Pressing her lips together, Kenzie looked away for a moment, then back to him. "She's doing okay."

"Gov was pretty torn up about it. Apparently he was a real good guy."

"Yeah, he was."

"Has to be at least a year ago now."

Sixteen months, five days and eighteen hours Kenzie silently estimated, glancing at the sun's position in the sky. "Your memory serves you well. It's been about a year and a half. She's getting back on her—" She was interrupted by the kids returning. Boot greeted them with a joyful bark.

"Hey, guys," she said as they came to a stop next to her. "This is a friend of Uncle Gov's, Mr.—" she stopped short. "I'm sorry, I didn't catch your last name."

"I don't think I gave it. Banks." He turned to the kids, extending his hand to Katie first. "Hi, I'm Bren."

"I'm Katie."

"Nice to meet you, Katie."

"You too," Katie returned politely.

He moved on to Mattie. "And you must be…"

Mattie gave Bren's hand an eager shake. "Matt."

"Since when?" Katie interjected. "Just call him Mattie," she told Bren. "He's just trying to be cool."

"Either is fine, Bren," Kenzie put in.

"Then I'll go with Matt. Nice to meet you, Matt. You've got quite an arm there."

"Thanks." He turned to his mother. "Can we play for a little while longer?"

"Just a few more minutes."

After the kids ran off with Boot, Bren commented, "Nice kids."

"Thanks."

"How old are they?"

"Katie is eleven and Mattie is nine," Kenzie told him, turning to straighten up the table. She'd already put the sub wrappers back in the bag, but she flattened and capped the water bottles. She was looking around for a garbage can when Bren stepped in.

"Here, let me get that." He took the trash from her, brushing his hand against hers in the process. Kenzie felt a rush go up her arm and settle in the pit of her stomach. She wondered if he felt it too because he froze momentarily before walking over to the Bear Box and disposing of the trash. Scolding herself, Kenzie turned her attention back to the kids. Behind them the sun was starting its lazy descent, bathing the basin in fiery vermillion light.

"It never gets old." Bren was standing next to her again, looking out over the water. "No matter how many times you see it."

She tucked the strands of hair blowing in her face behind her ear. "There's just something about the Tahoe sunset. Nowhere else compares."

"It's the indirect light reflecting off the clarity of the lake that creates the preternatural alpenglow," Bren commented as their eyes met. "And its unique, breathtaking beauty."

Kenzie nodded. Her heart was racing again. She was taking a couple of unsteady breaths when the kids returned with Boot.

"Can we go now?" Katie asked.

"Ah, yeah, it's getting dark anyway. Let's get Boot leashed up and grab his bowl."

"I'll walk out with you guys," Bren announced, grabbing his pizza box and water bottle from the far end of the table. They fell into step together and when they got to the parking lot realized they were parked next to each other. "What are the chances, huh?"

"Yeah," Kenzie seconded. "What a coincidence."

"How long are you guys taking care of Boot?" Bren asked as the kids and Boot piled into the car.

"About a month."

"Maybe I'll see you again then."

"Do you come here a lot in the evening?" Kenzie heard herself ask.

"When I feel like getting out a bit. It's more of a park that allows dogs than a dog park." He glanced over her shoulder at the lake. "And the view can't be beat."

Kenzie nodded in agreement. "I'm sure we'll be back. The kids seemed to enjoy it as much as Boot."

Their gaze lingered a bit until Bren said, "Well, take care. Tell Gov I say hey."

"Will do."

As Kenzie got into the car and drove away, the sun was slipping behind the mountains and darkness was falling over the lake. And she realized she was smiling to herself for the first time in sixteen months, five days and a little over eighteen hours. And she wasn't sure how she felt about it.

CHAPTER FOUR

Bren was curious by nature, a quality that came in handy as a writer. But perhaps the personality attribute that served him best was that he was observant. Plus he had a memory like an elephant. And he only remembered Gov having one sister.

Unfortunately, that revelation didn't strike him until after he'd gotten home. Specifically, when he was tossing and turning in bed trying to fall asleep. He'd put his foot squarely in his mouth. But who could blame him? He'd been more than a little starstruck.

He'd met McGovern Scott, Gov to most, a few years ago at Hues of Blue. The first time or two had been happenstance. They were each eating alone at the bar and struck up a conversation. Gov had recently moved back to town from the Bay Area and had taken a job at a construction company in Reno. Bren had been traveling quite a bit then and had just returned from Greece. He'd been writing a book with a storyline rooted in Greek mythology and had gone to the motherland to do some research. He'd spent a month there getting inspired and another two weeks *being* inspired by a real-life Greek goddess fresh off a divorce. And very, very happy to be single again.

He and Gov were both getting their bearings that summer and became friends. Gov eventually remodeled Bren's main level, a project that had displaced him for a few weeks while the crux of the work was being done.

Bren couldn't write with all the racket, so he'd taken up residence at Incline Villages's premier lodging establishment, which just happened to be home to Hues of Blue. Not only did the restaurant have the best lake views on the North Shore, it also had Mac, local legend and everyone's favorite bartender. And no one knows what's what like a bartender. Mac claimed he could write a book but why bother? He had Bren for that.

The night after Bren met Mackenzie at the park, he found himself craving the short rib risotto at Hues of Blue. Along with a side of information. He wasn't going to beat around the bush or go on a fishing expedition. He respected Mac too much for that. Besides, Mac wasn't one to break confidences or engage in idle gossip. But he was a discerning listener and could separate fact from fiction. And he was smart. Mac knew when to keep his mouth shut and when to share. And with whom to do the sharing.

Bren double-timed the steps leading down to the restaurant. The place was hopping, typical of a July night. He aimed his gait for the only vacant seat at the bar, the last stool near the computer station. Not the quietest of spots, but it offered the best of both worlds. It was next to the window wall but also provided a bird's-eye view of the restaurant and Bren liked to people watch. It was good for business.

He scooted the barstool over a bit, away from the nearest patron, and took a seat. He'd seen Mac at the opposite end of the bar when he walked in and they'd traded a silent greeting. Bren was retrieving his phone from his pocket when a cocktail napkin appeared in front of him.

"Hey, Bren. Start you off with the usual?"

"Thanks, Casey. You pinch-hitting behind the bar again tonight?"

"Looks that way. It's becoming the rule rather than the exception, which is fine with me. The tips are good and I've got another year of nursing school to go. And it's busier here than at the hostess stand. The night flies by."

"That's good. How's your dad?"

"He's recovering well," Casey answered, inputing Bren's order in the computer. "Thanks again for the book. It's helping pass the time. He's going a little crazy away from the course."

"Good to hear." Bren resisted the urge to ask her what Jimmy thought of it. It was some of his best work.

"It helps that I'm home for the summer and working the late shift."

"I'm sure. Open heart surgery is no joke. Even for our resident golf pro."

"You're telling me. I'll grab your beer and be right back."

"Thanks." Bren watched her retreating back for a moment, then swung around and took in the room. It was an hour until sunset, but people were already staking claim to the tables and couches near the windows. Others were gathering around the fire pit outside, vying for spots on the stone benches surrounding it. He really should set a book here—*Murder in the Jewel of the*

Sierra. Bren filed that away and turning back around, found Mac delivering his beer.

"Wow. To what do I owe the honor?"

Mac gave Bren a slow smile that narrowed his dark gray eyes and deepened the whiskers of time around them. "Gov's in Maui, so I guess that puts you at the top of the food chain."

"I heard."

Mac scanned the bar and finding everything under control, retuned to Bren. "On Boot duty?"

"Actually, I have another source of information."

Mac's eyes filled with intrigue and began to shine. "Usually that's me. Do tell."

"Does Gov have more than one sister?" Bren got right to the point, along with his Sierra Nevada.

"Not that I know of."

"So no."

"Someone crawl out of the woodwork?" Now Mac's eyes narrowed in suspicion. "Because I've known Jay and Sheryl for years and I can't imagine…"

"No. Nothing like that. I was at the park last night and I met Gov's sister and her kids. They're taking care of Boot while Gov and Laurel are out-of-town."

Mac nodded in recollection. "He made a pit stop in here the other night, said they were heading out. I'm surprised they didn't leave Boot in L.A. with Laurel's mother."

"Apparently the mountains were calling the old boy. Anyway, back to Gov's sister. She lost her husband, right?"

Mac started with a sad shake of the head, "Probably going on two years ago now. He was a Marine. It was a training accident. When I first heard about it, I didn't make the connection. But when Gov came in the next night it was written all over his face. The moment I saw him, I put two and two together."

"Did you know him?"

"I met him at Gov and Laurel's wedding. Kenzie moved away after she got married and they lived overseas for years at a time. They were stationed at Twentynine Palms when it happened. She and the kids moved to Reno after he died."

"Kenzie," Bren thought out loud. That rang a bell that Mackenzie had not. Bren mentally kicked himself for not connecting the dots in real time.

"How's she doing?" Mac asked. "I know Gov was trying to step in, fill the void. He took the boy to a couple of Aces games. Apparently he's a big baseball fan."

"He's going to *have* baseball fans," Bren told Mac. "The kid has an arm, among other talents."

"Must run in the family."

"His dad play?"

"I couldn't tell you. But Gov did in high school and college."

Bren nodded. He and Gov had traded war stories. "So has Gov been holding out on me to spare my feelings? Because this kid's a natural. Like Hall of Fame material."

"We both know Gov's not that humble." Looking down the bar Mac said, "I've got to make my rounds. Are you eating tonight or just fishing?"

Bren shot Mac a shrewd grin. "You know I really come in for the company. But I could eat."

Mac slapped a menu down on the bar with a look of mock irritation. "In that case, I'll try to be less charming. I'll check back with you."

Bren watched Mac walk away around a sip of beer. He didn't bother with the menu but instead grabbed his phone. He'd done some rudimentary research last night when he couldn't sleep, but had been consumed with work all day. He didn't know Mackenzie's married name, so he'd given Mackenzie Scott a shot on Facebook to no avail. There were plenty of profiles under that name, but none of them were the one he was looking for. The one with the piercing blue eyes, silky blonde hair and a bright smile. He'd actually felt his heart skip a beat when she smiled at him. Not the first time— that smile had been more perfunctory. But when he'd complimented her son's abilities, her smile had been genuine, natural, wholehearted. Her entire countenance had softened, lit up. Bren found it enchanting, alluring and incredibly sexy. Like the rest of her. Despite her claim to the contrary, she'd gotten her fair share of her father's height. Which paired nicely with her shapely legs, perky breasts and slender frame. Her toned arms were lightly freckled, her lips full and pouty. The thought of them against his sent a shiver of desire through him. With a suggestive moan, Bren took a deep pull of beer. He had a clear visual of her in his mind, but what he needed was a last name. He'd like to know more about her, her husband and his tragic death. He'd noticed she was wearing a wedding set, so for all ostensible purposes she was married. Bren wondered if that was conviction, habit or mindset.

It suddenly occurred to him that she hadn't corrected him, hadn't clarified that it was she who'd lost her husband. That seemed odd, not that Bren had any experience with such matters. He'd never been in a long-term relationship, let alone married. Maybe she didn't want to talk about it. After all, she barely knew him. Bren found himself wanting to change that and started contemplating how to go about it without being obvious or insensitive. He'd have to get creative. Fortunately, that was another one of his strong suits.

"Refill?" Mac asked, reappearing before him.

"Sure. And I'll take the short rib risotto when you have a chance."

"Will do." Mac slid a plastic card through the reader on the monitor, then used it to tap the screen a few times. He traded the menu for a placemat and roll-up and started to walk away.

"Do you know Mackenzie Scott's married name?"

Mac turned back and shot Bren a wary look from under one raised brow.

"We both know I'll figure it out eventually, but in the interest of time…"

"Bishop," Mac answered after a moment. "The boy is named after his father if that helps."

"It does," Bren replied, going back to his phone. He felt Mac's eyes on him as he started scrolling. He clicked on the third link, figuring it was credible since it was from a government website.

Lieutenant Colonel Matthew W. Bishop, 41, died last week during a routine training exercise. No further details are being released at this time pending a thorough investigation. A decorated Marine, Bishop was currently stationed at Twentynine Palms, CA. He is survived by his wife Mackenzie and two young children.

"That was short and sweet," Bren said, shifting his gaze back to Mac.

"They usually are. I don't think there's much to say. No foul play, no blame to place. Just an accident, a lapse in judgement, a blink of an eye at the wrong time. You can keep looking, but ten bucks says that's all you're going to find or—"

"Someone would have found it by now," Bren finished for him.

"Right. Dare I ask why the interest?"

"Just curious. With her being Gov's sister and all."

"Ah, right," Mac said with a knowing tip of the head. "And it doesn't hurt that she's easy on the eyes."

Bren drained his beer. "No rust on you."

"Tread lightly, my friend. We all have baggage, but she's saddling a heavy load."

"Maybe she could use a little help with the carry."

"Maybe," Mac conceded skeptically. "But I'd run it by Gov first, let him give you his take on the situation."

"Well, Gov's on his long-awaited honeymoon. One of the many perils of hitching your wagon to that of a writer."

"Takes one to know one. By the way, your writer," Mac made air quotes with his fingers, "friend was in last week. He must be summering in town."

"I have no idea who you're talking about," Bren replied. Mac had him more or less figured out but they amused each another occasionally by playing this little game of chicken. The writer in question had a place in Incline, a little farther up to the mountain from his own. "Celebrity sightings abound this time of year. No one knows that better than you."

"That I do," Mac said as Bren's dinner arrived. "Saved again. This time by the kitchen."

"Thanks for the info," Bren said gamely, unwrapping his napkin. "I really appreciate it."

"Don't get ahead of yourself here, Bren," Mac cautioned, switching out Bren's beer for a fresh one. "Don't unleash that wanton imagination of yours. That girl has been through enough."

Bren met Mac's gaze. His lips were pressed together in a firm line and his expression had grown staid. "I know," Bren returned. "The last thing I want to do is complicate her life. Or mine."

"There's no way around that for her. From what I understand she's just now getting back on her feet, figuratively and literally. And she has two kids to consider. I know the stock she comes from. She's not just looking for a good time."

Bren was actually a little offended. He'd have thought Mac knew him better than that. He set his fork, yet to be used, down. "And I am?"

"I don't know. But I know she isn't. Just keep that in mind." Mac's tone was clipped.

"Message received," Bren said and meant it.

"Good. Enjoy your dinner." Mac turned on his heel and headed down the bar, leaving Bren to his risotto. As he ate, he thought about what Mac said about his imagination. For Bren not using his imagination was akin to not breathing. It had gotten him through a fatherless childhood, a host of teenage angst and an adult life spent largely alone. Writing was, after all, a solitary occupation. But Bren didn't need to use his imagination if the circumstances were real. He'd been instantly drawn to Mackenzie Bishop. And that had been anything but imaginary.

Bren glanced out the window and gauged the remaining daylight. He hadn't gotten to where he was in life by waiting to see what would happen, by sitting idly by while things played out. He'd gone after everything he'd wanted by making a move, taking a chance. So if he wanted to get to know Mackenzie Bishop better, he'd do what he'd always done. Go for it. But he'd heed Mac's warning. The last thing Bren needed was to suffer his wrath. Or worse, Gov's.

Bren took one last bite of his dinner and washed it down with a sip of beer. Standing, he threw down enough bills to cover his tab along with a healthy tip. He bid Mac good-bye with a nod and headed out the back.

The sun was still up, drenching the basin in unrelieved golden light. He heard the plangent hoot of an owl and the resounding chorus of crickets as he walked along the boardwalk, then cut through the hotel breezeway and around front to the parking lot.

Ten minutes later Bren was pulling up to the park. He scanned the lot as he walked toward the entrance, looking for a white SUV. He didn't find one but inside he found exactly what he was looking for. As he made his way to Mackenzie and Katie at the picnic tables, he noticed Matt playing with Boot at the far edge of the park.

As if suddenly clairvoyant, Mackenzie turned around just as Bren opened his mouth to speak. "Bren," she said with a winsome smile. "That's so funny. We were just talking about you."

"What? Really? Oh, yeah, that is funny," Bren managed lamely. God, she was gorgeous. Tonight her hair was pulled back in a sleek tail, exposing her long, elegant neck. He'd love to get his mouth on it. He'd start at her earlobe and make his way slowly down her throat to—

"Mattie was saying if you were here tonight, he'd ask you to throw with him," Mackenzie explained. "We talked to Gov earlier and he said you used to play baseball."

"Yeah, I did. I was a catcher," Bren replied, coming out of the trance. So she'd mentioned him to Gov. To check him out or as an aside to conversation, he wondered. "Sure. That'd be fun." He greeted Katie by way of a smile, then nodded in Matt's direction. "Did you bring a glove? We still have some light left."

"Right here." Mackenzie reached between she and Katie and produced a mitt and a baseball.

Standing next to her, Bren could smell her perfume laced with sunscreen. The scent of jasmine melded with sea and sand had an aphrodisiac-like effect on him and one organ in particular began to react accordingly. He reached for the glove and automatically started to loosen it. At least that gave him something to do with his hands. "So what did you guys do today?"

"We went to the beach *and* the pool!" Katie informed him. "In the same day!"

Bren had thought as much. They both looked like they'd gotten some sun. "That sounds fun."

"And I wore both of my new bathing suits! One to the beach and one to the pool!"

"Even better."

"Since Mattie was patient and cooperative all day, Mom said we could come here again. He gets bored at the beach sometimes. It's called compromising."

Bren laughed. In addition to being the spitting image of her mother, Katie was delightful. "I understand." His gaze drifted back to Mackenzie and held until Matt and Boot's arrival broke it.

"Mattie, look who's here!"

"I saw! Can you practice with me?"

"You bet." Bren handed him the glove.

"Let's go!"

While Mackenzie and Katie looked on, Bren ran Matt through a few drills to get a feel for his skill level. He already knew the boy had a strong arm and good footwork but he could also catch, put it right in the web. He was an All-American in the making.

"Next time I'll bring my mitt," Bren told Matt twenty minutes later as they walked back toward the picnic tables. "I'll have better control that way and that'll make the ball more consistent for you. And remember what I said about your elbow."

"Keep it up. My coach told me that too. And point my shoulder and take my time."

Bren felt a grin stretch across his face. "Right."

"Can you come back tomorrow?" Matt asked as they reunited with Mackenzie and Katie.

Bren looked at Mackenzie. "If it's okay with your mom."

"Sure," she replied, standing. "Thanks, Bren. I know Mattie really appreciates it. And I do too."

"I don't know who had more fun. It brought back a lot of great memories, reminded me of how much I loved baseball growing up."

"I'm going to love baseball forever!" Matt exclaimed as they started walking toward the exit.

"Where are you guys parked?" Bren asked. The kids had run ahead with Boot and he and Mackenzie were a few strides behind.

"We walked over. It's such a beautiful night."

"Let me give you a lift home then."

"Oh, no, that's okay. It's just a few blocks."

"I insist. This a safe area, but darkness falls fast in the hills. And you guys aren't wearing reflective clothing."

Mackenzie mulled that over for a moment. "Well, we did stay a little later than I expected. Um, sure. But only if it's on your way."

"It is," Bren lied. He lived in the opposite direction. "You'll have to direct me. I know of Gov's neighborhood, but I've never been a guest."

"Don't take it personally. In the two years that he's owned that house he's probably spent more time away from it than in it."

"I can relate. I've been out-of-town more than I'd like in recent years myself."

"What do you do, Bren?"

"I'm a writer," he told her, indicating with a nod where he'd parked. Bren hit the key fob, opening the hatch and conveniently ending the conversation.

"Wow. Your cargo area is spotless. Are you sure you want Boot in there?"

Bren shrugged. "That's what it's for. I just don't have much occasion to use it."

Mackenzie rounded up the kids, informing them of the change of plans. They all got in and a few minutes later were pulling into Gov's driveway. Bren shoved the car into Park and looked around appraisingly. "I've never been on this street. The old-growth trees are incredible."

"You should see it in the winter. It's as though Jack Frost took a paintbrush to the forest," Mackenzie said, unbuckling her seat belt as the kids got out with Boot.

"Pogonip," Bren put in easily.

Kenzie whooped with laughter. "Pogonip! I'd forgotten all about pogognip!"

Even her laugh was sexy. "Welcome to Tahoe."

"Thanks so much for the ride and for throwing with Mattie," she said, getting out of the car and shutting the door.

"My pleasure." Bren didn't know if he should mention meeting up tomorrow. Not just because he wanted to see her again, but because he'd really enjoyed his time with the kid.

Mackenzie laid her hands on her son's shoulders. "What do you say to Mr.—Bren?"

"Thank you," Matt said through the open window.

"No problem, buddy."

"See you tomorrow!" he exclaimed and ran toward the house with Boot.

Mackenzie gave Bren a hesitant look, then turned to her daughter. "Honey, would you help Mattie and Boot inside? You know the code. I left some lights on."

"Okay. Bye, Bren!"

Bren lifted his hand. "Bye, Katie."

Mackenzie watched them open the garage door and go inside. Then she turned back to Bren. "Please don't feel obligated about tomorrow. Mattie shouldn't have put you on the spot that way."

"He didn't. I had a blast. It made me feel young again."

"Yeah, kids tend to have effect on you."

Bren cleared his throat needlessly. "So, what time will you guys be heading over tomorrow?"

"We've been playing our days by ear. Maybe around seven? I can shoot you a text if you want."

Yes, I would like that very much, Bren thought. But he answered nonchalantly, "That'd be great. I'm usually finishing up around that time." He rattled off his number, looking on as she put it in her phone. In the glowing crepuscular light he could see how long and lush her eyelashes were. He'd kiss one, then the other, as she drifted off to sleep in his arms… He shook off the daydream when he realized she was talking.

"Thanks again. Good night."

"Good night." Bren watched as she walked up the driveway, through the garage and into the house. He waited until the garage door closed before he drove away. As he made his way home, he thought about what Mac said earlier, implying that he was just looking for a good time. Bren had certainly had his share of those but he'd actually had a great time tonight doing something simple, playing ball with a kid. A kid who'd lost his dad, too. Well, you can't lose something you never had, so Bren couldn't really say that about himself. But maybe working with Matt would fill some of the void he'd been feeling lately. And maybe, if the fates were kind and the stars aligned, Mackenzie would fill the rest.

CHAPTER FIVE

There was something about being in Tahoe again that put a spring in Kenzie's step, a song in her heart. That came as no surprise. But the jittery feeling in her stomach was a mystery. At first she likened it to a similar sensation she'd felt when she was pregnant. She was excited to meet her baby, knew she'd be a good mom, but was still apprehensive about all the unknowns. This feeling was like that but intertwined with something else, something vaguely familiar that she couldn't quite put her finger on. And it was driving her crazy.

Their third day in Tahoe began with a hike on the Tunnel Creek Trail. When Kenzie was a girl this had been home to the Ponderosa Ranch. Part of the television series *Bonanza* had been filmed here and in ensuing years the defunct set had become an amusement park. Her family had visited every summer to watch cowboys rope horses and gunslingers square off in the Old West. Mattie would have loved it. But today he was excited about hiking up to Monkey Rock, the massive boulder shaped like a gorilla.

Once that feat had been accomplished, complete with photo documentation at the summit, they had lunch at the trailhead cafe and headed home. In the spirit of compromise, Katie got to choose the afternoon's activity which was, not surprisingly, the beach. But Mattie was tired enough from the hike not to care and fell asleep under the umbrella while Kenzie and Katie read in the sun. The lake was a sheet of azure glass today and there wasn't a whisper of a cloud in the sky. It was a hot afternoon and a bevy of kids huddled near the shore, building sand castles or skipping stones. Boats pulling skiers and tubers zigzagged the lake and a catamaran skirted the shoreline. Tahoe was like food for the soul, Kenzie decided with contented sigh. She promised herself they would spend time here every summer, as much for herself as for the kids.

But despite how postcard-worthy the day was, part of Kenzie was wishing it away. She was looking forward to seeing Bren tonight. Her initial impression of him was that he was friendly, good-natured, courteous. And of course incredibly handsome. Plus his story checked out; her brother had vouched for him. But when he showed up again last night, Kenzie hadn't just been pleasantly surprised, she'd been ecstatic. And that feeling had stayed with her as she fell asleep. She'd had a dreamless night's sleep and had woken up with a smile on her face for the first time in... Oh, God! They'd started a new week! Sixteen months, one week and...She reached into her bag and noted the time on her phone. Thirteen hours. That was a first. She usually anticipated the milestones before they arrived.

The grief counselor would say that was a good sign. She was starting to move on, finally accept that Matt was really gone. But Kenzie didn't know if she wanted to accept it. She'd been told to start small, concentrate on getting through a day, then a week, then a month until that pivotal first year had passed. After that she could start focusing on the bigger picture—getting over it as opposed to getting through it. The next year would be easier, the following more so, and so on. But as much sense as that made, the thought of growing further and further away from Matt made her feel sad, lonely and guilty in a different way. What if someday he became no more than a distant memory? Like an old boyfriend or a childhood friend? No, that was ridiculous! He was her husband, her children's father, the love of her life. He'd always be with her. She glanced over at the kids. He was just as much a part of her as they were.

Kenzie could count the number of dreamless nights she'd had since Matt died on one hand. But not all of her dreams were bad. Sometimes they were gratifying, like watching a movie of happy memories. She didn't always remember the dream itself, just knew she'd been dreaming about Matt. Sometimes she woke with a feeling of comfort and peace, others with a racing heart and tears in her eyes. But not a smile. Never a smile. Not until today.

One of the things going through her mind last night as she drifted off to sleep was that she hadn't been honest with Bren. In her defense, she'd been caught off guard by his assumption that it wasn't she who'd lost her husband. Kenzie wasn't one to wear her heart on her sleeve and she didn't want anyone's pity, so correcting him hadn't seemed worth the trouble. She had no idea that she'd see him again, let alone that Mattie would take to him so readily. Her brother had never mentioned him and when she googled him all she found was links to books he'd edited over a decade ago. He probably just picked up whatever freelance work came his way. But he must be good at it because she'd also come across his address. Kenzie was no real estate connoisseur, but living anywhere in Tahoe was pricey and Bren owned a home mid-mountain. Maybe he had another source of income or family money.

In addition to clearing the air with Bren about her widowhood status, she needed to be mindful that Mattie had introduced himself as Matt. It could be as simple as wanting to be cool, like Katie said, but what if there was more to it? Was he trying to take on the role of man of the house? Wanting to be more like his dad? Or was he just growing up? And what if Bren took him under his wing and Mattie got attached? They were only here for a month. Then what? Later it would occur to Kenzie that she was really asking herself the same question but wasn't ready to admit it, let alone answer it.

"You okay, Mom?"

Kenzie shook her head from side to side, returning to the present. "Yeah. Just thinking." She gave her daughter a tender smile. "How's the book?"

"Good. I think Callie is going to end up going to the dance with her brother's friend after all. Not because she lost the bet but because she secretly likes him."

"Does he like her?"

"Yeah, that's why he made the bet. Because he was too shy to ask her."

It all starts out so simple, Kenzie thought with an inward sigh. How does it get so complicated? "Got it.

After you finish that chapter, we should probably head home. We can pick up something for dinner on the way to the park."

"Are we going to do that every night?"

"Not necessarily. What would you like to do?"

"I don't know. I just don't want to go there every night. I mean, the sunsets are pretty and I know we're here to take care of Boot, but maybe we could take him to do something else instead. We haven't gone to that old-fashioned ice cream parlor yet. Or the pizza place with the jukebox you used to go to when you were a kid. Maybe we could take Boot and eat outside."

Kenzie let out a contemplative breath."Tell you what. We'll go to the park tonight because I already promised Mattie. But we'll go to the pizza place tomorrow night, okay?"

"Okay," Katie agreed and went back to her book.

Kenzie tried to do the same, but her mind kept wandering. Who was she really appeasing by going to the park again tonight? Her son or herself? Well, it didn't really matter because one way or the other she had to set the record straight with Bren. She was Gov's one and only sister and she should have made that clear from the beginning. At the very least she owed Bren an explanation, at the most an apology. She'd had several opportunities to clarify the misunderstanding and hadn't. But the real question was why. Why hadn't she corrected him straightaway?

She could blame the kids for running up and suspending the conversation that first night. But last night she had no excuse. She couldn't say she was caught off guard; Mattie had grabbed his glove in the hopes of running into Bren. And even as Kenzie was telling him that might not happen, she'd found herself freshening up. She'd also had the opportunity to come clean when they were parting ways in the driveway. But doing that hadn't even crossed her mind, perhaps due to the thudding in her chest and the pounding in her ears. And the curl of trepidation and anticipation filling the hollowness in her stomach.

Well, she'd tell him tonight, work it into the conversation somehow. It was ridiculous really. All this indecision and avoidance was unlike her. She looked down at her left hand and out of habit nudged her diamond back into place. She'd taken to wearing her engagement ring behind her wedding band instead of the traditional obverse for fear the diamond would slip off her finger. She'd lost some weight and it tended to spin around on her finger now. She should really have the rings soldered together. After all, she'd be wearing them for the rest of her of life. Because you only find true love once in a lifetime. And Kenzie's once in a lifetime had come and gone.

*****

Bren loved researching and writing but he despised editing, particularly line editing. He hated going back through his manuscript with a fine-tooth comb, dissecting it word for word. He liked to think of it as an aggregate, not as pieces of one. He loved using words in different ways, taking a word and flipping it on its side to stretch its meaning. But line editing took all of that creativity away. Instead of being focused on the story, the setting, the characters, he had to focus on the fucking alphabet. It might as well be calculus or, he thought with a smile of remembrance, Greek. Except Elena had made learning Greek fun. And so, so easy.

To add insult to injury, he was in the sagging middle of the book. It was hard enough for him to focus and get through this necessary evil under normal circumstances, but now he had the added distraction of seeing Mackenzie tonight. He glanced over at his phone. Providing she texted him, which she had not. And it was after five. Bren could tell himself he was looking forward to playing ball with a future Golden Glove Award winner, but he'd be half-lying. He couldn't get Mackenzie out of his mind, not that he'd tried very hard.

Having had enough picking the fly shit out of the pepper for the day, Bren closed his laptop and went downstairs. Mountain living meant vertical living and his house consisted of three levels. He used the smaller of the two bedrooms in the basement for storage. His mother had given him three boxes when she moved to Arizona. One contained pictures, mementos and keepsakes from his youth. Another was full of legal documents, family heirlooms and the like. And the third and largest box was a cache of his achievements. Trophies, awards, newspaper clippings and yearbooks from high school and college as well as his internship portfolio. And right on top of that big plastic bin with the cracked lid was his baseball mitt. He'd had several growing up, but this one had been his favorite. He'd gotten it for his thirteenth birthday. His mom had even had his name stitched on it. It probably hadn't seen the light of day in decades.

The scent of musty leather filled the air as Bren began kneading it the way he had Matt's glove the night before. Funny how certain things come back to you, like riding a bike or driving on the right side of the road after a trip abroad. Or making love to a pulchritudinous woman like he did in his dream last night. Specifically, a blonde with bottomless blue eyes and a willowy body he'd spent a great deal of time exploring. And flawless porcelain skin and a luscious mouth he'd gotten to know like the back of his hand. A mouth that had gotten to know him just as well. One he'd like to sample in real life. But first she had to text him.

Bren slid the box back in the closet and closed the door. He went upstairs and forever the optimist, set the mitt on the table next to the door. Then he headed back out to the deck to check his phone. No new texts, but he'd missed a call from his agent. Not many ghostwriters had agents but Bren was the exception, as was the fact that he shared his agent with the author under whose name he wrote. At first he'd been concerned the arrangement would be a conflict of interest, but being a team gave them the upper hand when negotiating with the publisher. Unless they were both happy nothing got done. He was listening to Miranda's message when a text notification popped up. The number was unfamiliar but he recognized the area code as Palm Springs. He immediately tapped it.

Hey Bren, We're heading over to the park around 6:30. No problem if that doesn't work for you. Kenzie

Kenzie. He liked that she was comfortable enough to use her nickname with him. She actually looked more like a Kenzie than a Mackenzie in his opinion. Not that his opinion mattered. That was another thing he'd like to change.

Sounds good. See you then.

Bren sent the text, then listened to the rest of Miranda's message. She was checking in about the revisions. No need to call back since it was getting late in New York, but email her an update as to his progress. Part of him wanted to offer to drop off a flash drive up the hill to save everyone a step, but she wouldn't have been amused. They never communicated like that in writing. There would be no paper trail. Even the working title of the book was fake. Bren never saw the cover or knew the real title until his courtesy copy came in the mail. The process was buttoned-up from start to finish.

He would deal with that later, Bren decided, and headed upstairs to shower. The third floor of his house consisted of two rooms, a bedroom and a bathroom. His room shared the same unspoiled view as the deck—a horizon broken by snow-dusted mountains girdling an expanse of cerulean blue. He wouldn't even need blinds but for the early summer sunrise. Privacy was not an issue. Not that he'd had anyone to do anything private with lately anyway.

He'd like to change that too.

Bren was ready by six and decided he'd might as well head out. Grabbing his laptop from the deck, he plugged it into the charger on the kitchen counter, then locked up. He'd spared no expense when remodeling the main level. From the river rock fireplace to the reclaimed wood cabinets and floating staircase, Gov and Brody Construction had outdone themselves.

Grabbing the mitt and his phone, Bren went out through the garage and at the last minute detoured to check the mail. He was walking down the driveway to the mailbox when he heard someone call his name. When he looked over he found his next door neighbor standing in his driveway. Bren walked over to him and extended his hand in greeting.

"Hey, Greg. I didn't realize you were back."

"Just got in this afternoon. It's getting mighty hot in Phoenix."

"I heard." Bren shifted his gaze to Greg's Porsche parked in the middle of his otherwise empty garage. "The family coming up separately?"

Looking down at his feet, Greg shook his head back and forth lugubriously before leveling his stare with Bren's again. "The kids will be up at some point, but Livy and I are calling it quits. For good this time."

Bren wasn't surprised, but he didn't let it show. "I'm sorry. That has to be tough."

Greg gave Bren a lopsided smile. "It's been a long time coming and is for the best, but we were trying to wait until everybody was through high school. Joey's got one more year, but Livy drew a line in the sand. Not that I blame her. I haven't exactly been a model husband."

Bren had heard talk of Greg's womanizing and drinking escapades, but had never actually witnessed any such behavior himself. But most of the time when Greg was here his family was with him. Like many professional athletes, he was under the microscope and his every misstep was not only documented, but often blown out of proportion. Locally he was known more for his love of blackjack than anything else. For his family's sake, Bren hoped he hadn't gambled away his fortune. Greg Gentry had been one of the best third basemen to ever play the game.

"Feeling nostalgic?" Greg was asking.

"What?" Bren followed Greg's sightline to the mitt in his hand. "Oh, no. I met Gov's nephew the other day. Got an arm like a rocket. Great hand-eye coordination too. And he's fast. I said I'd practice a little with him."

"That's a dangerous combination. Shortstop?"

"Yeah."

"I'd like to have a look at him. I'm taking my private lessons on the road this summer. It'll keep me busy while I'm here and let's face it, I'm going to need the cash. How old is he?"

"Almost ten, I think."

Greg shook his head assuredly. "Perfect age for development." He reached into his pocket and handed Bren a business card. "Give his parents my card. Tell them to get in touch with me if they're interested. Does he live here?"

"Reno," Bren answered, shoving the card into his pocket. "I'll pass it along."

"Thanks," Greg said as his phone rang. He grabbed it out of his back pocket and read the screen. "My attorney. I'd better take it. Nice to see you."

"You too. Welcome back," Bren said as Greg accepted the call.

Bren took his leave and retrieved the mail, leafing through it as he walked back up the driveway. He threw it and the glove on the passenger seat and headed out. As he pulled away, he noticed Greg was still on his driveway, a painful look on his face and a troubled hand on his forehead. Bren almost felt sorry for him.

Despite getting caught in beach traffic, Bren made it to the park on time. He didn't have to look for Mackenzie and the kids this time because they were waiting for him at the entrance. Matt had an ear to ear grin on his face and his glove in his hand. He ran up to Bren.

"I knew you'd come! Mom said not to get my hopes up, but I told her you would!"

"Of course I came. I've been looking forward to it all day. I even dug up my old mitt. That way you won't have such a big advantage over me."

"Awesome!" Matt exclaimed as they walked over to his mom and sister. Boot was sitting patiently beside them.

Mackenzie greeted Bren with a bright smile. God, she had such a sexy mouth. Her lips shimmered with a hint of gloss and were slightly parted, like she was about to whistle. Or had just licked them. Bren found himself wanting to do the same. And not stop there. But he only said, "Hey, guys."

"Hi, Bren. Thanks so much for coming," Mackenzie said, handling her son a baseball.

"My pleasure. How's it going, Katie?" Bren asked.

"Better now that you're here," she replied flatly. "Mattie has been talking about nothing else all day."

"Well, then I guess we'd better get to it."

Mackenzie and Katie hung with Boot at the picnic tables while Bren and Matt headed to the far end of the park. Bren grew more impressed with Matt's abilities with each drill. Plus the kid had a great attitude. He was tractable, patient and unlike Bren at his age, not easily frustrated. But one important thing was missing—a bat. And for batting they needed more space and less company. Like a large open field or a big backyard. Bren's backyard was the side of a hill and his front yard shallow, but Gov's neighborhood was at a lower elevation and relatively flat. He was mulling over that possibility when Mackenzie joined them. "You guys almost ready? The park closes at dusk. We're pushing it."

"Five more minutes, Mom? Please?"

"Five more minutes. If it's okay with Bren."

"Yeah, sure."

"Bren, I'm counting on you to enforce the curfew."

"Yes, ma'am."

"We'll meet you two out front." Then she turned on her heel and walked away.

"Hear that, buddy? We're on the clock. Ten more throws and we're out of here. Let's make 'em count."

Ten minutes later they met Mackenzie, Katie and Boot at the entrance.

"Mom, can Bren get ice cream with us?"

"That's up to him." Mackenzie shifted her gaze to Bren. "Would you like to? My treat."

"Ah, sure."

"Do you want to follow us?"

"Yeah. I'm parked right here."

"You must have gotten here at just the right time. We're in the overflow lot across the street."

"Got lucky I guess," Bren replied. "Every once in a while that happens."

"Not to me. I never seem to get that lucky."

"Sure you do, Mom. We got that great spot at the trailhead this morning," Katie gently reminded her.

Mackenzie turned to her daughter. "You're right, honey, we did. I'd forgotten."

"So you are lucky after all."

She ran a loving hand down Katie's hair. "I certainly am. But what are the chances I'd get that lucky twice?" Then returning to Bren, she swallowed hard and confirmed, "So, we'll meet you there?"

"The one on Tahoe Boulevard that's been there forever, right?"

"That's the one."

They exchanged parting pleasantries and a few minutes later Bren was pulling up in front of the ice cream parlor. The A-frame building shared retail space with a novelty toy and candy store and still looked the same as when he was a kid. Despite driving by it hundreds of times, Bren probably hadn't been inside for twenty-five years.

He hadn't missed a thing.

From the life-sized bear sculpture that stood out front to the speckled linoleum floor to the smell of freshly baked cones, Bren was transported back in time. The writer in him would call the shop quaint, but it was really just a long, narrow space whose old-school charm made up for its desperate need for renovation. But it was clean and efficient and still family owned according to the story told by the framed photos that covered the walls.

The line snaked through the shop and spilled outside, which is where Bren found the Bishops and Boot. Mackenzie was leaning against the door, holding it open, listening to whatever Matt was saying. She glanced over and gave Bren a quick smile, then returned to her son. Katie was looking down, scrolling on her phone. Mackenzie tapped her hand and Katie immediately looked up, then greeted Bren with a smile of her own. As soon as Matt was done talking, Mackenzie lifted her gaze to Bren. "We were debating what to get. Mattie can't decide between Birthday Cake and Cookies and Cream. So he's petitioning for both."

"Double-scoop. Go big or go home."

"You're no help."

"How about you, Katie?"

"She gets the same every time," Matt inserted with a roll of the eyes.

"Because it's my favorite," Katie told her brother decidedly. Then she answered Bren politely, "Chocolate Chip cookie dough."

"Can't go wrong there."

Before Bren could ask Mackenzie her preference, the line advanced. It was a moot point anyway because she passed on ice cream. Bren placed his order and when he got to the register realized that Mackenzie had picked up his tab.

"You didn't have to do that."

"You didn't have to spend the evening with us."

"It was fun."

"It was. And this is my way of saying thank you."

"Thank you," Bren replied, wondering if she meant it was only fun for Matt. He was slipping his wallet back into his pocket when he came across Greg's card. "Oh, I almost forgot," he said as they walked outside to find the kids and Boot. "I have something for you." He handed it over.

She scanned it, then looked back at him with questioning eyes. "Greg Gentry? The baseball player?"

"He's my neighbor," Bren explained. "He lives in Phoenix most of the year, runs a youth sports academy there. He's here for the summer and is giving private lessons."

The kids had snagged a table and the two of them stopped walking just before reaching it. Mackenzie knitted her brow. "And he's interested in Mattie?"

"He will be once he sees him. He's good, Mackenzie. Really good. I thought you might want to look into it."

With a vacant nod, she looked back down at the card as if it had somehow changed in the last few seconds. Then her gaze returned to Bren. "So you mentioned Mattie to him?"

"I saw Greg as I was leaving tonight. I had my mitt in my hand, which begged the conversation. One thing led to another."

"Okay. Thanks."

"I'm sorry. I didn't mean to overstep."

"You didn't. I'm just surprised, that's all."

"Really? No one has ever told you that before? About him?"

Before she could answer, Matt shouted, "Bren, your ice cream is melting!"

Bren looked down. He'd yet to take a lick and ice cream was trickling down the side of the cone, almost to his hand. He made quick work of the drip. "I guess I got a little distracted."

"Let's sit down so you can eat that." Mackenzie took the last few strides toward the table, sitting down next to Katie. Bren took a spot on the opposite side next to Matt. Boot was lying in the grass at their feet. It occurred to Bren that they looked like a family, capping off a day at the lake with ice cream.

The kids were almost done with their cones and Bren played catch-up with his while the three of them talked about what they'd learned today, a dinner table tradition carried over from Mackenzie's childhood. Bren found it fascinating. Since it had just been his mom and him, they often grabbed dinner on the way home from practice or ate at the kitchen island. He was thinking about that when he realized the three of them were staring at him.

"How about you, Bren?" Mackenzie was asking. "What did you learn today? Good or bad?"

Since he couldn't say the first thing that came to mind, that she somehow managed to look more stunning every time he saw her or that he found the color of her eyes as transcendent a blue as Lake Tahoe itself, he went with, "Today I learned that some things never change. This place is older than me and the ice cream still tastes the same as it did when I was a kid."

"So is that good or bad?" Katie wanted to know.

"Good," Bren replied. "It's still the best ice cream around." Or maybe, he silently added, it's just plain old ice cream and it's who I'm eating it with that makes it so good.

"Have you always lived here?" Katie asked.

"No. I'm from Sacramento. But I came here a lot when I was growing up."

"Mom did too. But not my dad. He'd never been to Tahoe before he met my mom."

Bren gave a nod. Should he pretend he didn't know that their dad died? He didn't want to be either presumptuous or duplicitous, but there was no middle ground here. He was still debating that when Mackenzie cleared her throat and broke the silence.

"Okay guys, time to pack it in. We've had a long day."

"Can we go to the candy store?" Matt asked.

"Just to check it out. We'll come back for candy another night. Stay together."

"We'll be fine, Mom. I have my phone," Katie reassured her, taking her brother's hand.

As soon as they took off, Mackenzie got up and sat next to Bren. He experienced five-seconds of euphoria until he realized she did it so she could keep an eye on the kids. Boot adjusted accordingly, lying between them.

Neither of them said anything at first, watching the kids walk across the clearing and into the candy store. Then, satisfied they'd made it safely, Mackenzie turned to him. "Thanks for practicing with Mattie again tonight."

"You don't have to keep thanking me, Mackenzie. I enjoy it."

"I can see that. But I want you to know it means a lot to him. And it means a lot to me too."

Bren replied with a smile. He had a sneaking suspicion she was trying to tell him something. And he had an even stronger suspicion what she was trying to tell him.

She turned and looked unseeingly into the near distance, as if rewinding time. The sky was dark blue but not yet black and the mountain skyline was lit by emergent stars. Waves still pounded steadily against the shore, but their pace had slowed as the lake turned itself in for the night. Soft music and honeyed voices wafted through the air from the pier down the beach. Bren wondered if Mac was working tonight. He might need a beer after this.

"I haven't spent much time in Tahoe in recent years. I've lived away since I got married."

"Let me guess. It looks the same."

Turning back to him, she cocked her head to the side. "How'd you know I was going to say that?"

"Because everybody, including myself, says that. Tahoe is timeless. That's part of what makes it so special. Time is the one thing we can't make, control or buy. But Tahoe somehow defies all that, or comes damn close. It's atemporal, ineffability so."

"Wow," Mackenzie remarked with a reverent grunt. "I bet you're a fantastic writer. You certainly know how to put things in perspective."

Bren brushed that off with a shrug. "That's all writing really is. Conveying things in a way that resonates with people, that they can relate to, identify with, figure out for themselves."

"Intuition."

"Yeah, I guess. I've always been intuitive."

Silence hung in the air between them for a few clicks. Then Mackenzie puffed out a breath and declared, "Well, in case you haven't already figured *this* out, I'm Gov's only sister. The one who lost her husband."

"I know. I'm sorry."

"Thank you. I should have clarified things from the beginning."

"Why didn't you?"

"I'm not sure," she paused on a frown, then went on, "That first night I was taken off-guard by your assumption and to be honest, I really didn't expect to see you again. After that it never seemed like the right time. I've gotten out of the habit of telling people about Matt. At first it seemed that everyone just knew. And the subject doesn't exactly lend itself to small talk."

"I guess we both made some assumptions."

"I guess so. How'd you figure it out?"

"I connected the dots after I got home the night we met. But it was Mac who filled in the gaps. He said it was a military accident?"

"Yeah," Mackenzie affirmed with a nod. "Matt was training in New Mexico. IED disposal. All those years of overseas deployments and the unimaginable happens at home."

"Since I can't tell him, I'll tell you. Thank you for your service and sacrifice."

"That's kind of you to say."

"How are the kids doing?"

"Much better now. I think it's hardest on Mattie, not having a dad. We were used to Matt being away, but this is different. It even took me a while to wrap my head around the fact that he isn't coming back this time. I think that concept was even harder for them to grasp. But they're strong and brave and we're getting through it together. Kids are incredibly resilient. We all got counseling and my parents have been wonderful. We moved to Reno last summer, but I just bought a house a few months ago. This has been a nice break, but I miss it. It's home now."

"There's no place like home."

"True. And this is yours?"

"For the last dozen years or so. What started as a pipe dream became a goal, then a reality."

"And quite an accomplishment."

"Not compared to raising two kids alone. But the things that are really important to us usually end up coming to fruition. It boils down to priorities. And a little bit of luck."

She thought about that for a long moment, then flashed that smile Bren found so disarming. "You're absolutely right." Her eyes, liquid sapphires in the soft light, began to glisten. Bren wanted to drown himself in them. "Thanks for the reminder."

"Thanks for telling me about your husband."

"I'm sorry for the misunderstanding."

"No apology needed. And I'm glad to practice with Matt whenever he's up for it."

"In case you haven't already figured *that* out, he's always up for it."

"I'm pretty flexible, Mackenzie. Call me anytime."

"Thanks. And Bren?"

"Yeah?"

"Call me Kenzie."

"You got it, Kenzie."

CHAPTER SIX

Bren talked to or texted with his mother several times a week. There was no rhyme or reason to it, no turn-taking or schedule to speak of. But he usually initiated the calls and she was a big fan of texting. She was an early riser and Bren often kept odd hours depending on how his creative juices were flowing, so texting was convenient. Still, Bren wasn't surprised to get a morning call from her two days after his ice cream outing with Kenzie and the kids.

He should have been.

Claire Banks owned her home and car unencumbered and had her pension and savings for discretionary expenses. She didn't like it, but Bren also made sure she had a getaway or two a year. This year he'd given her a six-night cruise to the Mexican Riviera. When she called he assumed she wanted to tell him about it.

He was wrong.

"Are you up for some company?"

"Sure. And you're not company."

"You know what I mean. Are you drowning in work?"

"Not really," Bren lied. Miranda was increasingly impatient for him to finish his current project and get going on the next. "But you know how to entertain yourself if I get bogged down."

"That I do. But I have something a little different in mind this time."

"Shoot," Bren replied, half-listening as he read Miranda's latest email. Jesus, she already had a rough outline for the new book.

"Can I bring a friend?"

"Of course. Who this time?" He assumed Barb or Janet, maybe Joanie. But the two of them occasionally got into it about one thing or another, so he'd prefer one of the former.

He was wrong about that too.

"Bob."

Bren's head shot up. "Bob?"

"Yes."

"As in Bob*bie*?" Bren asked, referring to their neighbor in Sacramento. She had to be ancient by now.

"You mean Roberta? God no, she's long-dead." Claire paused through a breath, then elaborated, "Bob Carlson. The man I've been seeing."

Bren shut the lid of his laptop. "Seeing how?"

"We've gone out to dinner a few times, attended a couple of community functions together. He picked me up from the airport when I got back from the cruise. It was wonderful, by the way. Thank you again."

"My pleasure. So how long has this been going on?"

"A few months, give or take."

"A few *months?* And this is the first I've heard of it?"

"There really wasn't much to say before. But it's evolved into a more serious relationship and I want you to meet him."

"How serious?"

"About as serious as they come at my age."

Bren pressed the full force of three fingers against his forehead. His mother had never brought a man to visit before. In fact, his mother had had very few men in her life, that he knew about anyway. She'd dated occasionally when he was in high school and college, but no one special and nothing long-term. He didn't think she'd been seeing anyone lately. Not that there was anything wrong with it. She was an attractive, active sixty-five-year-old woman. There was no reason why she shouldn't have a social life.

"Brennen?"

"That's fine, Mom. When were you thinking?"

"I need to run it by Bob, but I wanted to talk to you first. Maybe in a week or two?"

That's new, having to run things by someone. "Okay. Let me know when you nail it down."

"Will do. Thanks, honey."

After they signed off, Bren threw the phone down on the deck table and looked out over the treetops. The lake was already bustling with everything from kayaks to SUPs to Woodies. Bren reminded himself not to let the summer go by without getting out on the water. Maybe he and Bob could do a little fishing, get to know each other that way. Uttering an oath his mother would scold him for, he reached for his coffee and took a sip. Ice cold. He pushed up with a snarl and went inside. He swore again when he realized the coffee maker had hit its time limit and shut off. He'd been up for hours, trying to get this round of revisions behind him. He poured what was left in the pot down the drain and started over. While the coffee brewed, he surveyed the kitchen. He'd ordered Chinese food last night and grains of fried rice still littered the counter. He was wiping it down when he heard a soft knock at the front door. He threw the sponge in the sink and drying his hands on a dish towel, went to answer it.

There Bren got his second surprise of the morning. A much more pleasant one.

"Kenzie," he startled.

"Good morning."

"Good morning," he returned, instantly buoyed.

She was dressed in shorts and a T-shirt and wearing tennis shoes and an apprehensive grin. Her hair, spun straw in the sunlight, fell in a single braid down her back. She held a Starbucks cup in one hand and gripped her shoulder bag in the other. "I'm sorry. Am I interrupting?"

"No, not at all. Please come in."

She took in the house appraisingly as she entered. When she saw the panorama through the open deck doors she stopped in her tracks. "Wow. Now that's a view."

Throwing the dish towel over his shoulder, Bren shut the door. "Oh, that? It's okay, I guess. Come on back." He led her through the living room and into the kitchen.

"Need a refill? I just brewed a fresh pot."

Her gaze drifted to the cup in her hand. "Yeah, sure. Thanks."

"Cream? Sugar?"

"Please."

He grabbed a mug and the sugar from the cabinet, then went to the refrigerator for the half and half. When he turned back around, she was sitting on one of the bar stools at the island, taking the lid off her cup. "Let's start from scratch." He set the sugar and cream down in front of her, then filled the mug before dumping his old coffee in the sink, filling his tumbler and joining her.

"Thanks," she said, doctoring her coffee. "I'm sorry for stopping by unannounced like this. Mattie is next door with Greg being evaluated. I'd planned on staying, but they're running through a bunch of drills and I didn't want to be in the way. I felt comfortable leaving him, but didn't want to venture too far."

"No worries. I'm glad you did. And he's in good hands with Greg. Where's Katie this morning?"

"In Tahoe City with a friend's family. They're staying over there this week and invited her to spend the day with them. They have a boat at the marina at Sunnyside. We dropped her off first thing, then grabbed Starbucks and came over here."

"It's a perfect day for boating."

"Or just about anything else," she added, reaching into her bag and pulling out her phone. "I asked her to check in occasionally. Just so I can visualize where she is."

It occurred to Bren then that this was the first time he'd been alone with her. He processed that through a drawn-out sip of coffee. She looked different today for some reason. More youthful and relaxed. She could pass for Katie's older sister instead of her mother. But she still smelled the same. That jasmine perfume really did a number on him.

"I'm glad it worked out with Greg."

"I guess we'll see." She put her phone down on the counter, face up. "Thanks for the recommendation. That's another reason I wanted to stop by. To thank you. Mattie was so excited to meet a real baseball player."

"If he sticks around town long enough, he's bound to run into another one or two. Or a football or hockey player for that matter. We're spoiled for choice when it comes to celebrities, especially this time of year."

"I'm sure. People who can live or vacation anywhere in the world choose to do so in Tahoe."

"True enough," Bren agreed.

"Like yourself." She held his stare over the rim of her cup.

He laughed self-disparagingly. "Hardly. But I can work from anywhere and I choose to do so here. I'll give you that."

Kenzie scanned the room, as if looking for evidence of such, and her eyes landed on the deck table where his laptop sat. It was shielded from the sun by the oversized umbrella that was just as necessary in Tahoe in the summer as chains were in the winter. "Is that what I interrupted? Were you writing?"

"Actually, I'd just hung up with my mother. But I got an early start today. Thus, the second pot of coffee." He brought his cup to his lips, then took another sip. This was not only the first time he'd been alone with her, it was the first time he'd seen her hair braided. He wondered how it would feel uncoiling between his fingers as she lay beneath him. He'd spread it out on the pillow, then bury his face in it as he rose above her...

"Bren?"

He shook off the fantasy. "Sorry. What were you saying?"

"Your mother. Is she okay?"

"Oh, yeah. She's fine. We were just catching up."

"Does she still live in Sacramento?"

She remembered where he was from. "No. She retired to Scottsdale a few years ago."

"That's nice."

"Yes, it's very nice. She loves it." He ended on an unintended snort.

"And your dad?"

"Not in the picture."

She nodded. "Got it."

Silence lagged between them for a moment, then Bren elaborated, "It was just my mom and I growing up. I never knew my dad."

Kenzie's eyes widened as if she found that inconceivable. Then she said,

"Well, she must have been a great mom because you appear to be a successful, well-adjusted adult."

"She was. Still is," Bren said and meant it.

"So why the snort?" she asked around a sip of coffee.

He hadn't realized it had been that obvious. Or maybe she was just that perceptive. If so, he was busted. "She's coming to visit, which is great. But she's bringing a friend."

Kenzie kicked that around through a grimace. "And you don't like her friends?" She took in the house again. "Because it looks like you have plenty of room."

"No, I like her friends just fine. Her *girl*friends. This time she's bringing Bob."

"And Bob is?"

"New."

"Oh, I see," she said, her eyes glinting with humor. "And you don't like this Bob?"

"I don't have an opinion one way or the other. I've never met him."

"So maybe it's the idea of Bob you don't like."

"Maybe," Bren admitted weakly. Or maybe it was the word serious that he didn't like. That was as shocking as Bob himself.

Just then Kenzie's phone pinged, suspending the conversation. She glanced down. "It's Katie, checking in. They're anchoring in Emerald Bay."

"That'll be fun. They can swim, explore the island, check out the castle."

"Knowing Katie, she'll be on the deck of the boat reading."

"Sounds familiar."

"I take it by your chosen profession that you were a big reader as a kid."

"I was, but I also loved the outdoors and sports. So a day at Emerald Bay would have presented quite a quandary. I would have wanted to be in two places at once; on the boat reading and in the water skiing or tubing. Making a living combining those two affinities also proved to be a challenge."

"Well, it looks like you did fine by it."

"Can't complain. But sometimes I—" Jesus, what had he almost said? He was saved by her phone again. This time the sound was more of a trill.

"Time to get Mattie," she announced, silencing the alarm. Reaching for her purse, she secured it on her shoulder and stood. "Thanks for the coffee and the company." She picked up her mug. "I apologize again for the surprise pop-in."

Standing, Bren took the mug from her and put it in the sink. "No need to apologize. Feel free to stop by anytime."

"Thanks." She smiled wide enough to produce the inkling of a crease at the edges of her eyes. They were swimming with delight and anticipation and weaved with uneasiness. Then Bren realized that was a reflection of his own.

"I'll walk out with you," he offered and fell into step with her. They found Greg and Matt in Greg's driveway and met up with them halfway between the houses.

"Hi, Mom!"

"Hi! How'd it go?" Kenzie asked, brushing back the strands of hair that had fallen onto his forehead.

"It was awesome!"

"Great!"

"Mattie's quite an athlete, as you probably already know," Greg commended.

"Thank you." Kenzie turned to Greg. "And yes, I'm starting to realize that."

"I'd love the opportunity to work with him. Maybe twice a week?"

"Sure."

"I'll put a schedule together. I can email it to you if you text me your address."

Kenzie pulled out her phone and typed. "Done."

"Love the efficiency," Greg remarked, his gaze lingering lasciviously on Kenzie for a few beats. Bren wondered if she noticed.

"It's a prerequisite to motherhood, I've decided. How much do I owe you?"

As much as he hated to, Bren took that as a cue to excuse himself. "I've got to get back to work. I'll see you guys around."

"Mom, can I show Bren what I learned?"

"Not now, honey. He has to work."

"Later?"

"We have to get Katie later. Maybe another time."

"Okay," he conceded glumly.

"Tell you what," Bren said, squatting down to be eye level with the boy. "While your mom and Coach Gentry settle up, you can give me the condensed version." He glanced up at Kenzie. "Is that okay? We'll hang in my front yard."

"Sure."

They exchanged good-byes and as Matt and Bren were walking away, Bren heard Kenzie laugh at something Greg said. He pushed down the irritation and focused on the kid. "So you had fun, huh?"

"Yeah! I've never met a real baseball player before!"

"You're a real baseball player," Bren pointed out.

"From the Majors, I mean."

"Lots of stories to tell there, I bet."

"He didn't tell me any stories," Matt said innocently. "Except that his dad used to play catch with him a lot when he was a kid. His dad played in the pros too."

"That's cool."

"My grandpa does that with me sometimes. Because my dad is in heaven."

Bren stopped walking, mostly because they'd reached his driveway, but also because Matt's tone had grown so forlorn. He put a strong hand on the boy's shoulder. "I know. I'm sorry."

"Thanks. Everybody says that." He looked down at his feet. "My mom says they're trying to be nice."

"She's right. They are."

"But it still sucks." His head jolted up. "I mean stinks. Don't tell my mom I said sucks. She says it's bad language."

Bren couldn't stop himself from chuckling. "You got it." Then he rubbed his hands together. "Okay. Show me what you learned."

Matt demonstrated some of the same things they'd worked on together— posture and footwork, agility. After a few minutes, Bren looked up to find Kenzie standing in the driveway, watching them. Her arms were folded across her chest and that infectious smile was back, bigger and brighter than ever.

"Hold up, bud," Bren said, nodding over Matt's head.

"All right, time to let Bren get back to work," Kenzie announced when Matt turned around to face her.

"Okay," he begrudgingly agreed.

"Thanks again for the coffee," she told Bren as they joined her.

"Anytime."

"I hope you didn't get too behind on things."

"I make my own schedule. It always gets done in the end."

"Well, I guess we'll see you around then." Putting her arm around her son's shoulders, she made to walk away.

Bren cleared his throat unnecessarily. "I'm still up for practicing with Matt anytime. Unless I've been replaced." He ended on a high note, but inside he wasn't so lighthearted. Greg had a lot of star power and the kid was understandably impressed.

"Thanks, but we won't be at the park tonight. I'm not sure what time we have to get Katie in Tahoe City. Boot will have to settle for the backyard. But we're here for another few weeks."

"Just let me know."

"Will do."

She was turning on her heel when Bren decided to go for it. "I could always pick up a couple of pizzas and come over some night. Gov's street is pretty level and with having an interior lot, he must have a decent-sized backyard. We could do some batting, running, timing drills. Things we can't do at the park. "

"Um, right. Yeah, sure. That would work."

"Great."

Just then Kenzie's phone pinged. Bren looked on as she grabbed it from her purse and read out loud. "It's Katie, asking for permission to stay overnight. They're going mini-golfing later and then out for pizza." Kenzie texted in reply. After a few seconds, she read on, "She has a change of clothes with her since she was dressed for the boat." She typed a few more keystrokes, then looked up and announced, "Well, it looks like a pizza kind of night all around, then."

CHAPTER SEVEN

Emma Godfrey-Williams and Kenzie had been friends for almost a decade. They came from completely different worlds but lived together seamlessly in the same one. Emma hailed from Texas, the great-granddaughter of an oil magnate on her mother's side. Her paternal lineage was less sexy, but equally impressive. The Godfreys had raised cattle in Texas for generations. Emma liked to say that if her mother's family didn't own it, or a piece of it in Texas, her father's family probably did. Not that she said that very often. She was incredibly humble for someone who had a myriad of reasons not to be. She was Kenzie's best friend in her adult life and Kenzie liked to think the feeling was mutual.

They'd met at Camp Lejeune when Mattie was a baby. It was the kids who'd originally brought them together. Emma had two boys the same age as Katie and Mattie. Kenzie joined the playgroup on base and the two women became instant friends. Emma's family had been stationed in North Carolina for two years by the time the Bishops arrived. Emma took Kenzie under her wing, brought her into her social circle and showed her the lay of the land. Their husbands deployed together the following year and Kenzie and Emma helped with each other's kids, kept each other sane and drank a lot of wine in the evenings. And as luck would have it, they ended up stationed together again at Twentynine Palms where Emma still lived.

John Williams hadn't been in New Mexico the night Matt was killed, but he hadn't been at home either. Which was why, Kenzie later learned, Emma had been up at such an ungodly hour to notice the lights on in her kitchen. John had been at a hotel because Emma had kicked him out of the house. Again.

Kenzie and Emma had a lot in common, but their marriages did not. John was a heavy drinker, one of those people for whom there is no gray area, no in between. He was either the best guy you knew sober or a raging alcoholic. And his mercurial drinking habits were only the tip of the iceberg. Perpetually trying to prove himself to his father, getting passed over for several promotions and marrying an heiress only grew the iceberg. And the chip on John's shoulder grew right along with it.

Emma had threatened divorce half a dozen times. But she'd eventually relent, let him come home. He'd be sober for a while, or be deployed and be forced into sobriety, and things would go along uneventfully for a while. When John was sober he was a great father and according to Emma, an incredible lover. Kenzie knew Emma and John would likely be separated or divorced by now if Matt hadn't died. Emma felt guilty that happily married Kenzie had lost her husband when her own marriage was often dysfunctional and contentious.

Kenzie was delighted when her phone rang and Emma's picture popped up on the screen. It had been a few weeks since they'd spoken other than an occasional text. John was deployed and Emma had been in Texas visiting her family.

"Hey!"

"Lovey," Emma said by way of greeting. Her voice sounded thin and raspy.

"Smoking again?"

"Is it that obvious?"

"Em…"

"I know, I know. But don't judge me until you've spent two weeks with an overbearing mother, a doting father and a melodramatic grandmother. She's been dying for so long I've lost track of what deathbed we're on."

Kenzie laughed without opening her mouth. "She's going to outlive you if you keep that up."

Emma took a drag. "Last one."

"Where are the boys?" Emma never smoked around the kids.

"Janie has them. I needed a minute. We got back last night and I wanted to get organized, stock up, etc."

Kenzie visualized Emma unpacking, doing laundry, sorting through weeks of mail in her picture-perfect house. Her houses always jumped off the pages of *Architectural Digest* within a month of her occupying them. She played it off as a self-indulgent hobby, but it was often the subject of speculation among the neighborhood women. Only Kenzie knew that Emma could buy the Mojave Desert if she wanted to.

The mention of their mutual friend brought a smile to Kenzie's face. Janie's twin boys were the same age as Katie and Emma's oldest and they frequency spelled each other. "How's she doing?"

"Janie? Fine. As annoyingly contented as usual. They got a new puppy while we were gone and she thought the kids would want to meet him. Gives me a couple of hours alone and entertains the twins at the same time. Everybody wins." Emma took another drag. "So, how are you?"

"Okay."

"That okay sounds almost as pathetic as my smoker's rattle."

"Then I'll try again." Kenzie cleared her throat and gave an overblown, "Great!"

"Now you're overcorrecting."

"I'm good, actually."

"Are you in Tahoe?"

"Yes, for another few weeks."

"So is it true? Does Tahoe heal all wounds? Mind, body and soul?"

"There is something about the rarefied air." Kenzie filled Emma in on what they'd been doing, ending with Mattie working with Greg Gentry.

"He's from South Texas."

"I didn't realize that."

"His dad played for the Astros. Anyway, let's just say he and I have a few digits in common. His family goes way back in old Texas money too. My grandfather and his were founding members of the country club where my parents belong. He lives in Tahoe these days?"

"In the summer. He lives in Phoenix for most of the year."

"That makes sense. I think his wife is from there. He's a bit of a legend in my neck of the woods in more ways than one."

"How so?"

"Well, his illustrious baseball career aside, he has a penchant for the ladies. And the cards. A chip off the old block from what I understand. Hopefully he banked enough coin to cover all his bases, so to speak. But there are worse things. He's relatively harmless and was an outstanding athlete. I don't think any of his kids took to it, so he's probably got a lot of pent-up knowledge to share. That'll be good for Mattie."

"It'd better be. He charges a small fortune."

"Speaking of fortunes, I rented a villa in Coronado over Labor Day weekend. There's plenty of room if you want to come down."

"That sounds wonderful," Kenzie replied. "But Mattie will probably have baseball and now with these private lessons, I don't think I could make it work. Where's John again?"

"He's in-country."

"Which one?"

"Your guess is as good as mine. But I have a feeling it's spelled with a lot of vowels."

Kenzie nodded. She didn't miss those days. "At least you know he's sober, or close to it, for the time being."

"That doesn't do us much good in the long run. Government sanctioned sobriety." She started to say something else, but swallowed it.

"Spit it out, Em. I can take it."

Emma began on a sigh, "If it were just the drinking I could deal with it. Help him. Give him an ultimatum—rehab or us. But it's more than that. The hang-up about my family money, refusing to accept the reality of never achieving his father's rank, let alone that of his brother. The mood swings, depression, lack of coping skills. It's a vicious circle of excuses. If John could feel any more sorry for himself, he would. He wants to be pitied, play the victim. When he's like that, there's no living with him."

"Have you told him that?"

"Not in so many words, but yes, I've tried. He doesn't, or refuses to, see it."

"I'm sorry, Em."

Emma took a long, slow drag, blew it out. "No, *I'm* sorry. This is so insensitive of me! It's just that I... forget it," she said, audibly stubbing out the cigarette. "Tell me what's going on with Katie. Is she excited about going to middle school?"

"Now you're pissing me off. If the tables were turned you would never put up with this sidestepping bullshit from me. Finish what you started."

Emma took a moment, then began on deliberate breath. "I'm starting to think that John isn't my lifelong love, if such a thing even exists. Maybe there really is a season for everything and ours has come and gone. Maybe we were meant to be together for a while, for the kids to be born, to get me out of Texas and out from under my parents' thumb. And maybe the time has come for me, for both of us, to move on. Maybe I'm trying to do the right thing for the wrong reasons by hanging on to something that's not meant to be."

"Square the circle," Kenzie said under her breath.

"Put simply, yeah."

"So what's holding you back?"

"For starters, I love John. And even if I didn't, he's the boys' father and a good one. I don't want to use the booze as a cop-out and whether we're married or not, I've got to help him stop drinking. I can't give up on him. That's not the same as giving up on us. But sometimes I wonder if my true love, if that does exist, is out there somewhere waiting for me. Or in a relationship and feeling the same way I am. And I don't want to wait until I'm old and gray, or even another decade until the boys are grown and flown, to find out."

Kenzie took a deep breath, blew it out slowly. "Em, I…Wow."

"I know, it's a lot. A lot to risk, a lot to lose. And I also know I'm the only one who can figure this out, make this call. And that I'm the one who has to live with the consequences."

"True. But don't sell yourself short in the process. You deserve to be happy inside."

"Most of the time the majority of me is. But the part that isn't is getting bigger and louder and stronger. And I think I need to start listening to the little voice inside my head again. The one that told me to take a chance on John in the first place, the one that told me to jump on a plane when my grandfather was dying, the one that told me not to try again for a girl. Because I'm starting to think that our season, John's and mine, is coming to an end. One way or another."

"Even if you never find that lifelong love and end up alone?"

"Yes," Emma all but whispered now. "Even if I end up alone." Neither one of them said anything for a few weighty ticks. Finally, Emma broke the silence. "See, I told you it was insensitive. I'm a terrible friend."

"Stop. You know better than anyone that Matt and I weren't living the dream, especially at the end. I know no one really is, but let's face it we weren't in a good place."

"You've got to stop beating yourself up about that. You guys were solid. The love and commitment was always there, underneath it all. That means something and it always will."

"Same for you and John."

"I used to think so, I really did. But lately I'm not so sure. I love him and I know I always will. But I don't know if I can live with him for the rest of my life. I feel like the John I fell in love with has been slipping away from me little by little for years. And now there's so little of him left that I miss him already, before he's even gone. For all I know, he feels the same way about me. I'm not the same person I was fifteen years ago."

Kenzie doubted that, but she kept it to herself. She sensed Emma had done enough dumping for one day, so she decided to lighten things up. "Now who's being melodramatic? Besides, wouldn't you miss the sex? With John, I mean? Could you ever find that again?"

"Well, there's only one way to find out!" Emma laughed. "No, that would say more about me than it would him. Plus, it's a bad example for the kids. I would never betray my marriage vows. But yes, I would miss it. I won't pretend I haven't thought about that, our incredible sexual chemistry."

"Doesn't that tell you something?"

"I didn't have much experience in the intimacy department before I met John. And you and I both know how lonely deployments can get. But I also know this would be different. No guaranteed pot at the end of the rainbow."

"Tell me about it. It's been so long I've probably forgotten how to do it."

"I'll come right back to you, Kenz. Like gangbusters."

"I just can't imagine."

"Maybe you should try to. Maybe you should start preparing yourself for that eventuality. Because it's bound to happen sooner or later."

"Yeah, I know." Kenzie heard the sounds of Emma transferring laundry to the dryer and hitting the start button, then putting in another load of wash. It made her smile to visualize Emma in her laundry room, neat as a pin and decorated to a tee. She'd forgotten how much she missed having her right across the street. Emma was like having a sister without all the complications of a sibling. Because as much as Kenzie loved her brother, he was complicated.

"How has Greg held up? Have the years been kind?" Emma was asking.

"I don't remember what he used to look like. But he's a good-looking guy, I guess. I hadn't really thought about it."

"Well, maybe you should start thinking about it. He's apparently getting divorced for real this time. Might be a good trial run. I'm sure he'd be more than happy to accommodate you."

"Em, I can hardly imagine kissing another man let alone anything else."

"Then don't imagine anything else. Start small. Well, not too small. You want it to be worth it."

"You're evil," Kenzie told her through a giggle.

"Never professed otherwise. All right, I've got to run. I'm taking Janie's boys for a few hours later because she has book club. I've got to jump in the shower before she drops everybody off. Plus all this talk of sex is getting me worked up and John is gone for three more months."

"Speaking of a trial run…"

"I know you're being facetious but you're right. That's a good way to think of it. A post-divorce celibacy trial run."

"You have a term for it?"

"I just might. Either way, I'm sexless."

"That makes two of us."

"At least you have a choice."

"Even if I were interested, with whom would I break my dry spell? You're not seriously suggesting Greg Gentry? The inveterate womanizer with the gambling problem?"

"There's got to be an eligible bachelor or two left in Tahoe. Doesn't your brother have any friends?"

"My brother isn't here, which is why I am. And the only friend of his I've met is Bren."

"What's wrong with him?"

"Well, nothing I guess. I don't know much about him."

"That's odd, because you've mentioned him half a dozen times in the last fifteen minutes."

"I have?"

Emma sighed, mocking excessive patience. "He's a writer, lives in the mountains, likes Moose Tracks ice cream like your dad, is a voracious reader like Katie and shares Mattie's love of baseball. He's an only child, yet still tolerable like myself, and was raised by a single mother in Sacramento. He's a Tahoe guy through and through, couldn't love living there any more. And lastly and most notably, he spends a lot of time at a dog park for a guy who doesn't have a dog." She paused, then ended on a breath, "Did I miss anything?"

"Yeah," Kenzie told her, feeling a smile snake across her face. "It's really just a park that allows dogs. And he's coming over for catch and pizza tonight."

"There you go. Maybe you found your whom."

"Now you're grasping at straws. For all I know, he's in a relationship."

"Did you see any signs of a woman at his house?"

"No, I guess not."

"He's alone in the evenings, brings takeout to the dog park sans dog and has plenty of time to throw a bullpen with a kid he just met. A darling little boy with a beautiful mother. Who just happens to be single."

"I'm not single, I'm widowed," Kenzie corrected. "There's a difference."

"You're right, there is," Emma allowed. "Right now anyway. But one of these days you're going to start thinking of yourself as a little less widowed and a little more single. And when that day comes, it'll be nice to have options. Bren might be one of them."

Kenzie didn't comment, just twirled her wedding rings on her finger and bit her bottom lip as Emma continued, "Plus he beats the hell out of a washed-up baseball player with a roving eye."

Kenzie couldn't deny that, so she didn't. "I thought you had to shower."

"I do. I'm undressing as we speak. Let me know how pizza goes. And Kenz?"

"Hmm?"

"You deserve to be happy inside too."

With the hollow tone of disconnection ringing in her ear, Kenzie stared at her rings and thought about something her mom used to say about words. About what a difference a word can make. A word has the power to change the trajectory of your life. Like saying yes to a marriage proposal. And the power to destroy it. Like the word she'd gotten in the middle of the night sixteen months, one week, two days and, she glanced at the clock on the microwave, eleven hours ago. Those words had changed everything forever.

The irony of Emma's situation was not lost on Kenzie any more than it was on Emma. Emma was contemplating ending her marriage and moving on, a thought that had never entered Kenzie's mind even in the worst of times. And Kenzie was struggling to move on after her marriage had been ended for her. So while the difference between widowed and single might be more nuanced than she'd thought, it also might not be as determinate as she'd assumed. Because at the end of the day, they were just words. And Emma was right; feeling guilty doesn't change anything. It wouldn't bring Matt back or change the way things had been between them those last days any more than denying herself future happiness would.

Kenzie chewed on that as she tidied up the house and threw together a salad for dinner. Six months ago she wouldn't have gotten through that conversation without tears running down her face, something Emma knew. Emma had obviously been feeling this way about John for a while, but didn't bring it up for fear of upsetting Kenzie. So Emma could sense it too, that Kenzie was stronger, ready to embrace life again instead of watching it go by from the sidelines. And maybe the day when she would start thinking of herself as less widowed and more single was closer than she thought. But she still couldn't conceive of another man's hands… The jingle of her phone drew her out of her rumination. Looking at the screen, she decided to ignore the coincidence as she answered.

"Hello."

"Hey, Kenzie. It's Bren."

This was the first time they'd spoken on the phone and his voice sounded deep, gritty, sexy. "I know," she replied breathily.

"Wow. I guess I've achieved add to contacts status?"

"Don't let it go to your head. I stopped answering numbers I don't recognize, so I programmed you in. I've got to practice what I preach to my kids."

"I'm going to pretend I didn't hear that and stick with feeling special. Is six still good for you guys?"

"Sure. But only if it works for you. I'm sure you have better things to do on a Saturday night."

"Actually, I don't." Silence stretched out between them for a moment before Bren picked up the conversation again. "So, what kind of pizza do you guys like?"

"Anything is fine. No aversions or allergies here."

"Great. See you in a bit then."

"Thanks again."

"Sure."

She'd no sooner put the phone down when Mattie strolled into the kitchen.

"Mom, I'm hungry."

"Well, grab a banana to hold you over because Bren will be here soon with pizza."

"Okay," So saying, Mattie grabbed a water bottle from the refrigerator and a banana out of the fruit basket on the counter. "Who were you talking to?"

"Emma."

"They just got home from Texas, right?"

Kenzie affirmed with a nod. "Were you and Sam texting?"

"Yeah. He was bored at his grandparents' house." Mattie paused, then asked, "Can we visit them sometime?"

"Yeah, sure." They'd had such a busy year that Kenzie hadn't given much thought to going back to Twentynine Palms for a visit. But seeing Mattie's sorrowful expression made her realize she should have.

"Soon?"

"Maybe. We have a lot going on this summer. I'm not sure when we could fit it in."

"Could they come here, then? Maybe Will and Cam too?" he proposed, speaking of Janie's boys.

So it was more about the people than the place. For some reason, that made Kenzie feel better. "That'd be fun, wouldn't it? Like a reunion?"

"Yeah. And both their dads are gone right now, so…"

He wouldn't be the only one, Kenzie thought. She took him into a one-armed hug. "Yeah, I know," she said with a catch in her throat. "I'll work on that, see if I can put something together, okay?"

"Okay," he replied, pulling away. "I'm going to finish my game. I have five minutes left."

Looking on as Mattie returned to his room, Kenzie ran the summer schedule through her mind. She could take Emma up on her Coronado offer, maybe see if Janie could go too. But that was around her parents' anniversary and she wanted to do something special for them since they'd done so much for her this past year. Then there was the matter of getting a job or going back to school.

Kenzie was weighing the pros and cons of all of that when a realization suddenly hit her. What if Matt wasn't the love of her life? What if her lifelong love was out there somewhere waiting for her? And it took an unspeakable tragedy for her to find him? And what if Emma's analogy about the seasons applied to her too? That for some people relationships— friendships, romances, marriages—served their purpose, ran their course and then came to an end. However that end came to be. And that this soulmate business was really nothing more than a fairy tale. For some people she qualified, thinking of her parents on the doorstep of their forty-fifth anniversary. She and Matt hadn't even gotten half that far. But they would have. Surely they would have, right?

But even if Matt wasn't the love of her life, even if he had to die to pave the way for a future Kenzie couldn't yet fathom, how would she know the difference? Recognize the signs? Trust her feelings? Trust another man not only with her heart, but with that of her children? Let alone all the intangibles. She'd never had a lover like Matt, someone with whom she was so compatible, so in tune with from the very beginning. Even if she met someone eventually, how could she help but compare him to Matt? It was probably never going to happen anyway, she told herself as the doorbell rang. She glanced at the clock. She'd been so lost in thought that she hadn't realized how much time had passed. She made it to the door just behind Boot.

"Pizza delivery for the Bishops," Bren announced merrily, holding three large pizza boxes in one hand and a bottle of wine in the other. He must have rung the bell with his elbow. He was dressed in jeans and a San Francisco Giants T-shirt, having changed out of the shorts and sweatshirt he'd been wearing when she'd stopped by this morning. His eyes twinkled as if he'd just heard a joke and the spark intensified when they met hers. She found herself unable to tear hers away.

"I'm sorry, did I get my wires crossed?" Bren asked. "I thought we said six."

Kenzie let out a breath she didn't know she'd been holding and blinked away the stupor. "Not at all. Come on in." She stepped aside, allowing him to enter.

"I know I'm a little early, but North Shore was surprisingly slow for a Saturday night in July," he said by way of excuse. "They fixed me right up."

"No problem. Here, let me help."

"I've got it. Just point me in the right direction."

"Straight back." Kenzie gestured with a tip of the head. Boot had taken the opportunity to relieve himself in the front yard and she waited for him to come back, then closed the door. When she got to the kitchen, she found Mattie and Bren debating pizza toppings.

"You gotta go with sausage, buddy," Bren was saying. "Pepperoni is for amateurs."

"You don't get the same coverage with sausage. There's a pepperoni in every bite."

Bren shook his head from side to side, feigning dissent. "At North Shore they use a sausage *patty*. They don't take any chances—no crumble and spread for them." Bren opened one of the boxes stacked on the kitchen island. "But to cover all our bases, I got us one of each."

"Wow! Awesome!"

"And I got a veggie one too. Figured your mom might like that."

"She will. We'll probably have to have salad too," Mattie scoffed.

"You gotta take the good with the bad."

Kenzie indulged in their male bonding session for a moment more, then joined the party. "Bren, this is enough to feed an army."

"You guys can have some tomorrow too." He handed her the bottle of wine. "I wasn't sure if you preferred red or white, so I played it safe with white."

"Chardonnay is perfect. Thank you." She went to the refrigerator. "Gov has a few Sierra Nevadas in here if you'd rather have a beer."

"Sure."

Kenzie handed him one, then got out the bowl of salad and set it on the counter.

"See," Mattie told Bren under his breath, "told ya."

"Okay, smarty-pants, do me a favor and give Boot his dinner and wash your hands."

Mattie obliged as Kenzie grabbed the corkscrew. When she started to open the wine, she realized her hands were shaking. What the hell was wrong with her?

"Here, let me get that." Bren, all smiles, appeared at her side and took over. She'd noticed his cologne when he arrived, but now that he was standing close to her she could break down the scent. Sandalwood and spice with notes of tobacco. She felt its virile, potent fragrance settle in the vee between her legs. Damn Emma and all her sex talk.

"Thanks. I'll set the table outside." Grateful for the diversion, Kenzie grabbed plates, napkins and silverware and went out the deck door. The evening was airy and moonlit and the aspen leaves flittered in the breeze as if about to take flight. She put the napkins under the plates so they wouldn't blow away and was heading back inside when Bren and Mattie came out. Bren was carrying the bowl of salad on top of the pizza boxes and a beer under his arm. Mattie had a glass of wine in one hand, a Coke in the other and a bottle of water under his arm. Men, she thought shaking her head, are all the same.

"What?" They asked in unison.

"Nothing. It just starts young."

Bren and Mattie looked at each other in bewilderment, then back at her. "What does?" Bren asked, putting the food down on the table.

"Never mind."

They doled out the pizza and, much to Mattie's chagrin, the salad. Bren and Mattie talked about baseball and how cool it was that Bren lived next door to a real baseball player. Bren downplayed that, saying how cool it was that Mattie got to take lessons from a real baseball player. Kenzie didn't say much; she was enjoying the banter. Bren declined a second beer and the two of them went to warm up in the backyard.

Wine in hand, Kenzie looked on. She hoped Mattie would always remember Matt playing catch with him, however few and far between those occasions might have seemed. Wiping a tear from the corner of her eye, she got up and cleared off the table and stowed the leftovers, condensing the pizzas and refrigerating the rest of the salad. She poured herself another glass of wine and checked her phone to make sure she hadn't missed a call from Katie, then went back outside.

Setting a couple of waters on the deck table, Kenzie watched as Bren threw to Mattie. It looked like they were working on bunting. Bren was saying something about using your legs and imagining catching the ball with the bat, not pushing it away. He was so good at breaking things down to a level a kid could understand. And he was patient, even his body language was relaxed. He really seemed to be enjoying himself as much as Mattie. And there it was again, that impalpable feeling, almost like a smile in her stomach, mixed with trepidation and laced with…yearning? No, it couldn't be! Before she'd likened this feeling to that of being pregnant, the excitement and anticipation of meeting her baby, but it was more intricate than that. Suddenly unable to sit still, Kenzie went inside and started needlessly wiping off the counters. She was scouring the sink when she noticed Bren and Mattie sitting on the deck steps taking a water break. She could hear their conversation through the open kitchen window.

"Did your dad teach you how to play baseball?"

Bren shook his head. "My dad wasn't around when I was a kid."

"Did he die?"

"No. At least I don't think so."

"What happened to him?"

"I'm not sure." Bren shrugged those broad, muscular shoulders. "I don't think he wanted to be a dad. Or he didn't want to be my dad."

Kenzie could all but see the wheels turning in Mattie's head as he tried to make sense of that. "Why? Were you bad?"

Bren laughed. "Not particularly. But he wouldn't have known either way. I never met him."

"Never?"

"Nope."

Mattie thought about that for a moment. "So your dad never saw you play?"

"Nope. But my mom never missed a game."

"My mom never misses a game either."

"That's because she's a great mom, like my mom. She's super proud of you. And I know your dad was super proud of you too."

"Yeah, I know. But he was gone a lot. He missed a lot of games."

"He wanted to be there. But he had to be away sometimes. So all of us can be safe and free to do things like play baseball and eat pizza and ice cream."

"I guess," Mattie half-heartedly agreed. "My mom says he watches us from heaven."

"Sure he does. He's your biggest fan."

"Really? You think so?" Mattie lightened.

"Absolutely."

"I bet your dad would have been super proud of you too. If he'd come to your games."

"Well, I guess we'll never know." Bren cleared his throat. "Okay, let's get back to it. We're burning daylight."

Kenzie didn't realize she was crying until the tears hit the back of her hand. That was one of the sweetest, most generous and most heartbreaking things she'd ever heard. She hadn't realized how much Mattie needed a father figure in his life. Not just to play catch with but to talk to about things she couldn't relate too. And no matter how hard her dad and brother tried to fill that gap, it wasn't the same. Mattie hadn't made as many friends in Reno as Katie had; his only social outlet was baseball. Kenzie had to do a better job of rounding him out. And to be honest, she could use a little rounding out herself.

She was thinking about that and how to go about it when Katie called. They made arrangements for Kenzie to pick her up tomorrow afternoon. Katie asked what she and Mattie were doing and for some reason Kenzie didn't go into much detail. She had no sooner disconnected when Bren and Mattie came into the kitchen.

"Private lessons weren't in the cards for me, so count your blessings," Bren was saying. "I went to the batting cages a lot."

"Can we do that sometime?"

"Sure."

"My grandpa took me a couple of times, but he only watched. He says he's too old to swing. But you aren't."

"I guess we'll find out."

"Great!"

Over Mattie's head, Kenzie mouthed, "Thank you."

Their gaze held for a long moment until Bren broke it with a nod. "Well, I'd better get going."

He started to turn on his heel, but Kenzie stopped him. "Here, I packed up some pizza for you. We'll never eat it all." She went to the refrigerator and grabbed two plastic bags. "I'll hold on to the veggie, though. It's my favorite, so thanks again. And I think you have a sausage convert."

"The patty speaks for itself," Bren replied, his eyes full of humor.

They walked Bren out and waved him off. Then Mattie went to take a shower and Kenzie headed back to the kitchen. When she passed the mirror in the hallway she realized she was smiling again. As she put the kitchen to rights, the game her family played at dinner when she was growing up came to mind. The four of them had to go around the table and say what they'd learned today, good or bad. Her brother often grumbled his answer and her father made something up half the time to appease her mother, but Kenzie had always looked forward to her turn. She usually had something prepared. Living with her parents had introduced the tradition to the kids and given her a new appreciation for it. So much so that Kenzie often found herself taking stock at the end of the day. And today she'd learned that the difference between being widowed and being single isn't as clear-cut as she'd thought. She would have felt that her life was over when Matt died if not for the kids. But maybe now it was time to actually start living again, instead of just getting by or getting through. Bolstered by her renewed sense of agency, she locked up and adjusted the lights. And unbeknownst to her, she'd be putting that new perspective to the test sooner rather than later.

CHAPTER EIGHT

When Bren said he'd practice with Matt anytime he'd meant it. That wasn't the problem. But he had one. And his name was Greg Gentry. Clearly Greg was attracted to Kenzie, a feeling with which Bren could identify. And although he'd initially been drawn to Kenzie for obvious reasons, Bren really liked Matt. He was easy to be around and fun to play ball with. Tonight had been one of Bren's best evenings of late.

Until he got home.

When Bren pulled into his driveway, he noticed Greg smoking a cigar on the front steps. Apparently Olivia Gentry's rules remained in effect even in her absence. Bren gave Greg a perfunctory wave, closed the garage door and thought no more of it.

Until a knock sounded on the front door five minutes later.

When Bren opened it he found Greg standing on the other side. The cigar was wedged in the corner of his mouth and the necks of two beer bottles dangled from the tips of his fingers. Even at fifty, he all but dwarfed the frame. He was still that built.

Greg removed the cigar with his free hand. "Got a minute?"

"Sure. Come on in."

Bren led him through the living room and out to the deck, switching on the outside lights as he went. They sat at the table and Greg set the beers down, then produced a bottle opener from his shorts pocket and popped off the caps. He slid one over to Bren.

"Thanks." Bren took a swig. "What's up?" They were neighbors and acquaintances, but not necessarily friends. And Bren's gut told him this was not a social call.

Greg snubbed out the cigar in one of the bottle caps, then laid it on top of it. "I was wondering how well you know Mackenzie Bishop."

"I just met her." Faking indifference, Bren shifted in his chair. "She's watching Gov's dog while he's out-of-town. I ran into her at the park and we made the connection."

Greg nodded around a sip of beer. "Is she married?"

"Widowed."

"Recently?"

"About a year and a half ago, I think. Why do you ask?"

"Her check listed her name, no husband, but she wears a wedding ring. When she filled out Mattie's paperwork, she only put herself down in the parental information and listed his emergency contact as her parents. Didn't seem as though there was a father in the picture."

"He was killed in a military accident."

"I'm sorry to hear that. On foreign soil?"

"No, he was stateside. I don't know the details," Bren lied.

"So is she available?"

"Available?" Bren repeated unnecessarily, feeling the hairs on the back of his neck stand up.

"To go out. Maybe grab a drink or dinner?"

"Uh, I think she's pretty busy with the kids. And it hasn't been that long since her husband died."

"Over a year, you said. That's a respectable amount of time to mourn. She might just need someone to get her over the hump, get her back out there. And I'm just the guy for the job," Greg finished with raised brows and a smile dripping with hubris.

Bren sent Greg a stoic look, but inside he was fuming. The guy was barely separated and was shamelessly pursuing a vulnerable widow. Where was Mac when he needed him? "I'd let that one ride, Greg. Mackenzie doesn't seem interested in dating."

"Well, there's only one way to find out."

"Wouldn't that complicate your divorce?"

"Nah," Greg grunted. "Livy and I have had an understanding for years. She doesn't want to drag things out any more than I do. We're splitting everything straight down the middle. And I'll make sure my kids are always taken care of. At least I didn't screw that up."

Charming, Bren thought. "She's only going to be here for a few more weeks."

"But she lives in Reno, right?"

"She does."

Greg dismissed that with a wave of the hand. "Quick trip down the mountain. I'm going to be working with Mattie all month. Hell, if things were to progress between she and I, I'd be willing to comp the whole damn thing. There's just something about her, you know?"

Bren studied Greg through a lengthy pull of beer. He needed to play this close to the vest. Greg was a professional athlete, a natural competitor. He could smell a challenge in the air. And Bren didn't want to encourage him by giving him the whiff of one.

"You didn't tell me she was smoking hot, man," Greg was still talking. "Next time give me a heads-up. My eyes nearly fell out of my head."

Bren gave Greg a contrived smile. "Come on Greg, you're used to beautiful women. And I don't just mean your wife."

"You've got me there," Greg chortled. "Not that I'm proud of it. But I've learned my lesson. Unfortunately not in time to save my marriage. But now I'm as free as a bird."

Tread lightly, Bren reminded himself. "Well, I suggest you take your nascent freedom elsewhere. Tahoe is teeming with beautiful women. You'd have no trouble finding one to have a drink or dinner with."

"You're probably right. But some women just stick in your head, you know? Like a tune you can't shake. I mean, she was sexy as hell in shorts and a T-shirt. I can't imagine how incredible she'd look all dressed up."

Bren could, had, in fact. He'd imagined Kenzie all dressed up, then he'd imagined undressing her. Slowly, using his mouth as much as his hands. And then her doing the same to him. "I think you're barking up the wrong tree here, Greg. Kenz—Mackenzie— seems like she's more comfortable in shorts and T-shirt than evening wear. I'd hate for you to set yourself up for disappointment."

Greg gave Bren a slow nod. So slow that Bren wondered if he was catching on to his self-serving dissuasion. "Well, we can't have that." Greg polished off his beer and stood. "Thanks for the info."

Bren rose and met Greg's steady gaze. His full head of side-swept hair was white-blond more from a lifetime in the sun than age, and his eyes a prominent gunmetal blue against his deeply bronzed and furrowed face. They both clocked in at just over six feet but Greg's shoulders were broader, more brawny. Still, Bren knew he could take him. Greg had twenty pounds and ten years on him.

"Thanks for the beer."

Greg picked up the cigar and the bottle cap. "I figured since you just got home I wouldn't be interrupting anything."

"Nothing at all. I'll take that," Bren said, reaching for the bottle. "I'll toss it in the recycling bin with mine."

They walked back through the house. Just before they got to the front door Greg turned to Bren. "Big Saturday night for you, huh? Home before ten."

Bren matched the innuendo in Greg's voice the same way he had his gaze. Unwaveringly. "Every night's Saturday night for me. I make my own schedule." He

116

opened the door. "But you know how that goes these days, right?"

"Heard that. You know, we should do this again sometime."

Keep your enemies closer, Bren thought and stuck out his hand. "Stop by anytime. I'm usually around."

Greg shook it. "I just may. See ya, Bren."

"See ya," Bren told Greg's retreating back. But inside he was saying *game on*.

*****

And a few days later, the games began. Bren was working on the deck when he heard a car pull into Greg's driveway. Normally he wouldn't give that a second thought, but Kenzie had mentioned that Matt had a lesson this afternoon. It was another one of those times when Bren's steel-trap mind came in handy. Now he considered it a gift from his mother. When he was a teenager not so much as he'd inherited it from her.

He heard a car door slam shut, then another. The thunk of an SUV, not the muted sound of a sports car. Diverse voices in the distance, several sets of footfalls. Bren listened for the sound of a car door closing again and an engine firing up, but heard neither. Maybe Kenzie was sticking around for the lesson this time.

Bren forced his attention back to his laptop. He'd finished the revisions on his work-in-progress more to get Miranda off his back than to beat his deadline. He never missed a deadline. But he'd made the mistake of skimming the outline for the next project. And it had intrigued him so much that he'd been trying to flesh out an angle since the sun came up, which was going on eight hours ago. No wonder he was starving.

Bren was heading into the kitchen to remedy that when he noticed someone coming up the front walk. Even through the blur of the beveled glass he recognized Kenzie's glossy hair and fluid gait. She'd stuck around all right, but not for the lesson. Bren's heart soared along with his spirits as he made his way to the door, opening it just as her foot hit the landing.

"Kenzie."

"Hi." She was wearing a breezy skirt and a sleeveless top that fell just above the curve of her breasts and hugged her abdomen like a glove. The thought of him doing the same tied Bren's stomach up in knots.

"I promise I won't make a habit of dropping by unannounced."

"What?" Bren blinked a few times. He'd let himself get lost in her eyes again. They looked ultramarine today as if trying to keep up with the lake. "Don't be silly. Please come in."

"Thanks." She stepped over the threshold. "I come bearing gifts."

It was then Bren realized she was holding a cup carrier with drinks and sandwiches. "What's all this?"

"The cupboards were bare at Gov's, so I took Mattie to get lunch before his lesson. You brought pizza over the other night, so I thought I'd return the favor. Do you have time for a quick bite?"

Bren wanted a bite all right, but not of the food. And he didn't want it to be quick. But he replied, "Sure. You must be a mind reader. I was just getting something to eat. Let's sit outside." He reached for the carrier. "Here, let me get that."

"I've got it. Lead the way."

He led her through the living room and out to the deck. Kenzie sighed in appreciation as she took in the view. "Bren, this is just incredible. You can see all the way across the lake and then some. I feel like I'm in a treehouse."

"When I first looked at the place, I liked it. But when I saw the view, I had to have it."

"Who could blame you?"

He pushed his laptop off to the side. "I'll grab some plates."

"Don't bother. We can eat off the wrapper. We'll have a picnic." She set the carrier down on the table, then handed Bren one of the sandwiches. "I played it safe with turkey and American on white. I figured if you wanted mayo or mustard, you'd have it on hand."

"Perfect. Thanks."

She distributed the drinks. "I went with regular Coke for the same reason."

"Can't beat the real thing."

"Yeah. I never did take to the diet stuff."

She didn't need to, not with that body. "Here, allow me." He pulled out her chair.

Kenzie looked back at him in awe as she sat. "Thank you. Your mama sure raised you right."

Sitting across from her, he replied around a laugh, "So I'm often told."

She smiled and unwrapped her sandwich.

"Where's Katie today?"

"She's with the Westins again. Katie and Morgan were in the same class last year and became instant besties. Morgan has older twin brothers so she's the odd man out. They're going rafting, then spending the afternoon in Truckee. Katie is going to stay the night with them. It's a nice change of pace for her, but I miss her."

Bren swallowed his first bite. "I'm sure."

"But I'd better get used to it," Kenzie went on. "She's at that age. Sleepovers, hanging out with friends, becoming more independent."

"I remember."

As they ate, they talked about their childhoods, college years, jobs. Kenzie's time at USC overlapped with some of his at UCLA. She'd met her husband and gotten married a few years after graduation. Bren didn't have much to add in that regard but found himself oddly interested in Matt and their life together. Kenzie told him about her time abroad and they compared notes on travel. Among other commonalities, they had both been on safari in Africa. "Not long after that I found out I was pregnant with Katie," she elaborated with a dreamy smile. "We were so glad we took that opportunity when we did."

The next thing Bren knew, Kenzie's phone buzzed. "Ten-minute warning." Standing, she started to tidy up like she had that first night at the park.

Bren joined her, halting her hands with one of his. Hers were silky and smooth, like a spring rose on a dewy morning. "I've got this. You go get Matt. He'll be excited to tell you what they did today."

"He'll want to tell you too, so maybe we could go over together," Kenzie suggested casually.

Bren felt the smile crossing his face all the way down to his toes. "Yeah, sure."

They gathered the trash and Bren threw it away in the kitchen. As they headed for the front door Kenzie said, "Gov mentioned Brody did your remodel. It looks great."

"Thanks," Bren returned, wondering if his name had come up in more than one conversation. "I'll give you the ten-cent tour sometime if you want."

Pausing at the door, she turned to him. "I'd really like that."

Bren felt something take hold inside him then, something he'd never felt before, something so profound that it stole his breath for a full ten-seconds. It grew and spread, dovetailed in his gut, then pulled him under. It wasn't a slow tumble and fall or as if he'd been struck by a bolt of lightning, but instead a feeling of immense joy infused with gratification and contentment. Like coming home after a long trip or achieving a hard-fought goal. Or falling in love. His mind went blank, his mouth dry. But somehow he managed, "Maybe next time."

"Great."

When they got outside, Greg and Matt were just coming around from the backyard. Greg's hand was resting on Matt's shoulder and the kid was listening raptly, shaking his head in acknowledgment of what Greg was saying. Bren found himself smiling again, this time for a completely different reason. There was nothing quite like that thrill, that feeling of excitement and satisfaction tinged with just enough self-doubt to keep you on your toes, of realizing that you were good at something you loved. That you had what it takes.

And then Bren's smile got even bigger. The look of shock on Greg's face when he saw Bren and Kenzie approaching together was priceless. In fact, Bren would have traded a month's royalties for it without reservation. Greg's countenance fell as the realization sank in, but he caught it with the same celerity he had all those ground balls and line drives back in the day.

"Mom!" Matt broke away and ran to his mother. "Guess what? I took two-seconds off my time! I got the ball back to first in six-seconds!"

"Wow! I'm so proud of you!"

"Next time we're going to focus on footwork. And I need to watch more games. So I can learn to guess where the ball is going to go."

"Well, I'd much rather you do that than play video games."

"Me, too!"

"So I take it things went well?" Kenzie asked Greg.

"Very," Greg affirmed. "He's a great kid. Not just athletic but cooperative and focused. He's a coach's dream."

"Thank you."

"Thank you for letting me work with him." Greg shifted his gaze to Bren. "Hey, Bren. Just happen to be around today?"

"You know me, Greg. I'm a homebody," Bren responded, matching his snarky tone.

"Well, thanks again. We'll see you next time." Kenzie started to lead Matt away.

"Actually," Greg put in hastily. "I was wondering if you had time later to go over a training plan for Mattie."

Kenzie gave Greg a questioning look. "Oh, I thought we already did that."

"That was just a preliminary one. But now I have a better idea of his strengths and the areas I want to hone in on. I'd like to keep working with him after school starts as well. I can come to you for that. A buddy of mine owns a training facility in Reno. Indoor-outdoor, year-round, top-notch. I talked to him about working with Mattie there, especially after the weather turns. He's glad to help."

"Um…okay."

"I can put something together this afternoon. Maybe we could discuss it over a drink later?"

You bastard, Bren thought. Greg obviously pulled that out of his ass. And right in front of the kid too.

Kenzie opened her mouth slightly, closed it again. "I don't think that'll work, Greg. It's just Mattie and I tonight. My daughter is with a friend. Not that I leave the kids home alone much anyway."

"Well, maybe Bren here could help us out. If your daughter is otherwise occupied, Mattie could hang out with him for a bit, catch a game on TV. The All-Star break just ended, so the boys will be raring to go. In fact," Greg addressed Bren, "I think your Giants are playing at home tonight, aren't they Bren?"

Bren met Greg's calculated stare with one of his own. "You know, I'm not sure. I've had my nose to grindstone lately, haven't kept up with the schedule."

"Well, let's see here." Greg reached into his pocket and retrieved his phone, then started scrolling. "Yep. The A's at the Giants. Seven o'clock."

"Can we, Mom?"

Kenzie looked first at her son, then more beseechingly at Bren. Pressing his lips together to hide his clenching teeth, he sent her a tight nod. At least if Matt was him, he'd see Kenzie later.

"Yeah, I guess. I mean, if it's okay with Bren."

No, it was most certainly *not* okay with Bren. But what other choice did he have? Look like an ass in front of Matt? And petty to Kenzie? Tip his hand to Greg?

"Sure." Bren's tone was more brisk than he'd intended.

"Great," Greg preened. "It's Tuesday, so some restaurants are closed. I'll find a place and let you know. Pick you up around six?"

"I'll drive myself," Kenzie countered after a pause. "I'll have to drop Mattie at Bren's anyway."

"I'll come to your place, Kenzie," Bren decided out loud. "You'll be closer to town to meet Greg that way." And not alone with him, he added to himself. "And Greg," Bren went on as the idea took hold, "Hues of Blue is open seven days a week. The bar is a great place for a drink and not too loud for conversation. And the staff is top-notch," he finished patronizingly.

Greg, despite looking a little deflated, still managed to give Bren a taste of his own medicine. "Excellent suggestion, Bren. They also have a full dinner menu if we decide to make a night of it."

Before Bren could come up with a rejoinder, Kenzie interjected, "Dinner won't be necessary, Greg. But Hues of Blues is perfect. I'll meet you there at six-thirty." Then turning to her son said, "Time to get going. Boot will be crossing his legs."

They exchanged good-byes and the three of them walked down the driveway to Kenzie's car. After Matt got in, Kenzie turned to Bren. "I'm sorry Greg put you on the spot like that. I can cancel."

"Don't worry about it. I'll be nice to have someone to watch the game with. And Greg put both of us on the spot." But what Bren wanted to say was, *Yes, cancel and I'll still come over and we can all watch the game together.* But he only said, "I'll see you around six."

Kenzie drove away and Bren headed home. As he walked up his driveway, he noticed Greg was standing on the front steps. He gave Bren an upward nod, then went inside. But the silent message passed between them. *Game on.*

And to Greg that's all it was—a game. Another notch in his belt, another check in the win column. But to Bren it was the opposite of that. He couldn't get Kenzie out of his mind, not that he wanted to. He thought about her day and night, even when he was working. And that was a first. After all, there was nothing romantic about the female characters in his books. The women in his stories used their beauty, their bodies, their brains, as weapons, as a means to an end without remorse. And Bren wasn't going to let Greg inveigle Kenzie like that. She clearly had a good head on her shoulders, but was still a little frayed around the edges. And Greg wasn't going to be the one to smooth out those edges. Not on Bren's watch.

CHAPTER NINE

"*Where* have you been?" Kenzie demanded in a high-pitched whisper. Phone to her ear and out of Mattie's earshot, she wandered the deck.

"In a movie. It's hotter than hell here today. My bra feels wetter than when I was nursing. What's going on?"

"I have a date! That's what's going on!"

"Wow, that was a quick turnaround. I take it pizza night went well. There's just something about the simple things."

"Not with Bren! With Greg Gentry!"

"Well, give him my best. And send a picture if you can. I'm dying to see what he looks like now."

"Emma!"

"Okay, tell me what happened."

Kenzie brought Emma up to speed, ending with an exasperated, "Now what do I do?"

"Exactly what you said you would. Meet him for a drink, nurse a glass of wine, be your congenial self and hear out his plan for Mattie. Then after an hour, say you have to get home. Easy-peasy."

Kenzie stopped walking. "You think?"

"You have no other choice, for Mattie's sake at least."

"Emma, what have I done?"

"Nothing but be a good mom. You were a little blindsided, but you handled it. Now see it through."

"I guess you're right," Kenzie agreed with borrowed conviction.

"Of course I am. I'm great at solving everyone else's problems. It helps me avoid my own."

"Anything new with John?"

"No. He's been a little incommunicado."

"Is that good or bad?"

"Good. I know he's okay and there's no chance of us getting into it. Or worse, pussyfooting around the issue which is even more exhausting. He emails every couple of days and I share that with the kids. He'll be home in October."

"And then?"

"Then we'll transition, adjust, put out pumpkins and scarecrows. And see about the rest."

"You sound a little different this time, about the rest."

"Every time is a little different, a little closer. And this time it feels closer to right. But hope, and to a lesser extent oil, springs eternal. My grandfather, the eternal optimist, taught me that. And if he hadn't been one, I wouldn't be sitting here today, deciding between these two ridiculously expensive villas in Coronado. They had a cancellation and offered me an upgraded unit. But who needs a balcony off *every* bedroom?"

"Emma." Kenzie had to laugh. Emma somehow managed to say things like that without sounding the least bit braggadocios.

"You have your first world problem of the day, I have mine."

"I think mine beats yours. Today, anyway."

"It just might. Everything's going to be all right, Kenz. Things always work out. One way—"

"Or the other," Kenzie finished for her. "I know. You just have to make that way the right way."

"That's another thing my grandfather used to say. And things turned out pretty well for him."

"And, subsequently, for you."

"There's no denying it, so I won't try. But there's more to life than money, although it does come in handy. It gives us choices. Silly ones like I'm making now and important ones like you made earlier. You put your son first."

"I guess. Thanks. You always have a way of making me feel better."

"Likewise. Call me later to let me know how it goes."

"I will."

"You've got this, Kenz. Don't overthink it."

"Okay, Sheryl."

"I'm taking that as a compliment."

"It was meant as such."

After they disconnected, Kenzie took a long, determined breath, let it out and went inside. She found Mattie in the family room, watching the Cubs and the Cardinals duel it out. Gearing up for tonight, she thought. Walking to the bedroom, she decided she'd better do the same.

She hadn't packed anything appropriate for an evening out, not that she wanted to give Greg the impression that's what this was. But she'd thrown in a romper that was borderline dressy. She'd brought exactly three pairs of shoes; flip-flops, tennis shoes and a pair of wedges. So a green romper with black espadrilles and a denim jacket it would be. As Emma would say, easy-peasy.

Kenzie was debating if the romper needed a quick once-over with the iron when a realization hit her. Why did Greg assume she was single? Because only her name was listed on her check? Because she was here alone with the kids? Or had Mattie told him about his dad? That would be unusual for Mattie; he wasn't one to talk about Matt unless prompted. Many women had their own bank accounts, so that would be a bit presumptuous on Greg's part. And for all Greg knew, her husband was on a business trip or otherwise occupied. She threw in a load of laundry and decided to find out, starting with the least likely possibility.

"Do we care who wins here?" Kenzie asked, sitting down on the couch next to her son.

"Well, we never want the Cubs to win, so yeah."

"And?"

"Cards are up five to three, top of the sixth," Mattie informed her as the broadcaster threw to commercial.

"All right. Hey, did you tell Coach Gentry about Dad?"

Mattie turned to face her. "No. Why?"

"Just curious." Kenzie decided to take the rare opportunity of having her son's undivided attention to delve a little deeper. "So you're fine with hanging out with Bren tonight?"

Mattie shrugged. "Yeah. Why wouldn't I be?"

"Just making sure. I won't be gone long."

"He's cool. And he knows a ton about baseball. Almost as much as Coach Gentry. Except he never played in the big leagues." Mattie looked down into his lap. "And his dad was gone too. But in a different way."

"Yeah, I know," Kenzie replied softly around the lump forming in her throat. Kindred spirits, united in loss. After all, a loss is a loss, no matter the reason. The game came back on and Kenzie decided that was enough grilling for today. Plus, she needed to figure out dinner. Mattie would be hungry by the time she left and the least she could do was have something here for Bren. She patted her son's thigh and stood. "Let me know if the Cards pull it out."

Kenzie walked into the kitchen and did a quick survey of her options. There was always pasta. She had sauce and spaghetti but didn't have beef for meatballs. But she did have plenty of Parmesan cheese. So quick and easy meatless spaghetti it would be. Two problems solved, one to go. She mulled over the possibilities throughout the afternoon and decided it mattered less how Greg knew she was technically single and more that he did. At least she wouldn't have to rehash the whole thing. She put it out of her mind and kept the laundry going and got ready. She set the kitchen table, scooped out Boot's dinner and was letting him out in the front yard when Bren pulled up. The dog did his business and ran to the car, overjoyed.

"Well, hello there." Bren greeted Boot with scratches behind the ears. Kenzie wondered again how those hands would feel on her body. Strong and powerful, yet gentle, sensuous. Shuddering a little, she pushed down the thought and tried to focus on the matter at hand. She was probably just nervous about tonight she decided, watching Bren and Boot walk up the driveway. And unlike Greg, Bren felt so safe. No ulterior motives or hidden agenda to worry about with him.

"Come on, boy." Bren's stride was so long, he outpaced Boot. He carried a paper grocery bag in his arms and wore a lively grin on his face. When he reached Kenzie his eyes met hers and the grin widened, deepened. Their stare held for a few seconds before Bren said, "And hello to you too."

"Hello," Kenzie greeted, forcing herself out of her own head. "Thanks for coming over. Come on in."

Bren headed for the kitchen with Boot on his heels. He'd barely breached the threshold when he sniffed the air saying, "I don't know what that is, but it smells incredible."

"It's jarred spaghetti sauce doctored with a few spices and thickened with Parmesan cheese. And incredible is a bit of a stretch."

"Not to my nose. I can't remember the last time I had Italian food that wasn't takeout."

"Well, I guess tonight's your lucky night."

Setting the bag on the island, he met her eyes again, this time more affectingly. "I guess it is."

Kenzie let out a breath she didn't know she'd been holding. That feeling was sweeping through her again, the one she couldn't quite put her finger on. Her heart was racing, her stomach reeling. And then there was the buzzing in her ears...

"Hey, Bren!" Mattie came running into the kitchen.

"Hey, yourself!"

"Can we go out back and pitch some balls?"

"Later. Your mom has dinner ready."

"It'll keep," Kenzie said, grateful for the distraction. "Just boil some water in the microwave to reconstitute the pasta whenever you guys are ready to eat. Can you handle that, Bren?"

"Yep. I'm a wiz at boiling water in the microwave." Turning, he reached inside the bag. "I brought some ice cream—Cookies and Cream and Moose Tracks. I didn't want to risk both of us getting in trouble with Birthday Cake too." He glanced at Kenzie out of the corner of his eye. "And I picked up a some baseball cards. I collected them when I was a kid." He handed Mattie a stack. "Is that still a thing?"

Mattie shuffled the shrink-wrapped packs in his hands. "Not really. But we have a box of my dad's old cards." Considering, he looked up at Bren again. "Thanks. Now maybe I'll start my own collection."

"You're welcome. I still have mine if you want to look at them sometime."

"That'd be cool. Maybe you and my dad had some of the same ones."

"Could be."

"And I got a bottle of wine for your mom and some beer for your Uncle Gov. If he comes home to an empty fridge on account of me I'll never hear the end of it," Bren added as he finished unloading the bag. He shifted his glance to Kenzie. "Can I stick this stuff in the fridge?"

"Sure. Thanks." Kenzie would have loved a glass of wine to calm her nerves, but she knew she'd have one at Hues of Blue and had to drive.

"I'll grab my gear from the garage and meet you out back," Mattie told Bren.

"Sounds good," Bren said, then turned to Kenzie. "Am I allowed to drink on duty?"

"Of course." She laughed. "I do."

"Great." He put the ice cream in the freezer and the wine and beer in the refrigerator, reserving one. Then he twisted off the cap, took a sip and said, "You look nice."

"Thanks. I hope this is dressy enough."

"For Hues?" Bren snorted dismissively. "You might be overdressed." His gaze lingered through a long pause before he said, "It's a beautiful evening. The sunset will be spectacular."

"Oh, I'll be home long before sunset."

That seem to surprise and amuse him. "Will you?"

"I'm staying an hour, ninety minutes tops. That should be plenty of time to review a training plan, don't you think?"

"Absolutely." Bren took another sip. "But you know how those things go. One thing leads to another."

"One thing will not be leading to another tonight. I tried to make that clear earlier."

Just then Mattie stuck his head in the back door. "Ready?"

"You bet." Bren set the beer down on the island. "Can Boot come out with us?"

"Sure. I'll be out shortly to say good-bye."

Kenzie watched Bren take his leave. But instead of going to get her purse and jacket, she found herself staring out the window. Mattie was in his element, his expression intense, his eyes laser-focused on Bren as they warmed up. After a few pitches, Bren walked over and standing beside him, gripped the ball with his fingers and twisted his wrist, then extended his arm forward and pretended to throw. He handed the ball to Mattie, who imitated the technique. Then Bren clapped his hands and jogged back across the yard. Mattie threw to him, incorporating what Bren had demonstrated. Kenzie looked on as they went back and forth a few times, then went to the bedroom to grab her things. When she looked in the mirror, she realized her eyes were moist. She blotted them with a tissue, grabbed her jacket and purse and went out back.

"I'm heading out. See you guys in a bit."

"Bye, Mom."

Unlike Mattie, Bren looked up. "Hold up a sec, bud." He walked over to Kenzie and met her eyes. "Have a nice time."

"I'll try. Thanks for holding down the fort."

"We'll be fine. Nobody boils water in the microwave better than me."

She laughed without opening her mouth, then started to walk away. But Bren grabbed her hand and squeezed it reassuringly. She nodded in understanding and took her leave through the house.

The drive to Hues of Blue was short and uneventful. Kenzie pulled up to the entrance, handed her car off to the valet and went inside. When she got down to the bar at lake level, she saw Greg standing near the hostess stand, looking at this phone. He'd dressed up a bit as well, wearing jeans and a polo shirt as opposed to the shorts and T-shirt she'd seen him in earlier. With a resigned sigh she pasted a smile on her face and approached him with a friendly, "Hey, Greg."

Greg's head shot up. A suggestive smile spread across his face as his eyes filled with appreciation and lust. "Hey, Kenzie. Thanks for coming."

She didn't remember telling him to call her Kenzie, but she let it slide. That was the least of her worries. She couldn't deny it was nice to have a little male interest, but Greg was the wrong male and any interest he had in her aside from Mattie was purely physical. But it was an hour of her time for her son.

"Sure."

"There aren't any tables available right now, but something might open up in a bit. We can grab a drink in the meantime."

"Okay." Apparently she hadn't made herself clear earlier after all Kenzie thought, taking in the room. She hadn't been to Hues of Blue in years and it looked the same as she remembered. Under other circumstances, she would love to spend the evening here, enjoying the sweeping views and mellow vibe. But tonight was not that night.

She was taking a fortifying breath when she felt a tap on her shoulder. When she turned around, she was instantly enfolded into Mac's arms.

"Hey, stranger."

"Mac!"

"It's so good to see you."

"You, too." She took her voice down a few notches. "You have no idea."

"I think I might," Mac replied flatly, pulling back. He turned to Greg. "Welcome back, Greg."

"Thanks, Mac. Long time no see. You haven't changed a bit."

"Not much changes around here."

"True. Anything you can do to change the table availability tonight? Or lack thereof?"

"That's not my department, but I think a couple of spots just opened up at the bar. Better grab 'em while you can."

"I guess that will have to do," Greg conceded, gesturing with outstretched arm. "After you."

Kenzie walked toward the bar, finding two open seats at the far end. She quickly took the stool closest to the window. As Greg sat down next to her, Mac assumed his position behind the bar. He set a cocktail napkin down in front of each of them.

"What's your pleasure tonight, folks?"

"Ladies first."

"I'll take a Chardonnay. Dealer's choice, Mac."

Mac nodded in acknowledgement. "Greg?"

"Sierra Nevada."

"Coming right up."

As soon as Mac took his leave, Kenzie dove in. "So Greg, tell me what you have in mind. It's going to be a little challenging, juggling all of this baseball once school starts."

Seeming a little put off that Kenzie was getting right down to business, Greg began on a breath, "I'm thinking two or three sessions a week for the remainder of the summer. Then we can look at Mattie's school schedule and go from there. The weekends might be a little hit-and-miss at times with me commuting between here and Phoenix and Mattie's travel team schedule."

"I haven't made a decision about travel baseball yet."

Greg pulled back in surprise. "Really? Because Mattie will definitely make a team. At his age, it would only be local tournaments during the school year. Most traveling would be done over the summer if that's your concern."

Kenzie had done some research and found travel baseball to be a huge time and financial commitment. Mattie wasn't even ten yet and she had Katie to think about as well. She didn't want to over-schedule her son and overextend herself financially. But she also didn't want to deprive him of the experience and any future opportunities that might result from it. Maybe she should talk to Bren about it.

Before she could reply, Mac returned with their drinks. "Start a tab, folks?"

"I'll cash out, Mac. I'm just having one tonight." Here at least, Kenzie silently added, reaching for her purse.

"Keep it open, Mac. One tab." Greg handed Mac a credit card.

"You don't have to do that, Greg."

"I know. I want to. This was my idea."

"Thank you."

"My pleasure."

Greg put his wallet back in his pocket and produced a piece of paper. He laid it down on the bar, unfolded it and smoothed it out. It was a spreadsheet in calendar form. So he really did have something prepared. Maybe she'd misjudged him. Through a sip of wine, Kenzie looked on as Greg began explaining his training plan for Mattie.

"I take a holistic approach to coaching. When I was growing up I didn't play baseball all year-round, even in South Texas. I also played football and basketball and swam competitively. Each sport develops different muscles, fine-tunes movement, promotes mental fortitude and confidence. Nowadays kids tend to focus on only one sport. We have indoor facilities to play summer sports in the dead of winter and winter sports in the dog days of summer. For instance, Phoenix is one of the fastest growing markets for youth hockey." Greg paused for a sip of beer, then continued, "Instead of nurturing the whole athlete through multiple sports, there's cross-fit training and specialized workouts aimed at filling in the gaps. But the old-school method works best in my opinion. I want Mattie to run, shoot baskets, swim, hit golf balls. That will not only improve his pitching and batting skills, but help his footwork become second nature." Greg looked up from the paper and met her eyes. "Am I making sense?"

"Absolutely," Kenzie replied. "Thinking back, my brother and I played different sports depending on the season. Now it's a full-time job just to keep up with the sign-ups and practices for baseball. Let alone the cost."

"I know. My soon-to-be ex-wife dealt with the logistics and I just showed up when I could. We were a good team, that way at least," he finished more to himself than Kenzie and took another sip, prompting her to do the same.

"I can work with you on the cost of the lessons, especially if you decide to do travel ball," Greg went on. "It's really important that Mattie becomes part of a strong team. Baseball is a team sport and winning is a team effort. There's always going to be a star player or two, but the whole is always worth more than its pieces."

"I understand. I'll give it some thought."

"I know it's a lot to take in."

Kenzie sent Greg a kind smile. She was feeling more relaxed than she'd expected and it was nice to get out. She couldn't remember the last time she'd done something like this.

Greg slid the paper over to her. "This is your copy. If you're okay with it so far, I'll build out the schedule for the next few weeks."

"That's fine."

"Great. So—" Greg was interrupted by Mac's reappearance.

"You guys doing all right?"

"I'll have another," Greg told him, emptying his glass.

"I'm good, Mac. I have to get going."

"You sure you can't stay?" Greg asked as Mac walked away. "The sunset's going to be one for the books."

"I'm afraid not. I promised Mattie I'd catch the end of the game with him," Kenzie lied, remembering Bren had said the same thing about the sunset.

"Another time, then."

Kenzie started on a breath, "I don't think so, Greg. I'm pretty busy with the kids."

"Yeah, that's what Bren said," Greg sneered.

Kenzie, glass in hand, froze. "Bren?"

"Yep. But you can't blame a guy for trying."

"When was that?" Kenzie asked, setting her wine down without taking a sip.

"Saturday night. We had a beer, got to talking. I'm sorry about your husband."

So that's how Greg knew. "Thank you."

"He didn't mention our conversation?"

"No."

"I'm not surprised."

"Oh?"

"I could tell myself he doesn't want the competition, but I know better. Bren wouldn't back away from a fight any more than I would. But he's got this code of honor, this deep-seated morality when it comes to playing fair. Bren is one of those guys who should've made it to the show but didn't. That's part of why. You've got to step on some toes on your way to the top and even more if you want to stay there. Not everybody has the stomach for that."

"But you do."

Greg gave her a clever smile. "That I do. Come by it honestly, too. Bren could have been a real jerk about staying with Mattie tonight. But I knew he wouldn't be. Despite the fact that he's obviously interested in you."

"We're just friends," Kenzie heard herself say. But she couldn't ignore the way her stomach sank when she said it.

"No need to explain. I can't say I blame him," Greg said as his second beer arrived, delivered by the young woman who'd been manning the hostess stand earlier.

She gave Greg a closed-mouth smile. He really was a decent guy. But he was looking for something Kenzie wasn't ready or willing to give. She wondered if she ever would be. "Speaking of Bren, I told him I wouldn't be long. I really do need to get going." Reaching for her purse, she slipped off the bar stool.

Greg didn't attempt to dissuade her this time. Instead, he stood offering, "I'll walk you out."

"Thanks, but don't bother. Enjoy your beer. Thanks again for the wine."

"Thanks for meeting me."

"It was nice. Mattie and I will see you on Thursday."

"I'll look forward to it."

Kenzie walked through the restaurant and toward the stairs, feeling Greg's eyes on her back. Stopping at the hostess stand, she found the young woman back at her post.

"Can I help you?"

"I was wondering if Mac was around? I wanted to say good-bye."

"I haven't seen him lately. He might have left."

"Already?"

"I was surprised to see him at all. Tuesday is his day off."

"Oh, I didn't realize that."

"It's our slowest night, so the Assistant Manger can usually handle the bar with me helping out here and there. Something must have come up that brought Mac in. Can I give him a message for you?"

"No, that's okay. I'll catch him another time."

They exchanged parting pleasantries and Kenzie made her way up the stairs and outside. She gave her ticket to the valet and was admiring the pearly gray light filtering through the trees when she noticed movement out of the corner of her eye. There, walking briskly through the parking lot, was Mac. And just as he turned toward his car, he caught her gaze. Even with the distance between them, she could see his lips curve upward, his eyes crinkle at the edges. He raised his hand in greeting, then brought it to his mouth and blew her a kiss. Lifting her hand in an absentminded wave, Kenzie looked on as he got into his car and drove away, apparently having handled whatever had brought him in on his day off.

"All set, ma'am."

Distracted, Kenzie hadn't realized the valet had returned with her car. "Sorry." She walked over to the driver's side and handed him a bill. "Thanks."

"Thank you. Making it an early night?"

"Yeah," Kenzie replied, settling herself in the car. "Just a quick drink."

"Well, try to catch the sunset later. Tonight has all the makings of a corker."

Fastening her seatbelt, Kenzie met the young man's eyes. "You're the third person who's told me that tonight."

"What a coincidence."

"Yeah," Kenzie replied with a sigh. "Tonight's been full of them."

CHAPTER TEN

When Kenzie walked into the house, she found Mattie and Boot asleep on the couch. Mattie was half-covered with a blanket and the TV was on, but turned to low volume. She drew the blanket up around his shoulders before following the sound of running water to the kitchen. There she found Bren, dish towel thrown over his shoulder, wiping out the microwave. The table was cleared off and a place setting sat on the island.

"Hey." Turning to face her with a smile, he closed the microwave and dried his hands on the towel.

"Hey." She walked over to him. "You didn't have to clean up."

"I know. I didn't want you to come home to it. We saved you some dinner."

"I think I'll start with a glass of wine."

She started toward the refrigerator but Bren stopped her. "I've got it. Sit."

Kenzie obliged, suddenly spent. She watched as he poured generously from the bottle he'd brought, noting he'd already uncorked it. He set the glass down in front of her on the island.

"Thanks. Mattie hit the wall, huh?"

"That kid plays hard, eats like a horse and then passes out. I don't know where he puts it."

"Probably another growth spurt. And he's always been a napper."

"Will he sleep tonight?"

"Yep." She took a sip. "This is good. What is it?"

"Rombauer."

"Fancy."

"I figured it was a safe bet. So how'd it go?" Bren asked, grabbing his beer and leaning against the island.

Kenzie cocked her head to the side and took a longer, more contemplative sip of wine. Maybe it was the relief of being home, of having the meeting with Greg behind her, but the cobwebs were starting to clear. "Do you want to sit outside? It's such a lovely night. Unless you have to get going."

"I don't. Have to get going, I mean," Bren quickly clarified.

She let him follow her out the back door. Once they were settled at the table, surrounded by the symphonic susurrus of the aspens and the percussive drone of katydids, Kenzie answered the question. "Actually, better than I expected."

"Oh, how so?"

Kenzie shifted her gaze from the backyard to Bren. He was fidgeting in his chair, crossing and uncrossing his legs. "Well, for starters I can't remember the last time I was out in the evening alone. I felt like I was back in high school breaking curfew."

"Recalcitrant teenager, huh? I never would have guessed it."

"Hardly. Being late occasionally was the extent of my teenage rebellion. But I honestly can't remember the last time I was out at night without the kids."

"How'd it feel?"

"Simultaneously liberating and unnerving." Kenzie took another protracted sip, closed her eyes and let the buttery wine slide down her throat.

"And?"

She opened her eyes. Bren's, nearly black in the milky light, were glued to her as if riveted. She couldn't remember the last time that had happened either. The last time a man had looked at her so intently. "Now I'm not anxious at all."

"Good to know. But I meant with Greg."

"Good. Even better now that I've figured out what was really going on."

Bren opened his mouth, shut it again. "Help me out here."

"Mac is off on Tuesdays."

"Okay."

"Today is Tuesday."

"Last I checked, yes."

"This was your doing."

"Mac's day off or the day of the week? Because I don't carry *that* much weight around here."

Kenzie shot him a dubious look from under raised brows.

After a moment, Bren started on a defeated breath, "He's Gov's friend."

"And yours," Kenzie pointed out.

"And mine. But more Gov's. And you're Gov's sister."

"And I can take care of myself."

"I'm sure you can. You just haven't had to lately."

"Haven't I?"

"Not that way."

"And you know this because?"

"I'm intuitive, remember?"

Against her better judgement Kenzie laughed, then look another sip of wine. "Touché."

"So, honestly, how was it?"

"Nice, actually. Greg had a detailed training plan well in hand and gave me some good advice." She summarized what Greg had proposed ending with, "He really wants Mattie to do travel ball. I was going to ask your opinion about that."

That seemed to please him. Bren began with a smile, "The importance of teamwork in baseball can't be overstated. When I was growing up things were different, simpler. Now travel is an integral part of club sports. That would have been a stretch for us financially and there's no money-back guarantee. But Matt is worth the investment of time and resources because on top of his natural talent, he wants it. He's willing to put in the work. At the end of the day, athletes are built, not born."

"That's what Greg said."

On a sharp inhale, Bren stiffened and drained his beer. "What else did Greg have to say?"

Kenzie knew they weren't talking about Mattie anymore. "He said you were a good guy. And that your personal code of ethics and high moral standards likely held you back in baseball, among other things. He said you told him about Matt."

"I did," Bren answered without hesitation. "He asked me if you were married. I said that your husband was killed in an accident. I'm sorry if I spoke out of turn."

"You didn't. It's not a secret. But why didn't you tell me? About the conversation?"

Bren started on a helpless shrug. "It's none of my business for one thing. And I wasn't sure what was transpiring between you and Greg."

"Nothing has, or will, transpire between Greg and me. I hope that doesn't complicate things for Mattie. Or you, for that matter. Hopefully I haven't made things awkward between you and your next door neighbor. "

"Don't worry about that; we aren't close. Greg can be an overweening ass to be honest. But when it comes to baseball, he's fully committed, completely objective. He won't treat Mattie any differently. He's won't let anything cloud his judgment or decisions there."

"That's a relief."

After a quiet moment, Bren picked up the conversation again. "So Greg said I didn't have the chops for the pros, huh?"

"I think he meant it as a compliment."

"Doubt it," Bren scowled. "And he's probably right. But I'm actually more interested in the other things."

"The other things?" Kenzie polished off her wine.

"He said my upstanding character held me back in baseball, among other things. I'm curious as to what those other things might be."

What was she thinking, saying that? "That was just me paraphrasing. I don't think he meant anything by it," Kenzie backpedaled.

"I wouldn't put it past him, trying to look like the hero, playing the poor Bren card."

"You know what? Just forget I said that."

But Bren wasn't done taking Greg to task. "First he puts you on the spot and then he uses your son like a pawn in a game of monkey in the middle. I have half a mind to—"

"He said you were interested in me," Kenzie blurted out. "And that your sense of rectitude prevented you from being a jerk about tonight, about staying with Mattie. And about standing in my way. Or his."

Bren's face went blank. He actually looked a little panicked.

There was no going back now, so she might as well go forward. "So are you?"

"Am I what?"

"Interested in me?"

"We've become friends."

"As more than a friend?"

"You just lost your husband. Tragically, suddenly."

"Yes. That isn't in question and not what I asked." Bren was sitting at the head of the table and Kenzie was seated on the side next to him. In an uncharacteristic move, she leaned forward, closing the small space between them. Both of their forearms rested on the table now and their hands nearly touched. She met his eyes.

His were agitated, conflicted, troubled. She likened it to the eddy of emotions swirling around inside her.

He took a deep breath, let it out. "What if I am?"

"Is that why you're doing all of this?"

Bren seemed genuinely confused. "Doing all of what?"

"Why you're here tonight? Why you're so good with Mattie? Why you kept showing up at the park, brought us pizza and ice cream and baseball cards?" Something inside Kenzie needed to know. But it cost her.

Looking into her eyes, he laid his hand on hers. "No."

Before she could process that, give herself permission to believe it, she heard the screen door slam behind her. "Mom?"

Pulling his hand away, Bren sat back in his chair. Kenzie stood and clearing the emotion from her throat, went to her son. "There's my sleepyhead. How was the game?"

"It's still on. Bren, wanna watch the last couple innings? Giants are up five to two."

"Sure thing. I'll grab a beer and be right there."

"I'll get you one. I want a Coke anyway."

"Thanks, bud."

"Mom, you can watch too."

"Well, thank you."

Mattie turned back toward the house, then stopped short. "Oh, Katie called. She tried to call you but you didn't pick up. She's back at the lodge. She texted you."

151

"Okay. I'll check my phone."

"Can I have ice cream?"

"Sure. But then have water instead of Coke."

"I know."

Kenzie started to follow Mattie inside, but Bren pushed up and grabbed her arm. "The attraction came later, I promise. And it isn't why."

She nodded. "I'm not ready."

"I know."

"I don't know when…if…I'll be."

"But if you were?"

Kenzie glanced away for a few seconds, then looked back at him. She owed him the same brutal honesty he'd given her. "If I were, I would be."

Bren's face broke into a huge grin. His eyes began to dance victoriously. "That's fantastic!"

"It is?"

"Absolutely. You're saying I have a chance."

"But I have no idea when, if…"

"That's fine. I'll wait."

"I can't ask you to do that."

"You aren't." He shrugged. "I'm volunteering."

"Bren…" Kenzie amazed.

"Is that okay?"

"Ah, yeah. Sure. Of course."

"Awesome. Now let's get you some dinner and a refill. And I think I'll forgo another beer for ice cream. I feel like celebrating all of a sudden."

Kenzie could only stare in disbelief as Bren picked up his bottle and her glass from the table. Then he went to the door and held it open for her. "Shall we?"

She followed his direction and walked into the kitchen. Mattie was nowhere to be found, probably already in the family room with his ice cream. Still thunderstruck, she looked on as Bren topped off her wine and put a plate in the microwave. While it warmed, he got the Moose Tracks ice cream out of the freezer and scooped some into a bowl. By the time he was done, the microwave was beeping.

"Bren, you coming?" came Mattie's disembodied voice. "It's the bottom of the eighth."

"Be right there."

"Go on. I'll get that and check my phone. I want to connect with Katie before it gets too late. I'll be right in."

Bren smiled by way of reply and headed for the family room, ice cream in hand.

Kenzie grabbed the plate from the microwave and set it on the counter. She wasn't all that hungry, but Bren had gone to the trouble of making a plate for her, so she'd at least take a few bites. She dug her phone out of her purse and saw the missed call and text from Katie. They were going to roast s'mores on the beach. She'd call again after that. Kenzie texted that she'd keep her phone close by.

By the time Kenzie wandered into the family room, it was the top of the ninth. She ate quietly, not wanting to interrupt, while the guys chatted about players, strategy and stats. Fifteen minutes later the game was over.

"That puts the Giants in first in their division, right?" Mattie asked Bren.

"Yep. We'll see if they can hold on. October is a long ways away."

Mattie turned his attention to his phone, made a few comments about other team standings that Bren seconded, then started scrolling, lost in his own world.

Kenzie was sitting on one end of the sectional with Mattie and Boot sprawled out on the other. Bren, from his spot in the chair next to the couch, shifted his gaze to her.

"Turn out okay?"

"It's great. Thanks again."

"You did all the work."

"You boiled the water, cleaned up the kitchen."

He dismissed that with a wave of the hand. "Child's play."

Kenzie gave him a half-smile. There was something so wholesome about him, so endearing and familiar. She'd barely known him a week but felt like they'd been friends for years. She prided herself on being an excellent judge of character, but Bren almost seemed too good to be true. The vibration of her phone in her pocket brought her back to the now. Assuming it was Katie, she answered without looking at the screen.

"Hi, honey."

But the chipper voice that greeted her was not that of her daughter. "Well, hello darling."

"Gov?" Kenzie replied around a laugh. "I thought you were Katie."

"No such luck. Everything good there?"

Kenzie, phone to her ear, picked up her plate and headed for the kitchen as she spoke. "Yeah. Boot's fine, sleeping in the family room. We were just watching the Giants game."

"Mom of the year."

"I have no excuse to be anything but."

"True."

"How's everything with you?"

"It's Maui, so nuff said. Laurel is at a book signing, mixing business with pleasure. Speaking of that, I have a favor to ask you."

"Sure."

"You might want to reserve your answer until you hear what the favor is."

"Okay. Shoot."

"Laurel saw someone on the beach reading her book. I convinced her to go up to the woman and introduce herself. One thing led to another and she mentioned that her book club is reading *Christmas in Tahoe*. She invited Laurel to come to their next meeting and speak."

"How exciting!" Kenzie said, rinsing off her plate and putting it in the dishwasher.

"It is, but that's where the favor comes in. They meet monthly on Friday nights. As in *next* month. How would you feel about staying with Boot for an extra week or so?"

Shutting the dishwasher door with her foot, Kenzie's gaze floated to the family room. Mattie and Bren were watching the Giant's press conference. She brought the next few weeks' schedule into her mind. "That would probably work. Mattie can't get enough of it up here and Katie's pretty flexible."

"And you?"

She looked on as Bren, now standing in front of the TV, gestured at the screen, illustrating something to Mattie while the game highlights played. Finding herself smiling again, she said, "It would work for me. I'm a glorified babysitter and Uber driver at this point."

"Thanks. I owe you one."

"Don't worry about it."

"If you have to go down to Reno, just let me know. I can always ask Bren to take Boot in a pinch."

"Actually, I could ask him myself. He's been practicing with Mattie." For some reason, she failed to mention that he was actually there now.

"That's nice of him. He tends to downplay his athletic prowess, but he had a lot of potential. If he'd stuck with it, who knows how far he would've gotten."

"That seems to be the consensus."

"What?"

"Nothing. Anyway, it looks like he's done all right for himself."

"For sure. But you never really get over giving up on that boyhood dream. The loss of what might have been stays with you."

Kenzie certainly didn't want Mattie to feel that way or resent her later if they didn't give baseball their all. And if that meant travel ball, she'd find a way. "I think we'll be fine with Boot. But I'll keep Bren in mind." More and more often it seemed, Kenzie admitted to herself.

They traded good-byes and just as she was disconnecting, Katie called. They caught up on her day and made arrangements for Kenzie to pick her up in the morning. She was about to head back to the family room when Bren walked into the kitchen. He had his ice cream bowl in one hand and her wine glass in the other.

Handing her the wine, he asked, "All good with Gov?"

"Yeah. In fact, they're having such a good time they're staying a little longer." Kenzie recounted Laurel's beach encounter. "I guess being a writer yourself you can appreciate that."

"That is pretty cool," Bren agreed with a smile.

"Has that ever happened to you?" Kenzie asked, taking a sip of wine.

A faraway look came into his eyes. "No."

"Something to look forward to then."

"I won't hold my breath."

"You never know."

"Actually, I do. Hear from Katie?"

"I did. She's in for the night."

"And I have a feeling you are too. I think I'll make it unanimous." He set his bowl in the sink.

"I'll walk you out."

Bren said good-bye to Mattie and Kenzie gave him the five-minutes-to-shower warning. Once they were outside and stopped at his car, Bren asked, "We're good, right? About before?"

"Yeah," Kenzie told him truthfully. "I appreciate you being honest with me."

"Likewise."

"Thanks again for staying with Mattie. And for the wine and the ice cream."

"Thank you. It's been quite a while since someone made me dinner." He paused, then finished hopefully, "Maybe we could do it again sometime?"

"I'd like that."

"So if Gov is extending his stay, does that mean you guys are too?"

"I might have to make a trip or two to Reno, but for the most part we'll be here."

"Mattie said he has a lesson on Thursday."

"He does."

"Maybe I'll see you guys then."

"Sounds good."

"Well, thanks again."

He was stepping away from her to get in the car when Kenzie heard herself say, "I'm not looking for a father for my son, Bren."

Bren stopped short and turned on his heel. "That's good, because he already has one. He just isn't here anymore."

"But you are."

"Only if you want me to be. And not just because of Matt. That goes both ways."

She granted him that with a thoughtful nod. "I'm a package deal."

"I know. I like your package." He grinned mischievously.

She smiled back at him, but managed to maintain her serious tone. "It's never going to be casual for me. It can't be."

"Well, maybe for the first time in my life I don't want it to be casual for me either. And since we're on the same page in that regard, maybe we could just see where things go? We don't have to write the next chapter yet."

"But I have no idea when that will be. When I'll be ready to even start thinking about the next chapter."

Bren shrugged. "I'm not going anywhere. Plus you didn't say if this time, so I'll take that as a step in the right direction." He took her hands in his. "I'm not trying to replace Matt. But I can't imagine he'd want you to be alone forever. Or for his son to never hit a curve ball into the stands."

Cocking her head to the side, Kenzie sent him a puzzled look.

"It's the greatest feeling. Ever," Bren emphasized with good humor. "Okay?"

"Okay." The next thing Kenzie knew she was falling against him. His arms circled her waist and she buried her face in his neck. He smelled like Tahoe— woodsy and earthy with a hint of smoke. He tightened his arms around her, pressing her into him. She'd forgotten what it felt like to be held like this, to have a man's strong arms around her. She closed her eyes and wallowed in it, in feeling safe for the first time since Matt died.

She felt Bren's hands travel gently up her back, then return to her waist. His heartbeat quickened, his breathing grew ragged. She could feel her own pulse jumping, her breaths becoming shallow. He swallowed hard and kissed the top of her head, then pulled back. Their eyes met and held. His were stormy, full of hesitancy and struggle. She wondered if he saw the same in hers.

His gaze dropped to her mouth and her name slid off his lips just before they captured hers. Her arms wreathed his neck and her eyelids went to half-mast as his mouth began to move over hers. He tasted sweet and chocolaty from the ice cream and tangy and hoppy from the beer. But most of all, she could taste longing and desire in his kiss. And that sent the spool of want gathering in her stomach spiraling.

Her tongue made room for his and she melted into him. He explored her mouth slowly, thoroughly, sampling layer by layer, stopping only to pull on her bottom lip and start his ravenous journey all over again. His mouth was supple, his kisses unhurried and luxurious. Kenzie felt like she was being swept off her feet, floating through the air, light as a feather.

Then he stopped.

Still holding her against him, he rested his forehead against hers. He let out one stabilizing breath, then another, before lifting his head and meeting her eyes. The struggle in his had tempered a bit, making room for relief. "You have no idea how badly I've been wanting to do that. But I shouldn't have done it tonight. I'm sorry."

"I'm not," Kenzie realized out loud.

"But you just told me you weren't ready. I shouldn't have—"

"Kissed me after I all but threw myself at you?" She dropped her arms to her sides. "I should be apologizing to you!"

He released her. "For what? Letting me take advantage of you?"

"For giving you mixed signals. And you did nothing of the sort. I was a more than witting participant."

A smile threatened the corners of his mouth, but his tone stayed earnest. "I meant what I said. I'm not going anywhere. If all you have to give me now is friendship, that's enough."

"Do you kiss all your friends like that?"

"Not a one."

She shot him a look from under her lashes. "Then I guess we can't be friends."

He brushed back the errant strands of hair around her face. "You can take advantage of me next time if it would make you feel better."

"Such the gentleman."

"Well, I'm no Greg Gentry or anything." He gave her a boyish grin.

"He does have a lot to offer. A house in the mountains, baseball lessons…"

"I have a house in the mountains. And I still have a pearl or two of wisdom left to share."

"Among other things, remember? Besides, Greg wants a bedmate. And I want…"

"More?" Bren finished for her.

She looked at him for a long moment. You, she thought in utter astonishment. I'm really starting to think I want you. But she only said, "Yes. But of what I'm not sure." Her voice sounded thick, felt unreliable. And her usually cast-iron stomach was threatening to betray her.

Seemingly unfazed, Bren said evenly, "That's okay. I can be sure enough for both of us until you figure it out. If you'll let me."

Overcome, Kenzie could only nod and fall back into his arms.

He held her for a long moment, then leaned back and cupped her face. "I'm going to take off before we get ahead of ourselves and start writing that next chapter." He kissed her again, then got behind the wheel. As he backed up, he raised his hand in a final wave.

Kenzie reciprocated, watching as he cleared the driveway. She waited until he was out of sight before turning toward the house. The last sliver of the sun was dipping behind the trees, shrouding the sky in soft, velvety light. She laughed humorlessly.

Turns out she'd caught some of the sunset after all.

CHAPTER ELEVEN

The morning was clear and bright like most Tahoe mornings. But Bren's head was as foggy as a San Francisco night. It wasn't that he hadn't slept. He'd slept, dreamed, woke, gone back to sleep and dreamed some more. But the last thing he felt was rested.

If he was in a good place with the day's work, Bren had no trouble sleeping. Something about the mountain air and the satisfaction of meeting his goals along with a few beers usually did the trick. But if his workday was out of whack, he had trouble unplugging. If he was stuck in a rut or didn't have his head in the game, he tossed and turned all night and had nightmares about never getting another publishing contract and dying a feckless pauper.

But work hadn't been the issue the last two nights. It was Kenzie. He'd been writing their next chapter in his dreams. Rather graphically. Bren was a little hazy on the details, but he knew one thing for sure. The dream always had a happy ending. Several of them.

He'd lied a little, of course. The attraction had been instant, the moment he'd laid eyes on her that first night. And while his intentions with Matt weren't performative, when it came to Kenzie Bren couldn't say the same. God, he wanted her. And not just physically. He wanted all of her. Her sense of humor, her mind, her heart *and* her body. Although not necessarily in that order. She was beautiful, smart, witty and affable, yet still grounded. She was unlike any woman he'd ever known.

She said she was a package deal, but to Bren she was the whole package. And strings? She understandably needed them. And maybe for the first time, Bren wanted them. Even if he was borrowing some of them from a dead man. So if time was what Kenzie needed, time is what he would give her. But he wouldn't mind an ETA, a timeframe with which to work. He was only human after all.

But what Bren didn't know when he woke up all groggy and aroused was that his restless night would be the least remarkable part of his day. In retrospect it made sense, it just wasn't his first thought when his phone tore him out of his erogenous fantasies.

"Brennen?"

"Mom?"

"Did I wake you?"

Bren moved the phone from his ear to his face and noted the time. Jesus, it was after nine. "Sort of. But I need to get up anyway."

"I'm sorry, honey."

Sitting up, Bren shook off the daze and let his eyes adjust to the light. "No problem. What's up?" It occurred to him that this was the second time in as many weeks his mother had called him in the morning. He wondered if Bob had something to do with that. Maybe he was also an early riser, Bren grumbled to himself.

"What's your schedule like next week? We were thinking about coming up for a few days."

We. Whether his issue was with Bob, the relationship itself or simply the idea of him, Bren might as well get used to it. Because it was happening. "I'll make it work."

"Great. I'll book the flight and forward you the itinerary. We'll rent a car at the airport and drive up. That way you don't have to worry about picking us up and we can explore while you're working. Bob has never been to Tahoe."

"Sounds good. Talk to you later."

"Bren."

His mother rarely called him that. It was a nickname he'd grown into as an adult.

"Yeah?"

"Thank you. I know this is…different."

Bren took a reluctant breath, let it out slowly. His mother had been there for him his entire life, often at great personal sacrifice, and she deserved the same unconditional love and support she'd so unstintingly given him. "If he makes you happy and treats you well, I'm honored to meet him."

"He does. And just so you know, Bob said the same thing about you."

After they disconnected Bren sat there for a good five minutes, thinking. He'd never been uneasy about introducing a woman to his mother. Claire always said she'd love anyone he loved, because when you love someone, you love whoever they love. She'd always put her money where her mouth was and now it was his turn to do the same.

Bren raked a weary hand through his hair. The day was already far from ordinary, but that made coffee no less essential. He threw on a sweatshirt and headed downstairs. He got the coffee brewing, grabbed his laptop, went out on the deck and gave himself a moment to take in the lake. The water dazzled like a ballet of incandescent flashbulbs exploding in the sunshine, reminiscent of his first trip to Tahoe. And Bren was no less entranced this morning than he'd been all those years ago. The image of the basin that day was embedded in his mind, as he'd somehow always known it would be. That had never happened to him with anything or anyone before or since. Not until now, not until Kenzie.

The image of Kenzie that first night was carved in his mind just as indelibly as his first glimpse of the lake had been three decades ago. And she was becoming just as woven into the fabric of his being as Tahoe had long ago become. But unlike Tahoe, Bren couldn't promise her to himself. She had to do that in her own time, on her own terms, in her own way. He understood and respected that, had no choice otherwise. But it was already proving to be quite a challenge.

As much as Bren enjoyed women, he'd never had a problem controlling himself around them. He'd been raised to be gentlemanly and respectful and to never cross that proverbial line without explicit consent no matter how hot and heavy things got. But the other night he'd had trouble keeping himself in check. He'd wanted to touch Kenzie everywhere, explore her from head to toe. He'd wanted his hands running through her hair, his mouth on her breasts, his erection deep inside her. The dress she'd been wearing was more revealing than anything he'd seen her in before and he'd wanted to untie the sash and let it unravel around her as she did the same in his arms. He'd wanted to mutter her name as he fed on her mouth, her throat, the valley between her breasts. He'd wanted to pick her up, feel her legs cinch his waist, hear her lecherous pleas in his ear. He knew he could have pushed her a little, not all the way into bed, but farther. But she'd had a few glasses of wine and a stressful night and Bren wouldn't take advantage of that. Their first time together deserved better; at the very least a clear head and absolute certainty. Because when Kenzie was ready, when she wanted him the way he wanted her, there'd be no regrets, no second thoughts, for either one of them. Writing was not Bren's only strong suit; making a woman feel like a woman was front and center in his wheelhouse. No negative feedback or bad reviews there. And not a single rejection.

Bren heard the high-pitched beep of the coffee maker, indicating the pot was brewed. He returned to the kitchen, poured the equivalent of three cups in his tumbler, took a hearty sip and went back outside. He sat, opened his laptop, and logged on. He usually started the day by going through his email and deleting the superfluous messages before getting down to work. He was doing just that when he came across a message from Miranda. The subject line read CALL ME ASAP. The body of the email was blank. Like his mother, Miranda had the upmost respect for Bren's unconventional sleep schedule and rarely called him before noon. He dug his phone out of his pocket. She answered on the first ring.

"Good morning." The background noise indicated she was in a restaurant. Miranda was a buck ten soaking wet and despite living in New York City, as far from a foodie as one could get. This was undoubtably business lunch.

"Is it? You tell me."

"That depends on your perspective. Remember that as our conversation proceeds."

"Playing hooky?"

"Hardly. Quarterly Roundup."

"Is that where you guys decide who gets who for what?"

"More or less," Miranda replied, stepping away from the cacophony and lowering her voice. "Shoot me. At least during COVID we didn't have to pretend to like each other in person."

"Poor baby."

"Thank you for the sarcastic support. But because of you, I get a temporary reprieve from the catfighting."

"To what do I owe the pleasure?"

"I overnighted your new contract. You need to have it notarized and overnight it back. You know the drill. We're hitting the ground running with this one."

"Already? I was going to take a breather."

"Not in the cards, my friend. And I'll believe that when I see it. You can't sit still anymore than I can."

She was right. But Bren only said, "Why the rush?"

"Because the powers that be say so. And that urgency is reflected in your advance and royalty scale as well as your bonus structure for meeting all your deadlines."

"I always meet my deadlines."

"You might need some additional incentive to meet these."

"Because?"

"Because you've never written a book this fast. You already found a way in, right?"

Bren rested his hand on the side of his head and shut his eyes. "Maybe."

"So, yes."

"I jotted down some ideas, a few story arcs, did some preliminary research. But I've been buried in revisions. And there's more to come."

"I can get you some help with that. And the research."

Bren jolted up in his chair. Collaboration was as unheard of as communicating in writing. And not the way Bren worked, of which Miranda was well aware. He'd known Miranda for almost twenty years and trusted her implicitly. But something felt off.

"Okay?"

"Do I have a choice?"

"Not really. I mean you could walk, but you won't." She took her voice down another peg. "Look, I know this isn't our usual modus operandi. But for some reason this project is flying under the radar, literally and figuratively. Your fingers are going to be flying on that keyboard. But you're good under pressure, the contract is solid and the money is out of this world. For both of us."

"Sounds too good to be true."

"All I know is what I've been told, what I've told you. I need you to trust me. You know I'd take a bullet for you."

She would. And the feeling was mutual. "I know. I do."

"All right, then." Miranda heaved a sigh of relief. "The package is guaranteed by noon. Get it back out this afternoon for morning delivery tomorrow."

He'd have to drive to Reno for that. "Will do."

"Thanks. I'll be in touch."

Bren disconnected and took another pull of coffee, barely tasting it this time. He claimed to be intuitive and that attribute was being put to the test. He may not know what was really going on, but he knew one thing—Miranda would never do him dirty. They were in this together, like they had been with everything else from day one. If he was on a need-to-know basis, so was she.

He and Miranda Sheffield's paths had crossed when Bren was freelancing, picking up random jobs to make ends meet. Miranda, fresh out of grad school, was doing grunt work for a literary agency to learn the ropes. She was instantly impressed with Bren's talent and work ethic. And she liked his attitude. He was hungry, driven and just the right amount of cocky, much like herself. She'd even pitched Bren's books to a couple publishing houses, one of which he wrote for now. But no one had room on their roster for an unknown author or the resources to make him otherwise. And Bren was running out of time and money. Pipe dreams don't pay the bills any more than manuscripts that gather dust in slush piles.

But Miranda wasn't willing to give up. She'd heard that one of the agency's aging marquee authors was struggling with the rigorous deadlines and aggressive pace inherit to publishing. He still had the ideas, the aptitude, the ambition, but at his age lacked the stamina to write for twelve hours and then hop on a red-eye for the next stop on a book tour. So he'd have to do one or the other. And names sell books.

But Brown doesn't hand out degrees to non-starters and Miranda had an idea. How about hiring a writer, not a pool of freelancers or a team of editors, but a journeyman writer? One of those guys who should have made it but didn't. One of those guys who had everything going for him but the billing. One of those guys who didn't want to give up, but was staring down the barrel of trying to get blood from a turnip. A guy like Brennen Banks, a young, talented, struggling writer with a Hemingway complex who was smart enough to know that this was the chance of a lifetime. Miranda knew her standpat boss wouldn't hear of it, so she went over her head, to the president of the agency, risking her job and professional reputation. Despite being the grandson of the hoary agency founder and to the manor born, Harper Leary III was approachable, open-minded and forward-thinking. And he loved the idea.

Within a week's time, Bren found himself on the payroll at Leary and Leary. After two successful books and at Miranda's insistence, he resigned from the agency and declared work for hire status. Thereafter, she negotiated on his behalf with the publisher. Bren's current work-in-progress was his twelfth book with them. Miranda had gotten promoted to partner and they had both gotten rich. And the highly esteemed, world-renowned writer had gotten even richer. And older.

Older, Bren said under his breath. Time, he reminded himself, is the one thing we can't make, control or buy. And maybe Warren Holden was running out of it. Bren googled him, knowing he probably wouldn't find anything he didn't already know. But it gave Bren pause that Holden was almost ninety years old now. The headshot was probably at least a decade old, but there was a clip from a recent interview and he appeared to be in decent health. Bren found himself oddly transfixed by the video, as if there was something eerily familiar about it, particularly Holden's mannerisms. Deciding he'd likely come across it in prior searches, Bren brushed it off and read on. Holden was quoted as saying he was busy putting the finishing touches on his next book, due to be released in November. Bren laughed soundlessly. Apparently the revisions he'd been working on were right on schedule.

The ring of the doorbell interrupted his sleuthing and he rose to answer it. He and the delivery man were on a first-name basis due to the frequency of his visits. Bren greeted the tall, balding man with a smile. "Hey, Rodney."

"Hey, Bren. I take it you've been expecting me?" Rodney used his phone to scan the envelope in his hand before handing it over.

"That I have. Thanks." Bren stuck the envelope under his arm.

"Sure thing. This one needs a signature. They want a time stamp too." Rodney gave Bren the phone.

"Do I have to sign in blood?" Bren joked, using his finger to scribble his name.

"I wouldn't be surprised. My supervisor met me at the truck with this first thing this morning. Our mountain deliveries usually carry a disclaimer—not guaranteed by noon. But I guess you're just that special."

"Lucky me." He handed the phone back to Rodney.

"Thanks. Have a good one."

"You too."

Bren closed the door and returned to the deck. He pushed his laptop over, threw the envelope on the table and sat down. Tearing it open, he found a large sheaf of papers and a prepaid return label and envelope. Bren immediately flipped to page seventeen and let out a long, breathy whistle. Miranda hadn't been kidding about the schedule or the royalties. Both were accelerated. And staggering.

He turned back to page one and started skimming. Most of the contract was boilerplate; they'd worked out the fundamentals years ago. To the point that Bren no longer bothered with legal counsel. He knew what to look for and everyone knew he knew, not that Leary and Leary or the publisher would dare screw him. They all had too much to lose.

Bren took another sip of coffee and read on. The working title of the book was catchy, *Dusk at Dawn*, and he wondered if the illustrious author himself had come up with it. It not only stood to reason, it mirrored Bren's initial thoughts and the overall concept he envisioned for the book. Maybe they'd actually use it this time.

Bren thumbed through the remaining pages, then turned his attention to the paragraphs Miranda had flagged. The dates were beyond tight, but he could do it, piecemeal it in if he had to. He wouldn't have the luxury of his usual time-to-sit cushion but Miranda was right, he performed well under pressure. He was self-disciplined and resourceful by nature and the obscene advance would make up for the sleepless nights and long days when he wanted to pull his hair out. And giving up what was left of the summer.

But one thing the money might not make up for was getting to know Kenzie better. He'd been looking forward to spending some of his downtime with her and the kids. And of course there was his mother's visit and getting acquainted with Bob. He'd have to work that in somehow. He wouldn't let her down.

Bren scrolled through the rest of his emails, logged off and headed for the shower. If he was going to get these contracts to New York by morning, they'd have to be in the pipeline before five. Miranda had included a draft of the agreement for his reference so he wouldn't have to make a copy. He could get the contract notarized, drop off the package and head home.

His mind was already racing, gearing up for the challenge, as he walked upstairs. He could feel the determination building, his blood start to pump, the adrenaline brewing inside him. He would need every ounce of it, all that energy and moxie, to meet those deadlines without comprising the quality and integrity of his work. But Bren knew he would.

To Bren, nothing quite compared to the excitement of creating something out of nothing. Something that was solely his own, something that lived, breathed. To turn an idea into a tangible, intelligible entity. To bring the characters dancing around in his head to life, give them names and faces and pasts and dreams and voices. Because that's why we read books and watch movies and listen to music. To escape our world, our problems, ourselves, and be transported somewhere else, become someone else, for an hour or two. And for Bren to know he was the one providing that escape was a high like no other. To see the story burning in his head take shape, take on a life of its own, fueled him, yielded tenfold the effort he put forth. It was the only thing he'd ever experienced that rivaled sex. Although Bren had a feeling making love with Kenzie would give that conviction a run for its money.

Bren was halfway down the driveway when he noticed Greg in his backyard giving a lesson. The boy looked older than Matt, maybe twelve or thirteen. Greg was crouched down in a catcher's stance waiting for the ball. Bren tapped the brakes and watched as the boy wound up and threw. Meatball, right down the middle, at least a single. Greg rose and walked over to the boy, put a hand on his shoulder and said a few words. The boy nodded in understanding. Just as Bren was releasing the brake, Greg looked over and their eyes met. The men exchanged an upward nod, then Bren continued backing down the driveway. Despite being full of himself and some of his questionable proclivities, Greg was a decent guy. And he loved baseball. As Bren was driving down the street, he wondered what time Matt's lesson was today. Hopefully he'd be back in time.

The ride down the mountain was uneventful and despite it being lunchtime by the time he got to Reno, traffic manageable. Bren dealt with the package, took a picture of the receipt and sent the tracking number to Miranda. Then he grabbed lunch and headed back up the mountain.

And that's where his lucky streak came to screeching halt.

Traffic often backed up on Mt. Rose Highway in the summer months. All it took was one tourist not accustomed to the mountain roads to come around a curve too fast or a truck driver who didn't double-check his brakes to jam everything up. Usually it was a temporary slowdown that was quickly remedied.

But not today.

A semi had jackknifed about halfway up the mountain. Cars were backed up for miles in each direction and neither lane was moving. Swearing under his breath, Bren shut off the engine and opened the sunroof. The afternoon sun was high in the sky, a deep lapis-blue against the asymmetrical, buff-colored cliffs. Thankfully the rocky hillsides were secured with nets to prevent landslides or else they'd all be sitting ducks.

He'd might as well settle in since it looked like he was going to be here for a while. Unbuckling his seat belt, Bren reached behind the seat and grabbed his laptop. He didn't go far without it when he was in the middle of a project or had a tight turnaround and currently he checked both of those boxes. He glanced down at his phone in the center console. As per usual, he had no signal on this part of the mountain. He might not be able to find out what was going on up ahead, but he could get some work done.

Bren rested his laptop between the steering wheel and his stomach and settled in. The next batch of edits from his current project weren't back yet, so he'd work on some preliminaries for *Dusk at Dawn*. He looked back over his notes, refreshed his memory and dove into writing mode. He didn't do outlines anymore, but in this case he decided go back to basics and make an exception. He didn't have a second to spare and it was a good way to organize his thoughts.

He got into a groove and hit his stride. It wasn't until horns began blasting behind him that Bren realized cars were moving in front of him. He glanced at the clock, having had no idea how much time had passed. He lifted an apologetic hand to the driver behind him, tossed his laptop on the passenger seat and got going. Only one lane was open and traffic was inching along, but at least they were moving. The sun was starting to set, casting lengthening shadows on the triple-tiered rows of bottle washer pines as he drove through the pass and headed for home.

By the time Bren got to town, it was nearly seven. He'd obviously missed Matt's lesson and wondered if Kenzie had stopped by. They hadn't made plans per se, but there seemed to be an understanding that they'd see each other today. And the last thing Bren wanted was for her to get the wrong impression, to doubt his assertion that he wasn't going anywhere. Because as much as it surprised him, he meant it. The way he felt about her was completely different, altogether real and not subject to change.

Stopped at a light, Bren glanced at his phone. He had a signal again and hadn't missed any calls or texts. He wasn't sure what, if anything, that meant but the next thing he knew he was taking a detour. This was around the time Kenzie and the kids usually took Boot to the park. Maybe he could catch up with them there.

The park was packed and the parking lot full. He drove up and down the aisles and not seeing Kenzie's SUV, did the same in the overflow lot across the street. He doubted they'd walked; she seemed a little uneasy about doing that again. He had every intention of going home after that. God knows he had plenty to do and he'd gotten on a roll in the gridlock. He could capitalize on that, keep the momentum going into the night. But on a whim, Bren headed in the opposite direction.

When he pulled up in front of Gov's house, Bren saw an unfamiliar car in the driveway. Maybe Katie's friend, the family she'd stayed with in Tahoe City, was there. But if his memory served him correctly, they'd have gone home by now. Maybe a friend of Kenzie's from Reno was visiting, wanting to take advantage of the lake while she was in town.

Bren killed the engine. Should he forget the whole thing and head home? He didn't want to be rude, intrude if she was entertaining. He could text her, see if it was okay for him come by, but then what? Drive around for fifteen minutes and pretend he wasn't already there? That was ridiculous, juvenile, high school behavior. And high school was so far back in his rearview mirror that Bren could hardly remember it. But he sure as hell remembered what it felt like to hold Kenzie in his arms and kiss her. And he wanted to do it again.

Tonight.

Lights were burning in the living room and Bren could hear indistinct voices and rolling laughter coming from the backyard as he walked up to the front door. He paused on the stoop, visualizing Kenzie out on the deck graciously entertaining her guests while the kids and Boot played in the yard. They'd probably grilled out at the end of a long, summer day. He found himself wishing he'd been there. He rang the bell and waited. After a few seconds he heard approaching footfalls. Then the door flew open.

"Bren." Kenzie's startled expression became an allover grin. "Hi."

"Hi," he returned on a breath, remembering the first time she'd stopped by his house. He hoped she was as pleasantly surprised as he'd been that day.

"What a nice surprise." Her eyes began to sparkle and Bren thought she looked more beautiful than ever, if that was even possible.

"Is it? It looks like you have company."

"It isn't company, it's my parents. Please come in," she invited.

He obliged without breaking their shared stare. He didn't want to miss a second of her smile. But this time something was different. For the first time he felt like she wasn't just smiling, she was smiling at *him*. He found himself powerless against it. Unable to stop himself, he reached out and brushed her arm with the tips of his fingers, then slid his hand down to hers. She took it slowly, tentatively.

"You sure?" Bren asked.

She shook off whatever she was thinking with a few quick nods. "Of course. I'm just surprised to see you. We missed you earlier."

Bren's heart all but took flight. "I wondered if you came by. I got stuck on Mt. Rose. A truck jackknifed at the pass. It was a parking lot for hours."

"You got tangled up in that mess?"

"Yeah," he affirmed, too happy now to be bothered by the inconvenience. "I went by the park. To see if you guys were there."

"Oh." Her smile deepened. "We didn't go tonight. My parents have been here all day."

"That's nice." He simply could not take his eyes off of her. Or let go of her hand. But she didn't seem to mind.

"They needed their grandchildren fix," Kenzie explained matter-of-factly. "And they enjoy spending time at the lake, especially with the kids. It reminds them of when Gov and I were young. Plus I think my dad really wanted to meet Greg Gentry."

Bren couldn't blame him. He'd been a little in awe himself at first. But not nearly as much as he was of Kenzie right now. "It's a guy thing."

"Must be. Have you eaten?"

"Dinner?"

"Yeah."

"Um, no."

"Do you like tacos?" she asked simply.

"Yeah, I like tacos."

"Would you like to join us?"

Yes, Bren thought, I absolutely would like to join you. And then take you home with me and join you in a completely different way. But he only said, "I don't want to impose."

"You wouldn't be."

"Then, sure. Thanks."

She dropped his hand and closed the door, then started walking toward the kitchen. "Come on back. You know the way."

A silvery voice greeted them as they entered the kitchen. "Kenz, should I start warming the—Oh, hello."

Bren found himself looking into the face of a woman who could only be Kenzie's mother. Gov had gotten her caramel-colored eyes, but save that she was an older, shorter version of Kenzie. Her blonde hair was a shade darker and her figure more mature, but otherwise Kenzie was a dead ringer for her.

"Mom, this is McGovern's friend Bren Banks, who I was telling you about. Bren, meet my mother, Sheryl Scott."

So she'd mentioned him to her mother. Now Bren's heart all but leaped out of his chest. He extended his hand. "Nice to meet you, Mrs. Scott."

"Sheryl. It's lovely to meet you, Bren. Mattie told us about you helping him with baseball. And of course introducing him to Greg Gentry!"

"Guilty on both counts."

"Well, it's very nice of you. Thank you."

"He's a great kid. I don't know who has more fun."

On a blithesome smile, Sheryl's eyes drifted to her daughter, then back to Bren. Then her smile turned knowing and her eyes filled discerningly. "I imagine it's a toss-up. In my experience boys will be boys no matter how old they get. I was just about to warm the tortillas and set the table. Can I set a place for you?"

"That would be wonderful."

"I'll warm the tortillas, Mom."

"Then I'll get right to the table."

"The outdoor placemats and silverware are in the laundry room cabinet."

Sheryl took her leave and Kenzie walked over and popped the baking sheet of tortillas sitting on the counter into the oven. Then she turned back to Bren. "Would you like a beer? I've already got a glass of wine going."

"Sure. But I'll get it. What can I do to help?"

"No water to boil tonight," she replied with a playful smile, bewitching him all over again. "But you could grab some plates from the far cabinet and set them on the island. Everyone can make their own plate in here, assembly line style, and take it outside."

Bren did as instructed while Kenzie retrieved cheese and condiments from the refrigerator. While they doled them out, Bren asked about Matt's lesson.

"It was a family affair today. Mom took Katie to the bookstore and Dad went with Mattie and me. Mattie worked on infield throwing and sidearm motions. And something Greg referred to as the gator chop."

"So reflex and reaction drills."

"If you say so."

"How'd he do?"

"My dad or Mattie?"

Bren chuckled. "Both."

"Mattie did very well. And Greg was really nice to my dad. They talked about the good old days of baseball and a lot of players I've never heard of. My dad was like a kid in a candy store. And he couldn't believe that this was the first he'd heard of Greg living here. I have a feeling Gov is going to get an earful about that."

Before Bren could comment, Matt burst into the kitchen with his grandfather.

"Hey, Bren! I didn't know you were coming over!"

"Hey, yourself! Neither did I. It just sort of happened. I wanted to hear about your lesson." He walked over and extended his hand to Kenzie's father. "Bren Banks, Mr. Scott. It's nice to meet you."

The older man returned the handshake. "Jay. Likewise."

"We went to your house to tell you about it but you weren't home," Matt announced.

"Sorry about that, bud." Bren looked back at Matt. "I got stuck in traffic. So how was it?"

"Okay. We didn't really pitch or hit that much. Just a bunch of running and sliding drills."

"I know those aren't as much fun, but that's how you train your body to react in the moment."

"That's what Coach said. It's called donkey work."

"Right."

Jay and Bren exchanged an amused look. Then Jay said, "Kenzie, Mom sent me in for napkins."

"In the pantry, Dad. And you can tell Katie that dinner's almost ready."

"Will do." Jay got the napkins and went out to relay the message. Fifteen minutes later they were all sitting down at the deck table with their tacos. Dinner conversation went from baseball to the book Katie had gotten today and lastly to what Bren did for a living.

"I'm a writer," Bren answered, hoping that would suffice and they would move on to other topics.

"How exciting! Fiction of nonfiction?" Sheryl asked.

"Ah, fiction."

"Anything we would have heard of?"

"Probably not. I do a lot of freelance, some editing and development work, this and that. Behind the scenes stuff," he replied offhandedly. This wasn't his first rodeo.

"As a former English teacher, I can tell you there's much more to writing and publishing than meets the eye."

"Fortunately for me, there is."

"I just finished a good book," Jay entered the conversation. "An espionage thriller. *The Last Foreigner*."

Bren's last release. He looked over at Jay. "I'll have to look for that one."

"I really enjoyed it. I don't want to spoil it for you, but I didn't see the ending coming. Not by a long shot."

Bren tried to hide the pride rushing through him. "Good to know."

"You've read several by that author, haven't you, Dad?"

"I have. And he keeps getting better and better. I already pre-ordered his next one. It won't be out until the end of the year."

Black Friday, Bren silently added and changed the subject. "Katie, you sound like quite the bookworm yourself."

"Yeah, but I like romance novels."

"YA, age-appropriate, romance novels," Kenzie quickly qualified.

"So did Kenzie. And *Nancy Drew* mysteries. I still have those up in the attic," Sheryl added.

"Mattie only reads when he has to for school," Katie informed Bren.

"Reading is boring," Matt announced. "I'd rather play baseball."

"I get that," Bren said. "I was always torn between sports and reading. So I ended up doing a little of both. And when I got older, the books won."

Matt thought about that for a moment. "What books did you read?"

"All kinds, but mostly mysteries and thrillers. And books about sports."

"Mattie has read some of Mike Lupica's books," Kenzie put it.

"He's a good writer, especially for kids your age. I might be able to get you an autographed copy of his most recent one. I have some connections."

"Really? That'd be pretty cool," Matt said with a meditative frown.

"I'll see what I can do." Bren glanced over at Kenzie with a wink.

"Thank you," she mouthed.

Silence fell over the table for a few seconds until Sheryl stood. "Kenz, Dad and I will clean up. Finish your wine. Bren, can I get you another beer?"

"No thanks, Mrs.—Sheryl. I've got some work to do yet tonight." He started to rise, plate in hand, but Sheryl stopped him.

"Sit. The kids will help." She turned to her grandchildren. "Guys, grab some dishes and bring them inside please."

"Thanks, Mom," Kenzie said, handing her mother her plate.

After the four of them went into the house, Bren turned to Kenzie. "That was delicious. Thank you."

"It's the seasoning. My friend Emma's secret recipe. If I tell you, I'll have to kill you."

The irony of the statement was not lost on Bren. "So I guess that means you'll have to make them for me again sometime."

She didn't commit to that, only said, "I'm glad you liked them. And that you came by."

"Me, too. But I should get going. Duty calls." Grabbing his beer, Bren stood.

"I'll walk you out," Kenzie said, rising.

In the kitchen Bren exchanged parting pleasantries with Jay and Sheryl, then tracked the kids down in the family room before following Kenzie out front. Darkness had fallen, cloaking the basin in delicate, creamy light. Bren likened it to how it would feel to have Kenzie's body, damp from organism, pressed to his. He closed his eyes and took a cleansing breath. That image was not helping his self-restraint.

"Thanks again for letting me crash your party," he said when they reached his car. "Your parents are great."

Kenzie nodded in agreement. "I wouldn't have gotten through the last year without them. Did you finalize things with your mom and Bob?"

"I did. They're coming next week. I'll have to juggle some projects, but I couldn't say no."

"Of course not."

They were standing within a few breaths of each other, staring expectantly into each other's eyes. Bren could only assume his reflected the struggle he felt inside. But he wouldn't rush her. He'd given them both his word. He tipped her chin and laid a soft kiss on her lips. He had every intention of stopping there, but her lips parted and one kiss turned into two, then three. Her arms ringed his neck and she met him kiss for kiss, surrendering her tongue to his. He dove deeper wanting, needing, more. He licked, nibbled, tugged, tasting the sweet flesh of her mouth, devouring it. On bated breaths his tongue meandered down her throat, circling the hollow notch at the base of her neck. The murmur she made as he made his way back to her mouth was so erotic Bren felt himself start to grow and harden, but somehow he willed his hands to stay glued to her waist.

But something inside Bren snapped, turned primal, when she scrapped her tongue across his teeth. Instinctually his hands went to her butt, thrusting her against him. He could feel his erection throbbing, his heartbeat thundering, his control slipping away. He wanted her legs entwined with his, her center flush against him, her breast in his mouth. He wanted his hands on her, everywhere at once, as he turned to steel inside her. He wanted to feel the waves of pleasure ripple through her before letting himself go and joining her. She was either coming home with him or he was going home to a cold shower. And even in his current state of delirium, Bren knew she wasn't coming home with him.

He left her mouth on sawed-off breaths and buried his face in her hair. Need was raining down on him, soaking him to the bone. "I had to stop. I can't be responsible for my actions much longer."

Kenzie wrapped her arms around his middle as their heartbeats synced, settled. "I could say the same," she panted against his neck.

"I meant what I said before. I won't rush you."

"That's the problem. I think I want you to. I was devastated this afternoon when you weren't home. I didn't realize how much until I saw you tonight."

So he had read her right. He'd almost been afraid to believe it. Bren angled out of her embrace just as her eyes fluttered open. They were swimming with lust and rimmed in strife.

"You have no idea how happy I am to hear that. But your eyes tell a different story."

"They do?"

"Yeah. You okay?"

"Okay isn't a strong enough word, but it'll do. I guess we got a little carried away." Then her face fell and she looked around in alarm. "Oh God! Do you think anyone saw us?"

Bren couldn't help but laugh. "I doubt it. It's pretty wooded and dark around here." But he hoped the kids or Kenzie's parents weren't near any windows. That would be tricky to explain.

"Still, maybe we should stop doing this."

"Kissing or kissing in the driveway?"

"Kissing in the driveway. I feel like a randy teenager."

She had no idea. Bren was ready to explode. "One more." He cupped her face and brought her mouth back to his. His hands were making their way into her hair when she suddenly stiffened and pulled back.

"Bren, I can't… I'm sorry…" Taking a step back, she looked at him with eyes full of realization and shame.

"No, *I'm* sorry. I let myself—"

"No! It's not you! It's me!" She trudged a tormented hand through her hair. "God, that sounds so cliché. I'm completely unprepared for this and woefully out of practice! I don't know what's right or wrong. Let alone how I'm supposed to feel! And I don't know what I'm doing!"

"Tell me about it. But it's different for you, complicated. I don't want to make that harder, add to it."

She stared at him in silence for so long that Bren almost spoke, offered to slow things down. But before he could, she sighed and said, "You're not. You're just..." She searched for the words. "Unexpected, unintended, unsettling and absolutely wonderful. All at once." Her voice caught and her eyes filled. "And I'm..."

"Scared?" he supplied.

"Yeah."

"Me, too."

"You are?"

"I'm terrified."

"Why?"

"Well, for starters, I've never been here before. Not by a long shot. But you have."

Furrowing her brow, she stared at him blankly.

"You were married," he explained easily. "I've never been married or close to it, but I assume being in love is a prerequisite."

Kenzie gawked at him. "You're in love with me?"

"I really think I am."

"Bren..." With dropped jaw, she looked away.

"I don't need the words back. And they're not meant to pressure or upset you. I didn't plan on telling you like this, or this soon. But it just came out."

"Yeah," she said on a breath, returning to him. "That has a way of happening."

"I'll have to take your word for it. Now, as much as I hate to, I really do have to go."

She nodded. "You said you had to work."

"I have a hard-and-fast deadline. And you need to get back to your family."

"Knowing my mother, the kitchen is spotless and the kids are brushing their teeth as we speak. But, yes, I do. My parents will want to get going."

Bren brought her to him and kissed her one last time, slow and sweet. She kissed him back, then on a hug released him and walked up to the house. When she got to the front door, she turned and gave him a wan smile, then went inside. And unbeknownst to him, fell into her mother's arms and sobbed.

CHAPTER TWELVE

"Then what happened?"

"He got in his car and drove away."

"And what did you do?" Emma wanted to know.

Kenzie let out a jagged breath. "Cried to my mother."

"Oh, Kenz…"

"I'm the worst person I know."

"You didn't ask for this, seek it out. It just happened."

"Matt's barely been gone a year and—Oh, God," Kenzie cut herself off.

"Now what?"

"Today is Matt's birthday!" Kenzie threw a horrified hand over her mouth.

"I thought it was coming up."

"How could I have forgotten?"

"You didn't forget. It's ten o'clock in the morning."

"It should have been the first thing I thought of when I woke up. I should have said something to the kids, made sure they were okay. Last year we got a cake and sang 'Happy Birthday' to Daddy in heaven."

"Then get a cake, sing 'Happy Birthday.' The day has barely begun."

"I'm an awful person, a terrible wife."

Emma sighed. "No, you're not, you're human. And you're doing a very human thing. You're healing."

"By making out with another man?"

"How was it, by the way?"

When Kenzie didn't answer Emma prompted, "That good, huh?"

Kenzie swallowed the ache in her throat, tried to ignore the way her heart was chasing it. "Incredible."

"I'm listening."

"God Emma, I felt so alive." Kenzie closed her eyes, basked in the memory. "So wanted and sexy and…"

"Horny?"

"Yeah," Kenzie reluctantly admitted. "That too."

"You're allowed, Kenz. It doesn't cheapen what you and Matt had."

"It might. A little." Kenzie dropped down into a deck chair. "I got really worked up. Carnally, let's say."

"Now you're just being mean."

"Em, I'm serious. I feel like I'm cheating on my husband."

"You just have to get used to it. Of course it's going to feel a little foreign at first."

"That's the problem. It didn't feel foreign or strange or wrong. At least not in the moment."

"That's because it isn't. You met several widows in that support group who had moved on."

"Not after a year and a half!"

"There's no timeline for grief."

"This was about as far away from grief as you can get."

"That's a good thing. You're finally getting some closure."

"I guess you could call it that."

"I told you you'd get back in the saddle when the time was right."

"Since we were out in the driveway the time was definitely not right, but I get your point."

"Details. What did your mom say?"

"She was surprising supportive. I don't mean of me, that's not surprising at all. Of Bren, the idea of him. And of him and me."

"I hear a but."

"But," Kenzie dragged out the word. "She's concerned that I'm overthinking it. And if I don't push myself out of my comfort zone now, I'll regret it later."

"Buy the shoes. Classic Sheryl."

"Easier said than done."

"Once you do it, it won't be."

"Nice play on words."

"Wow, I wasn't even going for that," Emma congratulated herself. "What else did she say?"

"It's what she didn't say. I could see it in her eyes. She's not going to let this go. She's already thinking about what to serve when he comes to dinner."

"Love her."

"But there's something I haven't mentioned, to you or her." Kenzie paused, puffed out a breath. "Bren told me he's in love with me."

There was dead air for a few ticks. Finally Emma said, "Wow. He really puts it all out there, doesn't he? What did you say?"

"Nothing. I was in shock. But he made it clear he didn't expect reciprocation. And that he's willing to wait until I'm ready for a relationship."

"Sounds like a man who knows what he wants."

"That makes one of us."

"I think you do know. And it scares you."

So apparently Kenzie could add mind reading to the list of Emma's talents. "Who said I was scared?"

"He's not going to die, Kenz."

"God, Emma. I hadn't even thought of that!"

"Yes, you did. On some level, whether you know it or not."

Had she? Hidden under the inconceivable thought of being touched by another man, the effect a relationship would have on the kids and the guilt she still felt about where she and Matt were when he died, was going through that again what she was really afraid of?

"Well, if I didn't before I will now."

"He's not going to die," Emma repeated. "At least not anytime soon."

"I guess that could be part of it. And I should work on coming to terms with that. But the physical intimacy, spreading my already overextended self thinner, the guilt about the way things were between Matt and me at the end. I don't know if I have it in me to overcome all of that."

"Now who's playing with words?" Emma teased. But then her tone turned serious. "Kenz, those feelings are just as human as your—how did you put it—carnal reaction."

"Don't make me sorry I told you that."

"Look, you're not going to abstain from sex for the rest of your life, so you'd might as well take the plunge sooner rather than later. And for God's sake, when you do, let yourself enjoy it. As for the rest, you're the best mother I know, so the kids will be fine. You don't have to make a conscious choice to put them first, you just do. And unlike myself, you always seem to have a smile on your face while you do it." Emma paused, took a sip of what was likely her third cup of coffee of the morning, then continued, "And the die is cast on that fateful day, so stop beating yourself up about it. You and Matt might have had some loose ends, but your last words to each other were the three most important words you can say to someone."

"But I still feel so guilty."

"Then work on coming to terms with that that too. Nothing will change what happened, least of all punishing yourself. Life goes on. You have to go along with it."

"I know. You're right. I'll try."

"That's my girl. When will you see Bren again?"

"I'm not sure. His mother is coming to town. With her new boyfriend."

"Oh, this just keeps getting better and better."

"How so?"

"All this new relationship energy." Emma sighed longingly. "There's just something about emergent love. The enchantment, the exhilaration, the freedom. No expectations, no baggage. Not to mention the heightened passion, the open-minded give-and-take, the easy flow."

"Jesus, Emma. Maybe you should date Bren. Or his mother's boyfriend for that matter. And we haven't exactly defined our relationship, if you can even call it that."

"Don't tempt me. And I don't think you can call it anything but a relationship."

"The visit will be a distraction if nothing else. It'll buy me some time to sort things out."

"You don't need time, Kenz. You need to get out of your own way."

"Even if I manage to, what would the kids think?"

"I don't know. Ask them."

"*Ask* them? How the hell do I do that?"

"You'll figure it out. You always do."

"Well, I'm not bringing it up today of all days."

"Granted."

They spoke for a little longer, thankfully about more mundane things, then signed off. When Kenzie went inside, she found both kids in the kitchen. She decided to rip the bandage right off. "I should have mentioned this earlier, but today is Dad's birthday."

"We know, Mom," Katie said casually as she filled her water bottle. "Can we get an ice cream cake again? That was his favorite."

"Sure."

"They had some at the place we went with Bren."

"Okay. We'll pick one up."

"Can he come over?" Mattie asked. "He likes ice cream so he probably likes ice cream cake. Plus the Giants are on later."

"Uh…I don't think so. He has to work."

"Even tonight?"

"Probably. He has a deadline." Kenzie, unable to ignore the perfect segue, decided to go for it. "Speaking of Bren, you guys like him, right?"

"Yeah." Katie shrugged. "He reminds me of Uncle Gov."

Kenzie wasn't sure how she felt about that. "He does?"

"Yeah. He talks to me like a grown-up instead of a kid, even though he doesn't have kids. And he has nice eyes."

Kenzie couldn't argue there.

"I like that he calls me Matt," Mattie chimed in. "Mattie is babyish since I'm almost ten."

"I'll try to remember that."

"You just like him because he likes baseball," Katie postulated.

"So?"

"Okay, guys. What's the consensus for today?"

"We decided on Sand Harbor," Katie informed Kenzie.

"Sounds good. But we need to get going or we'll never find a parking spot."

While the kids got changed, Kenzie packed a cooler with water bottles and made the executive decision to buy lunch at the snack bar. A special treat for a special day. They'd stop on the way home to pick up a cake and some candles, a bottle of wine. A busy day at the beach would be a good distraction for all of them, especially herself.

But the thought of a distraction only brought Kenzie's mind back to Bren. The kids obviously liked him, but that didn't mean they'd like her liking him, dating him, if that's what it was still called. Part of her felt like she'd already been dating him without realizing it; it just kept happening. And if she was being honest with herself, the more it did, the more she wanted it to. And the more she wanted him. But love? Love was a different matter altogether. She was nowhere near ready for that. But the way she felt around him...Gasping, she brought an astonished hand to her chest. Was she in love with Bren? No, that was ridiculous! She'd know if she were in love! She was forty years old, had been married for fifteen years! Kenzie slammed the cooler shut as if shutting out the thought.

But her mother's age-old advice was not so easily dismissed. Be receptive, take a chance, buy the shoes. Because if you don't and change your mind later they might not be there. She'd known right away with Matt, had bought the shoes right away with no regrets. But this time she had so much more at stake, so much more to lose. Bren said he could be sure enough for both of them until she was ready. But she didn't have that luxury. She had to be sure enough for all of them. She couldn't let the kids get used to him and then lose him too. Especially Mattie.

But that was for tomorrow, she told herself. Today was Matt's day. So they'd lay in the sun, jump off the rocks, rent a kayak, eat fast food and have ice cream cake for dinner. And sing 'Happy Birthday' to Daddy in heaven.

*****

Sheryl stood at the laundry room door, gazing into the garage at her husband. He was sitting on an ancient three-legged stool, legs spread wide, polishing his golf clubs. His broad shoulders hunched forward and his sinewy arms flexed as he worked. His hands, thick and calloused from years in the yard and on the golf course, were still nimble. At over six feet, he commanded a room the moment he entered it, those long legs eating up the floor. Silvery-white had replaced his jet-black hair over the years and his fresh haircut and short sleeves revealed a farmer's tan and his love for the outdoors. A powerful lover even at seventy, he'd been her first and only. And, she had no doubt, her last.

She walked over to him, wrapped her arms around his shoulders from behind and kissed his cheek. She felt his smile before she pulled back. "Ready for lunch?"

"Sure." Setting down the hybrid and wiping his hands on a rag, he turned to her. "What do you have in mind?"

"I made chicken salad."

"Sounds good. I'll be right in."

Instead of going back into the house, Sheryl walked to the third bay and leaned against the golf cart that had been Jay's retirement gift from the kids. Arms crossed over her chest, she opened her mouth to speak.

"I thought he was nice," Jay said before she could get the words out.

"How'd you know what I was going to say?"

Standing, he closed the small space between them. "How'd you know I had a taste for chicken salad?" His crystal blue eyes began to twinkle as he drew her to him.

"And yes, I noticed the way he looked at her."

"I'm more interested in the way she looked at him."

"Let me guess. The same way she looked at Matt?"

Sheryl shook her head. "It's more than that. The way she used to look before the bottom fell out." She leaned against him, felt the warmth and safety of his arms that had never wavered through the years.

He held her close, stoked her hair. "We see it, but does she?"

"She does."

"And?"

"She doesn't like it."

"It hasn't even been two years." Jay angled out of her embrace and met her eyes. "What's the rush?"

"There is no rush. I just don't want her to miss an opportunity to embark on a new relationship and regret it later."

"And you know that would happen because?"

"I'm her mother."

Jay laughed dryly. "Of course."

"She needs a push."

"She's a grown woman, Sheryl. And as far from a slacker as you can get. She's never shied away from a challenge and has weathered more storms than both of us combined. Let her do this her own way, in her own time."

"She won't." Sheryl bit her bottom lip. "Not without a little help."

"Uh-oh. I don't like where this is going."

Increasingly determined, Sheryl plowed on, "Haven't you been thinking about taking Mattie to another Aces game before school starts?"

"Sheryl."

"Check the schedule and I'll coordinate a girls' day with Katie. We'll keep the kids overnight. Then Kenzie won't have any excuses. And more importantly, nothing to do up at the lake."

"And you think that just because she has a night to herself she's going to rush into this guy's arms?"

"With any luck, yes."

"You don't know anything about him. For all you know, he's seeing someone."

"Not for long if that's the case, which I doubt. I haven't seen a look that smitten in a man's eyes since college."

"Is that so?" Jay tightened his grip around her waist.

She wreathed his neck. "And we both know how that turned out." She laid a long, loud kiss on his mouth. "I only want that for her, what we have."

"She and Matt had a good marriage."

"They did. But that doesn't mean she should be alone for the rest of her life because their time ran out too soon. She has half her life left to live."

"And you're going to make sure she lives it."

"Or die trying. But I need a plan. A good one. She's a smart cookie, our girl."

"Don't you mean a trap?"

"Don't be silly. I'm just nudging nature along."

"As opposed to letting it take its course."

"Tomayto, tomahto."

Rubbing her back, Jay began to nuzzle her neck. That spot just below her earlobe he knew got her going. "So that's how you knew, huh? By the look in my eyes?"

Steeped in the memory, Sheryl closed her eyes. "You were manning the door at the fraternity house. You let us in even though we weren't on the list."

"I liked the look in your eyes, too."

"Anything else you liked?"

"Plenty. Come inside and I'll show you."

"I guess the chicken salad can wait for nature to take its course."

CHAPTER THIRTEEN

"Mom."

"Hi! Is this a good time?"

"Ah, yeah. Sure." Kenzie stepped aside, allowing her mother to enter. "I thought we were meeting at Mt. Rose." She checked her watch. "In an hour."

"Well, I was out and about, running ahead of schedule, and I figured I'd save you the trouble."

"Uh-huh." Kenzie looked askance at her mother.

"I can just hang out until the kids are ready."

"Okay. Katie's packing and Mattie's in the shower."

"Great. That'll give us a minute to chat." She headed for the kitchen.

Now we're getting somewhere Kenzie thought, following her. Her mother was nothing if not intentional. In the kitchen, Kenzie nodded to the shopping bag Sheryl carried. "Whatcha got there?"

"Just a little something I picked up for you."

"For me?"

"Yes, for you. I can't buy my daughter a gift?"

"Of course you can." Kenzie accepted the box her mother pulled out of the bag. "Thank you."

"Open it."

Inside Kenzie found a pair of shoes. A pair of very expensive, black slingback platform heels with rhinestone buckles. She ran her hand over the glossy patent leather. "They're gorgeous."

"Aren't they sexy?"

"Ah, right. Sexy." She should have known. "That they are." Kenzie resisted the urge to ask her mother if she'd gotten herself a pair as well. But that was crossing the line, even for them. "I'll save them for the next time I have a night out." Like when hell freezes over, Kenzie added to herself as she set the box on the island.

"How about tonight?"

"Tonight?"

Sheryl shrugged. "You have a night to yourself. Why not?"

"Well, for starters I don't have anywhere to go, let alone anyone to go there with. And I certainly don't have anything to wear with these," Kenzie picked up a shoe, swung it from its ankle strap by her pinky finger, "outrageously expensive, peep toe, thin-heeled stilettos that are borderline FMPs."

"Got you covered." Undeterred, Sheryl reached into the bag again, this time producing a dress. A strappy, form-fitting black mini dress Kenzie hadn't worn in years.

"Did you go to my house and get that out of my closet?" Kenzie amazed as Sheryl displayed the dress, still on its hanger, between them.

"I just might have."

"I can't remember the last time I wore it," Kenzie muttered under her breath.

"I believe it. It was in the very back. Still in the bag from the cleaners."

Dropping the shoe back in the box with its mate, Kenzie took the dress from her mother as she racked her brain. Was it a wedding? New Year's Eve? "I think it's older than Mattie."

"It's the quintessential little black dress. It's timeless."

Kenzie met her mother's eyes. "What did you say?"

"Isn't that what you guys call it? LBD? What Chanel started years ago?"

"Ah, yeah. But what else did you say?"

"It's timeless. An ageless wardrobe staple that—"

"Timeless," Kenzie interrupted.

"Yeah. Timeless, sophisticated, unassuming."

"Like Tahoe."

"I guess," Sheryl agreed through a pensive frown. "The classic little black dress never goes out of style. Like the timeless, unassuming beauty of Tahoe."

"Ineffably so," Kenzie uttered, laying the dress on top of the shoebox and looking into the near distance unseeingly.

"I've never thought about it that way, but sure. There's something indefinable, indescribable, about Tahoe. And there's also something ineffable about a woman in a little black dress that evokes those same emotions."

Shaking off the undeniable parallel, Kenzie cocked her head and stared suspiciously at her mother. "Mom, what are you up to?"

"I'm not up to anything," Sheryl maintained inadequately. "I saw a pair of shoes I thought you'd like and I bought them. End of story."

Kenzie ignored the lame attempt at explanation. "How did you know I even had this dress?"

"I would have been disappointed if you didn't. To be honest, I was getting a little nervous. It took some looking." Sheryl walked over and gave Kenzie's arms an affectionate squeeze. "You kept it for a reason. And if there's any place to find out what that reason is, it's Tahoe. Tahoe reminds us that anything is possible, gives us the courage and clarity to live in the moment and go for it. You like Bren. He clearly likes you. You owe it to yourself to see where it could go."

Nodding, Kenzie swallowed the tears gathering in her throat, but she couldn't stop the one that escaped the corner of her eye. Her mother brushed it away with her thumb just as Katie entered the kitchen.

"Mom, where's my—" she stopped short. "Oh, hi Grandma! I thought we were meeting you halfway."

"Hey, baby girl!" Sheryl sidestepped and wrapped her arms around her granddaughter. "I felt like taking a drive. No halfway today."

"No halfway today," Katie repeated. "That sounds funny, doesn't it Mom?"

"No halfway today. Yeah, that is funny."

"Words to live by." Sheryl gave Kenzie a pointed look over Katie's head.

"Mom, what's wrong with your voice?" Katie asked.

"Nothing." Kenzie cleared her throat. "Just a frog in my throat. Are you ready?"

"Almost, but Mattie's hogging the bathroom and I need to get in there."

"Okay. I'll get him going."

Kenzie lit a fire under Mattie and fifteen minutes later she was waving the three of them off. She gave Boot a few minutes to do his business in the front yard and went back inside. It was the first time she'd been alone here and the house seemed eerily quiet. She had no idea what to do with herself, so she started straightening up, beginning in the bathroom. She threw the towels in the washer and made Mattie's bed, then moved on to the kitchen.

She stuck the dress in the bedroom closet along with the shoes, still in the box. She was back in the kitchen folding up the shopping bag when she realized it wasn't empty. Reaching inside, she found a book. *The Last Foreigner*, the book her dad had recommended to Bren the other night, Stuck to the front was a note: *Dad thought you might want to pass this on to Bren.*

"Dad, huh? You can stop now, Mom," Kenzie said to no one. "Message received."

Kenzie set the book aside and put the bag in the pantry. By the time she ran the dishwasher and wiped off the table and counters, her mom had texted to say they'd made it to Reno.

Deciding two could play this game, Kenzie replied: *Great! I'm getting ready to run an errand. Looking for my black push-up bra. I might not have brought it since it's the LAST thing I expected to need at the lake.*

It was only a few seconds before an ellipsis flashed across the screen. *So you found the book. Hmmm... Maybe ditch the bra altogether?*

Unbelievable, Kenzie thought, shaking her head from side to side. *Did you really expect me to wear that to drop off a book? In the middle of the day?*

No, I assumed you'd wear something else and know you have the dress, come what may. The first step is always the hardest. After that things have a way of taking care of themselves.

Before Kenzie could reply, Sheryl was at it again. *Contrary to popular belief, lightning can strike twice. Being outside your life looking in doesn't change the when and where. Buy the shoes. I love you.*

Kenzie replied in kind, then set the phone down and picked up the book. Lost in thought, she didn't realize Boot had rambled into the kitchen until she felt him against her leg. On a heartening sigh, she reached down and scratched his head. "How about we shake things up for our walk this afternoon, big guy? Maybe somewhere mid-mountain."

*****

Bren wrote through most of the night, finally crawling into bed around four. The last few days had been much of the same—lather, rinse, repeat. The work was a good—and welcome—distraction. His mother's visit would be another one. But after that all bets were off. He was at the end of his rope.

The words had escaped his lips without warning and Bren didn't regret them any more than he expected them back. But that didn't mean he had to like it. His brain knew be had to be patient, wait for Kenzie to come to him. But his favorite organ was yet to get the message. At least now he knew he wasn't alone in his struggle. She wanted him too.

Progress.

Inescapable exhaustion took over and sleep started to come easier by the third night. But before Bren's eyes were fully open each morning, his imagination was at it again. The thought of waking up next to Kenzie after being on top of her, under her and meshed with her all night sent his hormones into a tailspin. He pressed the palms of his hands against his forehead and blew out a long breath. He had to get a grip. Maybe a cold shower and some fresh mountain air would take the edge off. And oh yeah, there was that pesky deadline. But the writing he'd done so far was solid, really good. This book was burning inside him, begging to be set free. It didn't always happen that way and Bren was grateful for it.

Scrubbing his face, Bren sat up and got his bearings. Coffee was the first order of business, so he got that going and jumped in the shower. But that just brought his mind back to Kenzie. The dual rainfall shower hadn't gotten much mileage under his watch. Now he imagined her in there with him, beads of water dripping off the ends of her hair, clinging to her nipples, her bottom lip, as her body, slick and slippery, sidled up next to his. He wanted to take her from behind as the steam curled around them and the haze took them under. He wanted to climb with her, fly with her, watch her fall as waves of pleasure gave way to cries of ecstasy. And then explode inside her as she took that final dive. That scenario blazed inside him just as fiercely as the story raging in his head. And shared the same desperate need for release. But unlike the book, Bren couldn't put blinders on, put mind over matter and make it happen. He was at Kenzie's mercy. And as much as he enjoyed a coaxing simmer, a tantalizing smolder, his yearning for her was becoming a violent inferno. Something had to give. And soon.

It was close to noon by the time Bren finally sat on the deck and opened his laptop. It was another bluebird day and the lake sparkled like a mosaic of turquoise-blues in the unfiltered sunshine. This, Bren told himself for the umpteenth time, is surely what heaven looks like. But here on earth his deadline loomed so he took a hefty sip of coffee and got to it.

Bren knew the next set of edits for his work-in-progress would be waiting for him in his inbox. The editor was a night owl and he had a feeling Miranda was also carrying some of the load this time. She was the middle man on all correspondence to prevent an accidental breach anyway. And in addition to being Agent Extraordinaire, she was a damn good editor. That quarter-million-dollar Ivy League education sure comes in handy.

Not bad Bren decided, giving himself a mental pat on the back as he scrolled through the comments. Some pacing issues, a few lulls in the arc to address and he had a tendency to get caught up in the minutiae at times. Readers don't care how the gun was built, only who it's pointed at and why. And of course, he had a malapropism or two here and there, largely due to the fact that he was a horrible speller. He'd had his share of omnipotent editors in the past who treated his work like a riffable chili recipe, but that was no longer the case. Miranda saw to that.

Bren gauged the time required to address the changes and decided that with a little luck, he'd get through this today and get back to the new project tonight. One of Bren's professional strengths was his ability to compartmentalize, separate projects into mental boxes when he had multiple balls in the air. Unfortunately, Kenzie was much harder to appropriate.

He dug in and started hammering away, beginning with the last chapter. It was a trick he'd learned from being an editor himself. It forces the brain to slow down, process the story methodically, like reading out loud from printed pages as opposed to reading silently off a screen. It also flags inconsistencies or anachronisms in the story, especially when flashbacks were involved as was the case with this book. Writing nonlinear stories was more challenging than writing in real-time, but can really pack a punch if done well. And Bren tended to do it well.

The sun was still at full-mast when the doorbell drew Bren out of his writing cave. He glanced at the time, finding it was already after four. It wasn't unusual for him to lose track of time when he was deep in work mode, but considering he hadn't had anything but coffee today, he was surprised his stomach hadn't alerted him.

He walked through the house toward the front door hoping it wasn't Greg trying to build a bridge or a solicitor he'd have to rudely dismiss. He didn't know if he had the energy for either one. But standing on the other side of the door, backlit by the afternoon sun, was a much more welcome visitor.

"Kenzie."

"Hey."

"What a nice surprise."

"Is it? I texted you that Boot and I were going to be in your neck of the woods."

"I must have missed it. I've been working." Bren stepped aside. "Come on in."

"You sure? I don't want to interrupt. You said you have a tight deadline."

"Actually, I could use a break." Greeting Boot with a pat on the head, Bren resisted the urge to do the same to Kenzie with a kiss. She was dressed in shorts and a low-slung tank top that skimmed the tan line from her swimsuit just enough to tease him. He wondered what, if anything, she was wearing underneath. Her skin was glistening with sweat, bringing his shower fantasy back to mind. Bren felt his mouth start to water. "Did you guys walk all the way over here?"

"Oh, no," she replied, stepping inside and taking Boot off the leash. "I'm parked down the block. We felt like exploring a little today. And I wanted to give you this." She handed Bren a book he hadn't noticed she was holding.

Bren immediately recognized the jacket of *The Last Foreigner*. The cover was one of his favorites, not that anyone gave a damn. "Thanks," he said, finding himself disappointed she had a reason for stopping by.

"My dad couldn't say enough good things about it."

"I'll look forward to reading it." Bren tried to sound nonchalant as he shut the door. "Are your parents here again?"

"No," Kenzie replied with a shake of the head. "My mom dropped it off earlier when she picked up the kids."

"I was wondering where they were. I didn't think Matt had a lesson until next week."

"He doesn't. My parents wanted to spend some time with them before school starts, which will be before we know it. Dad is taking Mattie to the Aces game and Mom and Katie are going shopping."

"That's nice."

"It is, but to be honest, I'm not quite sure what to do with myself up here. I'm not used to both of them being gone, especially overnight."

"I bet. Come on back," he invited, leading the way to the kitchen. "Do you want something to drink?"

"I have water." She tapped the bottle attached to her hip as she followed him. "Boot might be thirsty, though. But I left his bowl in the car."

"No worries. I have an array of containers for him to choose from." Bren got out a plastic bowl, filled it with water and set it on the floor. Boot immediately walked over and began lapping it up.

"I don't know how you work out there. I wouldn't get a thing done with that view." Boot's leash in her hand, Kenzie gazed out the open deck door.

"I'm pretty discipled. I put my blinders on and go. Now I have trouble working inside."

She looked back at him. "What do you do in the winter?"

"I work here, in the kitchen. Sometimes I visit my mom in Scottsdale for a few weeks. She has a nice patio that overlooks the valley."

"It sounds like you and she are close."

"It's always been just the two of us, so yeah."

Boot, having all but emptied the water dish, trotted into the living room and laid down in a sunbeam by the window with a contented sigh.

"Well, Boot wasted no time in making himself comfortable."

"He's been here before. During the remodel."

"Right." She stood there, holding his gaze for a long moment, then said, "Well, I don't want to keep you."

"Would you like to grab something to eat?" Bren heard himself ask. "I know it's a little early for dinner, but I haven't eaten all day and I'm starving."

Kenzie glanced downward. "Oh, I'm not dressed to go out to dinner."

"You are in Tahoe."

"What about your deadline?"

Bren shrugged. "I need to eat eventually. Do you like burgers?"

"Um, yeah. I like burgers."

"My buddy has a place in Tahoe City. Best burgers in town."

She tipped her head toward the window. "What about Boot? He'll need dinner too."

"I think I still have some dog food from when Gov was working through my punch list." Bren mentally crossed his fingers as he walked over to the pantry. Bending at the knees, he rummaged through the bottom shelf and pulled out a small bag of kibble. "Does this stuff expire?"

"I don't think so," Kenzie replied, joining him as he straightened. "Not the dry stuff." She took the bag from him and opened it, then sniffed the contents. "It smells fine."

"So, what do you think?"

After a few seconds of deliberation, she gave him a shy smile. "I could go for a burger."

With an inward cheer, Bren suggested, "How about you get Boot squared away while I grab my laptop and lock up." He got another plastic container out of the cabinet and handed it to her.

"Okay. And Bren?"

"Yeah?" he answered as he started to walk away.

"Thanks."

He smiled at her. "You bet."

After their tasks were complete, they hopped in Bren's car and headed out. He opened the sunroof out of habit, then realized he probably should have asked Kenzie if she minded.

"Oh, no. I love the open air. It's worth the havoc it wreaks on my hair."

Bren turned to her. "Your hair looks great." Her usually straight hair was wavy and sexily disheveled from the wind. He loved how she tucked it behind her ear from time to time as they drove. And when she pushed it out of her face it looked like she biting the air. Bren felt himself start to grow. She was seducing him without even trying and it was driving him mad.

If Bren hadn't been so spellbound by her, he'd have thought to take the longer, more scenic route around the lake. But he went through town on autopilot. As they passed the ancient casinos of Crystal Bay, he asked what they'd been up to the last few days.

"We spent the day at Sand Harbor on Friday."

"Incline's hidden gem. Did you guys rent a kayak?"

"We did. A glass bottom one. I swear I could see a hundred feet down."

"The clarity of the lake has really improved. Between the Keep Tahoe Blue movement and the resurgence of the zooplankton, the lake is practically aging backwards."

"Aging backwards. That's an interesting way to put it."

"I'm sure there's a more scientific term, but that's what comes to mind."

"Either way, we had a great day. Especially considering—" Kenzie cut herself off.

"Considering?" Bren asked as they crossed into California.

She paused for so long before continuing that Bren almost changed the subject. They were stopped at a light when she finally turned to him. "Friday was Matt's birthday."

"Oh, Kenzie." He reached over and laid his hand on top of hers with a supportive squeeze. "I'm sorry."

"Thanks." She squeezed back. "And you have nothing to be sorry about. I shouldn't have mentioned it."

Bren had no idea how to respond so he didn't. Fortunately the light changed, forcing him to focus on the road. They rode in companionable silence, hands clasped, until they got to the roundabout in Kings Beach and Bren needed both hands to navigate the turns. But the rest of the drive was a straight shot, so after a brief internal debate, he rested his hand back on hers.

They wound through touristy Kings Beach and into the more residential Carnelian Bay, where the lake took center stage again. The beaches were rocky on this side of the lake; granite outcroppings led to the water's edge instead of the fine-grained sand of the North Shore. With both hands back on the wheel, Bren slowed his pace as they got into Tahoe City and its waterfront lined with ski shops and restaurants.

Bren nabbed a parking spot on the lakefront side of the street. Shoving the car into Park, he looked over at Kenzie. "Hungry?"

"I am. And I'm also very impressed. You practically did that one-handed."

"Years of practice. Not of parking, of baseball. Promotes dexterity."

"I guess."

"I'd be chivalrous and open the door for you, but I don't want to be that guy who holds up traffic."

"Don't be silly."

"Watch yourself."

They got out and met on the sidewalk. Bren reached for Kenzie's hand as they started walking. She grasped it hesitantly at first, but then let him wrap his hand around hers. Baby steps, Bren reminded himself, are better than standing still. The street was packed, nearly shoulder to shoulder in some spots. Bren drew Kenzie closer to him as they walked, heartened that she didn't seem to mind.

After a couple of blocks, he gestured with his free hand. "Not much farther."

"No problem. I'm taking it all in. When I dropped Katie off at Sunnyside, I was reminded of how quaint Tahoe City is. But I was driving so I really couldn't get a good look."

"I think the term is mountain modern. The spirit of old Tahoe with all the modern amenities."

"Wordsmith strikes again."

"I probably read that somewhere. Here we are." Bren slowed their pace and opened the door for Kenzie, then walked in behind her. There was a line of people in front of the hostess stand that Bren, grasping her hand again, lost no time circumventing. Leading Kenzie through the restaurant, he stopped at the bar straddling the back wall.

"Hey, Cole."

Uncorking the bottle of wine in his hand with a thunk, the floppy-haired bartender looked up. "Hey, Bren." He shifted his gaze to Kenzie and nodded. "Ma'am. Tom said you'd be in. Best I could do was a two-top. But at least it's outside."

"Thanks."

"Cinda's on break, so you'll have to seat yourself. It's the one with the Reserved sign."

"Will do."

"Hailey has the deck tonight. She'll be right out."

"No rush."

"Want me to get something started for you?"

"Looks like you're busy. We'll wait for Hailey."

As they were turning away, Kenzie let out a small laugh.

"What?" Bren asked over his shoulder.

"You might know as many people around here as my brother."

"I wouldn't profess to be Gov, let alone Mac. Tom, the owner, and I grew up together. We played ball from Little League through high school," Bren explained as walked toward the outdoor seating area. "Tom pulled the long straw in the roommate pool at Berkley. I'm not going to name any names, but this guy is a financial wizard, all but has a crystal ball and whatever he touches turns to gold. But he was shy, kind of nerdy and a bit of a loner. Tom is the polar opposite of that. Tom got him out of the dorm room, pushed him to join a fraternity, get involved on campus and subsequently introduced him to his wife. As a token of his undying gratitude, upon graduation he gave Tom some stock in a company he swore would change the world." They reached the table and Bren pulled out Kenzie's chair. "You not only use their products everyday, you have one in your purse."

"Wow," Kenzie said, sitting down.

"Yeah." Bren took a seat across from her. "Tom, being no slouch himself, ended up with concurrent degrees from Cal. He took advantage of a stock split in the mid-aughts, followed his dream and opened this place. He lived in a camper for the first two years until it got going. Now he has three locations, is opening a fourth in Maui, and lives on twenty acres outside of Truckee."

"Double wow. And you have a standing reservation?"

"Sort of. Tom was a late bloomer, struggled in reading in elementary school. My mom tutored him for free. Tom and his mom were on their own too, so we had a lot in common. Now we both live in Tahoe and he has the best burgers in town," Bren finished just as Hailey arrived at their table.

"Hey, Bren. Long time no see."

"Work's been keeping me a little closer to home. How've you been, Hailey?"

"I'll be better when this baby is out of me."

"I'm sure. You must be getting close."

"Five weeks, give or take."

"Good luck if I don't see you before the big day. Hailey, this is Mackenzie Bishop."

"Nice to meet you, Hailey. Congratulations."

"Likewise and thanks."

"Your first?"

"No. I have a little girl at home."

"Awe. Do you know what you're having?"

"A boy."

"I can relate to that dynamic."

While Kenzie and Hailey discussed babies, Bren looked over the wine list. "You liked the Rombauer the other night, right?" he asked Kenzie during a break in the conversation.

"I did. But there's plenty of other less expensive options."

"That you may not like as well." He handed the list back to Hailey. "Rombauer Chardonnay for the lady. And I'll take a Sierra Nevada."

"We only sell that one by the bottle, Bren."

"That's fine. We'll take home whatever she doesn't finish."

"Coming right up."

After Hailey walked away, Kenzie gave Bren a pointed look. "You didn't have to do that."

"I know. I wanted to. When's the last time you had a night off?"

"Let me think. Last…never."

"There you go. Thanks for spending it with me."

She gave him a slow smile. "I'm really glad I am."

He held her stare for a long moment, then picked up the menu. "So what looks good? They're known for their Bloody Mary Burger. It's got everything but the kitchen sink."

"I can honestly say I've never had a Bloody Mary Burger."

"No one had, which was exactly what Tom was banking on. When he started this place they only served brunch on Sundays and the Bloody Mary was their signature drink. It was actually a meal in itself, garnished with just about everything you can imagine. But brunch didn't really cater to families on vacation, travelers passing through. So Tom ditched the brunch idea and standardized the Sunday menu with the rest of the week and created a burger in the same vein."

"Tom sounds like a clever guy."

"He is. Out of necessity I suppose. And you'd hate to have all that tech stock money go to waste."

"So are you going for the Bloody Mary Burger?" Kenzie asked, perusing the menu.

"No, I'm not *that* hungry. It's meant to be shared."

"I'll share it with you."

"You will?" Bren said as their eyes met again.

"Sure. It sounds good."

"Okay. The Bloody Mary Burger it is."

Just then Hailey returned with their drinks and took their order. After she left, Kenzie picked the conversation back up. "Thanks, Bren. The wine is wonderful. And so is this place." She took in the deck, the dock leading down to the lake, the cove where the waves barreled against the rocks in the wind, then came back to him. "I feel like I'm a million miles away, not just down the road."

"The magic of Tahoe strikes again. So, other than Sand Harbor, any other adventures in the last few days?"

"Not really," Kenzie replied with a shake of the head. "We stayed close to home yesterday. We were worn out from a long day on Friday." Her voice trailed off as she looked down into her wine glass.

Bren reached over and took her hand. "I'm sorry, Kenzie. I'm sure it was a sad day."

When her eyes found his again, they were watery. "It was. But it was also a fun day. How sad could a day that starts at Sand Harbor and ends with ice cream cake really be?" She ended on a shaky laugh.

"You amaze me. You always find a silver lining."

"Well, I don't have much choice. I don't want the kids' childhoods to be defined by their dad dying."

"Will you tell me about him?" Bren heard himself ask.

She gave him an open-mouthed stare. "Matt?"

"Yeah. Unless it would be too painful."

"It wouldn't be painful. I just don't want to make you…"

"Uncomfortable?" Bren finished for her.

"Yeah."

"I won't be. I'd like to know more about him. It'll help me get to know you better."

She gave him a look of equal parts surprise and veneration, then began on a gulp. "We met at a wedding. Neither one of us knew many people there so we started talking at the bar. He was stationed in San Diego and I was living in Reno, working my first job out of college." On a moony smile, she closed her eyes as if reliving the memory. "He wasn't wearing his uniform that night. I might have been too intimidated to talk to him if he had been. He looked so handsome in his uniform." Shaking off the nostalgia, she returned to Bren. "Anyway, I gave him my number, something I never did, especially in a bar. He called the following morning and asked me to dinner before my flight home. Long story short, we started dating and got married. Katie was born two years later and Mattie quickly followed." She took a sip of wine. "Matt was a wonderful man, a great father. We built a good life together."

"You were happy. I can tell by the way you talk about him."

She had to think about that for a moment. It shamed Bren a little that he didn't mind. "I was. I always felt safe, loved. I never doubted his fidelity, his loyalty or his commitment. But Matt was a military man through and through. He came from generations of service and never knew, or considered, any other way of life. It was as much a part of him as me and the kids." She took another, deeper, sip of wine. "As much as I understood and appreciated that, admired it, it's hard to compete with. I wanted him to retire, only do twenty years. Although we'd never talked about it, made a plan, he assumed he'd be career military, serve thirty or forty years. It became an issue between us. In retrospect, he probably couldn't imagine his life without it. Like I couldn't imagine my life without him until he died. It's cruelly ironic."

Just then Hailey retuned to check on them, top off Kenzie's wine and offer Bren another beer. "Only one for me tonight," he declined. "I've got to work later."

"Your burger should be right up."

After Hailey took her leave, Bren decided it was as good a time as any to fess up. "Along those lines, I have a confession make."

That seemed to amuse her. "Do you?"

"Mac wasn't my only source of information about Matt. I did a little digging on my own. I'm sorry— the journalist in me couldn't resist. It sounds like he was a decorated soldier, had a distinguished career. But all of that comes at a price, I suppose."

"He did and it does. Matt did all the working and I did everything else."

"The everything else matters."

"It does. I never saw myself as a stay-at-home mom, especially in the long-term. But I love it, I'm good at it."

"Obviously."

She smiled, big and bright. "Now *I* can't imagine doing anything else. But I'll be imagining it soon. I'm going to be looking for a job once school starts."

"That's exciting."

"You know, it really is. I think it'll be good for me."

"You've been through a lot, Kenzie."

"I have. But we all have our challenges. I'm sure it wasn't easy growing up without a father."

"It wasn't, but your situation is different, more complex."

"I guess," she agreed with a nod. "And although I never would have wanted it, could have fathomed it, it forced me to grow, become stronger, by having to dig that deep. The sky fell, but I picked myself up and kept going. I never would have deemed myself capable of that before. There were days I wanted to curl up in a ball and sob. But I couldn't. And eventually those days became fewer and farther between." She stopped and took a breath, stared blankly into the near distance. "Matt made me so happy, showed me the world, gave me the greatest part of my life— my children. Even now, just thinking about it fills me with such joy and gratitude. Not because our life was perfect, but because it was ours. And what better way to honor it, and him, than to spend the day together at Sand Harbor and eat ice cream cake for dinner?" She returned to him with a weak smile and teary eyes.

Bren reached across the table and took her hand again. He was feeling a little teary-eyed himself, listening to her bare her soul like that. It made him admire her even more. "I can't think of a better one. Thank you for being so open, for telling me about him, about your life together."

She tried out a bigger smile. "Thank you for asking, for listening. Sharing memories really does help us heal. I never would have believed that before."

Their burger arrived, reminding Bren that it was just as sharable as advertised, and they dug in. The conversation went to the chronology of Bren living in Tahoe, how Gov acquired Boot and ways Bren could entertain his mother, and more importantly Bob, next week. Bren settled the bill while Hailey bagged the wine and they headed back toward the car. He was in no hurry for the evening to end, but sunset was an hour away and Kenzie had already passed on dessert so his options were limited. He was running possibilities through his head when Kenzie asked, "Do you mind if we walk off our dinner a bit?"

"Not at all. You read my mind."

"You sure? Because I know you have to work."

"It'll be there. I need to clear my head anyway."

Out on the street the crowds had thinned and the hustle and bustle of earlier was replaced by the peaceful ebb and flow of the lake settling in for the night. The sun was starting to set, its slanting rays casting long shadows over the lake as it yielded to the gloaming. Bren took Kenzie's hand as they strolled down Lake Street toward the dam. When they came to the Fanny Bridge she said, "Mattie and I drove by after we dropped Katie off. We couldn't believe how loud and fast the river was rushing."

"Between the healthy snowpack and the early spring, the flow rate and water level are finally getting back to normal."

They walked leisurely along the bridge and through the exhibit chronicling the construction of the dam and the management of the water downstream. They were heading back to the car when Kenzie turned to Bren. "This was fun. Thanks again."

"It was. And you're welcome."

Bren opened the door for Kenzie, then got behind the wheel. By the time they got back to Incline, the bottom half of the sun was sinking into the horizon.

"Caught you looking."

"I don't usually get to see the sunset from this elevation. It's already managing to outdo itself."

"You ain't seen nothing yet. Some feathery clouds snuck in while we were eating. The blue hour portion of tonight's program will be off the charts."

With humor shining in her eyes, she turned to look at him. "Do you know a little something about everything?"

"Just enough to be dangerous. I'm a writer," Bren told her easily. "It comes with the territory."

She laughed. "Uh-huh."

Five minutes later they were pulling into Bren's garage. Boot greeted them at the door, tail wagging, and immediately sidled up to Kenzie.

"Hey, buddy. Did you miss us?" she said, stroking his head.

"Does he need to go out?"

"I think he's okay. It hasn't been that long." She walked farther into the house, stopping to stare out the window over the kitchen sink.

Coming up behind her, Bren resisted the urge to wrap his arms around her. Instead, he rested his hands on her shoulders and followed her line of sight. Coral-tinted indigo light flocked the basin and the woodland beyond as the sun took its final gasps. "Mother Nature in all her glory."

Kenzie leaned against him with an appreciative sigh. "Do you get this every night up here?"

"More often in winter. But she's really putting on a show tonight. You must bring out the best in her."

She looked up at him. Her eyes, shimmering like stars in the pale glow of the moon, searched his. "It must be going around."

"Kenzie…" Bren muttered as his mouth covered hers.

She turned into him, raising her arms to link his neck. She fell into the kiss, then the next, rising to meet him, match him, give-and-take in equal measure. Their tongues teased, mingled, tangled. Every breath he took had surely been in her lungs first. Bren was clutching her so tightly against him he could feel her turgid nipples through her shirt. And had no doubt she could feel his burgeoning erection through his jeans. He was approaching the point of no return again. But this time was different. This time Kenzie was right there with him.

On serrated breaths she pulled her mouth away and moving to his top lip, yanked, bit, sucked, kicking every cell in Bren's body into overdrive. When she put her mouth on his again and began to feed, all the blood in his head rushed to his cock, sending arrows of want shooting through him. But when she rubbed her foot up and down the back of his calf, Bren started to lose hold of his moral compass and sense of decency. He tore his mouth away, released her and took a step back.

"You need to go," he panted.

Kenzie stared at him with sultry eyes and a heaving chest. "What if I didn't?"

"Then you're going to stay," Bren decided out loud without breaking their shared gaze. "And I'm going to make love to you all night long."

Her eyes fired with discernment, then softened to make room for her heart. No wonder she was so emotional, so torn. Despite her best efforts, she'd fallen in love with him. Pervasive happiness surged through him. But it was what she said next that tipped the scales.

"Promise?"

"Promise," he said and scooped her up.

Her legs circled his midsection and she threw her head back in devilish laughter as he carried her up the stairs. The third floor was dark, lit only by the moonglade bouncing off the water. Bren set her down on the bed, laid down next to her and gathered her in his arms.

She smiled up at him. "I thought you had a deadline."

"I do. But this seems more…pressing."

"Yeah," Her voice was low, thready. And more shaky than Bren would have liked.

He stroked her cheek with the back of his hand, then traced the contours of her mouth. "You sure about this?"

She nodded. "I love you too, Bren."

He sent her a grateful smile. "I know."

"You do?"

"As of about five minutes ago, yes. I could see it in your eyes. I was almost afraid to believe it."

She snuggled closer to him, tucked her head under his chin and twined her legs with his. "I almost can't believe it myself. But I do."

He kissed the top of her head, inhaled the scent of her, indulged in the feeling of having her curled up against him. "Well, believe this. You're the first woman I've ever loved. I've been waiting for you without even knowing it."

"I'll try to make it worth the wait."

"It already is."

She uptilted her head and met his eyes. "Show me."

"Be careful what you wish for." Rolling on top of her, Bren framed her face with this arms and went in for a kiss. "Or I might find myself in a hurry."

"That's okay. I'm in a little bit of a hurry all of a sudden myself."

He nuzzled her neck. "I don't want to miss anything."

"I won't let you," she muttered as he seized her mouth. He felt the moan in her throat as his tongue trailed lazily down her neck, stopping to nibble on her earlobe, then finding the valley between her breasts. She tasted bittersweet; the florals in her perfume mixed with the tang of the day. But most of all she tasted like woman. Succulent and feminine with a hint of sweet. He peeled off the tank top and tossed it aside along with his shirt.

"God, you're so beautiful." Her skin was kissed by the sun and sheeny with desire. Straddling her, he filled each hand with a breast and fondled. "I can't wait to bury myself in them, in you." Closing his eyes, Bren lingered in her cleavage before taking one breast in his mouth, then the other. He pulled, licked, sucked, while bringing her other nipple to point with his thumb. Uttering endearments, Kenzie squirmed beneath him, urging him on.

He left her breasts and kissed his way down her torso to her stomach. He wanted to keep going, taste her desire, but not this time, their first time. He used his teeth to slide her shorts down and helped her shimmy out of them. She kicked them and her shoes off while Bren made quick work of his own. He returned to her, running his fingertips up her silky legs, over her clean-shaved triangle, her sculpted stomach. He wanted to explore her unhurriedly, meticulously, tirelessly, but that was for another time. He had to have her now.

Bren climbed on top of her and ranged himself between her legs. His erection rested on her delta and he had to close his eyes and clench his teeth for a few seconds to garner enough control not to take her with the force of a runaway train. She reached for him but he stopped her. "Once you touch me, I won't be able to hold back. Let me touch you first."

In silent understanding, she spread her thighs just enough for his hand to cup her. He could smell her desire now, knew he'd find her wet and hot and ready for him. She quivered as he explored her slick folds, her delicate creases, her pulpy layers. A telling gasp escaped her lips when he dipped one finger, then two, inside her, sending a shiver of fresh want through him. He darted in and out, driving her up as she arched below him, coming undone in his hand as the arc of gratification took her under. And when his thumb began to rub her fleshy nub, she let out a growl so guttural Bren almost climaxed. Urgent affirmations escaped her lips as her legs fell open and her pelvis lifted off the bed. She spasmed, throwing her head back in rapture and release, drenching his hand as the orgasm rolled through her. Bren rode the swell with her, trying to keep himself in check, circling her madly with two fingers still inside her. And just when he thought she was coming down, she cried out again. On heaving breaths she fell back on the bed, her hands clutching the comforter.

"Oh, God. That was amazing," she ground out "I'm still tingling inside."

"I aim to please. But I can't wait another second to be inside you."

"Then don't." She wrapped her hand around him and guided him into her, instantly tightening around him. Telling himself not to thrust too hard, lest he pound her into oblivion, Bren began to move above her. She kept pace with him, increasing the friction as they fell into that intoxicating, instinctive rhythm, and their hedonic moans mingled in the heavy air.

Her legs banded his middle and her nails dug into his back as she rocked back and forth beneath him. Bren was on the brink, holding on by a thread, but he kept pumping, soaring above her. But when she extended her legs, pressing her abdomen against his and burying him even deeper inside her, Bren felt himself start to blow. The tip of him was touching the most remote part of her and he'd never felt this kind of arousal, this kind of attachment to a woman before. Bren tried to hold on, make it a hat trick for her, but his cock had other ideas. And just as she howled his name, he exploded and emptied himself into her, making love for the first time.

CHAPTER FOURTEEN

"Am I crushing you?" Bren asked. He was collapsed on top of her, his breaths coming out in jagged spurts, his heartbeat sprinting neck and neck with hers.

"Oh, no. I love feeling your weight on me."

He lifted his head and met her gaze. "You sure?"

She stroked the side of his face. "Yeah. I'm just a little…." She searched the room for the word.

"Sad?"

"No. I'm definitely not sad. Not after that."

"Good to know." He rolled off of her and molded her body to his. "Melancholy?"

She looked over at him. She could see the concern in his eyes, the uneasiness. But they didn't come close to trumping the love. She couldn't remember ever seeing such unadulterated love in a man's eyes before. Not even Matt's. And Kenzie knew he'd loved her. It tore her up inside because she knew Bren didn't see the same in hers. She laid a gentle kiss on his lips. "Maybe a little. But that's nothing for you to worry about."

Bren made a buzzing sound with his mouth. "Try again."

With a sigh she shifted onto her back and stared at the ceiling. "I was married for fifteen years and with Matt for two years before that. That's almost half my life. And I just had some of the best sex of my life with a man I've known for less than a month."

"And this is a problem because?"

"Because I didn't think of Matt once."

"Really? Because I can take it if you did."

"Not even for a second."

"Actually, I was kind of hoping you had."

She turned back to him in disbelief. "You were?"

He gave her a resigned smile. "It's bound to happen eventually. I was hoping to get it out of the way. I'm just glad it was my name that came out of your mouth in the heat of the moment. Especially if it was some of the best sex of your life." He flashed his eyebrows impishly.

"And that wouldn't have bothered you? If it had happened?" Kenzie amazed.

"Of course it would have bothered me. That's why I want to get it over with. But it's only natural. I have a couple of divorced buddies who've called their second wife by their first wife's name at parties. Parents call their kids by their siblings names all the time. It's not intentional, malicious or even a Freudian slip. It's habit, wiring, second nature. I mean, I hope that's all it would be. You loved Matt, had a life with him. I can't expect you to negate that to spare my feelings."

Kenzie was blown away. "Bren, I don't know what to say."

"Don't say anything. Just know it's okay if it happens."

She put her arms around his neck, brought him to her. "I'm really glad it didn't. And I'm really glad it was you."

"I'm really glad it was me, too. I want it to keep being me."

"I want that too." She felt her eyes begin to fill. "But it doesn't seem fair."

"That's for me to decide, right?"

Kenzie wondered what she'd done to deserve him. This kind, patient man who seemed to take everything in stride so readily, so imperturbably. She fell a little deeper in love with him. And suddenly wanted him all over again. "Maybe we should try it again. Just to be sure it wasn't a fluke." She sent him a naughty look as her hand found him. He immediately began to swell.

On a cutting breath, Bren closed his eyes. "I could get behind that."

"There's an idea," she said and began to fondle him.

His eyes flew open and narrowed, became tiger-like. "Your wish is my command. But if you keep that up it's going to be a fleeting wish."

"We've already had slow and sweet. I'm good with hard and fast."

"Kenzie…" he moaned. "You can't say things like that while you've got me in your hand, doing what you're doing. I won't be able to control myself."

"I don't want you to control yourself."

She felt his body stiffen and his breath catch. Then in one fell swoop he rolled on top of her and pinned her hands above her head. "You sure about that?"

"Oh, yeah," she answered, feeling his erection nudge her.

He was leaning down to kiss her when his face fell in realization. He lifted the hand that held both of hers, then moved in for a closer look. His thumb rubbed the third finger on her left hand between her knuckles. "You took off your rings."

She nodded against the pillow.

"You had them on at dinner."

"I slipped them in my pocket when you laid me down on the bed."

"Kenzie…" he awed, caressing her cheek.

"I didn't do it for you. I did it for me. I couldn't be with you and feel married. Not in any way."

Bren started to say something, but swallowed it. He laid a long, tender kiss on her lips as his hands snaked up and down her body, igniting tiny flames of want in their wake. His kisses grew more intense, urgent, complete. He was claiming all of her with all of him—body, heart and soul. Kenzie wanted to respond in kind, give back all that she was taking, but she could already feel the pressure building inside her. The ache of anticipation was sweeping through her again, carrying her away. Her breast was in his mouth and his hand was between her legs but it wasn't enough. She wanted him inside her again, filling her, leaving her breathless and spent. She reached for him. Finding him ramrod straight and oozing only added to the sweet torture.

"Bren. Now."

Flipping her over, he positioned her on her knees in front of him and entered her from behind. He slid one arm up her chest to lay crosswise between her breasts.

One hand gripped her shoulder while the other rested on her stomach, pressing him deeper into her. Kenzie's head snapped back as the full length of him tunneled into her.

"Oh, God. You're even harder than before."

"See what you do to me? I'm afraid I'm going to hurt you."

"You won't."

The pleasure mounted inside her as Bren began thrusting in and out at breakneck speed. She bent back to take him deeper still, eliciting a gravelly moan from both of them. Kenzie loved knowing she could do this to him, wield this power over him, render him as helpless as he did her. He pumped madly, growing more and more engorged as the orgasm amassed in the very essence of her, consumed her, then set her free. She peaked audibly, wondering how she'd gone so long without this, without him.

"God, that was so hot. Again. Come for me again."

"I can't. It's too much...Oh, Bren!... Oh, God, I am!"

"I'm about to burst. Come with me."

And just as Bren shattered inside her, Kenzie obliged him.

*****

Kenzie woke like she did most mornings—alone. And at first she thought it had all been a dream. A wonderful, satisfying, oversexed dream. But since she was lying naked in Bren's bed, it must have been real. She stretched her arms above her head with a contented sigh, feeling more rested than she had in years.

She propped herself up on her elbows and took in the room, something she hadn't had the time or inclination to do last night. The morning sun was streaking through the slats of thick Venetian blinds covering expansive windows. Dark, chunky furniture stood in sharp contrast to bare, camel-colored walls. There were very few decorative touches; just a trinket or two here and there and some vintage-looking bookends holding a collection of hardcover books. This was definitely a single man's bedroom. A man with whom she'd had sex three times.

After their second interlude, Bren had taken Boot out for the night while she checked in with her mom. Then she'd fallen asleep in his arms, the sound of his breathing in her ear soothing her like a lullaby. She'd woken in the night and turned into him, finding him awake and erect. She took him in and they made love again as Boot slept on the floor next to the bed. They hardly made a sound, letting their bodies guide them, their desires lead them, until they came together as one. It was one of the most uninhibited, intimate experiences of Kenzie's life. And she was determined not to feel bad about it. Or the fact that she already wanted to do it again.

Boot was nowhere to be found and since the air carried the scent of coffee and the upstairs of the house apparently consisted of only a bedroom with an en suite bathroom, Kenzie assumed he was downstairs with Bren. Reaching for her phone on the nightstand, she found a note. *I wanted to wake up with you, but couldn't sleep. I'll be on the deck working. I laid a robe out for you. I apologize that it's ten sizes too big. Take your time. I'll get Boot started on the day.*

God, he was just so cute.

Kenzie slipped into the robe, which was indeed quite roomy, slid her phone into one of the pockets, made the bed and headed downstairs. The deck doors were open to the morning and Bren was sitting at the table with his back to her. Boot was sprawled out in the sun near the railing. First things first, she decided and detoured to the kitchen for coffee. There was a mug and cream and sugar sitting on the counter next to the coffee maker. She poured herself a cup and went outside.

"Now I understand why they call it the lake of the sky," Kenzie said, coming up behind Bren.

"Hey." Shutting the lid of his laptop, he stood and turned to face her. He was wearing the same UCLA shorts and sweatshirt he'd had on the first time she'd stopped by, the day of Mattie's first lesson with Greg. How things had changed in a few short weeks, Kenzie thought. He greeted her with a kiss. A lingering, prolonged kiss that suggested it had been days, not hours, since he'd seen her.

"Good morning."

She swallowed hard. "Good morning."

"Sleep okay?"

"Oh, yeah. Your bed is very comfortable."

"Good to hear. Robe looks good on you."

"Thanks. It was very thoughtful of you to leave it and the note for me."

"I figured you'd go for your phone first, since the kids are with your parents."

"You certainly know your audience." She sent him a look rich in innuendo. "In more ways than one."

Taking the cup from her hand and setting it on the table, Bren hooked her waist and drew her to him. "I could say the same. I loved making love with you. I want to do it again. And again after that."

She found herself wanting to say me too. Kenzie tried to remember she and Matt being this way in the beginning, this amorous, this spontaneous, this open, before life got in the way of living. It seemed like a lifetime ago and she almost felt like a different person now, as if she'd been a bystander in someone else's life then. And of course Matt had been gone for such long periods of time that when he was home it became about family and work. Pushing away the introspection, she wreathed his neck. "For a guy with a deadline, you seem pretty easily distracted."

Bren started nibbling on her throat. "Yeah, it's quite a departure for me. I have an impeccable reputation. I never miss a deadline."

"I don't doubt it," she said, angling her head to the side. "A Renaissance man like yourself. You seem to have a wide range of talents. I'm pleasantly surprised you don't have a matching robe in a smaller size."

He stopped kissing her neck and righted his head. He met her lighthearted gaze with a serious one. "Kenzie, I don't do that, pick up women and bring them home. I don't stock spare toothbrushes or robes. I'm not like that."

Kenzie nodded ruefully, feeling like a complete ass. "I'm sorry. I didn't mean it that way. This is all so new to me. I don't know the protocol," she finished with a contrite smile.

He pecked her lips. "I could say the same. On that note, I know it's a little late, but are we good? I got a little ahead of myself last night and protection was the last thing on my mind."

To Kenzie's horror, it hadn't even crossed hers. She let her arms fall to her sides. "We're okay on my end. I never went off the Pill. The last thing I needed after Matt died was to mess with my hormones. But I'm not used to thinking about...other things."

"No worries there. I've always used a condom. And I haven't been with a woman in almost two years. But I should have offered. I'm sorry. I haven't been that hot and bothered in a long time. Maybe ever."

"Well, I've never slept with a man on a first date, so let's call it a draw."

Bren frowned. "It didn't feel like a first date. And it certainly wasn't a romantic one. We'll have to fix that."

"That's not what I meant. It's just that we've usually been with the kids. I know you're not used to that."

"I want to get used to it."

Kenzie knew he was speaking from his heart, but through no fault of his own he had no idea how divergent their lifestyles were. If he was serious about having a relationship with her, she had to be sure he knew what he was getting into. "I believe you mean that. But Bren, they won't be going to their dad's on Wednesdays and every other weekend."

"Good. How else will I get to know them?"

"Bren," Kenzie tried again. "They're my whole life. And I have many more years of raising them ahead."

"Of course they are. You're their mother. And you have a lifetime ahead with them. I'm just asking if you'll share part of that life with me."

He was too good to be true, Kenzie was sure of it now. But how long was she willing to wait for the other shoe to drop? Until it was too late and he had no choice but to move on? She might not be able to deny her heart any longer, but she wouldn't risk the hearts of her children. There could be no shadow of a doubt in her mind that Bren was clear on the trappings of family life. She reached up and touched his cheek. "That life is in Reno. And it's…" her gaze swept the vast mountain vista in all its splendor, "not this. It's not romantic or colorful or storied and sometimes it's altogether…"

"Ordinary?" he finished for her.

Lowering her hand, she met his eyes again. "Yes. Ordinary. It's early mornings and late nights and strep throat and science projects and bake sales and practice in the rain. It's bad dreams and skinned knees and forgotten lunches. And pizza when you're craving a steak and Coke instead of wine because it's your turn to drive. It's doing the same math problem over and over and watching the same TV show a hundred times. It's constantly being reminded that you didn't know what you didn't know. It's falling into bed at night completely exhausted knowing you're going to get up in six hours and do it all over again. And yet somehow it's still unbelievably wonderful."

"Of course it is." Bren shrugged. "It's love."

"Yes," Kenzie agreed, taken by his effortless, uncomplicated response. "Love. A love like no other. And nothing will ever come before it, nothing will ever change it, nothing will ever compare to it."

"Nothing should. I am who I am because of that love. Look, I know I'll never be first, but eventually I'd like to be in the running for third."

She marveled at him. "Bren…"

"I know I love you. I'm starting to believe you might let yourself love me. The particulars don't change that."

"They don't?"

"Not for me. I hope not for you either. I'm all-in, Kenzie. Or as far in as you'll let me be. But I'll warn you, I don't do things halfway. Not for long anyway."

"Neither do I," she said as the weight she'd been carrying on her heart suddenly lifted. She fell back into his arms. "I can't believe this is happening to me." She hadn't said again, she realized. But she didn't have time to dwell on it because her pocket started buzzing.

"It's probably Katie," she announced, as Bren released her. She reached inside and retrieved her phone. "Hi, honey."

"Hi, Mom."

"What are you guys up to?"

"Grandma's making chocolate chip pancakes."

"Yum. Your favorite."

"And last night she and I went shopping and out to dinner. I got three new shirts! And a pair of earrings!"

"Wow! Grandma spoils you. What are Grandpa and Mattie up to?"

"After breakfast they're going to the batting cages. Grandma said we could go to the pool. But I can't find my book. Is it in the room?"

"Um, I'm not at the house right now." Chewing her lip, Kenzie met Bren's gaze.

"Where are you?"

"I took Boot for an extra-long walk this morning. But I can look when I get back."

With a grimace and a conspiratorial thumbs-up, Bren sauntered inside.

"Okay. Grandpa went to look in the car to see if it's there."

"If not, I'll ask Grandma to stop by the bookstore and get you another copy. That way you'll have it for the pool today."

"Okay. She wants to talk to you anyway. Plus the pancakes are almost done."

"Enjoy. Love you."

"Love you, Mom."

"Good morning," Sheryl greeted.

"Hi, Mom. Thanks so much for having them. And for taking Katie shopping."

"It's my pleasure. Reminds me of when you were her age. Is it all right if they stay for the afternoon?"

"Yes, of course. If Dad doesn't find the book, can you grab Katie another copy on your way to the pool? I'll reimburse you."

"Sure. And don't be silly. No book on your end, huh?"

"I ran out. But she wants to read it at the pool either way. What time do you want to meet up? Or do you want me to come to the house and get them?"

"Whenever. Are you okay?"

"Yes, I'm fine."

"You sure? You sound a little raddled."

"I'm just not used to being alone here. I don't know what to do with myself."

"Relax. Enjoy the downtime. Did you give Bren the book?"

"Ah, yeah. He said thanks and he looks forward to reading it."

"Great! How did you spend your free night?"

Kenzie had never been able to lie to her mother and that had never been more annoying than right now. "Actually, Bren and I went out to dinner."

Sheryl made no attempt to hide her delight. "Wonderful! How was it?"

"It was lovely." Kenzie looked into the house and watched as Bren moved around in the kitchen. "Really lovely."

"I want to hear all about it! Did you wear the dress?"

Kenzie closed her eyes, took a couple of calming breaths. "No, Mother, I did not wear the dress. It was a spur-of-the-moment decision and a casual restaurant."

"But you had fun?"

"Yeah," she replied as Bren returned with the coffee pot. "I had a lot of fun," she went on as Bren topped off her mug and his tumbler, then handed her the mug. "It was a great night," she said to Bren as much as her mother.

"Kenzie, I'm so proud of you! That's such a big step."

"Thanks, Mom. I'll let you go. I'll touch base this afternoon."

"Everything copasetic?" Bren asked as Kenzie disconnected and slipped the phone back in her pocket.

"Oh, yeah. Everybody got what they wanted, especially my mother."

Sitting down, Bren gave her a confused look. "How so?"

"The book wasn't the only thing she dropped off yesterday," Kenzie replied, taking a seat next to him. "She bought me a pair of shoes."

"Okay."

"A very sexy pair of high heels. That just happen to pair nicely with a black dress that has been gathering dust in the back of my closet for years that she also brought up."

Tumbler in hand, Bren raised his eyebrows. "Is the dress sexy too?"

"Very."

"Nice."

"It is not nice! My mother is all but pimping me out! To you!"

He grinned smugly. "So, I made a good impression, huh?"

"To put it mildly." Kenzie took a sip of coffee.

"I bet you look incredible in the dress."

"It's been so long since I've worn it I hardly remember. I don't even know if it still fits."

"Well, we're going to have to find out."

"Are we?" she asked in good humor.

"Absolutely. We need to have a proper first date anyway."

"I can't let my daughter see me in that dress! Especially with those heels!"

"Then you can put on a little fashion show just for me. But no matter how good you look in it, I'm going to like it better on the floor."

"You're incorrigible."

Bren, clearly enjoying himself, barreled on. "Sounds like I owe Sheryl one. What's her favorite flower?"

Kenzie glared at him through slitted eyes but on the inside she was just as amused as he was. If she didn't know better she'd have thought Bren and her mother had planned this whole thing. It couldn't have worked out better for either one of them. And, Kenzie had to admit, for her. At least she knew she still had it in her. Now she just had to get used to it.

"Kenzie?" Bren was saying.

"Oh, sorry." She returned to the conversation. "What?"

"Do you want something to eat?"

"Oh, no. Thanks. I'll get going. I should probably take my mother's advice and do something self-indulgent with my alone time."

He gave her a wicked grin. "I can help with that."

She laughed. "You have to work. And I don't expect you to entertain me just because I spent the night."

Bren's expression immediately sobered. He relieved both of them of their coffee and took her hands in his. "Leaving you in bed this morning was one of the hardest things I've ever done. No deadline is worth you thinking otherwise."

"I don't," Kenzie said. "I didn't mean it that way. Honestly."

Before he could say anything, her phone pinged. Bren released her and sat back in his chair as she retrieved it. "My dad found the book in the car. Crisis averted," she read out loud.

"Book?"

Kenzie set the phone on the table. "Katie couldn't find her book and wanted me to look for it. Since I obviously couldn't do that, I asked my mom to buy her another copy so she has it for the pool this afternoon. She's almost done with it."

"If it's the one she got the other day, she's a speed reader."

"Good memory," Kenzie replied, touched that he would remember something so trivial about her daughter. "But this is a different one. Part of a series she's been reading all summer. She hasn't started the new one yet."

"She was telling me about that series. She had some ideas as to where the storyline was heading."

"She's been on point so far. The main character is falling for her brother's friend for real."

"Is that so?" He leaned over and planted a kiss on her lips. "As opposed to pretending?"

"It's a long story," she explained as he began going after her neck again. "It started out as a bet."

"Interesting. So, does Katie think it's going to work out?"

"Yeah," Kenzie managed breathily. "She's pretty sure it is."

Bren slipped his hand inside the robe, finding her. "And what do you think?"

"I'm feeling pretty good about it myself," she murmured.

He untied the robe, letting it fall open, before taking her hands and bringing them both to their feet. He slid the robe off her shoulders, walked her over to the lounge chair in the corner and laid her down. Then he stripped, laid on top of her and proved her right.

CHAPTER FIFTEEN

When Kenzie walked into Gov's house later that morning she and Boot were met with deafening silence. She'd been told you get used to it, to the kids being more independent, but she still found it unsettling. One day you're walking them into kindergarten and the next you're dropping them off at college, as her mother often reminded her.

A shower was the first order of business, so Kenzie threw her hair up and jumped in, realizing too late that she didn't have to rush. But what she did realize was that she could go to the beach and read without having to entertain or corral anyone. And she could fall asleep under the canopy of pines or walk over to the hotel pier and have a drink to no one's determent. So, with her mother's voice in her ear, Kenzie decided to do just that. And when she got there she was going to call Emma. If ever they needed a debrief, it was today.

Thirty minutes later Kenzie was at the beach spreading out a blanket and situating her chair on top. She wondered if Bren was a beach person. Matt had hated the beach. Like Mattie, he was always too antsy to relax for very long. There she went again, reflexively comparing them. There was still so much she didn't know about Bren, yet she felt like she knew him so well. But one thing she'd learned last night was that he was an extraordinary lover. Strong without being overpowering and generous without sacrificing his own pleasure. She'd wallowed in his climax as much as her own.

She took in the view with an appreciative sign. The crowds had thinned as July turned toward August, but there were still clots of people smattered around the beach and plenty of boats coming and going at the dock. The lake mirrored the vibrant blue dome of sky above, its pearl-tipped waves breaking against the fawn-colored shore. Lake Tahoe was, Kenzie decided, one of the few places on earth humans hadn't screwed up. Yet, at least.

If Kenzie remembered correctly, Emma's boys were at soccer camp this week. But Kenzie texted her to make sure. This was not a conversation for little ears. Not thirty-seconds later, Kenzie's phone rang.

"I bought the shoes," Kenzie said by way of greeting.

"The Jimmy Choo drop heels? Why? You know you can borrow mine anytime you want."

"Not the Jimmy Choo's! The *shoes*," Kenzie drawled.

"Oh, *those* shoes!" Emma exclaimed after a moment. "That's so much better. At least I hope it was."

"Oh, it was."

"No wonder you wanted to make sure the kids were gone. I'm going to put you on speaker while I get a cigarette."

"Damn it, Emma, you promised."

"You know this calls for it."

Kenzie heard the sound of Emma unzipping her purse and walking outside to the patio, followed by the whoosh of her sinking into a chair and the flick of a lighter. She started on a drag, "Go."

"Can you take me off speaker?"

"That good, huh?"

Emma obliged, leaving Kenzie unsure where to start. She hadn't recounted a sexual experience since she'd lost her virginity twenty-plus years ago. That hadn't been anything to write home about and this had not been that. "Should I feel bad talking about this? I mean we're not sixteen at a slumber party."

"Maybe, but you should have thought about that before you called me. Start at the beginning."

Kenzie began by telling Emma about Sheryl being the impetus for the whole thing. "I mean she obviously wanted to give me an excuse to see him, but I can't imagine she actually expected me to wear the dress, let alone spent the night."

"She might have. Sheryl's a pretty cool cat. I bet she and Jay still get down pretty good."

"Gross. Stop."

"Will you share her with me? My mother can be such an insufferable bore."

"Not if you keep making comments about my parents' sex life."

"Fine. I'll be good. Proceed. You went back to his place after dinner. Then what happened?"

"We were standing in the kitchen and I don't know, Em. I just…Maybe it was the wine or the sunset, but it just felt right and I let myself go."

"Right there on the kitchen floor?"

"No. But I wouldn't have been above it, that's how wound up I was. He picked me up and carried me upstairs and—" Kenzie stopped short as the memory came flooding back. "My rings! I took off my rings!"

"Jesus, Kenz! Why didn't you lead with that?"

"I just remembered! I can't believe I just remembered!"

"You took them off before you guys…."

"Yeah. I tucked them in my shorts pocket when we got to the bedroom. They're still in there."

"That's huge."

"I know it sounds stupid, but it just seemed wrong to be with him with my wedding ring on my finger."

"You went with your gut, followed your heart. And that's never wrong."

"Still, I can't believe I didn't miss them this morning."

"That's a good sign. You were ready."

"I guess. And you know what the worst part is? My mother knew before I did."

"Of course she did. She's Sheryl."

"It's annoying."

"No, it's maternal instinct, a mother-daughter thing. So you have that to look forward to with Katie."

But what Kenzie was really looking forward to was seeing Bren again. She'd loved having his hands on her, exploring her as if she were one of the Seven Wonders of the World. She'd never felt so cherished, so wanted. And the way he'd muttered her name and held her eyes so profoundly in his when he climaxed, Kenzie felt bonded to him in a way she'd never known. Not even with Matt. The guilt was starting to creep in again when she realized Emma was still talking.

"So when will you see him again?"

"I'm not sure. He's got a deadline from hell and I've got to start thinking about school starting, getting back in the swing of things at home and finding a job. And he'll have his mother visiting."

"So was it awkward this morning?"

"Awkward is not the word I would use," Kenzie replied, glad Emma couldn't see the sly smile spreading across her face.

It took a few seconds for Emma to read between the lines. "Whoa, whoa, whoa. You're holding out on me. Was there a round two this morning?"

"Close, but no cigar."

"Wait—how many times did you guys do it?"

"Four."

"*Four*? Kenz, that's gratuitous."

"Oh, please. You're one to talk."

"But we're not talking about me, are we? So were all four mutually successful?"

"Oh, yeah. Two with a multiplier."

"What a stud! I want to hate you but I love you too much to allow it."

"Em, it was incredible. Sensual, passionate, urgent, but not rushed. But how can I have had what might be the best sex of my life with a man I've known for a few weeks and not my husband of fifteen years, the love of my life?"

"Maybe you get two."

"Two what?"

"Loves of your life." Emma took another drag, then went on, "Look, you could write it off to not having had sex for a while, the first time at least. Or to the fact that you two just happen to be compatible in bed. But maybe there's more to it. Who's to say you can't have more than one love in a lifetime? And yes, I hear the irony of my words based on some of my recent personal revelations. But maybe Matt was the love of your life for part of your life, like I suspect John might be for mine. You had some good years together and got two beautiful children out of it. And maybe the love of your life for the next part of your life is Bren."

"You can't possibly think Matt had to die so Bren and I could be together?" Kenzie hadn't dared verbalize the thought before and hearing it out loud took her breath away.

"No... I don't know... Maybe? A lifetime is a long time. Marrying for love, especially lifelong love, is a relatively novel concept in the course of human history. One that originated in times of shorter life spans. Marriage was often little more than a mutually beneficial transaction. People married for land, money, procreation, power, to unite families for a greater good.

Just because we aren't supposed to be alone doesn't mean we only get one partner, one love, for all the stages of life."

"Listen to you, getting all philosophical."

"Well, I've had a lot of time to think with both you and John gone. And I think you're in a place where you've never been, a place you never expected to be. There has to be reason, a greater purpose, for that. You aren't the person you were fifteen years ago any more than I am. If you met Matt today, would you still fall in love with him? Would I still fall for John? Bren isn't who he was fifteen years ago either. Timing really is everything. Maybe this is your time, yours and Bren's."

"Bren did say he feels like he's been waiting for me without knowing it," Kenzie remembered out loud.

"There you go. Maybe part of you was waiting for him too. And maybe this next stage of your life is for you to share with Bren. That doesn't detract from the part you shared with Matt."

"That all sounds well and good in theory, but it's not that easy. It's not just me we're talking about. I'm a party of three. I have to be intentional."

"It sounds like Bren understands that, would be willing to make that a party of four eventually. You owe it to yourself to find out."

If Kenzie was being honest with herself, part of her already knew. She'd known that first night. But she only said, "You're right, I do. I owe it to all of us."

*****

260

When Bren opened the door on Wednesday morning he found two smiling, eager faces standing on the other side. The familiar one belonged to his mother. He hadn't seen her in a few months and whatever reservations he might have had about her visit instantly vanished. Her chestnut-brown eyes began to shine when they met his. She folded him into her arms and hugged him tight. Bren felt a rush of sentiment flow through him.

"Hi, Mom."

With a kiss on the cheek, Claire stepped back. She blinked away the tears that had dampened her eyes. "Hi, honey. It's so good to see you."

"You too." Bren extended his hand to the man standing next to his mother. He looked to be a few years her senior, with a full head of wavy gray hair and hazel eyes that leaned toward green. He had a tanned, fit look about him, as if he played tennis as opposed to golf, and his deep smile lines and wise eyes reminded Bren of Mac.

"Bren Banks."

"Bob Carlson. Nice to meet you. Thank you for your hospitality."

"My pleasure. Please come in. Can I help with your bags?"

"In a minute," Claire answered. "Let's get aquatinted first."

Claire, as comfortable in her son's home as her own, led Bob inside, leaving Bren to close the door behind them. When they got to the living room, Bob let out an appreciative whistle. "You weren't kidding about the view, were you?"

"Isn't it spectacular?" Claire seconded. "Pictures don't do it justice."

"Bob, Mom tells me this is your first trip to Tahoe," Bren said, joining them at the deck doors.

"It is," Bob affirmed, turning to Bren. "And I already regret it. I didn't know what I was missing."

"Isn't that always the way?" Bren commented. "Can I get you guys something to drink? I picked up a sandwich ring and some sides for lunch."

"How thoughtful. I'll take an iced tea, but I can get it."

"Don't be silly, Mom. You've already had a long day and it's not even noon." Then he turned to Bob, "How about you, Bob? Iced tea, beer, water?"

"I'll take an iced tea, thanks."

"Coming right up. You guys make yourselves comfortable."

When Bren returned with the drinks Claire and Bob were standing at the deck railing admiring what Bren thought of as Tahoe in a nutshell. The forest giving way to the lake, the lake becoming one with the shore and the mountains holding it all in the palms of its hands. He handed them each a glass of iced tea. "Nice change of pace from the desert, huh?"

"I'll say," Bob echoed. "I thought I'd died and gone to heaven when I moved to Scottsdale, but I might have spoken too soon."

"Scottsdale's nothing to sneeze at, especially in the winter. But Tahoe has a way of getting into your blood."

"Your mother tells me it got into yours at a young age."

"It did indeed. And I wouldn't have it any other way." Bren gestured toward the table. "Take a load off. I know you guys were up early."

Once everyone was seated, Bren got the ball rolling. "So Bob, tell me a little bit about yourself. You're originally from Ohio?"

Bob affirmed with a nod. "Born and raised a Buckeye. Lived there for sixty years, save my medical school years at Northwestern."

"Bob was a pediatrician, practiced for forty years," Claire added.

That explains the wise eyes and look of distinction, Bren supposed. He couldn't help but be impressed.

"My wife and I retired to Scottsdale five years ago. Unfortunately shortly thereafter she was diagnosed with cancer. She'll be gone three years in October."

"I'm sorry," Bren said sincerely.

"Thank you. We had a wonderful life together. Married for forty-two years, three daughters, seven grandchildren."

Bren sent Bob a smile. He already liked him more than he'd wanted to. "Are your daughters still in Ohio?"

"Two are, but my youngest married a Marine," Bob said around a sip of iced tea. "They're in San Diego now, probably for another year. Then likely on to

Virginia. They'd like to get the big moves out of the way before the kids get into high school."

"I'm sure." Until Bren met Kenzie, he'd know very little about military life. Now it seemed to be around every corner. "I have a widowed friend whose husband was a Marine. Until recently I had no idea the sacrifices military families make for the greater good."

"Oh?" Claire's ears perked up. "Who's that?"

"You don't know her, Mom."

"Well, we just might have to change that. She lost her husband in the line of duty?"

"It was training accident, stateside."

"It's always a worry," Bob remarked gravely. "Where was he stationed? My son-in-law might have known him."

"Twentynine Palms, but the incident happened in New Mexico. His name was Matthew Bishop. He was a Lieutenant Colonel."

"He would have outranked my son-in-law, but I'll make note of the name. Did they have children?"

"Yes, two."

Bob gave Bren a sad shake of the head. "My daughter has known several women whose husbands have been killed or injured in active duty. But I suppose there's no guarantee for any of us, no matter our profession."

But Claire wasn't about to let this go. "What kind of a friend is she, Brennen?"

"She's a new friend, Mom. You remember Gov. She's his sister, in town to take care of his dog while he's on his honeymoon."

"Well, this is the first I've heard of new female friend."

"There really isn't much to say," Bren told her, but the irony of his words were not lost on him. And knowing his mother, he wasn't the only one.

"I'll be the judge of that. How old are the kids?"

"Katie is eleven and Matt is nine."

"Such a shame. And you've gotten to know her?"

"I met her one night at the park and we made the Gov connection. Her son is taking lessons from Greg Gentry. I've thrown a little with Matt myself. The kid's going to be a star."

"Your mom tells me you were quite the baseball star yourself," Bob put in.

"Not compared to this kid. But yeah, I was all right."

"Both of my grandsons are playing summer ball. I was hoping to get back to Ohio to catch a game or two, but it doesn't look like that's in the cards this year. The kids will be back in school before we know it."

Bren gave a nod. "That's what Kenzie said. The summer flies by."

Claire leaned forward a little in her chair. "So, tell me more about this Kenzie."

Bren should have known he wasn't going to get out of this so easily. "She moved to Reno last year after she lost her husband. Her parents have been helping her get back on her feet."

"And you've been spending time together?"

"I usually see her when her son has a lesson. And we've had dinner together a couple of times."

"It sounds like you've gotten to know her quite well in a short amount of time."

Quite intimately would be more accurate, Bren smiled to himself. He had to stop himself from closing his eyes and reveling in the memory. Making love with Kenzie had been the best sexual experience of his life.

"Brennen?"

"Sorry," he said, returning to the conversation. "What?"

"How is she doing?"

"She's unbelievably strong, says she has to be for the kids, but I think she sells herself short. She has so much grit, so much courage and perseverance. She handles everything life throws at her with perfect aplomb and somehow manages to make it look easy. She amazes me."

"Well, she sounds wonderful. And just when I'd given up on you."

"Mom, we're just friends," Bren lied.

"Oh, Brennen, honestly. You've always been a terrible liar, which is probably why you're such a good writer. You should see the way your eyes light up when you talk about her. When can I meet her? All three of them?"

"Claire, at the risk of overstepping, you might be a little out of bounds here. I'm sure they'll be a time and a place for that."

Claire gave Bob a sidelong glance. "There absolutely is a time and place for that. Now is the time and this is the place."

"Thank you, Bob," Bren said, liking him even more. The he addressed his mother, "And you just might get your wish. She'll probably stop by tomorrow. Matt has a lesson."

"Terrific! With both children?"

"Likely. Unless Katie is with a friend or her grandparents."

"Even better. It's a good thing we had this little talk. Shame on you, Brennen. You usually keep me more in the know."

"Mom, you're always the first to know when there's actually something to know. I would appreciate your patience until then."

Claire looked at him long and hard, then relented, "Fine. But I don't have to like it, do I?"

Bren laughed. "No. You don't have to like it."

Over turkey sandwiches and potato salad, Bren learned more about Bob. He and his wife had been college sweethearts and she'd followed him to Chicago for medical school. They married during his residency and returned to Ohio to start their family. Bob never dreamed he'd have another woman in his life after his wife passed away, but apparently meeting Claire changed all of that. He was looking forward to introducing her to his daughters, but they decided Bob meeting Bren was the first order of business.

"I adore my daughters and have a good relationship with all three of them. But as is often the case, they were closer to their mother. It's obvious that you and Claire share a similar bond."

"I won the mom jackpot. No doubt about it."

"Brennen was a joy to raise," Claire gushed. "I always figured I must have done something right to have been given such a wonderful boy."

"You did *everything* right," Bren told her, then said to Bob, "Mom always made it look easy, but it couldn't have been."

"In my experience not much that comes easy is worthwhile. It's the tough stuff that builds character. I'd say she did just fine."

After they finished eating, Claire stood and began to clear the table. "I've got it, Mom," Bren told her. "Why don't you guys get settled. You know where everything is. I grabbed your bags out of the car while you were showing Bob around. They're downstairs."

"All right. Then we'll get out of your hair. I know you're working on a tight schedule."

Within the hour, Claire and Bob had gone for a walk and Bren was knee-deep in research. He'd taken Miranda up on her offer of help with the editing, but not the research. Although time consuming, Bren found research to be an invaluable writing tool. He often learned things that sparked an idea, particularly when it came to exotic locales. The part of the story he was writing now was taking place in Morocco, somewhere Bren had never been and knew little about. His calendar didn't allow for a working vacation to soak up local culture, so he'd have to make do with the Internet.

Bren was reading about Morocco's diverse architecture and heterogeneous culture when he came across a section about gender roles in Moroccan society. He was developing a female antagonist and hadn't quite decided what kind of character she was going to be. Initially, he thought she might be a double-agent, spuriously using the male protagonist for information, but he'd been leaning toward softening her up a bit, making her more vulnerable. Maybe she starts out as an antagonist but develops some bona fide feelings for the hero along the way. Then as the story evolves, she flips and they become dual protagonists, working toward a common goal. Or so it would seem. Bren decided he'd figure it out as the story unfolded, let the character decide for herself.

Creating a female main character only brought Bren's mind back to Kenzie. And it was more than just the physical, although he longed to touch her, be touched by her, again. She had such strength, such resilience. Her optimism and positivity were contagious. Plus she had a way making you feel like you were the only person the room. He'd especially noticed that with the kids, the way she talked to them, managed them. And she was incredibly intelligent. Not just educated, but street smart too. She was confident and opinionated, yet modest and open-minded. Every time Bren peeled back another layer, he found something more to love about her. In a word, she was extraordinary.

Suddenly a shiver of relevance ran through him. She was his mother.

CHAPTER SIXTEEN

Kenzie was making coffee on Thursday morning when her phone started ringing. She quickly grabbed it off the counter so it wouldn't wake the kids. She was pleasantly surprised to see her brother-in-law's name pop up on the screen.

"Good morning."

"More like afternoon here."

Kenzie glanced at the time. She'd slept in today. It was almost nine. "How are you, Mick?"

"Can't complain. How's my favorite sister-in-law and niblings?"

"We're your only sister-in-law and niblings," she reminded him around a laugh.

"True. But no less my favorite."

"We're fine. We're up in Tahoe."

"Oh, Tahoe," Mick said, his voice full of longing. "One of the few places I've ever been able to truly relax, escape reality. It's a whole different world. What are you guys doing there?"

"Watching Gov's dog while he's on his honeymoon." Kenzie glanced out the window at Boot sniffing around in the backyard.

"Nice he finally got around to it. They've been married, what, two or three years now? I know it was before..." Mick's voice trailed off.

"Two years," Kenzie supplied around a gulp. "Not long before Matt died."

There was a long, heavy pause. Finally Mick said, "I'm sorry I've been so out of touch. I've been working like crazy and was deployed for a few months."

"Don't be silly." Kenzie had always gotten along with Matt's family, but she hadn't considered herself close to them. Mick was five years Matt's junior and they hadn't lived near each other in decades. They saw Mick once or twice a year at most. She wondered if Matt's birthday last week had prompted the phone call. They hadn't seen him since the funeral.

"I've been thinking about you guys. I have some leave coming up and wondered if I could come out for a visit."

"Of course. We'd love to see you," Kenzie replied, doctoring her coffee.

"Great. I'll check out flights and text you some dates. You can tell me what works best. And I'll get a room. I certainly don't expect your parents to accommodate me."

"Actually, I bought a house a few months ago. You're welcome to bunk with Mattie or sleep on the couch."

"Wow, we have more catching up to do than I realized. I'll think about it. Let me work on the logistics and we'll go from there."

Kenzie filled Mick in on the kids, particularly Mattie and baseball. Matt had been a bigger sports fan than his brother, but Mick couldn't help but be impressed that Greg was coaching Mattie. Then Kenzie asked Mick if he was seeing anyone.

"I'm in a bit of a dating rut," Mick told her. "I don't think I'm cut out for a serious, long-term relationship anyway."

"That remains to be seen, Mick. You probably just haven't met the right person yet."

"Doubt it. Plus, I think Matt got all the family luck in that department."

They were wrapping up the conversation with Mick's promise to be in touch about his plans when Mattie rambled into the kitchen.

"Mom, I'm hungry."

"Well, good morning to you too."

"Good morning," Mattie said around a yawn. "Oh, sorry. I didn't know you were on the phone."

"Is that my favorite nephew?"

"It's Uncle Mick," Kenzie told Mattie, putting the phone on speaker.

"Hi, Uncle Mick."

"Hey, buddy! How've you been?"

"Good."

"Your mom tells me you've been playing a lot of baseball."

"Yeah, I'm in Little League and taking lessons. From Greg Gentry!"

"I heard! That's super cool!"

"And I've been practicing with Bren."

"Is Bren a friend from your team?"

"Kind of. But not from my team. He's really my mom's friend. But he used to play when he was a kid."

Kenzie shut her eyes and exhaled slowly through her nose.

There was a lull in the conversation as Mick processed that. Then he cleared his throat and said, "Well, keep up the good work. Maybe we can catch an Aces game when I come visit."

"Okay. They're really fun. I just went to one with my grandpa. Bren might want to go too."

"Sure thing. Well, I'll let you guys go. Kenz, I'll be in touch."

"Sounds good. Thanks for calling."

After they disconnected, Kenzie asked Mattie what he wanted for breakfast. He voted for pancakes and by the time they were ready, Katie was up. Once they'd eaten, the kids scampered off and Kenzie started putting the kitchen to rights. But the busy work did little to ease her racing mind. She had no idea how she was going to explain her and Bren's relationship to them. How much or little should she tell them? Should she ease them in slowly, a little at a time, or come right out with it? In fact, she and Bren had yet to define their relationship, let alone discuss how things would work after she went home. But in concentrating on what she did know, Kenzie believed Bren was sincere in his feelings for her, felt confident they were exclusive, that he understood her priorities, his place in her life. And she trusted him. And she trusted herself and her gut.

But her mind kept going back to what Mick said about escaping reality in Tahoe. What if this whole thing with Bren turned out to be nothing more than a summer fling? A passing fancy, a frothy dalliance of salad days and starlit nights that wouldn't stand the test of time, the pressures of everyday life. That would be much more detrimental to the kids, especially Mattie, than any lack of candor on her part. But Mick had clearly picked up on Mattie's comment about Bren, so she needed to come up with a plan sooner rather than later. Better it come from her than anyone else.

She hadn't spoken to Bren since she left his place on Monday morning. They'd exchanged a few texts and planned to touch base today. She knew he was buried in work and had his mother visiting. But even after spending only one night with him, she found herself missing him when she went to bed. The sex aside, she longed to be in his presence, even to do something as simple as grab a burger or have coffee on the deck. Although that memory just brought her mind back to sex. Their lounge chair encounter had been next-level. She'd never had such an all-consuming, mind-blowing orgasm come on so fast, run so deep and last so long. She wondered with a twinge of guilt if that said more about her or Bren.

Kenzie was also grappling with some guilt for taking her wedding rings off. So much so, she'd fished them out of her shorts pocket before going to get the kids on Monday night. If Katie didn't notice she wasn't wearing them, her mother surely would have. Taking them off when she was with Bren was one thing, taking them off for good was another. She was nowhere near ready for that. And if she wasn't ready to reconcile that with herself, she certainly couldn't reconcile it to anyone else.

"Mom, what time is my lesson?" Mattie asked, retuning to the kitchen.

"Noon," Kenzie replied, flipping her mind back to the present.

"Can we take Boot for a hike afterward?"

"Um, maybe. If it's not too hot."

"Katie will probably want to go to the beach again anyway," Mattie whined with an eye roll.

"It'll be too cold for the beach before you know it, so we might as well take advantage of it while we can. And she's been a trooper about baseball."

"I know."

"Go hop in the shower. We'll figure it out later."

Kenzie finished up in the kitchen, then went to get dressed. She found Katie reading in the chair in the bedroom they were sharing.

"How's the new book?"

"It's okay." Katie looked up. "A little hard to get into."

Kenzie sat on the corner of the unmade bed. "Maybe you just have to give it some time. What chapter are you on?"

"Three."

"What don't you like about it?"

"There's a lot of repetition, especially from the last book."

"How did that one end? I never asked you."

"They like each other for real and Leo fessed up about the bet."

"So you were right."

"Yeah, but Callie's mad because he should've just asked her instead of making a bet with Caleb in the first place."

"Caleb is her brother?"

"Yeah. They're twins."

"Well, honesty is always the best policy. But Leo's heart was in the right place."

"But now she feels like she can't trust him."

"Hmm. Yeah, I guess I can see that. But sometimes you have to give people a second chance. Maybe once she gets to know him better she'll feel more comfortable."

"Maybe."

"Is she mad at her brother too? For being in on it?"

"No. He didn't know they secretly liked each other. He thought it was all a game."

"Got it." Tapping her daughter's knee, Kenzie stood and started making the bed.

"Did that ever happen to you?"

"No," Kenzie answered, tucking in the sheet. "I never made a bet like that."

"I mean did you ever secretly like someone?"

Kenzie drew the comforter up, then walked over to the other side of the bed to straighten it. "No." The word came out flat.

"Has anyone ever secretly liked you?"

277

Kenzie fluffed a pillow, set it against the headboard. "Not that I know of."

"I think Bren likes you."

Kenzie hugged the pillow in her arms. She willed her voice steady. "You do?"

"Yeah."

Kenzie placed the pillow next to its mate. Reminding herself that honesty was the best policy, she sat back down on the bed in front of Katie. "Why do you think that?"

"Because of the way he stares at you. And he smiles a lot when he looks at you, especially when you're talking. You don't seem to notice."

For the second time in less than a week, Kenzie couldn't ignore the perfect segue that had fallen into her lap. She looked her daughter square in the eye. "I do notice. How do you feel about that?"

"Fine." Katie scrunched up her face. "Why?"

"Because of Dad. Would it upset you? If Bren liked me?"

"No." Katie shrugged. "It'd be nice for you to have a new friend. I know you miss Emma. You wanted us to make friends here and you should too."

Keep it simple, Kenzie reminded herself. Only tell her what she can understand, relate to. "That's sweet of you to say. But what if I liked Bren too? What if he became more than a friend?"

Realization snuck into Katie's innocent eyes. But they stayed bright. "Like a boyfriend?"

"Yeah."

"Would you go on a date with him? Like to the movies or something?"

"Maybe. And sometimes we'd all four do something together."

Katie thought about that for a moment. "That'd be all right, I guess." She looked down at her lap. "Would it happen a lot?"

"Not too much." Kenzie used her finger to tip Katie's chin up. "Honey, nothing and no one will ever be as important to me as you and Mattie. That will never, ever, change. I promise."

"I know. It's just that Dad was gone a lot before he was gone for real, so I'm kind of used to it being just the three of us."

"It would still be the three of us. It's just that sometimes Bren might be around or he and I might do something by ourselves. Like go out to dinner or to a movie that's not appropriate for kids."

"And we would stay with Grandma and Grandpa?"

"Yeah. And before we know it you'll be babysitting. Remember, we signed you up for that class."

Katie nodded. "For after I turn twelve. Morgan's parents do that sometimes. But she doesn't need a babysitter because she has older brothers. Unless her parents are gone overnight. Then her grandma comes to stay with them."

"Right. I wouldn't be gone overnight, though. So what do you think? Would that be okay?"

"Yeah, I guess."

Kenzie let out a sigh of relief. "Great. Thank you for understanding." She knelt down and brought Katie into a hug. "We're in this together, just like we have been with everything else. And we'll take it one day at a time, just like we have everything else."

Katie laid her head on Kenzie's shoulder. "Okay."

Kenzie clasped her tight. "All right. Now, about Mattie's lesson this afternoon. Bren texted and asked if we would stop by. Would that be okay?"

"That's fine. I've never been to his house."

"Well, you're in for a treat. He has a beautiful deck, perfect for reading in the sun."

"Can we take Boot? I think he gets lonely without us."

"Sure."

"You sure Bren won't mind?"

Kenzie smiled more to herself than her daughter. "Positive."

Kenzie still had that smile on her face when she and Katie knocked on Bren's door two hours later. But it instantly fell away when the door was opened not by Bren, but by an older man.

"Oh, hello."

"Hello! You must be Kenzie."

"I am."

The man extended his hand in greeting. "Bob Carlson. I'm a friend of Claire's, Bren's mom."

Kenzie took it. His handshake was firm, yet gentle and his viridescent eyes looked kindly into hers. "Nice to meet you. This is my daughter, Katie."

Bob's gaze, and his hand, shifted down to Katie. "Well, hello there, Katie." His grin widened. "You look to be around the same age as my oldest granddaughter."

Shaking his hand, Katie announced, "I'm almost twelve."

"Well, how about that? Ashley tuned twelve in April. I bet you're going to be in the sixth grade."

Katie affirmed with a nod. "This is Boot." She gestured to the dog, sitting patiently by her side.

"Hey, Boot." Bob petted Boot's head. "Come on in." He stepped aside. "Bren said you might stop by. I'm on door duty."

"Thanks," Kenzie said, suddenly wondering if she'd read too much into Bren's text. Maybe it was more of a suggestion than an invitation.

As they walked inside, Kenzie saw Katie's eyes widen at the view out the deck doors. Bob, noticing too, put in, "You must be a first-time guest. I had that same reaction myself."

Just then a woman rounded out of the kitchen. She was wearing a white shift dress over sun-kissed skin and bright red lipstick against teeth just as white. Her chin-length, mahogany hair gleamed in the sunlight and her mouth carried a smile that seemed to radiate through her entire body. And right now it, and she, was aimed at Kenzie.

"You must be Kenzie! I'm Claire, Brennen's mom." Taking one of Kenzie's hands in both of hers, she looked at Kenzie with the same sublime brown eyes that graced her son's face. "It's so nice to meet you!"

"Likewise. This is my daughter, Katie."

Unlike Bob, Claire didn't have to lean down to shake Katie's hand. They were about the same height. "Hi, Katie. I'm Claire."

"Hi."

"I'm sure Brennen will be down shortly. He was up most of the night working, I suspect. I just made some lemonade. Let's sit on the deck."

"Oh, I don't want impose."

"You wouldn't be," Claire insisted, leading the way.

In contrast to Kenzie's previous visits, the deck table was beautifully set with colorful plates and napkins. A pitcher of lemonade and six glasses sat on a tray next to a plate of cookies. The umbrella had been strategically placed to block the sun and throw pillows Kenzie hadn't seen before adorned both lounge chairs. Boot immediately made himself comfortable in the same spot where she'd found him on Monday morning.

"Please, sit," Claire invited with a wave of the hand.

Kenzie and Katie each took a seat while Bob and Claire did the same on the opposite side of the table. "This is lovely. Thank you."

"Of course," Claire replied, pouring them each a glass of lemonade. "Brennen mentioned your son is taking lessons from Greg next door."

"Yes. He loves it."

"I'm sure. How about you, Katie? Are you a baseball fan too?"

"No, not really. Only when I have to go to Mattie's games. I like the pool and the beach."

"Katie is a big reader," Kenzie added, nodding to Katie's book on the table.

"A girl after my own heart," Claire replied, passing the plate of cookies around the table. "I spend a lot of time reading at the pool at home."

"Bren tells me you retired to Scottsdale," Kenzie commented around a sip of lemonade.

"Yes, thanks to him."

"Oh?"

"Brennen is not only a wonderful, loving son, he's a generous one. He set me up in a gorgeous condo there."

And a humble one, Kenzie thought. He clearly undersells himself. Before she could comment, she heard his voice behind her.

"Good morning."

Kenzie looked over her shoulder to find Bren, the robe she'd borrowed thrown over shorts and a T-shirt, standing in the doorway. His hair was mussed and matted, with unruly tufts flying this way and that, and his dark beard scruffy and stubbly. Kenzie let out a muffled snicker.

"Brennen, there you are. I was wondering when you'd surface."

Bren's puffy, slitted eyes scanned the table disconcertedly before resting on Kenzie and softening, brightening. His perplexed frown became a wide grin. "Hey."

She felt the smile deep in her soul and returned a wobbly version of it. "Hey."

Bren moved onto Katie. "What's going on, Katie?"

"Mattie has a lesson so we came over. Mom said it would be okay."

"Of course it's okay." Bren took a seat at the head of the table, between Kenzie and Bob. "I'm sorry I wasn't up to greet you. I spent most of the night working," he told Kenzie as much as Katie.

"That's okay," Katie replied. "We just got here. Your house is really pretty."

"Thanks." Then he looked at Claire. "You've had a busy morning, Mom."

"Well, you mentioned Kenzie might stop by and I wanted her to feel welcome. We were just chatting over some lemonade, getting acquainted."

"Yes, I can see that."

"Let me pour you a glass." Claire leaned forward in her chair.

Bren held up a hand, palm out. "Actually, I could use a hit of coffee first." He started to get up.

"You just sat down." Claire rose. "I'll get it."

"Thanks, Mom."

Bob chuckled to himself, then stood. "I'll give her a hand. I think Boot could use some water." Patting Bren's shoulder, he said under his breath, "And you might need a little Irish in that coffee."

Bren laughed without opening his mouth. Then he turned to Katie asking, "How's the new book, Katie?"

"It's okay. I'm having a hard time getting into it. Mom said I have to give it a chance."

"Good advice."

"Can I go read in the chair in the corner?" Katie asked Kenzie.

"Sure."

After Katie got up, Bren turned to Kenzie. "I'm sorry wasn't up when you got here. I rarely set an alarm anymore. I have no idea what time I drifted off."

"No problem, *Brennen.*"

"Very funny." He glanced over at Katie, who was already settled with the book, then laid his hand on Kenzie's. "I've been thinking a lot about you, about us."

"Me, too." She laced her fingers through his.

"Look, I know now isn't the time or the place, but I don't want to sneak around."

"Neither do I."

"It took everything in me not to take you in my arms when I saw you. And it's more than just the physical. I miss *you.*"

"Bren, I—"

"Let me get this out. Obviously I'm not going to French kiss you in front of the kids. But maybe we could start slow, get them used to the idea of us being together. I know my schedule is crazy right now and you'll be going back to Reno soon, but maybe the four of us could go to dinner this weekend? And there's that adventure park near Tahoe City the kids might like. We could do some things together, ease them in a little at a time."

Kenzie leaned in, closing the small space between them, and placed her other hand on top of their joined ones. She took her voice down a notch. "Bren, before we do that, we have to be sure, really sure, this can work in the long-term. And in real time, not Tahoe time."

"I'm sure. Aren't you?" His heart was in his eyes and Kenzie was trying to find the words to reply in kind, while still making her point, when his face fell.

"You put your rings back on."

She nodded. "Yeah."

All the color drained from his face. "Why?"

"I had to."

He pulled his hand away. "Why?"

Before Kenzie could answer, Claire returned with Bren's coffee. "This should get your motor revving," she said, setting his tumbler down in front of him. "I made it extra-strong with just a dash of cream."

Bren sat back in his chair. "Thanks, Mom."

"Bob missed a call from one of his daughters," Claire went on, sitting down. "He wanted to check in, make sure everything was okay." She nodded toward the far end of the deck. "I see Katie found a quiet reading spot."

"She wants to finish her new book before school starts," Kenzie said, wringing her hands in her lap.

"Do the kids still have summer reading lists?"

"Ah, yeah." Kenzie shifted her gaze to Claire and tried out a smile. "Katie blew through hers. She wanted to get the required reading out of the way so she could get to the fun stuff."

"That sounds familiar, doesn't it Brennen?"

"Sorry, Mom. What?" Bren said around a sip of coffee, his stare still fixed on Kenzie.

"Katie reading what she has to first so she could get to what she wants to read."

"Yeah. Turns out Katie and I have a lot in common," he replied as Kenzie's eyes reunited with his. The love in them had turned to hurt. It broke her heart in two.

Claire looked first at Kenzie, then at Bren, and sensing something had shifted between them announced, "I think I'll go check on Bob, make sure everything's okay in Ohio."

Kenzie watched Claire go into the house, then with an oblique glance at Katie, turned back to Bren. "I put my rings back on because there would have been too many questions otherwise."

Bren lifted a single eyebrow. "Questions you aren't ready to answer?"

"It's just all happening so fast."

"For who?"

"I can't spring this on them. They've been through so much already."

"I know. That's why I want to start slow, let them get comfortable with the idea."

"Bren, I have to be prudent."

His mouth became a tight, straight line. "Are you having second thoughts? About us?"

"No, of course not, but I can't mess this up."

"That's qualified."

Kenzie started on a harried breath. "Let me unqualify it for you. Katie is at an impressionable age.

And Mattie already idolizes you. He'd be devastated if…"

"If what?"

"If we can't make it work."

"We *can* make it work. I'll come to Reno, you guys can come here on the weekends."

"I might not always be able to come here. And you have deadlines, commitments. Not to mention the sleeping arrangements," she finished on a whisper.

Silence hung in the air between them for a long moment. Finally Bren said, "What are you so afraid of?"

"Nothing."

"Bullshit. You're talking yourself out of this."

"I am not," Kenzie replied as her stomach begin to churn.

"Then what changed?"

"Nothing."

"For one of us something has," Bren countered sharply, his eyes pinned to hers.

Kenzie couldn't lie to him anymore than she could her mother. She was fighting a losing battle and they both knew it. "Bren, it's not that. I—"

The chime of her phone cut her off. "I have to get Mattie." She started to rise.

He grabbed her arm. "Don't you have ten minutes?" Then closing his eyes, he huffed out a frustrated breath. "I'm sorry. Would you please sit for a minute more?"

When she did Bren began again, "I promised I wouldn't rush you. I'm trying to keep that promise.

But there's no way I feel this way about you, a way I never knew was possible for me to feel, and you don't feel enough of something for me to give this a fighting chance."

Kenzie opened her mouth to speak, but he halted her with his palm. "I fell in love with you the instant I saw you, before I talked to you, touched you, knew your name. I can't explain it, put it into words, which really says something, all things considered. All I can come up with is lightning in a bottle."

"Bren—" Kenzie's jaw dropped as her hand flew to her heart.

"I'm not done." His voice was firm, forthright. "What happened between us was not a fluke, a one-night stand or a series of fortunate events. I haven't even known you for a month and I already can't conceive of my life without you. I don't want to."

"I'm not asking you to. I'm just asking you to give me some space, some time, to deal with the more complicated parts of my life." She set her hand on the table, palm up.

He grasped it and the heartbreak in his eyes eased a little. "I can do that."

"Thank you." Resisting the urge to kiss him, she squeezed his hand, then called to Katie, "Time to get Mattie."

"Can I finish this page?"

"She can hang here for a few minutes if she wants," Bren offered.

Kenzie rose. "Do you and Boot just want to stay here?"

"Sure."

"Okay. I'll be right back."

"I'll walk out with you. "

In the house they found Claire cleaning an already spotless kitchen, obviously making herself scarce. "Thank you for the lemonade," Kenzie said. "I'm going to run next door to grab my son. I'll be right back for Katie and Boot. She wanted to read a little more."

"I don't blame her. It's such a beautiful day," Claire remarked, hanging the dishtowel on the bar of the oven door. "Bob and I are about to head over to Tahoe City, so we may not be here when you get back. We're going to shop a bit and grab a late lunch. Brennen's friend has a restaurant there."

"Yes, we went there for dinner on Sunday night. It was delicious."

"Oh, I didn't realize that. Yes, Tommy has done quite well for himself."

"I take it all is well in Ohio."

Claire nodded solemnly. "It sounds like Jen is missing her mother a bit today."

"I'm sure."

The women exchanged good-byes and Bren and Kenzie walked outside. Bren barely had the front door shut behind him when he pulled Kenzie into his arms. She collapsed into him, feeling the angst of earlier fall away as his mouth moved over hers. Then, breath hitching, he buried his head in her hair and clutched her against him as if afraid she would slip through his fingers at any second.

"I'm sorry I got sideways with you before. But if you feel even a fraction of what I do, it's worth fighting for. For both of us."

"I know," Kenzie told him, starting to believe it for the first time.

He held her close for a moment more. Then he mumbled, "So, will this keep happening?"

"Will what keep happening?"

"Will I fall in love with you again every time I see you? Over and over? Deeper and deeper?"

"I don't know. No one has ever asked me that before. But I'd like to find out."

Bren leaned out of her embrace and laid his lips on hers. She felt his smile against her mouth. "Me, too."

With a peck, she cocked her head and met his eyes. "I'm going to hold you to that. By the way, your mom is great."

"Yeah, they broke the mold with her." He started to say something else, but swallowed it.

"I see so much of her in you."

"Since I wouldn't know otherwise, I'd have to agree."

Kenzie wondered if he was ever tempted to change that. These days it might be as simple as a few keystrokes. "How's it going with Bob?"

"I honestly can't find anything wrong with him. Yet," Bren finished with a grin.

"Good to hear. But now I really have to go."

"I know," he said, releasing her.

"I'll be back in a few minutes for Katie and then we'll shove off. I know you have to work."

Kenzie felt his eyes on her back as she walked down the driveway. She sent him a wiggly wave as she turned toward Greg's house. And for the countless time in the last month, found herself smiling.

*****

With his mom and Bob out of the house, Bren doubled down on his manuscript. First order of business was reading the last of what he wrote last night as it likely needed some shoring up. He'd crashed on the living room couch and eventually staggered upstairs just as the sun was teasing the horizon. The next thing he knew, he heard voices coming from deck. And one voice in particular not only got him out of bed, but had him splashing cold water on his face and brushing his teeth. And throwing on the robe that still smelled like jasmine.

He was trying to take Kenzie's attempt to slow things down as a compliment. She had to be intentional and he understood that. But when he saw her rings, Bren swore his heart stopped beating. He'd never had his heart broken and he didn't intend to start now. Kenzie could try to logic her way out of this all she wanted, but it wasn't going to work. This, as his grandmother used to say, 'twas meant.

Yep, Bren thought as he read on, this was where he'd started to get punchy. Pleonastic narrative, rambling dialogue, and apparently he'd forgotten where the comma key was situated on the keyboard. If Miranda could see him now, she might not be so gung ho on this whole thing.

Then, as if brought forth, Miranda's name appeared on his phone.

"Good evening."

"Oh, no. You know what time it is here. Not a good sign."

"Checking up on me?"

"Actually, no. I know better. Have a minute?"

"For you, I have two."

"I wanted to share something I happened upon. Something that is germane to our current situation."

"I'm listening."

"Warren Holden is canceling his press tour for health reasons."

Bren outlined the corners of his mouth with his thumb and forefinger. "I had a feeling there was more to all of this. Money doesn't talk this loud for the hell of it."

"Agreed. Plus this is the first I've heard of it. Not so much as a whisper in the wind around the office."

"And your ear is usually pretty close to the ground. Is your source credible?"

"Fair to middling. But where there's smoke, there's fire."

"Well, if anyone can get to the bottom of it, it's you."

"As a matter of fact, my plan is already in motion."

"I have no doubt. Let me know what you find out, but not necessarily how you went about it. "

"Naturally. And since I've got you, how's it going?"

"It's going. Some of it is brilliant, some of it is crap, most of it is somewhere in between."

"Well, if anyone can turn a frog into a prince, it's you."

"I already signed my life away, Miranda. No need for sweet talk."

"You know I mean it."

He did. "I'll have the first batch to you by morning."

"And a day early to boot."

"Don't get used to it."

After they disconnected, Bren got back to work. He cranked out ten solid pages, wrapping up the chapter and bringing him to just over the thirty percent mark. He could stop, beat his first deadline, but he knew he wouldn't. He could, however, go for something to drink, take a break to stretch his legs. He was rising from the deck chair when he heard his mother and Bob enter the kitchen from the garage.

"I wouldn't push too much, Claire. He's a grown man."

"I know. But I hardly got to spend any time with her. Or meet her son. There's no harm in reaching out, inviting them over for dinner. Who knows when I'll be back."

"Seems to me you're welcome here anytime. I think what you're really feeling is a loss of control."

Claire set the shopping bags she carried on the kitchen island. "That's ridiculous! I haven't controlled Brennen's life for decades."

"I don't mean that way. The way he talked about her yesterday? The way he looked at her today? Your boy has it bad, Claire. Real bad. And I have a feeling that might be new for him. And for you."

Bren looked on as his mother, put gently in her place, shook her head in agreement. "Maybe you're right. I don't know why I'm acting this way. I would love for him to finally find someone. I only want for him to be happy."

Bob put his arms around her. "Of course you do. You're his mother. No one will ever love him the way you do. Maybe you're just feeling a little insecure, a little worried, about your relationship changing. This is uncharted territory. For both of you."

"But not for you."

Bob chuckled. "No, I've been down this road. Nancy struggled with it at first with all three of them. It's natural."

Claire smiled up at Bob. "I wish I'd known her. But then I might not know you."

"I think you two would have been great friends. And no, you wouldn't know me. Not this way, at least. I'm a one-woman man."

"I wouldn't have it any other way. I pity any woman who would."

"Which is why you did what you did all those years ago and never looked back."

Claire nodded. "At first I didn't want to force a child on an unwilling man. But once I felt that first flutter in my belly, I didn't want to share him either."

"Well, I think you're going to have to share him now."

"I suppose it's only right. I've had him to myself for forty years."

Bob tightened his grip around Claire's waist. "Hopefully he's willing to do the same."

"I don't think you could have made a better first impression."

"The feeling is mutual. Turns out, Bren and I have a lot in common."

"Oh? How so?"

"I don't think he ever saw it coming either."

As Bren watched Bob lean down to kiss his mother, he decided to stop trying to find something wrong with him.

CHAPTER SEVENTEEN

They never got to the adventure park in Tahoe City, but Kenzie and the kids met Bren twice for dinner the following week. Claire and Bob had gone home and the Bishops weren't far behind, something Kenzie both looked forward to and dreaded. This would be a true test for she and Bren. She was going back to her life, a life she still wasn't sure he could fit into. And Bren would continue living his here. So close, yet a world away.

But if Bren shared those doubts, he didn't let it show. He'd honored his promise to keep things on the down-low, but it was clearly costing him. Once or twice he'd reached for her, then pulled back. They hadn't been alone since the night they'd spent together and Kenzie longed for his touch, his mouth, his hands on her. She was thinking about sex more than she had in years and her body was reacting accordingly. She closed her eyes on a deep exhale as the longing rushed through her.

But Kenzie didn't have the bandwidth to dwell on that today. Gov and Laurel's homecoming was turning into an impromptu party. Their flight had been cancelled so they'd jumped on an earlier one. Mattie had a lesson with Greg, so instead of Kenzie seeing them later at her parents' house, they would come straight home. Sheryl and Jay would pick them up at the airport, grab takeout and head up to the lake.

"Would you like to ask Bren to join us?"

Kenzie, knowing Bren wouldn't take the time to eat otherwise, was a step ahead of her mother. "I already asked him."

"Wonderful! Does he like barbecue? I ordered from Famous Dave's."

"Mom."

"What?"

"I need you to care about this less."

"What's the big deal? I'm inviting a mutual friend of you and your brother to dinner."

Wondering why she bothered, Kenzie began on a sigh, "It's not a big deal and the last thing I need is for you to make it one."

"So is he coming or not?"

"He'll be here."

"Excellent. We'll see you around five."

And just before five, Jay, Sheryl, Gov and Laurel arrived to much fanfare, mostly from Boot. After jumping on Gov and licking his face profusely, he remained glued to his side as Gov greeted Kenzie and the kids and went back out for the luggage.

"I'm sorry you had to see that," Laurel told Kenzie.

"Does that happen every time?"

"Pretty much. But this is the longest Gov has ever left him. Not that Boot knows the difference."

"It was borderline pathetic."

"Tell me about it. Thanks again for taking care of him and especially for staying longer. You're a real lifesaver."

"Thanks for letting us. I want to hear all about your trip. And the book signing."

"We'll get to that. I could use a glass of wine first. I know your mom's up for it. How about you?" Laurel wound her shoulder-length auburn curls into a perfect bun as they walked into the kitchen.

"Twist my arm. You know, I've seen you do that a hundred times and it never ceases to amaze me."

"It's all in the wrist."

Laurel opened the refrigerator. "You didn't have to re-stock, Kenz. I bought all that stuff for you guys. The least I could do was get you started."

"I know and it's appreciated. But I didn't want you to come home to an empty fridge." She walked over to the pantry and opened the door. "Or an empty wine rack."

"Bless you."

"Mac dropped off the Barbera. He said it's your favorite."

"It is, as is he. But a hot day like today calls for Chardonnay."

"I've got just the one," Kenzie stated, joining Laurel at the refrigerator. "You get the glasses."

"Coming through," Jay announced, entering the kitchen carrying a foil-covered pan with a bag of hamburger buns sitting on top of it.

"Need a hand, Dad?"

"Nope. I've got my number one assistant right behind me." He set the pan on the island as Mattie appeared with a bag of utensils and napkins.

"Jay, can I get you a beer?" Laurel asked, grabbing three wine glasses out of the cabinet.

"I wouldn't knock one out of your hand. But we've got one more load."

As Jay and Mattie exited the kitchen, Sheryl entered. "Laurel, I was told give you this without peeking inside." She set a duffle bag down on one of the bar stools. "As if I would."

"We went a little crazy with souvenirs and presents, especially for the kids. I had to buy that bag at the airport."

"You spoil them," Kenzie said, opening the bottle of wine.

"I'm allowed." Laurel grabbed two beers out of the refrigerator. "I didn't know you drank Rombauer, Kenzie. That's my mom's favorite Chardonnay."

"I didn't until recently. Bren turned me on to it."

"Bren? Bren Banks?"

"Reporting for duty." Bren entered the kitchen, carrying another rectangular pan with a large plastic bowl sitting on top. "Welcome home, Laurel. Where do you want this?"

"Ah, thank you. Right there on the island with the other one."

Bren obliged, then his stare met Kenzie's and held. "Hey."

She swore her heart sighed. "Hey."

Laurel's doe-like eyes darted between Kenzie and Bren. Then with a slight shake of the head, she addressed her mother-in-law, "Sheryl, can all of this sit for a bit while we have a drink?"

"Sure. Just throw the potato salad in the fridge. I'll inform the troops."

"Thanks. Bren, can I get you a beer?"

"I picked some up on the way over. I need to grab it out of the car."

As Sheryl and Bren took their leave, Kenzie stuck the bowl in the refrigerator. When she turned back around Laurel handed her a glass of wine. Then she leaned against the island, crossed her legs at the ankles and gave Kenzie a waggish smile over the top of her glass. "Okay, what the hell was *that*?"

"Is it that obvious?"

"I'm not exactly sure what *it* is, but yes."

"Bren and I have become friends. He's been helping Mattie with baseball." Kenzie hid behind a sip of wine.

"Ah, right, friends. Do all your friends inhale you with their eyes? Because I consider myself your friend and I don't do that."

Are all writers this annoyingly intuitive? But if she and Bren were going to give this thing a shot, there was no use in pretending otherwise, especially with her family. "We've sort of started…seeing each other."

"How much of each other? Because Bren was all but undressing you with his eyes."

Kenzie took another sip, reminding herself not to guzzle it since she had to drive down the mountain later. And apparently that told Laurel everything she needed to know.

"Oh my God! How long has it been going on?"

"It just happened!" Kenzie dragged a flustered hand through her hair. "We're trying to be discreet for now. For the kids," she added with borrowed conviction.

"Yeah, well, good luck with that," Laurel mocked sarcasm, then went on sincerely, "I'm happy for you, Kenz. It's time. And I want all the gory details. Seeing how Bren is the most eligible bachelor in Tahoe."

"You mean since you married my brother?"

"What about your brother?" Gov asked as he entered the kitchen.

"Bren and Kenzie are a thing."

"Shh!" Kenzie exclaimed in a harsh whisper. "Where are the kids?"

"Out front with Mom and Dad." Gov grabbed a beer out of the refrigerator, paired it with the two on the counter and scooped them all up. "Mattie wants to show me what he's been working on with Greg." Then he turned to his wife. "What did you say?"

"Bren and Kenzie are a thing."

"What does that even mean? And what does it have to do with me?"

"It means they're involved and it has nothing to do with you."

Gov shook his head of close-cropped dark hair from side to side. "Involved in what?"

"*Involved.* Biblically."

"Jesus, when did *that* happen?" Taking a shocked step back, Gov looked from his wife to his sister.

"Doesn't Mom want wine?"

"I'll come back for it. And an answer."

"Mum's the word," Laurel told his retreating back.

Gov hoisted the bottles in the air in reply and kept walking.

"Really?" Kenzie shot her a look of feigned condescendence.

"It was just a matter of time. I saved you the trouble. Spill."

Kenzie let out a resigned breath, then brought Laurel up to speed. "I already tested the waters with Katie."

"And?"

"She seemed fine with it."

"That's a good thing."

"I guess."

"So what's the problem?"

"I don't know. It all seems kind of surreal. But when I'm with him it's—"

Approaching footfalls cut her off. "I come in search of wine," Bren announced blithely as he entered the kitchen. "And since the beer I brought is warm, I'm taking Gov up on his offer to drink yours." He put the six-pack he held in the refrigerator, then he realized both women were staring at him. "What?"

"Nothing," Laurel answered. "I'll bring Sheryl her wine. How about you guys unpack the paper and plastic products and get out some plates? We can eat outside, the way God intended." Then walking past Kenzie she added in a whisper, "I'll stall everyone a bit, give you guys a minute to get reacquainted."

Once they were alone, Bren hooked Kenzie's waist. "What was that all about? Actually, I don't care. Can I give you a proper kiss now?"

Tossing a surreptitious glance over her shoulder, Kenzie wrapped her arms around his neck. "Why not? We're busted anyway."

He wrinkled his brow. "How so? All I did was say hi."

"Apparently that's all it takes with Laurel. You writers and your damn intuition."

With a smile in his eyes, Bren lowered his head and cupped her buttocks, crushing her against him as his mouth took hers, sending pangs of desire through her.

"God, you feel good. Can we go somewhere? Anywhere?"

She giggled. "No."

"Please? I'll make it quick."

"What would that even look like?"

He feathered her neck with kisses. "I'll make an exception. This one time only." He kissed his way across her breastbone, then started pulling on her earlobe with his teeth. Kenzie's head fell off to the side as his mouth made its way back to hers. "I want you. Right here, right now." His hands moved to the waistband of her shorts and he slid one inside, finding her damp.

"Bren, no! We can't!"

"I know. Just tell me you want me too."

"Can't you tell?" she asked against his mouth.

"I want to hear you say it. It'll help tide me over until next time."

"I want you too," Kenzie muttered as his mouth began to feed. She'd surely lost her mind, letting herself be swept away like this in her brother's kitchen with her children within earshot.

"Desperately."

"Desperately," she repeated on a breath.

Bren's tongue found hers just as the front door slammed loudly shut. Laurel was making her impending presence known.

"Places," Bren said defeatedly, releasing her.

Still striving for calm, Kenzie forced the world back into focus as they sprung into action. Bren was opening the bag of utensils and Kenzie was getting the plates out of the cabinet when Laurel entered the kitchen.

"All set in here?"

"Almost," Kenzie said. "Are we bothering with placemats?"

"To quote the legendary Ronnie Reynolds, let's not and say we did."

"Works for me."

Sheryl, Jay, Katie, Mattie and Gov filed in and the usual controlled chaos of a family dinner ensued. The conversation went from Laurel and Gov's trip, to baseball, to Katie starting middle school and finally to Bren.

"Sure you don't want one?" Gov asked as he returned to the deck with another beer for himself and Jay.

Bren nodded. "One's my limit tonight. I've got a long night ahead of me."

"Is this the same project you were working on a few weeks ago?" Jay asked.

"It is," Bren affirmed. "And it's a beast. Speaking of which, I'd better get going." Rising, he gathered his trash, then started clearing the rest of the table.

"Don't worry about that, Bren." Laurel waved him off. "It'll just take us a minute later."

"The least I can do is help clean up. Thanks again for dinner."

"Thanks for making the time. Especially since it sounds like you have a lot going on," Gov put in pointedly around a sip of beer.

"Yeah, well, it's of my own doing. Gotta make hay while the sun shines."

"I'll give you a call in a couple of days. Maybe we can grab a beer and you can fill me on what I've missed around here." Gov's gaze flipped momentarily to Kenzie as he extended his hand to Bren.

Bren didn't flinch as he returned the handshake. "Sounds good. I need an excuse to get out of the house these days."

After everyone exchanged parting pleasantries, Kenzie told Bren, "I'll walk you out."

Night had tucked in still and quiet around them, with only the stridulation of crickets and the tapping of a woodpecker to break the soundscape. The dark folds of the mountain shadows swaddled the basin in a giant bear hug. Bren did the same to Kenzie.

"Thanks for coming."

"You knew I would."

"Yeah, I knew you would."

Bren pulled back, planted a kiss on her mouth. "I'm glad of it. When will I see you again?"

"I don't know. I need to get home, get my bearings. We have middle school orientation for Katie and travel team tryouts for Mattie coming up. Greg is going home for a few weeks, so at least that's one less thing. And I applied for a few jobs."

"I didn't realize you decided to do travel ball. It's the right decision. If you're worried about expenses I can help—"

Beyond touched, Kenzie silenced him with a finger to the mouth. "Thank you. But I need to do this on my own. We're fine. I was just thinking ahead." She exchanged her finger for a peck.

"Got it. But the offer stands." He took her hands in his.

"You really don't do things halfway, do you?"

"This thing, you and I, might be the most important thing I've ever done. So no."

The tug on her heartstrings pulled a little tighter. Kenzie knew he didn't expect her to say me too. But for the first time, she wondered if him being in the running for third would be enough. For *her*. She squeezed his hands.

He squeezed back, released her and started to walk away. Then he whirled back around. "I love you, Kenzie."

"I love you, too."

"Text me when you guys get home."

"I will." She watched him walk down the driveway and get into his car. With a beep of the horn and a parting wave, he pulled away. She waited until his taillights were out of sight, then turned toward the house just as Gov was making his way out of the front door. Having anticipated this eventuality, Kenzie took her time walking up the driveway. She sat down next to him on the steps.

"Lockdown was officially lifted when Laurel heard Bren's car pull away and not one-second before. Something about respecting your privacy."

Kenzie couldn't help but smile. "Have I told you lately how much I love your wife?"

"No. And same."

"Something on your mind?"

"I thought I was done with the whole brother-in-law vetting thing."

"Me too. And I don't remember you vetting Matt."

"We bonded instantly over California Common beer and a mutual hatred of the Dodgers. It was love at first sight."

"And then you went and married a Dodgers fan."

"That I did. That was love at first sight too."

She smiled at him again.

"You okay?"

"Actually, I'm better than okay," Kenzie told him. "Most days anyway."

"Good to hear. I can't say you were when I went left. Most days anyway."

"That's probably true. And I'm still not sure how I feel about it."

"For what it's worth, I like you better this way."

"I think I will too, once I get used to it."

"And I like Bren. For you and for the kids. And for me if it matters."

"It does." She leaned against him, bumped her shoulder against his. "Of course it does."

"Do Mom and Dad know?"

"Sort of. Mom was an unwitting impetus leading to our….Biblical status. Don't ask."

"Don't tell."

Kenzie looked into the near distance and contemplated the sleepy night, fringed in cedars and pines. "This was the last thing I expected to happen. The last thing I would have wanted to happen."

"Laurel would say the same about me. I had my work cut out for me there."

Kenzie waved that away. "She didn't stand a chance. You never met a rule that couldn't be broken."

Now it was Gov's turn to smile. "I doubt Bren has either."

"Probably not. But I'm still not sure it could work. Or if it even should."

"Where there's a will there's a way. And knowing you both makes two wills I wouldn't want to go up against. But why shouldn't it?"

"It hasn't even been two years." The fact that she had to stop to think about it shamed Kenzie all over again. "It's been—"

"Seventeen months, five days, and," Gov paused to mentally calculate, "roughly twenty hours."

"Yeah," she realized, glancing at her watch. "Just about. Thanks for knowing that."

"Of course I know that."

Suddenly drained, Kenzie stood. "I need to get the kids home."

Gov joined her. "Want to stay one more night?"

"Thanks, but no. The car's packed and the kids are ready to go, whether they know it or not."

"I think Mom and Dad are ready too."

"I'll follow them down." Kenzie hugged her brother. "Thanks for the talk."

"No thanks necessary. Besides, I owe you one for taking care of Boot."

"Oh, I think we can call it even, all things considered."

As they broke apart and walked inside, Kenzie realized she was ready to go too. Ready to get back to her house, her life. Ready to find out if tomorrow was going to be the first day of the rest of it or the last day of another one. Or the unlikely combination of both.

CHAPTER EIGHTEEN

Bren studied himself in the mirror as he brushed his teeth. The pressure to make the impossible possible was starting to wear on him. His already sharp facial features had grown taut and his eyes were sunken and bloodshot despite the morning hour. Well, technically it was afternoon but since he'd just woken up, it was morning to him.

His stomach growled and Bren had to think about when he'd last had a real meal. It had to have been at Gov's last week. That was last week, right? Yeah, he self-confirmed as he lumbered downstairs. That had not only been his last real meal, it was the last time he'd been out of the house. Or shaved. Or heard Kenzie's voice.

Opening the cabinet, Bren swore under his breath when he realized he was out of coffee. But thanks to his lackadaisical housekeeping habits of late, yesterday's remnants still lingered in the pot. Far from ideal, but it would have to do. Bren filled a mug, popped it in the microwave and went out on the deck. The sun's reflection off the crystalline water was so refulgent that Bren felt it behind his eyes. And that only augmented the nagging headache a few hours of sleep hadn't been able to assuage.

Neither did the simultaneous shrill of the microwave and his phone.

First things first, Bren thought and grabbed the coffee. He took a sip and decided more credit should be given to day-old coffee. It wasn't half-bad.

"Checking up on me? Again?" Bren asked Miranda by way of greeting.

"That's clearly unnecessary. I just finished reading your latest submission."

"Such the overachiever."

"Takes one to know one. Bren, this is fantastic."

He'd thought so, but he was also delusional when he sent it. "I take it that means it meets your increasingly exacting standards."

"Blew them away. You've set a new bar."

"Don't get used to it. This one is killing me."

"Softly, apparently. It doesn't show. And you're two days early with the fifty."

"And change. I trust the check's in the mail?"

"You'll have it tomorrow." Miranda paused, then asked, "You okay? You sound like shit."

"I just woke up."

"Slacker."

"Speaking of which, what's going on with the edits?"

"I'm going to take those the rest of the way."

Bren almost choked on his second sip of coffee. "You're kidding."

"Don't worry. You'll get it back at galleys for a last look."

"When we're all but press-ready? Since when?"

"Since I spent the day reading *Dusk at Dawn*. Your head is where we need it to be. It needs to stay there."

She was right and Bren knew it. "Fine." He bit off the word. "But I'm keeping the research."

"On one condition. You take a break."

Bren let out a derisive snicker. "Oh look, a pig just flew by."

"I'm serious. You'll be better off for it."

"I will if you will."

"I have a book to edit. Seriously, when was the last time you showered? Changed your clothes? Got out of the house?"

"I'll think about it."

"Put it away for a day, clear your head. I'll be in touch. Ciao."

"Bye."

Around another sip of coffee, Bren decided Miranda had a point. If he jumped back on the treadmill now, he'd be at it all day and into the night and be even more burned-out tomorrow. He could clean himself up, run to the store, pick up his shirts at the cleaners. Maybe see if Kenzie and the kids were available for dinner, he thought, the mere possibility boosting him. But first things first, he'd hop in the shower, get his errands out of the way, then give Kenzie a call.

Turns out he didn't have to.

He'd just finished putting away the groceries and was sitting on the deck eating a sandwich when his phone rang. Bren wasn't one to customize ringtones, save Miranda, so when he saw Kenzie's name pop up on the screen, he quickly choked down a bite.

"Hey," he managed through a cough.

"You okay?"

"Yeah, went down the wrong way." Bren took a swig of water. "I was about to call you."

"So I take it that means this is a good time?"

"For you there is no bad time. I hope you know that."

"I do. But I also know you've been working like a fiend."

"I have. But I'm in a good place and wanted to see what you were up to tonight. Can I take you guys to dinner?"

"That's actually why I'm calling."

"Oh?"

"I find myself in a bit of an unexpected situation."

Bren's heart dropped. "You okay?"

"Yes, I'm fine."

"Thank God," he said on a sigh of relief. "So what's up?"

Kenzie paused as if for effect, then drawled, "I'm alone."

Bren's sleep-deprived mind was slow to process the words, let alone the potential meaning of them. "Can you be a little more specific?"

"I'm *alone*."

"For the evening?"

"For the night."

Bren swallowed hard. "All night?"

314

"All night," she confirmed in a languid voice.

"So would you like to go out to dinner?"

"Not particularly."

"Want me to pick up dinner and bring it over?"

"Dinner isn't what immediately springs to mind."

Bren, finally catching on, stood. "What does spring to mind?"

"You're a writer. Use your imagination. What would you like to spring to mind?"

His throat went dry. "Be careful what you wish for, Kenzie."

"Last time you said that things worked out pretty well for both of us. How fast can you get here?"

Bren balled up the sandwich wrapper, grabbed his water bottle and hightailed it into the house. "Forty minutes, give or take."

"I'll text you my address. And Bren…"

He grabbed his laptop off the kitchen counter, stuffed it in his bag. "Yeah?"

"Don't forget your toothbrush."

It took Bren every bit of that forty minutes to get to Kenzie's. He breezed down the mountain, but once he got to Reno he hit traffic. And getting more and more aroused by the second didn't help matters any. He blew out a recuperative breath, willing himself level. Getting a ticket or getting in an accident wasn't going to get him to Kenzie any faster.

Almost an hour later, he pulled into Kenzie's neighborhood and was instantly reminded of where he'd grown up in Sacramento. Cozy, well-maintained homes of various shapes and sizes, people working in their yards, kids riding bikes in the street. He drove by a clubhouse with a pool and tennis courts, took the next turn and found himself in a cul-de-sac. Kenzie's house dead-ended it.

He all but ran up to the door. It opened just as he raised his hand to knock.

Kenzie greeted him with a wolfish grin. Her eyes held a seductive twinkle and her voice followed suit. "Hey."

"Hey." Bren stepped inside.

She was in his arms before the door was fully closed. He gobbled up her mouth like a drowning man would his first gulp of air upon surfacing.

"What took you so long?" she muttered when he drew back.

"Damn traffic." He ran his hands down her arms, over her hips, up her back. "God, I've missed you."

"I guess. You answered on the first ring."

He cradled her face in his hands and met her eyes. "I always will."

She gave him a heartfelt smile, then knitted her brows. "You look tired."

"I'm exhausted."

"You should be in bed."

"Lead the way."

"I mean to sleep."

"If sleeping is what you had in mind, I'm losing my touch. And my mind."

"You were a little slow on the uptake." She ran her fingers through the hair over his ears, reminding him he could use a haircut. "It's unlike you."

"All the more reason to get me to bed."

"What if I wear you out? Deplete what's left of your reserves?"

"I'll chance it. I'm still young enough to bounce back."

"I guess we'll see about that."

"Where are the kids?" Bren asked as she took his hand and led him into the house. Later it would occur to him that her hands were ringless, but for now his one-track mind held course.

"Katie was invited to a sleepover at Open House this afternoon," Kenzie explained as they walked down the hall toward the bedrooms. "Mattie was already going to an Aces game with my Dad and spending the night with my parents."

"Divine intervention, no doubt about it."

Kenzie's room was at the end of the hall, situated in the back corner of the house. Unlike the rest of the house where daylight abounded, her room was dark. She stopped next to the bed and started unbuttoning her blouse.

"Allow me." Bren worked from the bottom, meeting her at the button between her breasts.

"You do the last one."

The blouse fell away, revealing bare breasts. He took them in his hands, began to circle her nipples with his thumbs. "No bra, blinds closed, bed turned down. You were ready for me."

She closed her eyes, let her head fall back. "I couldn't wait for you to get here. I almost started without you."

The thought made Bren wonder if he could get any harder and still do right by her. He eased her down on the bed and laid on top of her. "Then what are we waiting for?"

She grabbed the bottom of his shirt, tugged it over his head and jettisoned it. Then she ran her hands over his chest and shoulders with an expectant sigh. "So strong, so sexy, so hard."

He took one of her hands, brought it down to his cock. "Oh, I'm hard all right. See what you do to me?"

Both hands on him now, she unzipped his shorts and found him. "You almost made me come in my brother's kitchen. So I could say the same."

Bren set his jaw in an attempt to slow his pounding meter. He was already surging and they both still had their pants on. "You wouldn't have been alone. That would have sent me over the edge."

She rubbed the tip of him with her thumb. "And now?"

"What do you think?"

She released the button on his shorts, pushed them and his underwear down, then used her foot to finish the job. "There were some things we didn't get to before." Her voice was dark and full of challenge. "Things I've been thinking about." She took the full length of him in her hands and began to stroke. "Things I'd like to do."

She had no idea. "Yeah, same here. But I'm not going to last if you keep doing that."

"Oh, I think you will. We have a perfect record."

"Four for four," Bren managed, bringing her shorts over her hips and down, giving silent thanks they were slip-ons. "A personal best for me."

When she looked away, Bren brought her back to him with a kiss. "It's okay if it isn't for you."

"I know. But is it also okay if it is?"

Bren was floored. "Kenzie…"

"I've never felt that connected to a man before, not even Matt. I've never felt so free, yet so safe, so desired but still so loved."

He knew it wasn't the same, but he wanted to say me too. She'd made him realize what he'd been missing. Having sex and making love were two different things. Loving someone was the difference, feeling that love in return was the difference. *She* was the difference. But before he could, she raised her arms above her head, crossed them at the wrists and made him an offer he couldn't refuse.

"I want you to make me feel that way again. And again after that. "

Bren started with her mouth, then kissed his way down. Throat, breasts, stomach, thighs as she purred like a cat beneath him. Bren knew he could take her now, he was hard enough, but he wanted more. He wanted his mouth on her, his tongue in her, the taste of her on his breath. And he wanted to watch her come while he did it. It was the only thing that could compare to being inside her.

On his knees at her feet, Bren bent her legs, then pried them gently open. Settling himself between them, he burrowed his face in her center and began to lick. Long, lazy strokes, then short, quick ones as he held her thighs apart. Her head shot up when he began to suck, locking her eyes with his. Even in the dim light he could see the abandon, the yielding, in them. She was giving herself to him in another way, trusting him with the most intimate part of her. Babbling superlatives, she spread her legs father apart and gripped his head in her hands, wanting more, giving more, taking more. Bren would give her that, all of that, and then some. And he knew it still wouldn't be enough for either one of them.

The world around him slipped away as Bren explored every crack and crevice of her core. Burning appeals slid off her lips, his name rode on strangulated breaths and all the while her gaze stayed fixated on his. Until she began to fall. She bucked against him as her head flew back, her hands froze in his hair. Bren actually felt the orgasm trickle through her before her heady screams filled the air and she doused him in relief and gratification. Arms flailing limply, she slumped back on the bed, spent. But Bren wasn't done. With two fingers still inside her, he kept licking until she arched again and surrendered to the second swoon. Then, already halfway there, Bren crawled on top of her and joined her.

*****

Bren woke to the scent of sex hanging in the air and Kenzie's legs pretzeled around his. She was asleep on his chest, her hair cascading down her back like a satin waterfall. She was making a low, bassy rumble that he not only heard, but felt. He reached over and brought the sheet up to cover more of her, then pulled her arm up, bringing her closer. He'd missed waking up with her last time and had no idea when he'd have the chance to do it again. The day could wait.

The sun was up and Bren judged it to be around eight. He hadn't been up this early in months, nor had he slept as soundly as he had last night. They'd eventually gotten up and thrown in a frozen pizza, eaten in bed and made love again. Kenzie wanted to return his favor of earlier and was doing such a good job, Bren had to tap her head to stop her. He didn't want to do that to her, come that way. Instead, she'd slithered up and given him the ride of his life. A ride that had ended successfully for both of them. Bren started getting hard just thinking about it.

Her hand rested on his heart and he caressed her ring finger. Bren wondered if its nakedness was for his benefit or if she'd reconsidered, decided she was ready. While he could hold out hope the latter was true, he knew the former was more likely the case. The kids were away, so no questions or concerns there, and a night at home left no one else to notice.

No one but him.

But almost as noteworthy as her ringless finger was that he hadn't thought about *Dusk at Dawn* in over twelve hours. And that never happened when he was this immersed in a project, especially one this imposing. His characters usually loitered in the back of his mind, waiting in the wings for life to get out of the way. Another first, Bren decided and wondered what time Kenzie had to pick up the kids. Maybe they could all go out to breakfast before he got back at it.

Just then she started to stir beside him. A sexy combination of a groan and a hum came from her throat as her eyes fluttered open. A smile came into her eyes as she looked up at him. "Good morning."

Bren leaned down and kissed her. "Good morning."

"How long have you been up?"

He shrugged. "Five minutes."

"I'll make some coffee." She started to roll away, but Bren brought her back to him.

"Not yet. Let's stay like this for a little longer."

Kenzie snuggled back in, started playing with the hairs on his chest.

"Not much to work with there."

"Just the way I like it."

"I like waking up with you."

She kissed his shoulder. "I like it too."

"I want to keep doing it."

"Me, too. But it's—"

"Complicated. I know." He laid his hand on top of hers, threaded his fingers through hers and said what they were both thinking. "You took your rings off."

"After I dropped Katie at her friend's house. Before I called you."

Bren kissed her hand. "I like that even more."

He didn't expect her to say me too, but it still cut deep when she said, "I'm going to put them back on before the kids come home."

"I figured. I understand."

"I wonder if you do," she said after a long moment.

"I won't pretend it doesn't bother me, as selfish and petty as that sounds. And I also won't pretend I haven't thought about you wearing a different ring, my ring."

"Wow, you really must like waking up with me," she teased, looking up at him.

But to Bren it was no joke. He paused, took a breath, then looked into her eyes. "Not today, or tomorrow or next week. But someday. If that's not even a distinct possibility, I'd like to know now."

"If it wasn't a possibility, distinct or otherwise, you wouldn't be here, waking up with me, to begin with."

"Because you don't do things halfway either."

She held his steady gaze. "No."

Bren had come this far so he'd might as well finish it. "But ring or no ring, I want to belong to you. I want you to belong to me."

She looked down briefly, then back into his eyes. "I've belonged to you since that first night at the park. I just didn't know it yet."

He laid a gentle kiss on her forehead. "I think I did know. I just didn't know what it was."

"You get a pass. I should know better."

"You weren't looking for it."

"It was the last thing I was looking for."

"And now that you've found it?"

"I can't imagine not having it. That seems to be the way of things with me."

He rubbed the small of her back. "What time do you have to get the kids?"

"Katie, around ten. She'll text. Whenever for Mattie. He has practice at one." Running her hands through the hair at his temples, she looked at him from under heavy-lidded eyes. "Why do you ask?"

"How about we grab them and go to breakfast before I take off?"

"That is not what I thought you were going to suggest."

"I didn't mean right this second." Hands on her hips, he rolled over, bringing himself, and his erection, on top of her.

"I thought you weren't a morning person."

"I'm not."

"Could have fooled me."

With a kiss, Bren ran his hands down her arms, then entered her. "God, I love being inside you," he said around a contented grunt. "I just can't seem to get enough."

Cooing, she tightened around him. "No complains here."

Bren loved her thoroughly, achingly, not knowing when the next time would be. They came in unison, their mouths pressed as tightly together as their bodies, knowing they belonged to each other.

Thirty minutes later, after a cup of coffee, Kenzie hopped in the shower, giving Bren a chance to take in the house. Like the neighborhood, the house spoke to Kenzie's effortless beauty and refined style. Contemporary, comfortable furnishings, warm colors, neat as pin but still inviting. Sipping his coffee, he walked into the family room and looked at the framed photos on the sofa table. Kenzie and Matt's wedding picture, baby and school pictures of the kids, one of Mattie in his baseball uniform. A picture of the four of them at Disneyland and a Scott family photo rounded out the collection.

Bren picked up the wedding picture and studied it. Kenzie looked the same, he thought, likening her timeless beauty to that of Tahoe. She and Matt were gripping each other around the waist, beaming into the camera. Bren could see the overt love their eyes, the pure joy in them. He picked up a picture of Katie as an infant sleeping on Matt's chest, then traded it for one of Kenzie sitting in a hospital bed with a newborn Mattie in her arms and Matt standing beside her holding Katie. And in all the pictures, their eyes overflowed with that same joy and happiness. Bren surprised himself by being glad about that. It also helped him appreciate how hard it must be for her to let go, move on. And made him even more grateful she'd chosen to do so with him. He would do everything in his power to live up to that privilege and do right by her, by all three of them.

Bren was heading back to the kitchen for a refill when the doorbell rang. He detoured down the hall and called for Kenzie, then realized the shower was still running. The bell rang again as he was making his way back to the front of the house. Putting on a polite smile, he opened the door.

And found himself staring into the face of Matthew Bishop.

CHAPTER NINETEEN

When Kenzie came out of the bathroom and heard Bren's voice, she assumed he was on the phone. But by the time she was halfway down the hall, she realized he was talking to someone in person. Someone whose voice sounded familiar. Tightening the belt on her robe, she made her way to the front door.

"Mick."

"Hey, Kenz. Sorry I didn't call. I hopped on a MAC flight at the last minute and came straight from the airport. I figured if you guys weren't around I'd try my luck at the tables until we connected."

Kenzie swallowed the shock. "No problem. Come on in," she invited around a hug, then ushered him into the foyer. "This is Bren Banks, my…friend." She met Bren's strained smile with one of her own.

"Yes, we met. He tells me the kids are out and about. And it looks like I've caught you at a bad time. Maybe we could get together for dinner later? I'm staying at the Peppermill."

"That'd be great. The kids have been looking forward to seeing you."

"I'm sure they've grown like weeds." Mick turned to Bren. "Will I be seeing you later as well?"

"I was actually about to head out." Bren stuck out his hand. "It was nice to meet you, Mick. Thank you for your service."

Shaking Bren's hand Mick remarked, "Looks like you have the upper hand here, Bren. You seem to know all about me but I don't know anything about you. Other than you've been throwing some heat with Mattie."

"Bren is a friend of Gov's," Kenzie interjected, sidestepping closer to Bren and taking his hand in hers. "He lives in Tahoe and we got to know him during our time there. He's been wonderful to Mattie, to all of us."

Mick took that in through a slow shake of the head. "I see. Well, I guess I owe you that thank you right back."

"No thanks necessary. Matt's a great kid. I'll let you guys catch-up. Excuse me."

Mick watched Bren walk away, then turned to Kenzie. "I'm sorry for showing up like this. I should have called first."

"Don't worry about it. And Mick, it's not what you think." Then Kenzie realized it was exactly what he thought. And there was no reason to pretend otherwise. "On second thought, I take that back. It's exactly what you think."

"You don't owe me an explanation."

"Of course I do. Matt was your brother. For starters, you should know that this is a first. For Bren, or anyone else, to be around."

"He seems like a nice enough guy. I'm just… surprised."

"Believe me, so was I."

Mick looked down at his feet, shuffled them. When his eyes met Kenzie's again, his were wide, distant.

"Look, you know Matt and I weren't close, especially as adults. But I loved him and I know he loved you. I also know that he was super focused on his career, on ranking up. And I know the toll that can take on a marriage, the toll it took on my mother." He paused, took a breath. "Bad as it sounds, I always thought you were too good for him, to him. And maybe now you have a chance to be with someone more deserving of you."

"For the record, I never felt that way," Kenzie told Mick truthfully, not realizing he had. "Matt and I had our issues, his career being chief among them, but I loved him and we had a good life together. And to be honest, I've been having trouble moving on. Your support helps."

"I want what's best for you, Kenz. You and the kids are my family. The only family I have left."

"I know. Nothing will ever change that."

He nodded appreciatively. "Well, I don't want to keep you. I'll give you a call later." Mick leaned over, gave her a kiss on the cheek.

"Sounds good." Kenzie opened the door. "Thank you for coming all this way."

"Sure. I'll see you tonight."

Kenzie watched him walk out to his car, struck by how much he'd come to look like Matt. From the way he walked and talked, to the gray streaks now woven into his high and tight haircut. Kenzie felt her lips began to quiver, her eyes began to smart. Just when she'd started to feel as though she was ready to— Oh God! Bren! Shutting the door, she dashed into the kitchen.

She found Bren at the table typing furiously on his phone. Shoulders hunched and stance rigid, he seemed consumed in thought.

She came up behind him, leaned down and gave him a shoulder hug. "Hey."

He stroked her forearm. "Hey."

Swinging around, Kenzie sat down next to him. "Bren, I'm so sorry."

Setting the phone down, he met her gaze. The turmoil in his eyes had eased, but not the apprehension. Kenzie laid her hand on top of his, relaxing a little when he let her connect.

"Don't be. I was just thrown for a second when I saw him. I'd been looking at the pictures." Bren gestured with a tip of the head toward the family room. "He looks so much like Matt. I mean, I knew it wasn't him but—" he cut himself off.

"But your fecund imagination got the better of you."

"For a split-second, yeah. But not yours."

"At first I was so shocked to see him that the resemblance was lost on me. Mick is five years younger and it seems the older he gets the more he looks like Matt, although their personalities are as diametrical as can be. But yeah, it brought up some feelings I thought were buried." She felt her eyes start to well up again and pursed her lips to hold back the tears.

Bren nodded but fear had joined the apprehension in his eyes.

"Bren, this doesn't change anything between us. At least I hope it doesn't," she told herself as much as him.

"I know that." He pointed to his temple. "In here, I know that." He moved his finger down, aimed it at his heart. "But in here, it felt like a sucker punch to the gut."

"I'm sure. But things like that might happen from time to time."

"Two steps forward, one step back."

She nodded. "Don't give up on me, okay?" A tear rolled down her cheek and he brushed it away with his thumb.

"I couldn't if I wanted to." Bren paused, looked down as he continued, "Being here, seeing the pictures, seeing how happy you were, showed me another side of you, another facet of your life. It helped me understand the depth of your loss." His gaze returned to hers. Now his held pain. Her pain. "I'm so sorry, Kenzie. So incredibly sorry you had to go through that, are still going through that. All three of you."

She leaned forward, tightened her grip on his hand. "Thank you."

"And I'm so humbled, so grateful, that you're trying to move past that loss, that pain, and let yourself love someone again. To let yourself try to love me."

"I don't have to try to love you, Bren. You're easy to love."

He gave her meek smile. "My mom used to say that. But I always figured she was biased. Seems like you and she have a lot in common."

"Yeah, I'm getting that. And I'm sorry too. It never occurred to me to prepare you to come here or to put the pictures away." Her gaze swept the family room. "Matt is everywhere."

"Of course he is. This is his home."

"Not really. This is his family's home. But I wanted certain areas, especially the kids' rooms and the family room, to be the same as they were in California. So they felt at home here right away."

"I don't expect you to pack your old life away as if it never happened."

"I know. I don't intended to. But I need to find a happy medium between those two worlds. A lot has changed in the three months since I moved in here." Kenzie gave him a warm-hearted smile. "I can't keep up with the learning curve."

Bren leaned over, laid a soft kiss on her lips. "I think you're keeping up just fine. And speaking of learning, let's lighten things up a bit. I know it's early, but what did you learn today, Mackenzie? Good or bad?"

He remembered the game from the night they got ice cream. The first thing that came to Kenzie's mind was that she could lose him. Because in her own split-second of shock and confusion, she saw the hurt and dismay in his eyes. And in that moment, she wondered if he would decide it wasn't worth it. That she, them, with all their baggage, was too much. Because that terrified her, she went another way. "That you don't break. You were your same steady, unflappable self despite the awkward situation."

Bren shrugged. "On the outside. On the inside not so much. And Mick and I were in the same boat. He was just as surprised by me as I was by him. Well, almost." He gave her a coy smile. "Plus you said some nice things about me."

"I did, didn't I?" She cocked her head to the side, sent him a flirty grin. "And what did you learn today, Brennen?"

"That I believe in ghosts."

Bren wasn't trying to be funny, he was dead serious, but for some reason Kenzie started laughing. And then Bren started laughing and they sat there laughing for a solid two minutes. Finally, wiping tears from her eyes, Kenzie said, "I don't know why I did that. It just sounded so funny. I know you didn't mean for it to be."

"I don't either, but I feel a lot better."

"Me, too."

"Are you still up for breakfast?"

"Sure." Kenzie looked around. "But I need to find my phone, see if Katie texted, check in with my mom."

"How about you do that while I jump in the shower? I have not only my toothbrush but also a change of clothes in the car." Bren glanced down. "I think yesterday's wrinkled shorts and shirt have done enough damage to my reputation for one day."

"Between that and me coming to the door my robe, I think our reputations are set." She stood. "I bet my phone is in the bathroom. I'll hunt it down while you get your bag."

Rising, Bren gathered her in his arms. "I'm actually glad this happened. It makes me feel closer to you. Like we're in this together."

"Thanks for hanging in there with me and being so understanding."

"All-in."

"All-in," she echoed with a kiss.

As suspected, Kenzie's phone was on the bathroom counter. Katie had texted that she needed to be picked up at eleven and Mattie had already eaten with her parents so Kenzie and Bren were on their own for breakfast. They drove separately and ate at a place convenient to both of their destinations, then parted ways.

Kenzie arrived at Katie's friend's house just as woman she'd known in high school was pulling up. Shannon Springer got out of her SUV looking like she was stepping off the pages of *Vogue*. Throwing her oversized designer bag over her shoulder and jiggling the stack of bracelets on her arm, she sauntered up the sidewalk on platform wedges. The sillage from her perfume was so strong Kenzie picked up its scent before the two women met at the pathway leading up to the front door.

"Hi, Shannon."

"Hey, Kenzie." Shannon peered down her nose at Kenzie over massive sunglasses. "I'd say fancy meeting you here, but I've been behind you for the last ten minutes."

"I didn't realize that. But Katie mentioned Sadie was here."

"She and Bryn have been friends since kindergarten."

"That's nice."

"Did you enjoy your breakfast?"

"My breakfast?"

"I saw you at Metro Eats. I tried to catch your eye."

"Oh, sorry. I didn't see you," Kenzie said as they walked to the door.

"I'm sure not. He's gorgeous, by the way. Good for you, not wasting any time getting back out there."

Kenzie stopped, prompting Shannon to do the same. "Pardon?"

"The guy you were with. Mmm, mmm, mmm. Is it serious?"

"Oh, we're just friends," Kenzie heard herself say.

"Really? Because the chemistry between you two was palpable, even from a distance." Shannon held up her hands, palms out, making the column of bracelets slide toward her elbow. "No judgment here. I'd totally tap that if I were single." Turning on her heel, she started walking again.

Stunned into silence, Kenzie somehow managed to catch up to her just as the door opened. After everyone exchanged greetings, Kenzie begged off the conversation by saying she was late to pick up Mattie.

"Are we going to Grandma and Grandpa's?" Katie asked as they got in the car.

Buckling her seat belt, Kenzie turned to her daughter. "No, I told a little white lie. Grandma and

Grandpa are meeting us at the field later with Mattie. I just didn't feel like talking. This is one of those do as I say, not as I do moments."

"Okay. I'm tired of talking anyway. We were up late talking."

"So did you have fun?" Kenzie asked as she started the car, put it in gear.

"Yeah. The three of them have been friends forever, so I was afraid I might feel left out. But I didn't."

"Great! I'm so proud of you."

"They thought it was really cool that I got to stay at the lake for a whole month. And that my uncle lives there. I said maybe sometime we could all go up together."

"Sure."

"Bren's house is bigger and prettier though so I thought that might be better. Do you think that that would be okay?"

The thought of a gaggle of middle school girls invading Bren's bachelor pad put a smile on Kenzie's face. "We'd have to ask him."

"I bet he'll say yes since he likes you."

"Maybe." Kenzie cleared her throat. "So you told them about Bren?"

"Yeah. At first they thought I had two uncles but then I said Bren was your boyfriend."

So much for easing the kids, herself, and the Shannon Springers of the world in slowly. "And what did they think about that?"

Katie shrugged. "Nothing. Reagan's parents are divorced and her mom has a boyfriend. But he lives in Reno."

"Got it."

"Reagan doesn't go to his house though. Her mom visits him when Reagan is with her dad."

"Right." Kenzie turned into their subdivision, slowed down as the road curved in front of the clubhouse.

"Can we go to the pool after Mattie's practice?"

"Not today. We need to go school supply shopping. Oh, I almost forgot," Kenzie said, wondering how that was possible, "Uncle Mick is in town. We're going to meet him for dinner."

"Okay. If we're going shopping, I need an outfit for the first day of school. We're dressing up."

"We?"

"Yeah, the four of us decided at the sleepover. I'm going to text Morgan and tell her," Katie informed Kenzie as they pulled into the driveway.

Here we go, Kenzie thought as they got out of the car. As if the day hadn't already been eventful enough, Katie had apparently become a teenager overnight. And if Sadie was anything like her mother, it was going to cost Kenzie a pretty penny.

They had an hour before they had to leave, so while Katie took a shower Kenzie got Mattie's baseball equipment together and called Emma.

"Who cares what some bitch you haven't seen since high school thinks? She didn't even know Matt."

"Actually, I think I invited her to my wedding. God knows why. And she's not really a bitch, she's just bitchy sometimes," Kenzie replied in voice barely above a whisper, "of which this was one."

"Jealous is what she is. Bored, insecure and jealous."

"Jealous? Of me?"

"Yes, of you! You're beautiful, smart and amiable and it sounds like she's only one of those things. And unlike you, the pretty doesn't come naturally. It also sounds like there's trouble in her well-heeled paradise or she wouldn't be thinking about tapping Bren. And that's me saying that."

"I don't know, Em." Kenzie threw a pair of socks into Mattie's duffle bag. "Between that and Mick showing up, I feel like someone is trying to tell me something."

"No one is trying to tell you anything. Other than Shannon's a bitch and Mick left his manners at home."

"Or it's a cautionary tale."

"A cautionary tale of what? Letting yourself be happy?"

"I swear if one more thing happens today…"

"Life isn't baseball, Kenzie. Three strikes doesn't mean you're out. You're projecting."

"Projecting what?"

"Your fear of losing someone again, your unwarranted guilt about moving on, the anxiety over you and Bren not being able to make a relationship work. It's clouding your judgement, your sense of reason."

"If you say so."

"What's the first thing you thought when you saw Mick?"

"That I'm naked under this robe."

"Okay," Emma replied around a laugh. "The second thing."

Kenzie pressed her lips together, exhaled through her nose. "That Bren could cut and run."

"And how did that make you feel?"

"Distraught, heartbroken, wrecked," she admitted on a sigh.

"Bingo. And if you felt that way imagine how Bren must have felt."

"I don't have to." Kenzie told Emma the rest of the story.

"So he was just as terrified as you were. But in a different way, for a different reason. That isn't a bad thing."

"Two steps forward, one step back, like Bren said."

"I think you're looking at this all wrong, Kenz. This isn't a step back, but another one forward. You're finally getting some closure. And that closure only brings you guys closer. Bren also said that."

"I just can't shake this feeling of waiting for the other shoe drop."

"If it does, you'll pick it up like you have all the others. You've done it before and you can do it again."

"I guess."

"Well, I *know*." Emma paused, then continued with a smile in her voice, "The only shoe that's going to drop is the one off your foot when you wear those FMPs for Bren."

"I still can't believe she did that."

"She knew you needed a push then and I know you need a push now. So consider yourself pushed."

Kenzie zipped up the bag. "Fine."

"We always find the people we need. And I'm starting to think you need Bren as much as he needs you. Maybe even more."

Kenzie snorted. "Me and my instant family. And all the baggage that comes with us."

"Seems like he's up for the job. The kids are going to grow up and not need you as much. He still will. Things that are meant to be tend to come full circle."

"Any developments in your circle?"

"I think the time has come for me to stop trying to square our circle once and for all."

"You might feel differently when you see him."

"Maybe. This is the longest John's been gone in years. Maybe hell will freeze over and he'll come home ready to commit to sobriety and rehab. And all the feelings I've been struggling with will fall to the wayside when I fall into his arms. But I doubt it. Either way, I have two great kids and a gem of a best friend. Who I hope to see over Labor Day weekend."

"I'll let you know next week. I'll have a better grasp on things once school starts," Kenzie said as

Katie came in the kitchen. "I've got to run. Thanks for listening and letting me vent."

"Always. That's how it is with us."

After practice and school supply shopping it was time to meet Mick, so Katie's new outfit would have to wait for another day. When they got to the restaurant, they found him sitting in a booth in the back with a beer. He looked so much like Matt with his thick brows and wide chin, his deep-set eyes. Even the way he held his glass had Kenzie sucking in a breath.

"Uncle Mick!" Katie exclaimed, running to him.

"Hey, guys!" Mick stood. "Let me look at you!" He hugged Katie. "You're all grown up. And just as beautiful as your mama." Moving on to Mattie, he pulled him into for a side hug and a couple of slaps on the back. "And you, Mr. Baseball. Look at those guns!"

"I'm going to play on two teams this year!"

"Wow!" Then he turned to Kenzie. "We meet again," Mick greeted her with a kiss on the cheek.

"When did you see Mom, Uncle Mick?" Katie asked as she sat down.

"I rudely dropped by this morning unannounced." He glanced at Kenzie as she sat down next to Katie.

"I was at a sleepover."

"I heard."

"It was no problem Mick." Kenzie locked eyes with him. "I was up."

"I was at my Grandparents' house. We went to an Aces game last night."

"Did they win?"

"Yep. They win every time I go. My Grandpa says I'm their good luck charm."

"All right," Mick responded just as the waitress came over.

She took their drink orders, starting with Katie and ending with Mattie who was sitting next to Mick. "You look just like your dad," she remarked with a sweet smile.

"He's not my dad. He's my uncle. My dad's in heaven," Mattie innocently informed her.

The young woman's face turned ghostly white. "Oh, I'm so sorry."

Kenzie smiled at her. "No worries. It's an easy mistake to make."

After she walked away, Mick asked Katie what she was looking forward to most in middle school.

"Going to different classes," Katie answered. "And not having to wake up so early."

They ate and talked companionably. To Kenzie's surprise, the kids seemed unfazed by Mick's resemblance to Matt despite the waitress' comment. Mattie was especially chatty.

"This summer was the best because I got to play so much baseball. Plus it isn't as hot at the lake."

"Yeah, it sure is pretty up there."

"And my friends think it's so cool that I'm taking lessons from Greg Gentry and that I've been to his house."

"That is really cool."

"He lives next door to Bren. That's how we know him."

"Bren is my mom's boyfriend," Katie supplied.

Mick met Kenzie's gaze. "That's nice."

"He is too. And his house is really pretty," Katie went on.

"So you go there?"

"Not really," Mattie chimed in. "He mostly comes to Uncle Gov's or we meet him at the park."

"Got it."

"You know, I saw a game room over there," Kenzie put in, opening her purse. "You guys can play a few games while Uncle Mick and I finish our drinks." She handed Katie a twenty dollar bill, then slid out so she could exit the booth. "Ask the hostess for change. Ten dollars for each of you. Stay together." Kenzie watched them walk away, talk with the hostess and head over to the machines, then sat back down. "Mattie will shoot baskets. Katie likes the claw machine."

"I never had the patience for either. You didn't have to send them away."

"I know. But we didn't get much of a chance to talk earlier. And what Katie said about Bren…"

"Is none of my business. I was out of line stopping by like that."

Later Kenzie would realize why it was so important to her to explain things to Mick. It was her way of justifying Bren to Matt. "We're taking it slow, making sure everyone is comfortable, including myself. Bren has been incredibly patient and kind."

"Like I said before, he seems like a nice guy. Tell me about him. Has he ever been married? Have any children?"

"No on both accounts," Kenzie said around a sip of wine. "But he's great with mine."

"They seem to think so. He's from Tahoe?"

"Sacramento. But he's a writer so he can live and work wherever he wants."

"What does he write?"

"Actually, I don't know," Kenzie realized out loud. "Fiction of some sort. But he works long, odd hours. Whenever inspiration strikes, I guess."

Finishing his beer, Mick picked up his phone. "Banks, right"

"Yeah."

After a few minutes of searching, Mick looked up. "Nothing of note. Does he write under a pen name?"

"If he does he's never mentioned it." But then again, Kenzie reminded herself, I've only known him for six weeks.

"That's kind of weird, isn't it?" Mick stated more than asked. "If he works a lot?"

Was it? "He must do a lot of uncredited freelance work."

"Enough to live in Tahoe? Does he come from money?"

"No. He was raised by a single mother. A retired elementary school teacher."

Whom he apparently set up in a condo in Scottsdale, Kenzie reminded herself.

"Maybe he got lucky in the stock market."

"Maybe." But Bren had never mentioned investing despite having the perfect opportunity that night at his friend's restaurant.

"Doesn't matter, I guess. Just curious," Mick was saying. "Want me to do a little digging?"

"Sorry." Kenzie returned to the conversation. "What?"

"Do you want me to run him?"

"No. No," Kenzie reiterated decidedly. "I'm sure there's a perfectly logical explanation. We just haven't gotten to it yet." She glanced over to check on the kids.

"Let me know if you change your mind. He'd never know."

Kenzie focused on Mick again. "But I would."

Mick nodded in understanding. "Yeah. You would."

The waitress brought the check, which Mick instantly usurped. Kenzie finished her wine while he settled up.

"Ready?"

"Ready," Kenzie said, standing.

"After you." Mick gestured with open palm.

After the kids picked out their prizes, the four of them walked out to the parking lot together.

"How long will you be in town, Mick?"

"I booked three nights at the hotel. I have two weeks leave and no ticket home yet. I want to spend some time in the mountains, take a road trip down the coast, relax, decompress. That's why I rented an SUV." He tipped his head to indicate which car was his. "But I'd like to see you guys again before I take off. I checked the schedule and it looks like the Aces are on the road for a few weeks. Maybe we could do something else instead."

"Sure. We have some back-to-school shopping to do this weekend and Mattie has practice. School starts on Tuesday."

"Maybe I could come to practice, see the big guy here in action."

"Absolutely. I'll text you the info," Kenzie told him.

"Mom, you and I could go shopping while Mattie is at practice with Uncle Mick."

"Yeah! Then I don't have to go to the mall!" Mattie weighed in.

"Sounds like a plan. Thanks for dinner, Mick," Kenzie said, suddenly anxious to get home.

"It's great to see you guys." Mick gave the kids each a hug, then turned to Kenzie. "And it's great to see you all doing so well. Matt would be so proud."

"Thanks," Kenzie returned, bringing him in for a hug. He held her for a little longer than he had the kids and when his cheek grazed hers she shut her eyes on a sigh. His scent, his touch, his embrace was so much like Matt's. She clung to him even as her heart broke in her chest and her throat clogged with tears.

"Thanks for coming out," he said, pulling back.

Kenzie cleared her throat, swallowed the tears. "Of course. We'll see you this weekend."

They parted ways and everyone was quiet in the car on the way home. Once Kenzie got the kids settled for the night, she called Emma.

"Twice in one day. You okay?"

"Not really." Kenzie gave Emma the rundown as she unpacked the plethora of school supplies they'd bought. "Strike three. I'm out."

"It's not strike three and you're not out. And even if it was, it'd only be strike two. Mick doesn't get to count twice."

"When he hugged me good-bye, I felt like I'd traveled back in time. Like I'd fallen down a wormhole or something."

"Of course seeing Mick is going to stir up some emotions. That's only natural."

"It wasn't just that. His mannerisms, his laugh, his smile, are so Matt. Why didn't I notice that before?"

"Maybe you never paid attention or it wasn't as apparent before. Or maybe you were feeling a little melancholy today. Does it really matter? It doesn't change anything."

But Kenzie couldn't get past it. "Em, even the waitress though we were a family."

"You *are* a family. You just aren't *that* kind of family. But I'm surprised the kids didn't pick up on it more, especially Katie."

"I was too and until we hugged good-bye, I would have thought it was all in my head. So now I'm officially the worst person I know and headed for a nervous breakdown."

"You've had a day, that's for sure. You need a break, a reset, a chance to process. And there's no better place to do that than Coronado."

"I haven't ruled it out, providing schedules allow. Although part of me feels like we just got home."

"But this would be different, a true change of scenery. And what would you guys do over Labor Day weekend otherwise? The lake will be packed."

"I doubt we'd go up to the lake. Gov and Laurel are going back to L.A. for a few weeks. And Bren will probably be working," Kenzie said, deciding to store the supplies in the laundry room for now.

"Maybe it's good that you're home and Bren is bogged down with work. It'll give you a chance to work through some things. And realize you're being positively ridiculous."

"Very funny. But Mick did bring up a good point. Bren never really talks about what he's working on, yet he's always working. And he has virtually no online presence."

"So? He always seems to carve out time for you. And Mattie too."

"Yeah, I know." Kenzie agreed, sorting the supplies by child. "But if I'm thinking about it, he can be sort of elusive. He doesn't like to talk much about himself. Or his work."

"So he's private, humble. You know all you need to know about him, for now at least. You have a good gut, Kenz. Trust it. Trust him."

"I do. I did, right away. I left Mattie with him for God's sake. But when he said what happened to Laurel in Maui could never happen to him? He was acquiescent, doleful, almost regretful."

"Maybe he writes under a pen name and is really committed to maintaining that boundary, keeping his personal and professional lives separate. Or he's never written a bestseller, has accepted that he never will, and that eats at him a little. At least he's not full of himself. And if Gov had any concerns you'd know."

"True."

"I don't know what John really does," Emma added. "I don't even know where he's operating half the time. You can relate to that."

Kenzie looked at her rings, nudged her solitaire back into place. "I can."

"You're agreeing with my logic without necessarily believing it".

"You know me too well."

"I do. And right now I know you need to pour yourself a big glass of wine and try to put all of this out of your mind."

"That I can believe in wholeheartedly."

"Good. And to be supportive I'll do the same. Try to get some sleep."

"Yes, ma'am."

"That's more like it."

After they disconnected, Kenzie stowed the school supplies, reorganized Mattie's bag and poured herself that big glass of wine.

She took it with her as she checked the locks and adjusted the lights. Katie's light was still on, so she stuck her head in her daughter's room. "I'm surprised you're not asleep. You probably didn't get much sleep last night."

Katie looked up from her reclined position on the bed. "I just want to finish this chapter. But my eyes are getting heavy."

Setting her glass on the dresser, Kenzie went to the side of Katie's bed. "Not too much longer, okay? You need a few good sleeps before Tuesday."

"I know."

Kenzie leaned down to kiss the top of her head. "Good night."

She was almost to the door when Katie said, "Mom, you seemed sad earlier. Are you okay?"

Kenzie turned back around with a wistful smile. She had such a sweet girl. "Uncle Mick reminded me so much of Dad tonight. But I'm better now."

Katie agreed with a nod. "He looks like him, but doesn't act like him, so that helps. Dad was quiet and Uncle Mick is…animated."

"You're right," Kenzie agreed with a grin. "Uncle Mick is nothing if not animated."

"I wonder if it makes him sad to see us."

"That's a good question. I don't know."

"He seemed fine."

"Yeah, he did." About everything, Kenzie added to herself.

Katie went back to her book and Kenzie grabbed her wine and was leaving the room when Katie said, "Love you, Mom."

"Love you, baby girl."

Kenzie crossed the hall and checked on Mattie, finding him sound asleep. She covered him up and turned out his light. Walking back through the family room, she stopped at the pictures on the sofa table. She picked up the one from their last trip to Disneyland. The kids wearing mouse ears and huge smiles, Matt with one arm around her shoulders, the other around Katie and Mattie standing in front of them. It didn't seem possible that had been three years ago. Moving on to her wedding picture, she traced Matt's face with her fingertip. She'd been so happy, so sure that day and not the least bit nervous. And despite everything, she wouldn't change a thing. She'd do it all over again even knowing how it would end. She told herself that somehow Matt knew that, knew it had all been worth it.

Deciding that was a good thing, Kenzie washed her face and brushed her teeth. She climbed into bed, the bed she'd shared with Bren last night, and took solace in the fact that it wasn't the same bed she'd shared with Matt for so many years. She'd replaced the mattress when she moved. With her head next to the pillow that still smelled like Bren's cologne, she went to sleep and slipped into dreams.

And that's where the solace ended.

At first the dream was a happy one, like the movie of memories she'd experienced before. But then it became discombobulated. Katie taking her first steps, but in this house, not where they'd lived then. Matt leaving for deployment, but in his dress uniform, not cammies as was protocol. And Mattie was graduating from... high school? No, that couldn't be—Matt was there. Or was that Mick? No, it was Matt. In her favorite suit of his and the tie she'd given him for Christmas. The four of them were posing for a picture. Katie was wearing a UCLA sweatshirt like Bren's. No, it *was* Bren's! And Bren was the one taking the picture! They were all laughing, smiling into the camera. But now Bren was standing next to her and Matt was taking the picture! Then Matt was next to her again, leaning down to kiss her. But it was really Bren she was kissing. Matt was on her other side, waiting for her. He'd been waiting for her all this time. What was she going to do? She had to choose. Mattie was going to college, she couldn't put it off any longer. Matt had to know or he had to go back. If she didn't choose him, he had to go back. But Bren was smiling at her, calling her name...

Kenzie shot up in bed shaking like a leaf, dripping in sweat, her heart galloping in her chest. She took one frenzied breath after another as her eyes adjusted to the low light. Grabbing her phone off the nightstand, she let out a relieved sigh when she saw the date and that her screen saver was the picture of the kids at Monkey Rock. She pressed the heels of her hands to her forehead as her breathing slowed, then steadied.

She'd never had such a vivid, granular dream before. It must have been brought on by the stress of the day. She'd certainly run the emotional gamut. From the joy of waking up in Bren's arms, to the shock of Mick showing up, to the melancholy of reminiscing over the pictures, to the horror of having to make an impossible choice. A choice that would never have to be made, of course. Even on her worst day she still had her sanity. But the supposition gnawed at her as she tried to go back to sleep. And haunted her in dreams when the ump called strike three.

CHAPTER TWENTY

While Kenzie was having nightmares, Bren was living a wide-awake one. He felt like he was on a runaway roller coaster with no emergency stop, no off-ramp. It was like being on an incessant hamster wheel from hell.

She'd have chosen Matt, of course. No matter how Kenzie felt about him, there was no doubt in Bren's mind that she'd choose Matt in a heartbeat. He was her husband, her children's father. They'd made a life, a home, a family together. In Bren's version of the nightmare, Kenzie had jumped into Matt's open arms with cries of joy and tears of happiness. He'd held her tight, swung her around as tears streamed down his face, then promptly shown Bren the door.

And in that split-second of shock and confusion, Bren's whole world had crumbled before his eyes, leaving a crater of agony in his chest where his heart used to be. All because of the ghost of someone he'd never met and never would. In this world anyway.

To make matters worse, Bren wasn't only jammed up emotionally, he couldn't seem to write anything worth a damn. He'd always thought writer's block was nothing more than an excuse, an easy way out, a strategy to force the publisher's stingy little hand by threatening to be the domino that takes the whole row down in the eleventh hour.

He'd been wrong.

So he'd add that to the list of things he'd learned, along with believing in ghosts and that some things never change. But he'd also learned that whenever he was with Kenzie everything was better, brighter, made more sense. So maybe that's what he needed. It'd been a week since he'd seen her and he certainly wasn't making any progress here.

"Hey."

"You answered on the first ring."

"I always will."

See, it was already working. "I was wondering what you guys are up to tonight."

"Need an excuse to get out of the house?"

"More like an excuse to see you."

"You don't need one. At present, Katie and I are sitting in the bleachers at Mattie's scrimmage."

"Want some company?"

"Sure. We're going out for pizza later if you're interested. It's a first Friday night of the school year tradition with us."

"As it should be."

"It just started so we'll be here for an hour or so. If you can make it down in time, I know Mattie would love to look up in the stands and see you."

Rising from the deck chair, Bren shut his laptop. "I can leave in five."

"I'll text you the address of the field. It's near the high school."

Unlike his last trip to Reno, Bren made it down the mountain in record time. He caught the end of the scrimmage and met them for pizza afterward.

"Mom, can we get sausage for me and Bren?" Mattie asked.

"Bren and I," Kenzie corrected. "And yes, if Bren will eat it too."

"Since when do you like sausage?" Katie wanted to know.

"Since Bren brought it to Uncle Gov's. You weren't there."

"Thank God."

"More of a pepperoni girl, Katie?" Bren asked.

"Yeah. Or just cheese. Sausage is too spicy."

"That's the best thing about pizza. Everybody can get what they like."

Bren got the play-by-play on school, detailed teacher evaluations and homework projections and the biggest news of all—Mattie made the travel team. That called for some celebratory ice cream on the way home. After which the kids crashed in the family room, giving Bren and Kenzie some time alone on her deck with a nightcap.

"They're always exhausted the first week or two. And the middle school day is so much longer. It takes some getting used to."

"They both looked pretty tired. And so do you. You okay?"

"I haven't been sleeping well. And the alarm goes off at six again rain or shine."

"That's about the time I've been getting into REM."

Leaning back in her chair, Kenzie took a sip of wine. "This project must be something else."

"It's kicking my ass, that's for sure."

Kenzie cocked her head to the side. "Tell me about it." Her tone was leading, almost suspicious. Or maybe Bren was so out of sorts he was being paranoid.

"Not much to tell. Just a backbreaking deadline coupled with some writer's block. It'll pass."

Kenzie didn't comment, just gave him a closed-mouth smile and a nod.

"I know what's keeping me up. What about you?"

She took a moment before answering but her eyes never left his. "I've got a lot going on between school starting, baseball and looking for a job. And I'm debating going to Coronado over Labor Day Weekend."

"Oh." Bren hoped to be in the homestretch by then and thought they could get in some time on the lake before the weather started to turn. But he hid his disappointment behind a pull of beer. "What's going on there?"

"My friend Emma rented a villa and invited us to join her."

"That's nice."

"Knowing Emma, it will be very nice. She's my Texas heiress friend, although you'd never know it. The one whose family runs in the same circles as Greg's."

"Right. Your friend from Twentynine Palms," Bren remembered out loud.

"We go back farther than that, but yes. Her husband is deployed and the kids all get along so it would be fun."

"So what's the problem?"

"Baseball for starters. And I feel like we just got home, back in the swing of things. Plus the idea of a nine-hour drive doesn't thrill me but neither do the airfares."

"Yeah, they really jack them up on holiday weekends."

"But if Mattie has a tournament the decision will be made for me. I'll know next week."

"How long would you be gone?"

"Just Friday through Monday." Kenzie paused, then finished in a questioning voice, "I figured you'd be working anyway."

"Likely, but I can always find time for you." Bren met her dubious tone head-on. "You sure that's all that's been keeping you up?"

"That's not enough?"

"Of course it is. But you seem to have more than schedules and airfares on your mind."

"It's nothing for you to worry about."

Bren leaned forward in his chair. "Try me."

Slowly, deliberately, Kenzie set her wineglass down on the table. She started to say something but switched gears midway, instead contemplating the near distance for a long moment. Then she gave him a smile that didn't reach her eyes. "Really, it's nothing." She tapped his hand. "Thanks, though."

Bren didn't buy it, but he knew he wasn't going to get anything out of her tonight, especially when the kids could surface at any second. So he'd put it on the back burner, circle back later. "Okay. But if you change your mind, I'm here. Got it?"

She nodded and the smile became sincere. "Got it."

With a furtive glance into the house, Bren brought his hand to the nape of her neck and drew her in for a kiss. A long, slow, lingering kiss that made him want more but told her this was enough. That whatever she had to give him would always be enough.

Her hands slid up and cupped his face as she kissed him back, taking that in, taking it to heart.

They broke apart and keeping his eyes closed, Bren laid his forehead against hers. After a few beats, he eased back saying, "I'd better shove off."

As they stood, she reached for his hand. "Bren."

"Yeah?"

"Thank you."

"For what?"

"For tonight. For understanding." She paused. "For everything."

He squeezed her hand, felt her rings against his palm. "Things are a little up in the air for both of us right now. But like my writer's block, this too shall pass."

"Yeah," Kenzie agreed in a whisper. "I know."

In the house they found the kids passed out on the couch. Kenzie turned off the TV and spread a blanket over each of them. Then they walked out to his car and

Bren kissed her again, this time more passionately, as the amber glow of the streetlight burned above them and the insistent mimic of mockingbirds filled the air.

Leaning out of his embrace with a shake of the head, Kenzie remarked, "I've never heard so much birdsong as I have since I moved into this house."

"It's the Northern Mockingbird. They're notorious night crooners, especially when there's a full moon."

She smiled up at him. "You really do know a little something about everything, don't you?"

"Just enough to be dangerous, remember?" Bren brushed back the wisps of hair that had fallen into her face. "It's likely unattached males, looking for mates."

"Well, they're very persistent."

"Unattached males tend to be."

She laughed. "True. What happens when they find one?"

"They mate for life."

Slanting her head to the side, Kenzie gave him a leery look. "Do they?"

"That's my story and I'm sticking with it." Bren laid a tender kiss on her lips. "Good night."

"Good night," Kenzie returned, releasing him.

With the mockingbirds warbling in the distance, Bren got in his car and drove away. He didn't know if mockingbirds mated for life or not but he knew he did. As long as Kenzie was the one who answered his call.

But who did not answer his call the next day was Miranda. And that, like the unshakable feeling in Bren's gut, was not only unusual, but unsettling. And in his experience, things that were unusual and unsettling were rarely good. Even if they weren't necessarily bad, they weren't good.

He wouldn't go so far as to call it a breakthrough, but the evening had loosened him up a bit and Bren wrote through most of the night, coming up for air and calling Miranda as the predawn light broke through the ink-black sky. It was going on ten in New York and since Miranda considered sleep a wasteful indulgence in the best of times, her radio silence put Bren's gut-o-meter on high alert. Saturday or not, unless she was a Jane Doe in a hospital or dead in a ditch, something was off. Bren could feel it.

He finally succumbed to exhaustion and crashed in the bright light of morning. He was caught between the half-worlds of sleep and wakefulness when Tom Petty's signature twang roused him. Bren groped the bed for his phone and answered in a wooly voice, "Yeah."

"You called me."

Shaking off the blur, Bren opened his eyes. "That's right I did. You didn't answer, *American Girl*."

"I was…indisposed. And now I'm scared. You don't usually call me with good news, especially at that hour. Plus you remembered my favorite song, which means you're lucid. So unlike you when you're under the gun."

"It's your ringtone. I'm sending in another batch later."

"Bring it."

"I want my galleys."

"That's unfortunate. They're not ready."

"Then I'll pick up the edits again. I need to do something else for a day or two."

"No can do, champ. Keep on chugging."

Bren, now fully awake, sat up in bed. "What gives? I'm ahead of schedule."

"I know. Let's keep it that way."

Now Bren's gut-o-meter hit the red zone. "What aren't you telling me, Miranda?"

"I'm not telling you what you want to hear and it pisses you off."

"And rightly so."

"Granted. But put it aside and keep doing what you're doing."

"You know I will. But I find it hard to believe that you still haven't figured out what's really going on."

"You and me both. Go back to sleep for a bit, pound some coffee and get back to it. I'll authorize the payment, get the check out to the Hamptons for Harper to sign. You'll have it by noon Tuesday."

"That's the first thing you've said that makes sense."

"Here's the second thing. Keep your eye on the prize."

"Whatever you say, Miranda."

After a pause so long Bren almost disconnected, Miranda started on a shallow breath, "Look, I know all of this is out of the ordinary. But we've always been each other's ride or die and that hasn't changed. God knows we've been in the trenches together. And your house in the mountains and my apartment on the Upper

East Side beats the hell out of the trenches. *Dusk at Dawn* could ensure that never has to change. For both of us."

"I know that. You know I know that."

"All right, then. Text me when you submit. I'll look at it right away. I'm dying to find out if she sleeps with him for all the wrong reasons."

Bren cracked a cunning smile. "That's for me to know and you to find out."

"Parsimonious bastard. Ciao."

*****

While Bren grappled with Miranda's hemming and hawing in Tahoe, Miranda was doing some grappling of her own in New York. She'd put him off, for the time being at least. But Bren was smart, really smart, and he was a genius at research. And unlike most writers she knew, he actually liked it. He liked knowing the origin of things, the meaning of them, the reasons behind them. Like is an orange called an orange for the obvious reason? And what actually did come first, the chicken or the egg?

It would be irritating as all get-out if she didn't love him beyond measure, owe him her career, her apartment in Lenox Hill and her sense of self-realization and actualization. So basically, she owed Brennen Banks her life. And she not only loved him, she liked him. He was a man of his word, had more integrity than anyone she knew and despite his incontrovertible success, somehow managed to keep his ego in check. Which is why he'd put aside whatever qualms he had about what was really going on and keep plugging away on what may be his best book yet. Because he not only performed well under pressure, he came through with flying colors. And he probably knew the origin of that idiom too.

So annoying.

But if she figured it out, eventually he would too. Bren was like a dog with a bone when he got an idea in his head. So Miranda had a decision to make, a course of action to take, a choice to weigh that would irrevocably change both of their lives. It would be hard enough if it could stay between them, but it wouldn't, couldn't. It was bigger than the two of them, bigger than the agency, bigger than profit margins, bestsellers, pen names and confidentially agreements. And it was only a matter of time before it became public knowledge.

All of it.

Miranda doubted Bren had any idea. She certainly hadn't. But in retrospect, something about this project had smelled fishy from the beginning. She should have known something was up when Harper Leary, who was only a rung or two down from Bren on her list of favorite people, had been cagey, tight-lipped and strictly business when it came to anything *Dusk at Dawn*. And in contrast to his usual hands-off managerial style, wanted weekly updates on Bren's progress.

When she'd broached the subject with him she'd been told to keep doing her usual bang-up job and keep her head down. But Miranda hadn't gotten to where she was in life by taking no for an answer, so she'd pushed, used all the tools in her arsenal, personal and professional. Harper may not be able to be broken, but most people had their price. And just when she thought she'd gotten to the bottom of things, a trapdoor opened and that bottom fell out.

Their esteemed author Warren Holden was not only ailing, he was dying. Of pancreatic cancer for which he'd refused further treatment. He'd been given three to six months to live—two months ago. The publisher had cancelled the press tour for *Down and Dirty in Denmark,* Holden's Black Friday release, citing unexpected complications from a routine procedure. Then came the spin. Holden would conveniently use the downtime to get cracking on his next book. Turns out they couldn't have timed it better if they'd tried. And the house of cards still stands.

But that was only half of the story. And while consequential, it didn't hold a candle to what Miranda had stumbled upon next. Even the master scribe himself couldn't make this stuff up. After the initial shock, she'd tracked down the source, confirmed what she somehow already knew was true, had somehow always known. Suddenly it all made sense. No wonder Holden had so readily agreed to something that should have taken delicate convincing and skillful negotiation. Miranda wondered how long he'd known and who at Leary did. Had it been coincidence that their professional paths had crossed or had that been orchestrated from the start? That, Miranda decided as she stared down at the Park, was the million dollar question.

But what Miranda did know was that the clock was ticking. And not just for Warren Holden. For now her sources could be bought, but it was only a matter of time before the connection was made. She also knew she had to be the one to tell Bren. She wasn't sure how exactly, but it should come from her, in person, unvarnished and straight from the heart. And it would. As soon as he hit send on a hundred percent.

Because the last thing Bren needed now was a distraction. And this would be a distraction to end all distractions. Not to mention what would happen if the press got a hold of it, which they would when Holden died. So they needed him to hang on until at least the end of the year. Even if he didn't make it until *Dusk at Dawn* was released, at least a reasonable amount of time to have written it. Then come what may. For all of them.

So Miranda didn't really have a choice. Not because she'd figured it out, chased it down. Because she wouldn't let Bren be blindsided. Not for all the money in the world. Maybe she'd hand-deliver his final advance installment as an excuse to visit, tell him that way. Feeling a little more in control with the inklings of a plan, Miranda requested the check and went back to bed and her date.

*****

"Yeah!" Emma exclaimed. "I'll get wine, the basics, snacks and treats for the kids. We can wing dinners. Text me anything else I should have on hand. I'll bring some things from home, order the rest and pick it up on my way to the villa."

"I can google grocery stores in Coronado same as you, moneybags."

"Don't squash my enthusiasm. I need this almost as much as you do."

"Okay, I guess that makes sense, since we're not getting in until later. But we're splitting the bill down the middle."

"Fine. Send me your flight info. We'll be there with bells on."

"We can get an Uber so you don't have to backtrack to the airport."

"Don't be silly. We have a half-day that Friday, so we'll drive down in the afternoon, check in, get settled and grab dinner in San Diego while we wait for you guys."

"I appreciate it. The kids are going be so excited."

"Same here. It'll be here before we know it."

"I can't believe we've already been back in school for a week."

"Tell me about it. I'm exhausted, still adjusting to those early mornings."

"Me, too. "

"Speaking of sleep, any more crazy dreams?"

"Nothing like that one. But I've been dreaming about Matt a lot again, like I did right after he died. In one dream he and Mick were interchangeable. "

"So you remember the dreams when you wake up?"

"Sometimes eidetically, other times vaguely. I'm not sure what, if anything, that means."

"Dreams can be very powerful. They reveal things we're afraid to think, feel, say, even to ourselves. Maybe you're subliminally justifying Bren to Matt via Mick. In a way, telling Mick about Bren was almost like telling Matt, asking for his approval, his blessing."

Kenzie, who had been unloading the dishwasher, mulled that over as she put a stack of plates away. "Actually, that does kind of makes sense." And for some odd reason, made her feel better.

"Dr. Williams at your service. I've got to run. It's almost dismissal."

Kenzie glanced at the time on the microwave. "I need to grab Mattie at the bus soon myself."

They signed off and Kenzie started on the top rack. The busy work let her mind wander. She'd tried to get that terrible dream out of her head, but talking with Emma had brought it back to the forefront. She'd have chosen Matt, of course. He was her husband, her children's father. They had almost two decades of history, had shared a life, made a family together. But Bren had become so important to her in such a short amount of time. She felt so good when she was with him, so much like herself. Had she lost some of that, some of herself, over the years? If Matt hadn't died, would that part of her been gone forever?

But maybe that was just the way of it. Marriage, motherhood, life, couldn't help but leave a mark. At times it wore you down and at others it lifted you up. And Kenzie couldn't deny that Bren lifted her up. But then why couldn't she shake these doubts about him? And about making it work?

Maybe Emma was right. She needed a break, a reset, a true change of scenery to clear her head. For the second time in— Kenzie did the mental math— seventeen months, two weeks, six days and twelve hours, her life had done an emotional one-eighty. And as she put the last of the glasses away, she hoped that the unofficial end of summer would bring an official end to her doubts about Bren. And that the change of seasons would change her misgivings into convictions.

CHAPTER TWENTY-ONE

Bren couldn't deny he was disappointed that Kenzie was going out-of-town for Labor Day weekend. But, he conceded as August became September, it was probably better this way. If Matt had a tournament, Bren would have been tempted to go to the games. If Greg had been in town, Bren would have tempted to stick around for the lesson to make sure he wasn't coming on to Kenzie. She had no interest in Greg, but Bren still wouldn't put it past him. The more you win, the more you hate to lose. And Greg was used to winning.

He'd averaged about three hours of sleep each of the last four nights. Three out of four of those nights Bren had pushed his laptop aside, laid down on the couch, and conked out. But he was making real progress, some serious headway. And keeping Miranda happy enough to have not heard from her again. He had two chapters to go and two endings written in his head. He just had to get it out, make sense of it and polish it up. Then he could get back to the land of the living and Kenzie.

He hadn't seen her since that night almost two weeks ago, but they'd texted, spoken a couple of times. She seemed to be as busy as he was. Since none of the jobs she'd applied for had panned out, she'd decided to sub until something materialized.

That was good, they could work with that, Bren decided. She'd be on the same schedule as the kids and once he got this behemoth behind him they could see each other on the weekends, maybe a weeknight here and there. He'd be available to go to Matt's games, see her that way. Maybe they could take the kids to a pumpkin patch when the weather took its inevitable turn. He'd love to take Kenzie away for a long weekend, to wine country or one of the little towns on the coast, but he didn't want to pressure her. They'd agreed to take it slow, ease the kids into the idea of him being a bigger part of their lives. So he'd follow her lead, fall in line with whatever she thought was best, take what he could get and be glad of it. They'd figure out what the future looked like in due time. He'd have to be patient, keep the faith and take the long view.

But that was easier said than done, Bren reminded himself and took in the view for which he paid so dearly. The days were already getting shorter and they'd barely flipped over the calendar. Another Tahoe summer was all but in the books and he hadn't been able to enjoy hardly any of it. In fact if not for Kenzie, it would probably go down as a lost summer. But there was always next year. Maybe he'd buy a boat, Bren considered through a deep pull of coffee. He'd toyed with the idea over the years, but could never justify the expense for his amusement alone. But now he had other people to share it with. And if *Dusk at Dawn* proved to be the bestseller he thought it was going to be, he'd have no reason not to give it some serious thought.

So he'd better get back to it.

Bren pulled up the file and started reading the last few pages of what he'd written last night. Doing so reoriented him with the story and shifted his mind into writing mode. Not bad, he thought with a mental pat on the back. At least he hadn't mixed up the character's names or forgotten what country he was writing about. So he could function on twelve hours of sleep over four days. Good to know.

To say he'd started the penultimate chapter would be an overstatement, but he'd made some rudimentary notes, sketched out a couple of exit strategies. He was at a pivotal point in the plot and had some loose ends to tie up. His protagonist had fallen for the female main character hook, line and sinker. Or at least that's what Bren had been trying to depict. But he'd incorporated some foreshadowing, interspersed a few Easter eggs here and there to raise the protagonist's, and the reader's, suspicions. Was the hero turning a blind eye to her wily ways or playing it cool, trying to lure her in, gain her trust? Double-cross the double-crosser? Bren's goal was to evoke sympathy and create conflict, yet still leave the reader guessing. He wanted his books to be hard to put down because the reader didn't know what would happen next. He didn't necessarily want them to be right about it, but he also didn't want them to be disappointed by it. And he had to be careful not to insult his audience, make them feel stupid. There was a fine line between surprise and satisfaction. Because page-turners don't make bestsellers, endings do. Endings make careers. And ruin them.

Right now the stakes were sky-high for both of his protagonists and the tension was even higher. They not only wanted to come out of this alive, they seemingly wanted to come out of it together. But even though she'd saved his life, could he really trust her? Or was that the twist at the end? He beats her at her own game. But where is the reader satisfaction in that? Or does he save her from a no-other-way-out death wish, proving both of their feelings are sincere? Then they kill the bad guy, save the world and ride off into the sunset together. Staring at the screen unseeingly, Bren pressed his thumb and index finger against his mouth. That could work. Redemption, victory, survival. The guy in the white hat saves the world and gets the girl. Or should it be the other way around?

Maybe, Bren thought, stretching his arms out in front of him and wiggling his wrists. Just maybe. Or maybe that was trite, predictable and campy. But he rubbed his palms together and took a stab at it to see where it would go. Which turned out to be pretty far, considering he was still at it at what most people thought of as dinner time. No wonder he was so hungry, he hadn't eaten all day.

Pushing up with a sigh, Bren rolled his shoulders and rotated his head from side to side. It was an exercise he used to get his blood flowing and clear his mind after a particularly tiring writing session. And a shower never hurt either. The scalding water rushed over him, bringing with it the clarity Bren sought. He'd finish this weekend. Then he'd have a clean slate when Kenzie and the kids got back. He'd catch up on some sleep during the week and be bright-eyed and bushy-tailed by next weekend. He knew Miranda was stringing him along about the galleys; some of them had to be ready for marketing purposes if nothing else. But she was right, first things first. So he'd kick it back into gear tonight, keep chugging along and bring it home by Monday. And then everything would fall into place. Or would have, if only he'd heard his phone.

*****

Miranda knew Bren was getting close, was going to make it. She could hear it in his voice the last time they spoke, sense it in what he'd been batching in. But what she'd woken up to this morning had been nothing short of genius. He'd surely pulled another all-nighter. And the most intriguing thing about it was that he'd labeled it 'A'. Bren was writing two endings. So the best might be yet to come.

He'd done that in the past, but she'd never been privy to the runner-up. But this time Bren didn't have the luxury of his sit and simmer time. So for the first time in ages, he wanted her opinion.

Fortunately for both of them, she was good at giving it.

She was also good at getting what she wanted, which is why despite it being a holiday weekend, she called Leary's CFO and authorized Bren's check for his final installment as well as his bonus for beating his deadline.

By nearly a week.

And while David was at it, he'd might as well cut hers too. Then messenger them both out to the Hamptons, where Harper was waiting, pen at the ready. Or would be. He was her next call. And while the checks were being signed, sealed and delivered, she'd be booking her flight to Reno.

Last-minute flights were always pricey but with it being a holiday weekend, they'd be outrageous. She'd be expensing that, along with hotel, transportation and incidentals. Right now she had a golden ticket and she planned to make the most of it.

With rare exception, Miranda hated traveling. As a native New Yorker she didn't see the point. But the circumstances called for it and if nothing else, Tahoe would be a nice change of pace. The only downside was there were no decent hotel rooms available. No problem, she could always crash at Bren's if nothing opened up. It might even help to soften the blow. Plus she hadn't seen him since the last time he was in New York, almost two years ago.

She needed to throw in some laundry, pack, water the plants, order a car for the morning. And mentally rehearse how she was going to tell someone who meant the world to her something that was going to rock his world and change his life forever.

So this definitely qualified as an exception.

But if anyone deserved to know the truth Bren did. She also had to keep his mother in mind. Miranda had never met her, but knew she and Bren were close. And that she was one of a handful of people who knew about their arrangement. But did she know the rest of it? That was another can of worms Miranda didn't want to open. But she would. She'd do it for Bren. She'd do anything for Bren.

CHAPTER TWENTY-TWO

Monsoon rains inundated the desert southwest, grounding planes from Tucson to Denver. Including, despite the clement weather in both Reno and San Diego, all Friday evening flights between the two.

After four hours of waiting at the airport, the Bishops' flight was finally canceled and they were rebooked on the first one out the next day. And although Saturday was clear across the region, Friday's weather had stranded planes and crews all over the country. The best the airline could do this time was a Sunday afternoon flight, but Kenzie didn't see the point in going to Coronado only to turn around and come home the next day. So she took the flight credit and for the second time in twelve hours mollified the kids with In-N-Out Burger.

They'd gotten up at the crack of dawn for no good reason and everyone, including Kenzie, was a little cranky. She wasn't one to sleep during the day, but she told the kids to lie down, even just to rest and promised to do the same. Mattie was out cold for a couple of hours and Katie catnapped. Kenzie actually fell asleep for a little while herself.

They headed to the pool for a few hours in the afternoon after which Katie invited Morgan to sleep over and they grilled out for dinner. Kenzie watched the end of the Giants game with Mattie and then let him go to his room to play his video game. She thought about texting Bren to let him know their trip had been cancelled, but knew he was dialed into work in all weekend. He'd been putting in a lot of late nights lately, trying to wrap up his current project. What that project was, however, still remained but a mystery.

Kenzie found herself missing him, not just tonight but in general. Maybe it was because the kids were back in school and she had more time to herself, but he never seemed to stray far from her thoughts. With a sip of wine, Kenzie studied her rings. Her gut reaction to Bren's comment about wearing his ring had been oddly ambivalent. Part of her had been taken aback and the other part over the moon. Neither she nor Bren were spring chickens and she couldn't date casually if she wanted to. But marriage? So soon? Seeing her finger naked was hard enough to get used to. And thinking of anything naked only made her miss Bren more.

God, she loved making love with him. She loved the feel of his hands on her body, the way his mouth chased them. Every time she climaxed felt like the first time. And as incredible as their first time had been, it seemed to somehow get better and better. Kenzie had no complaints about her sex life with Matt, but she didn't remember each time topping the last, even in the beginning. There it was again, that nagging comparison weaved with guilt, preying on her mind and taking the wind right out of her sails.

If Emma were here, or her mother for that matter, they'd both tell Kenzie to get over herself, remind her that she had a life to live and not living it wouldn't change anything. And that Matt would want her to be happy. She would've wanted him to be happy if something had happened to her, wouldn't she?

Then suddenly it all made sense. She'd been happier since she met Bren than she'd been in the last eighteen months, two days and—she glanced up at the clock above the mantle—nineteen hours. And if she was being honest with herself, maybe even before that. And that was okay. Actually it was not only okay, it was nothing to feel guilty about or apologize for. So Kenzie decided it was time she stopped. Emboldened by her newfound lease on life, she reached for her phone. It was time to give happiness a fighting chance.

*****

Miranda couldn't get a direct flight to Reno and due to thunderstorms in what she considered the flyover states, she found herself stranded at O'Hare airport for several hours on Sunday. She used the time to give *Down and Dirty in Denmark* another pass. She'd lied about the galleys, of course. They were already in the hands of media outlets and street teams, as was typical with tentpole releases. But she'd keep her word and make sure Bren got one last look. Once *Dusk at Dawn* was put to bed that is, which she hoped it would be by the time she was wheels down in Nevada.

She hadn't let Bren know she was coming. Miranda told herself she didn't want to break his stride but she knew part of her was equivocating. She had to tell him what she'd discovered sooner rather than later, but wasn't sure how or when to do it. She'd rehearsed a couple of scenarios in her head, but hadn't settled on one, so her plan was to ring the doorbell, read the room and go from there. She'd start with the check, of course. Nothing softened a blow like a big, fat check. Well, there was another way, but it didn't apply in this situation.

By the time Miranda landed in Reno it was mid-afternoon local time. She had to admit it was pretty out here. You could actually see the sky and the air was definitely cleaner. Since she hated driving almost as much as she hated traveling outside the tri-state area, she grabbed an Uber at the airport in lieu of renting a car. She was making small talk with the driver, an older man named Nick with a laid-back disposition that was reflected in his driving, and checking emails on her phone when she saw one from Bren. On the subject line was a single letter—'B'.

"Yes!" Miranda exclaimed under her breath, pumping her fist in the air. He'd done it. Twice over. He was done.

"Good news?" Nick asked.

"Very," she answered without looking up. "Definitely worth the price of admission."

"That's good, seeing how you came all the way across the country."

"Nick, you are absolutely right," Miranda responded absently, opening the attachment. "Absolutely right."

Miranda became so engrossed in the manuscript that she didn't notice they'd not only made it up to the lake, but were on Bren's street.

Nick gave a long whistle. "Nice digs. So this is where the one-percent live."

Closing the file, Miranda looked up. "Do yourself a favor and take the long way out of town, down Lakeshore Boulevard. Then you'll see where one-percent of the one-percent live. Part of the year anyway."

"I just might."

"It's right here," she informed Nick as they approached Bren's house.

As Nick pulled into the driveway, Miranda added a healthy tip on to the ride, then threw her phone in her purse. "Just pop the trunk, Nick. I can grab the bag myself."

Nick obliged and two minutes later he was pulling away and Miranda was knocking on Bren's front door. When he didn't answer, she texted him to no avail. He'd sent the email two hours ago, after which he'd probably crashed.

Miranda retraced her steps down the front walk to the driveway. Bren may lean toward the cerebral, but he was also literal, matter-of-fact and pitifully predictable. She lifted the keypad cover on the garage and punched in Bren's birthday and the enter key. The garage door immediately started rising. She shook her head in soundless laughter. "Unbelievable."

Miranda walked through the garage, feeling the hood of Bren's car as she passed it. Ice-cold. He'd likely been holed up for days. She found the kitchen and living room empty and no signs of life on the deck, where she knew he wrote in the warmer months. Putting down her bag and removing her heels, she tiptoed up the stairs. Bren's bedroom door was ajar so she knocked softly and after getting no response, peeked in.

Bren, fully dressed and spread eagle, was sound asleep on a bed that looked like it hadn't been made in weeks. Fluorescent yellow earplugs stuck out of his ears and a sleep mask covered his eyes. With an adoring smile, Miranda shut the door and went back downstairs. She'd might as well make herself comfortable. It could be a while.

She went to the kitchen for a bottle of water and found little else in the refrigerator. Taking a deep swig, she surveyed the room. There were dishes piled in the sink, coffee stains on the counters and the garbage can was on the verge of overflowing. She needed to break down both endings, be ready to offer her opinion when Bren woke up. Deciding the best way to do that was with busy hands, Miranda rolled up her sleeves and got to work.

Since it was all but empty, Miranda started with the refrigerator, wiping it out and throwing away anything questionable. Finding the dishwasher just as empty, she loaded it and scrubbed the sink and the counters. She took out two bags of garbage and shook out the rug in front of the sink. That earned her a glass of wine and a shower, after which she threw her towels in the washer along with a dish towel that smelled as if hadn't been washed in…ever. Then sporting comfy sweats and wet hair, she poured a second glass of wine and settled in at the deck table with her laptop. She was leaning toward the first ending Bren had written, but had mentally highlighted a few pros and cons of each. She was putting her thoughts into words when the doorbell rang. She saved her work and jumped up to answer it.

When Miranda looked through the peephole, she saw a woman. A blonde, leggy woman dressed to the nines in a black mini dress and to-die-for stilettos. Maybe Bren had been fitting in some extracurricular activities after all. She opened the door with a smile. "Hi."

The woman's perfectly proportioned, exquisitely contoured face fell. "Hi," she replied after a moment.

"Can I help you?"

"Is Bren home?"

"He's sleeping. I'm Miranda. Would you like to come in?" She stepped aside hospitably.

The woman tightened her grip on the bottle of wine in her hand. "Ah, no."

"You sure?"

Her bemused gaze left Miranda and swept the house searchingly. "Yeah, I'm sure." She stood up a little straighter. "Thanks, though." With a tight nod, she turned on her heel.

"But you're all dressed up," Miranda called to her retreating back.

The woman stopped mid-stride, quite an impressive feat in those heels, then spun back around. "Yeah, I'm all dressed up," she agreed flippantly.

"Did you guys have plans?"

"No. It was supposed to be a surprise. Well, kind of," she quickly amended. "I texted him."

"So did I. But when that man sleeps, he sleeps like the dead."

The woman gave a simper and a noncommittal grunt.

"Maybe you can save the surprise for another time."

"Maybe."

"Can I give him a message?"

"No, I'll catch up with him later. In fact, don't even bother to mention I stopped by."

Miranda shrugged. "If you say so."

"I do. Nice to meet you." She turned and started walking down the path again.

"Wait! I didn't even catch your name."

"It doesn't matter," she replied and kept walking.

Miranda had a feeling it did. But she only shouted, "Nice to meet you, too."

The woman lifted her arm in a motionless wave and made a beeline for her car.

Miranda stood at the door for a moment, watching her drive down the street. Bren hadn't mentioned he was seeing anyone, not that they talked about that kind of thing much. The woman had a soigné look about her and was probably around Miranda's age. But whoever she was, she had great taste in shoes.

Figuring she'd feel Bren out about it, decide whether to break girl code and tell him she'd stopped by, Miranda went back out to the deck. It wasn't her cup of tea, but she understood why it appealed to Bren. He liked the quiet, simple life and had gone to great lengths to carve one out for himself. She dreaded having to upend it, but they'd been through the wringer before and come out on the other side in one piece. This was just a different kind of wringer. Better they go through it together like they had the others.

She topped off her wine and dove back into work just as the sun began to set. There was something about the alpenglow, she'd give Bren that. But between getting up at three a.m. and the wine, Miranda started getting loopy not long after the sun went down. She hadn't heard a peep from upstairs, so she decided to call it a night. She locked up and turned out the lights, then crashed in Bren's guest room. It could wait until morning, Miranda decided as she nodded off. It could all wait until morning.

*****

Bren woke to a closed bedroom door and the smell of freshly brewed coffee. He pulled the earplugs from his ears and reached for his phone. It was eight o'clock on Monday morning. He'd been asleep for nearly eighteen hours.

But he was done. By the grace of God, or some other higher power, he was done. He shoved an incredulous hand through his hair. He'd actually done it. But what he hadn't done was shut his bedroom door. He never shut his bedroom door. And unless he'd chosen last night of all nights to start sleepwalking, he hadn't made coffee either.

Considering two people knew his garage code—his mother and Gov—and the former was currently in Scottsdale and the latter in L.A., and burglars weren't known for being either considerate or conspicuous, Bren was at a bit of a loss as to what was going on.

He sat up, moved his head back and forth a few times to stretch out his neck. He'd slept in his clothes, so at least whoever was here hadn't gotten a gratuitous peek. It also saved him a step. Operating under the assumption that the coffee bandit was friendly and known to him, he did them both a favor by brushing his teeth before heading downstairs.

The first thing Bren noticed when he stepped off the stairs was that his kitchen was spotless. The second thing he noticed was that the deck doors were open and the last thing not only explained the aforementioned but the closed bedroom door and the coffee.

Miranda.

Her thick mass of ebony curls rested halfway down her back and acted as a makeshift silhouette against the white light of morning. She sat cross-legged and barefoot in the deck chair, laptop open in front of her, coffee mug off to the side. Very much at home, she'd adjusted the umbrella to her liking and made herself a bagel.

So now Bren knew *how* things were the way they were, but he still needed to know *why*. Miranda didn't do anything without a reason and a cross-country trip would need a reason. A damn good one.

He'd get to that, but first things first. Bren went to the kitchen and poured himself a cup of coffee, using the mug she'd set out. He would've preferred his tumbler but it was nowhere to be found. It had probably seen the same fate as the sink full of dishes he'd been meaning to tackle. Fueled up, he made his way out to the deck.

"If I'd known you were coming, I'd have baked a cake."

"You don't know how to bake a cake or have the slightest desire to learn," Miranda replied, without looking up. She hit one last key with a flourish, then stood and turned to him.

"There's the man of the hour." She threw her arms around him, nearly spilling his coffee, and laid a loud kiss on his cheek. "Nice stubble." Drawing back a little, she pinched his jowls, making him pucker. "You look like shit."

"Thanks. I feel like shit, so it's only fitting."

"Well, it's nice to see you nevertheless."

Bren took a seat, prompting Miranda to do the same. "And why exactly is it that you're seeing me?"

Miranda, sloe-eyed with rich umber skin to match, cocked her head to the side. "I wanted to congratulate you in person. You're a miracle worker. And I have your check to prove it."

"And yours, no doubt."

Miranda adjusted a little in the chair, tucked her reed-like legs underneath her. "And mine."

"Did you read both endings?"

"I did."

"And?"

"You stuck the landing either way. It's up to you."

Bren laughed contemptuously. "Since when?"

"Since you, back against the wall and against all odds, knocked it so far out of the park we not only won the series, but the pennant and the championship."

"Nice sports analogy."

Miranda sat up a little straighter in the chair and gave him self-satisfied smile. "Thank you."

Bren took a wary sip of coffee. "But you could have told me that over the phone."

"Yes, I could have. But I couldn't give you this over the phone." Reaching into the bag at her feet, she retrieved a book and handed it to him. "Lupica's people sent it over the other day."

Bren set the book on the table, flipped to the title page. "That was quick."

"I called in a favor."

Bren sent her a knowing grin. "I bet you did."

"Not that kind of favor. Who's Matt, by the way?"

"A friend of mine's son."

"I hope it's a good friend. It was a big favor."

"She is. Thank you."

"She." Miranda's eyes flashed insightfully. "You're welcome."

"So let me get this straight. You flew all the way out here on a holiday weekend to congratulate me in person and deliver a book and a check that could have been overnighted."

"Don't worry. I'll be out of your hair tomorrow."

"Why?"

"I missed you."

Bren was about done with this little game of cat and mouse. "Miranda."

"Fine. There is another reason for my visit."

"I'm all ears."

"Holden is on borrowed time," Miranda informed him around a sip of coffee. "His condition is terminal. Thus the urgency, the secrecy."

Bren shrugged. "At the risk of sounding insensitive, I'm not shocked and you shouldn't be either. We thought as much."

"That's not all." Unfurling her legs, Miranda leaned forward and covered Bren's hand with hers. Swallowing hard, she looked down for a moment and when she returned to him tears had doused the spark in her eyes. "God, this is one of the hardest things I've ever had to do."

Bren felt fear rise up inside him. Miranda was a lot of things, but dramatic was not one of them. Setting his mug on the table, he took the hand that covered his.

"Miranda? Are you okay?"

"Yes, I'm fine." She shook her head from side to side. "It's nothing like that. Actually, it's not even about me." Pinching the bridge of her nose, she closed her eyes briefly before training them on him again and starting on a breath, "Bren, you aren't just Warren Holden's ghostwriter. You're his son."

If Miranda's gaze didn't hold so earnest, her expression so pained, Bren would have started laughing. But they did, so he didn't. He just sat there in stunned silence.

He saw Miranda's mouth moving, heard her voice, but couldn't seem to process the words she was saying. Something about Holden following his career, watching him from afar. It's unclear if he knew who Bren was before agreeing to work with a ghostwriter or if the truth came to light somewhere along the way.

"Bren? Did you hear me?"

"Yeah. I mean, no. What?"

"I said—"

"I heard what you said," Retrieving his hand, Bren cut her off. "I mean how do you think you know this?"

Miranda leaned back, crossed her legs. "Something about this whole thing felt off-kilter from the beginning. The money alone is beyond egregious. So I did some digging, shook some trees."

Typical, Bren thought. Miranda never could let anything go. And that was part of why he was where he was today. "Sounds like you got more than you bargained for."

"I think we both did. Bren, you're taking this incredibly well."

"Because it's ludicrous, farcical and absurd. Miranda, you're smarter than this."

"I am and I thought so too at first. But you know very little about your father."

"You're forgetting about my mother. She knows who I write for."

"We've long suspected Warren Holden is a pen name."

"So?"

"Think about it. You're both prolific, robust writers. In fact, I've never seen two more compatible writing styles. Holden could live anywhere in the world, has multiple homes, but spends more time here than anywhere else. You've always said Tahoe was in your blood. Maybe it really is."

Bren waved a hand in the air. "Coincidence."

"Does your mother have her Master's?"

"Yeah." Bren shrugged. "She finished it when I was in high school."

"Finished being the operative word. When did she start it?"

"I don't know. What does that have to do with anything?"

"Everything. You don't know because you weren't born yet. Claire Banks was enrolled at Sacramento State as a graduate student in 1982. She withdrew after one semester. She completed the program in 1999."

"Okay."

"There was an adjunct professor who taught night classes there at the time. His name was Holden W. Greer. Your mother was his student."

"Your point?"

"I think Holden W. Greer's pen name is Warren Holden. And I think he's your father."

Bren's scalp began to tingle. "You got all that from shaking a few trees?"

"They were really good trees."

"Let me guess. Your friend at *Weekly*?"

"For starters. But it was really her contact, an entertainment reporter out of L.A., who sussed it out."

Now Bren was even more confused, but he'd always liked puzzles so he'd play along. "What does an entertainment reporter from L.A.want with Warren Holden?"

"There's been talk of movie options for years, you know that. But Holden's people want a green light guarantee and that's not how Hollywood works. No guarantee, no rights. She got wind of a deal actually being put together and ran it down. She stumbled across the paternity information, brought it to Mia. They go way back."

"How do you," Bren made air quotes, "stumble across that kind of information?"

"From what I've been able to cobble together, it started with one of those ancestry DNA tests and snowballed from there. You know better than anyone what you can find with a little elbow grease and a deep dive on the Internet. Especially if you have the right incentive. Like exclusivity or blackmail."

"Blackmail?"

"Look, even I haven't been able to get Holden's true identity out of anyone. There has to be more than privacy at stake here."

"And God knows you tried."

Miranda smiled at the memory. "That I did. One of my few failings."

"Not all of us can be bought."

"So I've heard."

"Well, I don't believe it," Bren told himself out loud.

"I didn't either." Reaching into her bag again, Miranda produced a file folder. "There's coincidence and evidence and then there's science. And all three are in here for your eagle-eyed perusal. I have an electronic copy as well if you'd prefer."

Bren took the folder from her outstretched hand and promptly dropped it on the table. "No, thanks."

"Your prerogative. But there's only so much I can control; it's going to come out sooner or later."

"Let it."

"Bren, not believing the truth doesn't make it any less true. At the very least you need to talk to your mother about this. You also have to prepare yourself to be ousted."

"That's more your problem than mine."

"Is it?"

"I'm not the one doing the ousting, so yeah."

"I can't believe how well you're taking this. I may have underestimated you."

"That's unlike you."

"It is. As is your reaction." Miranda cocked her head to the side speculatively. "And that's not all. You seem different. Calmer, relaxed, almost humble. It's out of character and honestly, a little off-putting."

"Maybe because I wrote a book in a month that should have taken a year and I'm basking in the accomplishment. Sue me," Bren finished wryly.

Miranda disagreed with a grunt. "It's more than that." Knitting her brows, she nodded at the book on the table. "Who's Matt again?"

"I told you. A friend's son."

"A female friend?"

"Yes," Bren dragged out the word.

"With long blonde hair and legs up to here?" Miranda raised her hand, palm down, to chin level.

Bren felt his jaw start to throb. "Miranda, what did you do?"

"I answered the door."

"To whom?"

"A woman."

Bren jerked forward. "What woman? When?"

"Last night. You were asleep."

"Why didn't you tell me?"

"I am telling you," Miranda said matter-of-factly. "Despite the fact she asked me not to. I'm breaking girl code. You're welcome."

Bren didn't know what girl code was and he didn't care. "What did she say?"

"She said she was surprising you. Well, kind of. She texted you but you didn't reply. We bonded over the shared annoyance."

In a hurry to get downstairs, Bren hadn't checked his messages. He patted his pockets, pulled out his phone. "What else did she say?"

"Nothing, not even her name. I asked if you guys had plans because she was all dressed up."

Bren swore under his breath. "Let me guess, a black dress and high heels," he said, tapping Kenzie's number.

"Yep. And she was smoking like a wildfire out of control."

"Tell me you were decent when you answered the door," he said tiresomely as the call went to voicemail.

"Of course I was. I'd just gotten out of the shower."

Shutting his eyes, Bren counted to three. "Perfect. How did she seem when she left?"

"In a bit of a hurry to be honest,"

Panic surging through him, Bren jumped up.

"Where are you going?"

"To Reno. I have to go to her, explain."

Miranda stood, followed him into the house. "Wait! We have to talk this through, come up with a strategy."

"That's the least of my problems right now."

"Finding out Warren Holden is your father and him being exposed as a fraud is the least of your problems?"

Bren grabbed his wallet and keys off the kitchen counter and headed for the door. "As of about two minutes ago, yes."

"Bren!"

Hand on the knob, Bren turned and met Miranda's exasperated gaze.

"Who is she?"

"A woman I've been seeing," he replied, praying that was still the case.

"I didn't know you were seeing anyone."

"Well, now you do." He turned the handle, started to step into the garage.

Before he could, Miranda leaned over his shoulder and slammed the door shut.

"Miranda, I don't have time for this," Bren said without turning around.

"Trust me, you don't not have time for this."

"Expose Holden, don't expose Holden. Leak the story to get ahead of it or don't. I really don't care." He started to turn the knob again.

"What about your mother?"

That had Bren spinning around. For the first time in his life, his mother hadn't been his first thought. "I'll handle my mother. Give me a couple of hours. But I need to do this."

Miranda's eyes, softer now, clung to his. "You're not just seeing this woman, you're in love with her, aren't you?"

Bren nodded. "Yeah."

Now her eyes misted over. "No wonder you seem different, happier, vulnerable. You've never loved a woman before, have you?"

"No. Not like this anyway."

"Well, for God's sake, don't screw it up."

"I'm trying not to. Can I go now?"

"Hold on a sec."

Bren looked on as Miranda ran back out to the deck. When she returned, she held the book for Matt. "Take this as a peace offering. What woman could resist a guy who gets her son an autographed copy of a book hot off the press?"

Bren accepted the book and the sentiment with a shaky smile. "What am I going to tell her?"

Miranda shrugged. "The truth."

"All of it?"

"Do you trust her?"

"As much as I trust you."

"Then you have nothing to lose."

"What if I lose *her*?"

"Does she love you back?"

"Yeah. I mean, she must right? For me to feel this way?"

"Yes or no."

All-in, Bren reminded himself. "Yes," he affirmed. "She does."

"Then you won't. And if you do then she doesn't and you would have eventually anyway."

"Thanks… I think."

"Have you talked about a future together?"

"Yeah." Bren's voice waffled as he qualified, "A little."

"Then she was bound to join our little club sooner or later. And there's no time like the present. After all, the truth is what brought me all the way out here. Maybe this is part of why. Maybe the time to tell the truth has come. For all of us."

Bren felt the emotion swimming in Miranda's eyes fill his chest. "Maybe I have loved a woman before. Just in a different way."

Miranda smiled through her tears. "I'll take it. But only your mother is allowed to come ahead of me in line."

"Deal."

"And the feeling is mutual, by the way."

"I know."

Miranda rested her hands on his shoulders. "You need to prepare yourself for a firestorm. A big one, but fix this first. With any luck, maybe you won't have to go through it alone."

"You going to bail on me?"

"Never." She grabbed his ball cap off the hook, handed it to him. "Now get out of here."

CHAPTER TWENTY-THREE

Hunched over on her hands and knees Kenzie thrust the hand shovel into the ground, breaking up the dirt in the flower bed. The impatiens and petunias still had some life left in them but she wanted to get her fall bulbs in. She knew it was not only too early, it was also a waste. And her mother, who'd been tending her garden much of the summer, was going to kill her.

Oh, well.

She needed something to do to keep her hands, as much as her mind, busy. And wear herself out so she wouldn't be up all night again. Because when you're asleep, it's impossible to feel simultaneously sorry for and furious with yourself. You also can't throw a pity party for one and go through an entire box of tissues.

How could she have been so wrong? About Bren, about letting herself love someone again, about trying to build a new life with him, not only for herself, but for the kids.

What the hell had she been thinking?

Well, she wasn't going to let that happen again. She'd be perfectly happy here alone, watching her children grow up in their new home. She'd get a job, make some new friends, look out for her parents. Get that dog she'd been putting off. Play catch with Mattie, make the most of Katie's middle school years before she outgrew her altogether. She'd build that new life all by herself. Because she was done. She'd never trust another man again. And she'd be fine. She'd been fine before and she'd be fine again.

Kenzie thought she'd handled herself, the whole thing really, pretty well. When Bren hadn't texted her back, she'd assumed he was catching up on some sleep after a long night of working. He didn't seem to mind surprises, so she decided to give him one. Her parents had been thrilled to take the kids, not only last night, but today as well. They'd gone out to dinner and a movie last night and were going to a neighborhood party today. It might not be Coronado, but it was something to do on Labor Day.

Kenzie had been pleasantly surprised that the black dress still fit and the heels were actually comfortable. She'd put her back into getting ready, breaking out the diamond earrings her parents had given her for her fortieth birthday and painting her nails for the first time in ages. So much for that, she huffed under her breath, studying the dirt that had settled into her nail beds. But most notably, she'd taken off her wedding rings. For good this time, or so she'd thought. She'd put them in her parents' safe in the same velvet box Matt had given her the diamond in the night he proposed. She'd decided to save them for Katie or for Mattie to pass along someday. So much for that too she thought, plucking a perfectly heathy plant out of the ground and tossing it into the garbage bag on the grass next to her. She'd get them back tonight when she picked up the kids.

She'd packed an overnight bag, picked up a bottle of wine and headed up to the lake. She'd run through a couple of scenarios in her head. If Bren wasn't home, she'd wait for him at Gov's. If he was tied down with work, she'd amuse herself in town until he was free. She could go to the store, make dinner, relax a bit while he finished up. Of course that would have required a change of clothes, but she had that covered too.

But what she hadn't counted on was the door being opened by the most beautiful woman in the world. Miranda, she'd said her name was? Yes, Miranda, with her flowing knotless braids damp from the shower, dark, exotic eyes and magnificent bone structure. And she was not only at ease in Bren's home, she was comfortable enough to take a shower and get into cozy sweats without a stitch of make-up on. Not that she needed any. And to top it off, she was charitable and welcoming. She'd invited Kenzie in as if they were old friends.

Maybe she and Bren had an open relationship? An on-again, off-again type of thing, a relationship of convenience? And apparently Kenzie being out-of-town had proven to be extremely convenient. The booty call had come at just the right time.

What a complete and utter fool she'd been.

He'd called twice this morning, the calls coming within fifteen minutes of each other. So either Miranda had broken girl code and told him, or she'd gone on her merry way. Bren probably thought nothing of Kenzie not answering. She was in the air for all he knew. She reached into her pocket and retrieved her phone. No more missed calls or new texts.

Oh, well.

She used the bulb planter to make a hole, then ripped open another bag of bulbs. She was throwing a handful of them in when she heard rapidly approaching footfalls. When she looked up, Bren was rounding the house to the backyard.

"There you are. Thank God," he said breathlessly, stopping in front of her.

Kenzie straightened up slowly, met his frazzled gaze. In wrinkled jeans and a raggedy T-shirt, he looked like something the cat had dragged in. He was wearing the same Giants cap he'd had on the night they met at the park. Kenzie couldn't help but think of it as a full circle moment.

Chest heaving, he reached out to her. She took a step back.

"Bren, what are you doing here?"

"Looking for you. I tried calling. Miranda told me you came by."

"Yeah." Kenzie returned sharply, resting her hands on her hips. "I came by,"

"I know what you must have thought. Please, let me explain."

"Explain why the most beautiful woman in the world, fresh out of the shower, answered the door while you were in bed?"

"It's not what you think. And you're the most beautiful woman in the world."

His attempt at humor just made Kenzie madder. "Well, did you change the sheets at least?"

He gave her a baffled frown. "Change the sheets? I never want to change those sheets again. I had the best sex of my life on them."

"When? Last night?" she snapped, looking away so he wouldn't see the tears building in her eyes.

"Kenzie, look at me." When she didn't he yanked her by the waist and brought her to him. Then, tilting her chin up, challenged, "Look me in the eye and tell me you really believe I could be with another woman."

When she couldn't, Bren released her and began to pace. "That's what I thought. Hell, I couldn't think about another woman if I wanted to, let alone anything else. You consume my every thought, you're in my every breath, every beat of my heart is searching for the beat of yours."

Against her will, Kenzie's disillusioned heart began to melt. Hearing it out loud made her realize how ridiculous and petty she'd been. And jealous. That had been a first. Kenzie opened her mouth to speak, but Bren kept going. "Change the sheets?" he repeated. "Hell, I've hardly been in the bed! The last time I spent any time in that bed was with you."

"Bren—"

Stopping in front of her, he held up a hand. "I'm not done. Let's get something straight. The last time I made love was with you. The next time I make love will be with you. The time after that will be with you. Last time, next time, every time, you." He cupped her face in his hands and looked pleadingly into her eyes. "There will never be anyone else for me but you. Now and forever, there is only you." He feathered a kiss across her lips, tasting the tears running down her cheeks before brushing them away with his thumbs and gathering her in his arms as her body shuddered with sobs. He kissed the top of her head. "Okay?"

Swallowing the ache in her throat, Kenzie nodded into his chest. "I'm sorry I jumped to conclusions. It's unlike me to be so presumptive and impetuous."

"I'll take it as a compliment. I would have been outside my mind if the roles had been reversed," Bren admitted, pulling back. "But why were you at the lake to begin with? I thought you guys were in Coronado."

"Weather cancelled our flight on Friday and the ripple effect the rebooked one on Saturday." Kenzie gave him a sheepish smile. "I've been doing a lot of thinking. About you, about us. I missed you. I decided to surprise you."

He whisked away the hair that had fallen into her face. "I would have loved that. But where are the kids?"

"My parents were more than willing to take them. Especially when the my mom heard my plan."

Bren grinned mischievously. "My biggest fan. I heard your plan included a black dress and high heels."

"Miranda told you that?"

"Yes, among other things. Can we sit down? I have something to tell you while you're in a forgiving frame of mind."

Kenzie's stomach dropped as Bren led her to the deck table. "So Miranda is…"

"My agent, one of my oldest, dearest friends, someone without whom I wouldn't be where I am today and perhaps most relevant to the matter at hand, a lesbian," Bren said as they sat down.

Kenzie felt her jaw drop. "You're kidding."

"Trust me, there was a time when I wish I were. It just goes to show you can't judge a book by its cover." He paused, then finished with a grimace, "Which in my line of work is a bit of a paradox."

"I guess so. But that explains why she didn't seem the least bit threatened by me. If she was interested in you, the claws would have come out. I guess I was too blinded by jealousy to think it through."

"Now that we've cleared the air, I kind of like this side of you," Bren said with a smug smile, clasping her hands in his.

"Well, I don't. So don't get used to it."

"As long I get a raincheck on that outfit reveal. And you weren't the only one surprised to see Miranda. I woke up to her sipping coffee on my deck."

"But you said you and Miranda don't have that kind of relationship."

"We don't. We actually have an even more intimate one." Bren took a breath, blew it out through his nose. "I haven't talked about this in a long time, never really, so bear with me. You're about to join a very exclusive club. Only a handful of people know what I'm about to tell you. But first, do you trust me?"

"Bren, I know I overreacted before. It won't happen again."

He shook his head from side to side. "I don't mean that way. I'd like to think in your heart you knew you had my fidelity. I mean trust *me*. As a person, my integrity, my word."

"Yes, of course. I trust you around my children," Kenzie said and meant it.

"I appreciate that, and try to keep that in mind as I move through this, but this is different. I'm violating ironclad contracts, inciting civil litigation and risking financial ruin. Not just for me, but for Miranda as well. But none of that matters more than you. And just so you know, Miranda is on board with this."

Despite the warmth of the day, Kenzie felt a shiver run through her. "Okay."

"It's about what I really do, how I make my living. Who I am professionally."

"Well, you are a little vague about it. It has occurred to me that things don't add up, especially when I couldn't find anything you'd published."

Bren wagged his eyebrows. "Mackenzie Bishop, did you google me?"

"In the beginning. I'm sorry. I was curious. I—"

He cut her off with a kiss. "I'm flattered. And it's a logical assumption that my lifestyle is not supported by freelance work."

"That thought has crossed my mind," Kenzie admitted nervously, looking into the near distance. She couldn't imagine Bren would do anything illegal or unethical. But sometimes people aren't who they appear to be. And she'd only known him for two months...

"I'm a ghostwriter," Bren spit out.

Her gaze found his again. She wasn't sure what she'd expected him to say, but that was not it. "You're a ghostwriter?"

"Yes. I write books for a famous author."

"That's what this is all about? That's what you were afraid to tell me?"

"It wasn't that I was afraid. I couldn't, still shouldn't. But I want to spend the rest of my life with you and I don't want to base that life on a lie, even if it's only a lie of omission."

Kenzie laughed without opening her mouth. "Well, I have no leg to stand on there."

"That was different. That was a mistaken assumption on my part that got away from you. This is the kind of lie that breeds suspicion, mistrust, resentment. The kind that tears people apart. I can't risk that. I can't risk losing you. I was afraid I already had. I can't go through that again."

"I know the feeling." Kenzie leaned over and pressed a kiss to his lips. "But you don't have to prove yourself to me. I don't need to know about your work."

"It may not be up to you. Or me, for that matter."

Kenzie straightened up again. "Now I'm really confused."

"It's going around. This is a multi-faceted issue with a lot of moving parts. I was going to tell you about the ghostwriting eventually, but recent events have moved up the timeline. And raised the sakes considerably. I'll get to that in a minute."

Kenzie's eyes darted back and forth as she tried to keep up. "Okay."

"It's the reason Miranda is here, why she showed up at my door in the first place. Actually, she let herself in when I was asleep, but that's neither here nor there," he added lightly. "But I need to start by telling you who I write for."

"No, Bren, you don't," Kenzie protested. "I trust you, every part of you. It doesn't matter."

"It does and you'll see why in a moment." Bren pressed his lips together, took a breath as if searching for the words. "I write for Warren Holden, your father's favorite author."

Kenzie pulled her hand from his, brought it to her mouth. "Oh my God, Bren! You're one of the most renowned writers in the world."

"Thank you, but that's a matter of opinion. And I've only been writing for him for fifteen years or so. He was well-established long before I came along. Plus, there is often significant collaboration, depending on the project. But I've never met him."

"Thank you for telling me. And rest assured your secret is safe with me. But lots of famous authors have ghostwriters. What's the big deal?"

Bren's posture stiffened as his eyes grew distant, absent, almost catatonic.

Alarmed, Kenzie joined their hands again. "Bren, what is it? You're scaring me."

His eyes focused on her again and came slowly back to life. "I'm sorry. I haven't had a chance to process this yet and it's hitting me all of a sudden. But the real reason Miranda is here, why she flew all the way out here, was to tell me that Warren Holden isn't just my phantom author, he's my father."

*****

For some reason hearing himself say it out loud made it seem almost plausible. The realization washed over Bren as he stared unseeingly into Kenzie's eyes. The next thing he knew, she was jumping up and wrapping her arms around him. He pulled her down into his lap and buried his face in her hair.

"Bren, oh my God, Bren," she cooed.

Suddenly spent, Bren pressed his lips to her neck and drank her in. She smelled like freshly tilled earth and the shampoo from her shower. The relief that she still loved him, trusted him, wanted him, flowed through him, bringing tears to his eyes. He wanted to stay like this forever, basking in the sanctuary of her arms. He hadn't been held like this since he was kid.

She pulled back and laid the palms of her hands on his cheeks. "Do you want to tell me about it?"

He nodded. When she started to get up he drew her back down. "Can we stay like this while I do?"

"Yes, of course." With Kenzie's head against his shoulder, Bren recounted the conversation with Miranda.

"That's it? Just hearsay and rumors?"

"No, there's a folder full of proof."

"Well, what did it say?"

"I don't know. I didn't read it."

Kenzie reared up, stared at him in astonishment. "You didn't read it? Why?"

"All I could think about was getting to you, to explain. I was out of there like a bat out of hell."

She gaped at him, open-mouthed. "You just found out that your father has been in the periphery of your life, under the guise of your namesake author for years, and all you could think about was me?"

"Getting to you, yeah. And losing you. When you didn't answer, I was terrified it was too late. I don't know if any of this is true, but I know you are. Nothing else matters."

"Bren…" Kenzie muttered, bringing a remorseful hand to her chest. "I'm so sorry. I should have had more faith in you, in us."

"It doesn't matter now."

"Well, what about your mother?"

"My mother knows who I write for. She, Miranda, a couple of agency employees and now you are among the select few. She wouldn't have kept it for me. She doesn't know."

"Don't take this wrong, but how could she not?"

"She hasn't seen or heard from my father in over forty years. And their relationship was relatively brief from what I understand. She didn't follow Holden's career; she'd have no reason to since she knew the truth."

"But I can't believe she didn't recognize him somewhere along the line."

"He's never been one for the limelight. And attending a book signing or other such event is self-directed. Why would she go to something like that when she knew the truth? Unlike the talk show circuit an actor goes on before a movie premiers, promotions leading up a book's release tend to be faceless. The cover gets more press than anything else. And Holden isn't one to put his picture on the jacket. She would have no reason to make the connection, if there's a connection to be made."

"So what are you going to do?"

"I need to look at what Miranda has in that folder. If it pans out, I'll talk to my mom, work through it with her."

"And if it does, then what?"

Bren started on a sigh. "I haven't gotten that far yet. To be honest, I'm sort of numb to the whole thing. And I still don't know why anyone other than us would care about the paternity aspect of this coming to light. But if the ghostwriting comes out, it not only tarnishes Holden's reputation but jeopardizes how I make my living. Successful writers form a connection with their readers based on trust. Depending on how this goes, I might have just busted my ass for a book that will never be published."

"Or you'll finally get the credit you deserve and become a bestselling author in your own right."

"I doubt it, but thanks."

Kenzie didn't say anything for a long moment, then asked, "If it's true, would you want a relationship with him? Before it's too late?"

"Why? He certainly doesn't want one with me. I'd rather keep thinking of him as the asshole I never knew."

"But now you could know him. What if this was his roundabout way of looking out for you?"

"By hiding in plain sight? Not to mention leaving my mother high and dry."

"I get that. But I don't want you to regret this later."

"The only thing I'd regret is losing you."

Settling back in, she laid her head against him again. "I think we're good there."

"Jesus, what a day. It's not even noon and I feel like I ran ten marathons."

"It's probably the adrenaline rush wearing off. What can I do?" Kenzie asked, looking up at him.

"Can you just sit here with me for a while? Then I'll go home, deal with it all."

"I can do that, but it doesn't seem like nearly enough."

Bren stroked her hair. "It's everything. You're everything."

She tightened her grip on his middle. "Do you want me to go with you?"

"Thanks, but I need to figure this out on my own. And you'll have to get the kids at some point."

"I'm always here if you change your mind."

He kissed the top of her head. "I know."

Despite having slept for eighteen hours, Bren drifted off. When he woke, Kenzie was asleep against him. He dug in his back pocket, shimmied out his phone. Now it really was noon. He couldn't put it off any longer, he had to face this, come to grips with it one way or the other. And he would, but at the moment he was too content having the woman he loved asleep on his chest. A woman he'd all but asked to marry him. A woman, he now noticed, who wasn't wearing her rings, despite what she must have thought. That gave Bren hope. And the courage to do what he had to.

He didn't want or need a father at this point in his life, but he sure as hell wanted to be one. If Kenzie would let him, that is. She'd come to him, that was a good sign, a promising first step. So that would be his next order of business. A ring, a plan, a future. But first he had to get through this cannonade, try to salvage his and Miranda's careers, protect his mother from any collateral damage. Then he could get this monkey off his back once and for all and they could start writing that next chapter.

In the stillness of the backyard, Bren let his mind wander. If Warren Holden was his father and knew it, how long had he known? Had he kept tabs on him, even as a kid? And if so, why? He resisted the urge to google Holden W. Greer. Miranda would have whatever there was to be found waiting for him in that folder, all tied up in a bow. So he'd stay here for a little longer and enjoy the view he decided, tightening his arms around Kenzie again.

*****

When Bren got home two hours later, he found Miranda in the kitchen. The cabinet doors were flung open, their contents stacked on the counters. The washer and dryer were both cranking and every window in the house appeared to be open.

Hair up in a clip on the back of her head, Miranda turned and greeted him with a hopeful smile. She tossed the sponge she held in the sink and dried her hands on the dishtowel thrown over her shoulder. "Well, did we win?"

"We won," Bren confirmed.

"Yeah! It was the book wasn't it?"

"Actually, I forgot to give it to her. What's going on here?"

"I couldn't sit still, wondering if you were able to make this right. So I decided to do a little fall cleaning. Or spring cleaning. Or just cleaning."

"Thanks."

"So you kissed and made up?"

"Something like that. I'll spare you the details."

"Thank God for small favors."

"Miranda, I need to look at that folder."

She walked over to him, laid her hands on his shoulders. "We'll do it together. Like we have everything else."

Because his throat threatened to close, Bren cleared it. "You know, this doesn't change anything between us."

"It changes everything between us," Miranda disagreed lightheartedly. "But change is the only true constant in life. You have to change right along with it. So I'm taking care of you for as long as I can before I get replaced."

"I could never replace you. You know where all the bodies are buried."

"That I do. Let me show you what I dug up on another front."

They walked out to the deck. The folder was still in the middle of the table where Bren had dropped it. Miranda handed it to him. "Do you want to look at this alone first? Then talk about it?"

"No, unless you want to get to back to your stress cleaning."

"It'll be there."

They sat down next to each other and Bren opened the folder. The sheath of papers inside was separated into stacks held in place with different colored paper clips.

"Really?"

"I know, I know. I'm the poster child for anal-retentiveness," Miranda said, reading Bren's mind. She picked up the first set of papers, held together with a blue paper clip. "This is a timeline of sorts. In 1980 Holden W. Greer, who was working at an advertising agency, starts teaching a course at Sacramento State University. He was married with three children at the time."

"Okay."

Miranda removed the paper clip and flipped to the next page, then pointed to a flow chart. "This family tree—"

Bren curled his hand around Miranda's wrist. "I don't care."

"You don't care? Bren, you have siblings."

"Half-siblings," Bren corrected. "And maybe I do and maybe I don't. But either way, I don't know them and they don't know me. So I don't care."

Miranda started to say something, but swallowed it. "Noted. But it's all here if you change your mind."

"I won't. Besides, it looks more like a March Madness bracket than a family tree to me," Bren quipped.

Miranda was not amused. "You know, I spent a lot of time on this."

Bren blew his cheeks out, released the air along with Miranda's wrist. "I know. I'm sorry. Proceed."

"All right, that's more like it."

Miranda skipped through a couple of pages, then stopped on the last one. "Let's start with Mom. Claire Banks was enrolled at Sacramento State for the 1982 summer and fall sessions. She withdrew midway through the fall semester and did not return in the spring."

Bren's birthday was in April. "How did you get your hands on her transcript?"

"I didn't. This is part of what the entertainment reporter flushed out. And you don't need a transcript to confirm enrollment. But Mia did her own due diligence. Your mom was a straight-A student."

"Tell me something I don't know."

"I'm trying to."

"Fine."

"Greer teaches for a few more years, then takes a job at an advertising agency in San Francisco. He and his family relocate to Marin County and in 1989, he and his wife divorce."

"Warren Holden's first book series was set in San Francisco," Bren recalled out loud.

"Among others. He still owns a home in Pacific Heights." Miranda replaced the paper clip, flipped the papers over and put them facedown on the lefthand side of the folder. "It wasn't until the mid-nineties that Greer's publishing career really started to take off. He bounces around from publisher to publisher for a while until he finds a home with our very own Reardon and Powell. He adopts the pen name Warren Holden, reclaims the rights to his early titles and Reardon and Powell republish them under his pseudonym."

Bren still didn't know what all of this had to do with the cause du jour and it was starting to try his patience. "Can we just fast-forward a few decades and get to it?"

"No, we can't. And you'll understand why soon enough." Miranda grabbed another cluster of papers, held together with a yellow paper clip. "By this time, Greer has achieved enough success to write full-time for a living, but the *Crawford Chronicles* was the juggernaut that changed everything. Book One was his first bestseller and the subsequent titles in the series topped the charts. During that time, he also remarried and had another child."

"And I need to know all of this why?"

"You'll see." Miranda spread out the papers and used her index finger to illustrate. "His second wife is from the East Coast and as you might have guessed, is considerably younger. She wanted to raise the baby closer to her family, so they bought a home in Connecticut. Holden starts spending more time in New York, becomes interested in the business side of publishing, even considers starting his own imprint with his eldest son at the helm. Junior comes out for a visit and as luck would have it, mentions a short story he read in one of the airline magazines. The writing style reminded him of his father's work." Miranda paused and gave Bren a thin smile. "Thoughts?"

"I probably wrote those pieces seventeen, eighteen years ago."

"This was in the late-aughts from what I could piece together."

Tipping his head back, Bren rolled his eyes skyward. "Okay, now we're actually getting somewhere."

"Oh ye of little faith. Anyway, Junior found the story so intriguing he thought it had potential as a springboard for a book. In fact, the premise reminded him of the series Holden was developing."

Bren rubbed the back of his neck. "The *Foreigner* franchise."

"Yep."

"So how did we get here from there? None of this proves anything."

"I'm getting to that. The real purpose of Junior's visit wasn't to discuss running an imprint for his father. He and his siblings were concerned that Holden was overextending himself and it was aging him. By now he would have been in his seventies. Their mother had recently died and they didn't want a repeat performance. I think it was the son's idea to hire a ghostwriter."

"It was your idea."

"It was," Miranda conceded with a nod. "But great minds and all of that. It sounds like all of this went down not long before we approached Holden with the idea. That could be part of why he didn't put up much of a flight. And apparently somewhere in there the missus gave him an ultimatum. Workaholics, even rich ones, make terrible husbands. Remember that. Nobody wants to be that guy who gets divorced twice, especially at his age. No thinking woman would touch you after that."

"But what does all of this have to do with me? I mean, other than the obvious."

"I think Junior checked you out, vetted you. Before you went underground you and your work were easily accessible. Your web site was your resume. You were looking for work."

"Begging was more like it. But like Kenzie said, this sounds like a lot of hearsay and rumors."

Next to him, Miranda pulled back with a wide grin. "Kenzie, is it? Well, Kenzie is not only beautiful but smart."

"I already know that. What I don't know is where this DNA test comes in."

"One of Holden's granddaughters submitted the test with some friends for kicks. She asked her mother, Holden's daughter, about the results. Your name came up."

"How? I have very little family. Someone related to me would have had to do one of those tests too, right?"

"Right."

"I'm the only child of an only child."

"Yes, but your mother isn't."

Miranda tidied up the papers and moved on to the next stack, held together with a red paper clip. "Your grandmother had a sister who had children and each of them had children."

"Aunt Lucy. She was older than my grandmother and passed away several years before her. I remember my mother talking about her cousins, meeting them once or twice as a kid, but we were the only ones in California. They all lived in the Midwest."

"The power of technology knows no bounds."

"So one of those genealogy databases matched one of them to Holden's granddaughter?"

"Yes and eventually to you."

"How?"

"Legwork, hustle, process of elimination, social media mining and cross-checking. Your mother is connected with your cousins on several platforms." She pushed the paper over to him. "You'll need to get swabbed to confirm."

"I won't."

"Then don't. But all roads lead to Rome. I just wanted you to have all the information, be prepared, so you weren't blindsided. It's just a matter of time before it comes out—the ghostwriting, the paternity, all of it. Whether or not Holden lives to see it is the only question."

"I need to talk to my mother," Bren said, glancing down at the paper. Unlike the color-coded family tree Miranda had put together, this graphic looked more like the results of a blood test—tiered percentages and numbers separated into columns on a bar chart. Bren couldn't make heads or tails of it.

"You do and I'll leave you to it." Miranda stood. "I have a kitchen to put back together anyway." She started walking back into the house.

"Miranda."

She turned and met his gaze.

"Do you think he knew? From the beginning? And that's why he chose me?"

Miranda crossed her arms over her chest, tilted her head to the side. "*I* chose you. But I know what you mean. No, I don't, at least not at first. I think it was happenstance, fate, destiny, whatever," she finished on a shrug.

"But if it's true, he likely knew this whole time and didn't reach out to me."

She nodded sadly. "So it would seem. That's his loss more than yours, exponentially so. But maybe this was his roundabout way of looking out for you, the only way he knew how, after all this time."

"That's what Kenzie said."

Miranda's sympathetic frown became a broad grin. "I like this Kenzie. She sounds like the real deal."

"She's all that and more. I have excellent taste in women."

"You do indeed. And don't you forget it. You okay?"

"Yeah, it's just weird, you know? This monumental thing that could change everything feels like nothing."

"Give it some time. And remember, it doesn't change who you are or what you've accomplished. The proof's in the pudding there."

"Thanks."

"Now, call your mother and get that over with. We'll deal with the rest as it comes. And in the meantime, I have a feeling you have some ring shopping to do."

CHAPTER TWENTY-FOUR

Summer's electric-blue sky had been replaced by autumn's warm amber light as Halloween quickly approached. Between the drama surrounding Bren, school and baseball, Kenzie was just now putting out her fall decorations. She'd intended to tackle this yesterday, but had spent most of the morning on the phone with Emma and had only gotten the inside done. John retuned from deployment and had agreed to counseling as well as Alcoholics Anonymous. Emma was cautiously optimistic.

The movers had stacked the orange and black plastic bins in the garage as instructed. Kenzie needed a step stool to reach the last one and was walking into the house to grab it when she heard a car pull into the driveway. She changed course and reached it just as her mother stepped out.

"Mom." Kenzie greeted her with a hug. "What are you guys doing here?"

"We were in the area running errands and grabbed some lunch. I thought you might like something. I know you get busy during the day and don't take the time to eat." She handed Kenzie a white paper bag. "It's a chicken sandwich and coleslaw. I didn't think you'd want fries."

"Ah… thanks," Kenzie said as her father rounded the front of the car and joined them. "But the closest one of these is twenty minutes away," she pointed out, nodding to the logo on the bag.

"It's such a nice day we felt like taking a drive to see all the pretty fall colors," Jay readily explained.

Kenzie smelled a rat, but only said, "Got it. Do you want to come in?"

"Actually, we were wondering if today's a good day to pick up the kids after school for an end of the week treat. Mattie doesn't have practice tonight does he?"

"No," Kenzie replied. "But he has a science project due next week and we were going to shop for supplies this afternoon. And Katie is going home with Morgan after school. They're having a sleepover tonight. I dropped off a bag for her earlier."

"Now that you mention it, I remember Katie telling me about that." Sheryl paused as if for effect. "Here's an idea. How about we grab Mattie after school and take him shopping for the supplies? Send me the list. He can eat with us and spend the night. Then you're off the hook for dinner and can have a relaxing Friday night all to yourself."

Now Kenzie smelled two rats. She narrowed her eyes in suspicion as she looked from one parent to another. "Wow, we couldn't have planned that better if we'd tried."

"I know! Can you text Mattie to let him know and tell the school to put him in the car line? We have everything he needs for the night at the house."

"Sure thing, Mom."

424

"Well, we have another stop to make so we'll be on our way." Sheryl leaned in, kissed Kenzie's cheek. "Enjoy your lunch."

"I will. Thanks again."

"Bye, honey," Jay called, walking around to the driver's side of the car.

"Bye, Dad."

Kenzie looked on as Sheryl settled herself in the passenger seat. Just as Jay started the engine, she lowered her window. "The decorations look great. Are you almost done?"

"Yeah. Just one more box to open."

"Decorating the first year in a new place always takes longer. Now that you're not rushed, you can take a some time for yourself when you're done."

"Some time for myself?"

"Yeah. Take a nice long shower, get dressed, primp a bit."

"Ah, right, primp. For a relaxing night at home." Crossing her arms over her chest, Kenzie nodded slowly at her mother. "I just might."

"Great! Talk to you later."

"Bye," Kenzie called as they drove off. She didn't know what those two rats were up to, but she had a feeling it had something to do with Bren. In the month since the incident with Miranda, they'd seen each other a few times a week, but never alone. Sometimes he came over for dinner or the four of them went out. He'd come to some of Mattie's practices and all three of his games. Since Greg was coaching Mattie in Reno, Kenzie hadn't been up to the lake since that fateful night. Maybe that's what she'd do with her free evening—head up to Bren's. Not a surprise this time as she'd learned her lesson there. But she could finish up here, get ready and be there by six. They could have dinner and a little alone time. Yes, an end of the week treat was exactly what she needed, Kenzie thought with a roguish smile. And she knew just what to wear.

Reaching into her pocket, Kenzie retrieved her phone. First order of business was to text Mattie and let him know about the change of plans. He wouldn't see it until after school, but at least he'd understand why he was being put in the car line. She called the school and authorized the change, then called Bren. When he didn't answer, she texted him and asked him to give her a call.

Kenzie went through the last box of decorations and decided she already had enough displayed. She tidied up the garage, showered and dressed and had just finished applying her make-up when the doorbell rang. Phone at the ready in case Bren called back, she went to answer it.

But when she opened it she found none other than Bren standing on the other side. In a departure from his usual attire, he was wearing dress pants and a sport coat with an open-collared button-down shirt underneath. His face broke into an appreciative grin as he took her in. "Wow. I figured it was my turn to surprise you. But it looks like you beat me to it."

Before Kenzie could ask him what was going on he stepped inside. Kicking the door shut, he hooked her waist and brought her to him. Then he covered her mouth with his and kissed her like he'd never kissed her before. The kiss held more promise than passion, more affection than longing. It was familiar, yet somehow new, fresh, different. Like everything had changed between them while staying wonderfully the same. She felt herself fall in love with him all over again.

He pulled back with a final peck. "The dress looks beautiful on you, by the way. I plan to relieve you of it later, but thanks for wearing it."

"Bren, I called you to see if—"

"I know," he beamed, cutting her off. "I love it when a plan comes together. Let's get going."

"Get going where?"

"We're going on a date."

Now Kenzie smelled three rats. "I have to get my purse."

"You don't need your purse. You have your phone if anything comes up."

"But I need my—"

"You don't need anything. I have everything covered." Bren opened the door, then gestured with open palm. "After you."

Kenzie looked back into the house. "But I need to—"

"You don't need to do anything. Everything's taken care of," he told her, nudging her along and closing the door behind them.

Kenzie stepped outside to find her second surprise of the night—a stretch limousine parked in front of the house. A man in a black suit and tie wearing a chauffeur cap stood next to it.

"Bren, what's going on?" she asked, turning back to him.

"I'm taking you on a proper first date. We still haven't had one," he explained easily, taking her hand in his.

Butterflies filled Kenzie's stomach as she let him lead her down the walk. When they got to the limo the man opened the back door. "All set, Mr. Banks."

"Thanks, Tony."

The chauffeur tipped his cap at Kenzie. "Ma'am."

"Thank you." Kenzie said, sliding onto the cool leather seat.

Bren got in next to her. "Okay so far?"

"It's wonderful. Thank you."

"Champagne?" Bren asked, nodding to the bottle chilling in an ice bucket on the console between them.

"Ah, sure," Kenzie answered as the limo started moving.

Bren poured two glasses, handed one to Kenzie and then clinked his against it. "To us."

"To us." She took it sip. "Mmm, delicious."

"Mac gets all the credit there."

The rats had her woefully outnumbered. "Mac, huh?"

"He thought you'd like it."

"What's not to like?" Kenzie said around another sip. "But, Bren, what is all of this?"

"It's our first date."

"Is this how you treat all your first dates?"

"Only the ones I'm madly in love with," he replied with a silly grin.

Kenzie wondered how many times you could fall in love with someone in one night. Laying a hand on Bren's thigh, she leaned over and kissed him. "You don't have to woo me, you know. I'm already done for."

"All the more reason. I want to keep it that way." Bren paused, parted his lips as if he was going to say something else, but swallowed it. Instead, staring unblinkingly into her eyes, he skimmed his fingertips along her jawline and kissed her tenderly, deliberately, poignantly. And that was when Kenzie realized what was different. About the kiss, about tonight, about Bren. It was the future. She could see the future in his eyes, feel it in his touch, taste it in his kiss. It took Kenzie a full ten-seconds after he pulled back to catch her breath and steady the hammering of her heart. When she did she saw they were on Mt. Rose Highway.

"We're going up to Tahoe?"

"You haven't been able to make it up to the lake lately. It's such a pretty time of year in Tahoe. And I know the changing colors is one of the things you missed living away."

Kenzie didn't remember telling Bren that, but she did remember having that conversation with her mother on more than one occasion. Rats four, Kenzie zero. But deciding there was no harm in it, she replied graciously, "I have. Thank you for knowing that."

The hillsides came alive with the variegated colors of fall as they ascended the winding mountain road. Yellow and gold aspens shimmered vividly along side blazing red maples and mountain ashes aglow in orange and rust. Pink and purple wildflowers dotted the meadows amongst bowering willows stubbornly hanging on to their bright green leaves. Streaks of high-altitude mare's tail clouds scuttled the boundless blue sky on the telling autumn wind.

When they got to Incline, Kenzie assumed they were going to a restaurant but instead Tony veered toward Diamond Peak and drove up into the hills. The fluttering in Kenzie's stomach turned to hollowness when they pulled up in front of Bren's house.

"You know, I was planning on coming up here anyway. You could have saved yourself a lot of trouble and just called me back."

"Then Tony wouldn't have had anything to do tonight," Bren replied with a shrug.

Kenzie just shook her head on a sigh of laughter.

Tony exited the limo and opened the door, then offered his hand to help Kenzie out. The men exchanged a few words before Tony bid them good night and took his leave.

"After you." With an upward nod, Bren pressed his hand against Kenzie's lower back and aimed her toward the front door. When they got there it was immediately opened by a man with a silver-blond man bun and a weather-beaten face wearing black pants and a white dress shirt. He extended his hand in greeting.

"Good evening. You must be Kenzie. I'm Tom Callahan, an old friend of Bren's."

Kenzie shook his hand. "You own the restaurant in Tahoe City."

"Guilty. But tonight Backcountry is coming to you."

"Your Bloody Mary Burger was the best burger I've ever had."

"Thanks. I'll pass that along to the chef. But Mr. Deep Pockets here," Tom tipped his head at Bren, "has chosen a more upscale menu for tonight." Stepping back, Tom swung open the door and for what seemed like the hundredth time in the last hour, Kenzie lost her breath.

Bren's deck had been transformed into an elegant bistro. A round table draped in white linen and two Chiavari chairs stood in place of his wrought iron set. Candles burned in its center and china and crystal gleamed from its edges. Tableside a bottle of wine chilled in a shiny silver bucket. But as lovely as all of that was, it paled in comparison to the backdrop on which it sat. The sun was starting to set, saturating the basin in iridescent, cotton candy-colored light.

"Tahoe is known more for its romantic sunsets than its romantic restaurants," Bren said as they stepped inside. "So I decided to improvise. I hope it'll do."

"Oh, it'll more than do," Kenzie managed, turning to him. "But Bren, you didn't have to do all of this."

"I know. I wanted to, should have months ago. I missed so much time with you because I was so focused on the book, under so much pressure. And then with everything that's gone on lately…I want you to know that will never happen again. I'll never ignore you like that again."

"You didn't ignore me," Kenzie told him truthfully. "You were always there for me, for us."

"Not when that whole thing happened with Miranda. If only I'd heard my phone…"

"You were asleep."

"For eighteen hours straight because I hadn't slept in days, weeks really. I don't want to live like that anymore."

"That was an outlier, an exceptional period of time. It doesn't define you. Or us."

"No, *you* define me. I've been thinking a lot about that. And about time. Time stopped when I met you. It stopped again when I thought I lost you. I don't want to waste any more of it."

Just then Tom, who had made himself scarce, came in from the kitchen. "We're ready whenever you are, Bren."

"Give me a sec," Bren told him without taking his eyes off of Kenzie. "I had this whole thing planned— expensive wine, a romantic dinner, big swing at the end. But you don't care about any of that and I can't keep this inside for one more second." Bren reached into his jacket pocket and pulled out a small black box.

Intuition snuck in to join the hollowness in Kenzie's stomach, sending it flip-flopping. She sucked in a breath as Bren got down on one knee in the middle of the living room.

"I know this may seem fast. I know you said you needed some time. We don't have to get married right away if you say yes. I know you have the kids to consider. You can talk to them first, see how they feel about it. Or we can talk to them together in case they have questions for me. But I don't want them to feel like we're ganging up on them."

"Bren…" Kenzie said on a gasp.

"I know you've been down this road before. I know you and Matt had a good marriage. I'll try not to compete with that and still do my best to make you happy every day. I'm going to screw up sometimes. Tell me when I do so I don't keep doing it. But whether we make it official or not, or until we do, I'd like you to have this. I've noticed you haven't been wearing your rings lately, even around the kids. I know we haven't talked about this in certain terms, but I love you more each day and I know that's never going to change."

Kenzie opened her mouth to speak, but Bren kept going. "Endings make books. Make mine. Be mine. Marry me." He opened the box to reveal an octagon-shaped sapphire stone set on a white gold band surrounded by what had to be a hundred tiny diamonds.

Rendered speechless, Kenzie could only look between Bren and the ring in complete wonderment.

"I know it's not a traditional engagement ring, but the color reminded me of your eyes. And it's nothing like your other one. I thought that was a good thing. Even if you're not ready to give me an answer tonight, I'd like you have this and keep it until you are ready. And every time you look at it, I want you to remember how much I love you. But you can take as much time as you need."

"Bren, I don't—"

"In terms of living arrangements, I was thinking a mixed bag might be best," he barreled over her. "A yours, mine and ours type of thing. But whatever you think works best for the kids is fine with me. I can move to Reno and we can come up here on weekends, breaks. Or I can go back and forth as to not disrupt their routine." With a deep breath, he lifted the ring from its velvet pillow and took her hand in his. His was shaking as he looked up at her expectantly. "Kenzie, will you marry me?"

"No," Kenzie replied on a hitched breath.

"No?" Bren's face went slack, all the color drained from his face. His mouth fell open as he jerked back. He was turning away in incredulity when she grabbed his chin and brought him back to her. The hurt and disbelief in his eyes broke her heart. And told her everything she needed to know. She'd doubted him once, she wouldn't make that mistake again.

"Do you want to know why?"

"Nothing has to happen right away," Bren reiterated nervously as he scrambled to his feet. "And we can work out the living arrangements however you feel is best. I'm flexible."

"It's not that. Besides, Katie already has plans for a sleepover at your house," Kenzie told him mildly.

"She does?"

"Oh, yeah. And just wait until *Down and Dirty in Denmark* comes out with your name on it and you become a famous author overnight. That will only add to the appeal. You'll have to get back to me after the sleepover, see if that changes your mind about this whole thing."

"More like the bastard son of one. But at least I'll be credited as co-author in the small print."

"This time. For *Dusk at Dawn* you'll get top billing."

"I'll believe it when I see it. And I'm not going to change my mind. So, what's the problem?"

"Bren, I don't want any more children at my age."

"I know. I was kind of hoping you'd share the ones you already have with me."

"But your mother would never have grandchildren of her own."

"Can't she be in on the sharing? You can't have too many grandparents."

Beyond awed, Kenzie could only shake her head. "Yes, of course, but that's not all."

"What is it then? You wouldn't even have to change your initials."

"Well, if that's not reason enough."

435

"Kenzie, you're killing me here. We don't have to get married if you don't want to. But I just thought—"

"Well, you thought wrong," Kenzie interrupted, her voice taking on a superior tone. "You rent a limo, turn your deck into a candlelit restaurant, buy me a beautiful ring, tell me you love not only me, but my children. You enlist my parents' help, so clearly you've got their approval, not to mention that of my brother who endorsed you from the get-go. You're not only a kind, patient, handsome man but a successful one too. And comfortable in your own skin on top of it. But most importantly, I love you. I love you in a way I didn't think I'd ever get to experience. In fact, I think you knew I loved you before I did. Of course I want to marry you. I'd be a fool not to. But we do have one huge problem."

"What?" Bren bewildered on a weary breath.

"You must think I'm not very smart. You're giving me way too many outs." Kenzie held her left hand out in the air between them. "So ask me again, like you mean it."

With a full-body sigh of relief that had him dropping his chin to his chest, Bren looked down at the ring in his hand. Then he raised it to the tip of her third finger. "Kenzie, I love you more than I thought possible. Will you share your life with me, share your family with me? Will you do me the greatest honor of my life and marry me?"

"Yes, yes, yes!" She jumped into his arms before he could get the ring on. "I thought you'd never give me a chance to say yes! Thank you for loving me, for loving us, for letting me love you for the rest of my life. And for the best first date ever."

He lifted her up and swung her around. "Thank God. You had me worried there for a second."

"I'm sorry. I didn't mean to. I was in shock, happy shock, and then I couldn't get a word in edgewise."

"So you don't want to wait? To get married?"

"Not unless you do."

"Tomorrow wouldn't be soon enough for me," Bren told her, setting her down and slipping the ring on her finger.

Kenzie, nestled in Bren's arms, stared at the promise sparkling on her finger. And realized that she was happier than she'd been in...forever. So it was time to stop counting.

EPILOGUE

A bone-chilling wind bit and howled under a leaden sky raw with winter. Billowing whitecaps crashed against the shore with a vengeance in protest and denial, framing the lake in a pewter froth. Tahoe had a handful of days like this each year when it was too cold to snow and the basin's ceiling hung so low that the peaks on the eastern shore seemed to have gone the way of the sun.

To Bren's mind it was a perfect day for a funeral.

The dense grove of evergreens flocked with snow and encased in ice provided a makeshift shelter from the sting of the wind, but that wasn't why he'd chosen this spot. Bren was following the tried-and-true investment rule of last one in, first one out.

So far all was going according to plan.

Bren looked on as a tall, broad man in a black suit with hair matching the sky stood at a wooden podium in front of a shiny black casket. Bren couldn't make out what he was saying but he didn't really need to. His somber expression and tight-lipped frown told Bren everything he needed to know. He was flanked by a shorter man with salt and pepper hair also dressed in black and a statuesque brunette wearing a dark wool coat. Next to her stood a younger man dressed accordingly. She held his hand as the older man spoke.

United front. Nice touch.

The man finished speaking and stepped toward the casket, tapping the top of it with his hand twice as he walked by. The second man followed, knocking the bottom of his clenched fist against it a few times as he passed. The woman came next, kissing her fingertips before doing the same. Bringing up the rear was the younger man, who paused at the casket and bowed his head before walking over to a woman dressed in black sitting in the front row. He helped her up and led her out. The crowd stood and dispersed, the first two rows heading for the trio of limousines parked along the lane, others to the dozens of cars that lined it. Several men wearing sympathetic grins and dark suits hung back, waiting for the mourners to clear out before lowering the casket into the ground.

As they did, Bren turned to his mother. "Ready?"

"Ready."

"Let's go." Bren offered his arm and like any good son, escorted his mother out of his father's funeral. He couldn't wait to get home. His beautiful wife and two perfect kids were waiting.

The End

Christmas in Tahoe
by Martha O'Sullivan
(copyright 2022 by Martha O'Sullivan)

CHAPTER ONE

Laurel Reynolds always had a plan. For as long as she could remember, she went to bed knowing the next day's agenda. Even as a teenager—school, practice, hanging out with friends. College threw in studying, sorority activities and football games. Adulthood added work, domestic duties and social obligations. But now, for the first time in three decades of living, she had no idea what she was doing tomorrow, let alone the next day.

And she liked it.

But she was the only one. Her mother thought she'd completely lost her mind, her boss thought she needed an intervention and her best friend was convinced it was the divorce talking. And as Laurel watched the pastel haze suffuse the mountains and dusk fall over the lake, she had to admit that one had legs. Why, they had collectively argued, would the senior managing editor and heir apparent to publisher of *L.A. Digital* magazine, with a trendy apartment and a bright future, want to move to a sleepy little town in the mountains to write a novel.

Alone.

But that was all she wanted to do. Part of her had always wanted to be an author, but the rest of her, the practical, ambitious, realistic part, knew that was a pipe dream. It was nearly impossible to make a decent living as a writer in this day and age. She'd only landed the job she had because she'd fallen into a college internship, worked her ass off and stayed on after graduation for peanuts. Much of which had been facilitated by her ex-husband. She used to feel guilty about that; now she considered it paying it forward.

Laurel slowed her pace, anticipating the upcoming change in elevation. When she was a girl, the view from the curve on Lakeshore Boulevard wasn't as obstructed as it was now. Before the waist-high guardrail and sign prohibiting cell phone use, this had been her favorite part of the drive. She still remembered goosebumps erupting on her arms as the lake came into view. First it only teased, peering out from behind the forests of massive trees and panorama of snowcapped mountains. Then suddenly it emerged, a boundless expanse of cobalt blue, the crests of its waves gleaming like millions of tiny diamonds in the sunlight. And if Lake Tahoe could hold its own for millions of years, through droughts and wildfires, long, harsh winters and scorching hot summers, surely she could face her fear of failure and make something tangible out of the ideas that had been running amok in her head for what seemed like just as long.

By Christmas.

She found herself pulling onto the shoulder at the vista at the top of the hill. She got out of the car, zipped up her jacket and filled her lungs with the crisp, fresh mountain air. Walking to the lookout, she took in the lake with its rugged, rocky shoreline, the rows of bottle washer pines casting lengthening shadows over the water, the crashing of the waves in the evening wind. Resting her forearms against the rail, she took a few deep breaths, shut her eyes and indulged herself in the summers of her childhood. The scent of sunscreen melded with pine straw and cedar filled the air, wall-to-wall sunshine warmed her cheeks and sand, coarse and silty, coated her toes. Squeals of laughter rose up from the beach where children buried each other in the sand and watched as sandcastles were washed away in the afternoon drift. Boats zigzagged the lake, towing tubers and skiers as jet skis skirted the shore, leaving a trail of white in their wake. Her mother stood in ankle-deep water, a hand shielding her eyes from the sun, making sure Laurel didn't venture past the buoys. Every so often a melody floated through the air as if on butterfly wings, its harmony as familiar to her as the voice that carried it.

She opened her eyes, damp now, and returned to the present. Clusters of lights dotted the mountainside and the docks were illuminated from below, awaiting the handful of boaters who would be out at this hour this time of year. The sheet of azure glass that was Lake Tahoe at sunrise was long gone, giving way to a steady pounding as the lake settled itself in for the night. And that ebb and flow, as comforting to Laurel as a lullaby, took with it the last little bit of doubt that she was doing the right thing.

She'd rented a furnished house in town, something that had taken some wrangling and persuading on her part. Most single-family homes here only leased annually, were partial to locals and preferred to have some mutual acquaintance or common thread between the two parties. When offering to pay over asking didn't move the needle, Laurel pulled the nostalgia card and did a little name-dropping. After all, she'd spent many summers here as a child and wanted to return to her Tahoe roots. To those carefree, seminal, fundamental years on which she'd based her life. That, and oh, by the way, her grandmother was Ronnie Reynolds. And although the property manager didn't seem to be old enough to recognize the name, let alone appreciate the zeitgeist of Southern California in the seventies, Laurel had a feeling that the property owner was. In fact, she'd put money on it. She'd done her homework; she was a journalist after all. The little house on the corner of Village and Southwood had been owned by the same person since the sixties. A person who must treasure it enough to never have sold it in the last fifty years despite its value increasing tenfold. And that person was likely right around the age of someone who would appreciate the music and culture of Southern California in the seventies. In fact, it wasn't outside the realm of possibility that said owner had crossed paths with her grandmother or her mother back in the day, either here or in L.A. where he apparently lived. The leasing agent, her skepticism bordering on condescending, had finally agreed to humor Laurel and run the request by him.

So it had come as little surprise when she'd called back within fifteen minutes and in a considerably friendlier tone of voice, congratulated Laurel on securing the property for seven months at the advertised price and not a penny more. The only caveat was that the house was scheduled for some maintenance and repairs which likely wouldn't be completed until late May. That was fine, Laurel had insisted. She could put on her noise-cancelling headphones and escape into her writing hole, such as it was. By day's end, she had mailed a cashier's check for the deposit and signed an electronic lease beginning May first.

Which was tomorrow.

But for tonight she was treating herself to the best hotel in town, a nice dinner and a couple of glasses of wine. Straightening up, she took a bolstering breath, tapped the top of the guardrail in farewell and left the sunset behind. And she was still in that wistful state of mind when she arrived at the hotel ten minutes later. The lobby was an updated version of the way she remembered it, a refined, rustic decor of rich leathers and warm tapestries with lodge-themed rugs accenting the hardwood floors. Once in her room, she freshened up, changed into jeans and a sweater and headed across the street to the hotel's lakeside restaurant. She should be tired from the drive, but between the brisk evening air and the rush of making it to her intended destination, she felt more alive than she had in months. Her grandmother had always told her to listen to her gut, that anything was possible if she wanted it badly enough. And Laurel was about to see if Ronnie Reynolds was right about that too.

*****

McGovern Scott walked into Hues of Blue loosening his tie. The only thing he hated more than wearing a tie was wearing dress shoes. But he couldn't take those off, so he went with the lesser of two evils. Shoving the tie into the pocket of his suit coat, also among his least favorite things, he made quick work of the stairs. With an upward nod to the hostess indicating his intention, he made his way to the bar. Despite the calendar claiming it was shoulder season, the place was hopping. Whoever coined the phrase location, location, location must have done so here. Hues of Blue was the only lakeside restaurant and bar combination in town, with not only an upscale hotel but a high-end casino to boot. And the floor-to-ceiling windows with unparalleled views of Lake Tahoe didn't hurt.

There were a few empty stools scattered around the bar, but he set his sights on one at the far end, near the prep area and computer station. Not the most desirable spot to some, but it was close to the windows and he knew most of the staff, at least in passing. He'd spent the day with clients who had more money than he thought possible, so the idea of being around people more like himself was appealing. He'd barely settled himself in when a cocktail napkin followed by a beer in

445

a frosted glass appeared in front of him. He didn't have to look up to know Mac was working.

"Thanks."

"Gov," Mac greeted, sliding a plastic card through the reader on the side of the computer monitor and using a corner of it to tap the screen a few times. "I'll take the liberty of assuming it's a start-a-tab kind of night," he stated more than asked.

"What gave it away?"

"I bet there was a tie to go with that dress shirt and the suit looks almost as awkward on you as you probably feel in it."

"Hey," Gov mocked insult. He opened one side of the coat, proudly displaying the label.

Mac's dark gray eyes crinkled at the edges in amusement, accentuating the whiskers of time around them. "Big spender. What's the occasion?"

"Jack Brody is too damn good at his job, that's the occasion. We knock one teardown out of the park and suddenly he's the most popular contractor this side of Stateline. Dragging me to so many client meetings, I had to buy two new suits."

"Sounds like a good problem to have. How'd it go?"

"Oh, we got it," Gov told him with a good-humored snicker. "Who knew people could have not only three, but four homes, each one bigger than the other."

"So where's Mr. Wonderful tonight?"

"Probably halfway down the mountain by now." Gov took a sip. "New baby at home. I don't think things

446

could be going any better for the guy. I told him to buy a lottery ticket."

"Good to hear. Brodys are good people."

"Can't argue with you there," Gov said and meant it. "How have you been?"

"Busy. We've been short-staffed all spring. No one just comes for ski week and spring break anymore."

"Don't I know it. Didn't you tell me last summer that you were getting too old for the night shift?"

Now it was Mac's turn to snicker. "Yeah, well until I get too rich for it, I'll be working it." He laid a menu down in front of Gov. "I've got to make my rounds. I'll check back in with you."

Gov watched as Mac walked down the bar to greet a couple who'd just arrived, then went back to his beer. He grabbed his phone from his pocket and checked his texts, then scanned through his email messages. He was about to turn his attention to the menu, see if they'd changed it up any, when he saw her out of the corner of his eye. He actually felt his jaw drop, his head tilt slightly forward in wonder. Later, he would realize he was trying to decide what was most captivating about her. Was it the auburn hair, flowing just past her shoulders in long, loose curls? Her bright, infectious smile as she conversed with the waiter? Or was it her coffee-colored eyes dancing in the soft light against her flawless porcelain skin? Even with the distance between them, the chatter of the bar all around him, he could somehow make out her voice. Velvety, a little husky, yet inviting and warm. He looked on as she handed her menu to the waiter, then nodded in reply at his parting words. Gov was still in a state of awe when he realized that Mac had returned.

"What's the verdict?"

Gov turned back around and sent Mac a blank look.

"A little dinner to go with that beer? Which you've hardly touched, by the way. Usually the first one goes down pretty easy."

"Ah, yeah." Gov looked unseeingly at the menu. Then he handed it back to Mac. "Actually, surprise me."

Mac chuckled. "Since we both know the offerings by heart, that's not much of a stretch for either one of us." He stowed the menu behind the bar and took his leave.

But Gov was already focusing his attention back to the redhead. From his vantage point at the bar, he had little more than a profile view of her. He couldn't imagine how beautiful she must be face-to-face when she looked this mesmerizing from the side. By now there was a glass of wine sitting on the high-top table in front of her. He watched as she intermittently sipped it and tended to her phone, her lips curving upward every so often as she typed.

Gov couldn't remember the last time he'd found himself so starstruck by a woman. He loved looking at women, no doubt about it, but just the sight of her actually *did* something to him, *moved* something in him. Like some mechanism he'd never known was there had been triggered. And he wanted to keep it on.

Mac was nowhere to be found, so Gov got the attention of a passing waiter. Five minutes later Mac reappeared with a glass of wine in his hand and a confused look on his face.

"Did you order this?"

"Yes, I did," Gov replied readily, taking the glass from Mac and sliding off the bar stool. "Keep my dinner warm, will you?"

He felt Mac's gaze on his back as he made his way through the bar. Once he reached the woman he'd planned to give himself a moment to take her in, to selfishly indulge himself in her beauty, but she lifted her chin and gave him a curious look the second his shadow crossed her. He started to speak, flash that smile he'd been told was disarming, but froze. He prided himself on being smooth with women, cool under pressure, in control of any situation. But for some reason his tongue was tied and his mouth was unable to form enough syllables to string a sentence together. His eyes were working just fine though; he simply couldn't take them off of her. He'd been right; she was even more stunning up close. The begging to be touched curls accentuated her high cheekbones and her doe-like eyes were soulful and deep-set behind thick lashes. Her mouth was heart-shaped and just pouty enough to be sexy. And right now it was broadening into a nonplussed, closemouthed smile. She was staring at him, eyebrows raised in anticipation and head cocked to the side inquisitively.

Finally, Gov heard himself say, "I thought you could use a refill." He set the glass of wine down on the table next to her half-empty one.

"Ah, thank you," she said, without taking her eyes off of him.

She wasn't going to make this easy. "May I join you?"

She exhaled a short breath of contemplation, then gestured with open palm to the chair across from her. "Sure."

Gov couldn't believe how happy that made him. He took a seat, setting the beer he'd forgotten he was holding down on the table. Now that they were one-on-one, he could see the tiny flecks of gold in her sable eyes, the splattering of freckles that dotted her nose, the subtle plumpness of her bottom lip. He could also see, as she cupped the glass in both hands and fidgeted her fingers a bit, that she wore no rings. He extended his hand. "McGovern Scott."

She offered hers across the table in kind, holding his eyes in hers all the while. Her soft, small hand fit perfectly into his. "Laurel Reynolds. Nice to meet you."

"The pleasure is all mine, Lauren."

She opened her mouth slightly as if to say something, but swallowed it. Instead, she took a sip of wine. "Hmm. Lovely. You have excellent taste."

"So I'm told. The waiter said you ordered the best Cab they had by the glass."

She slanted her head to the side. "I did. And this isn't it."

"No, it isn't. It's one of their signature reds. From a small vineyard in Amador County."

She thought about that for a moment. "And it's a Cab, not a Zin? From Amador?"

"Someone knows her varietals," Gov said, impressed. "It's actually a Barbera. The owner of the vineyard frequents the restaurant when he's in town. They usually keep some on hand for him."

She nodded at that, as if she understood how such things worked. Just as she finished another sip, the hostess appeared. "Ma'am, your table is ready." She glanced briefly at Gov, then back to Lauren. "Dinner for one, correct?"

"Yes," she confirmed, rising. Now Gov could take in the full-length of her, from the neckline of her sweater that showed just enough cleavage to make his mouth water, to the narrow indentation of her waist and the willowy curve of her hips. He had to stop himself from grunting appreciatively as he stood.

She picked up the glass he'd brought her and with a polite smile said, "Thanks again for the wine."

"My pleasure. Enjoy your dinner." He'd intended to ask for her number—after all she'd accepted the drink, wore no rings and was dining alone. But before he knew it she was gone, being led through the bar toward the restaurant. All Gov could do was watch as she walked past the stone hearth and then disappeared behind the mahogany doors at the far end of the room. He stood there for a long moment, still a little thunderstruck, until he heard someone ask if he was leaving. Shaking off the reverie, he answered accordingly, grabbed his beer and returned to the bar. There he found Mac and a fresh draft waiting for him.

"Well, that was short and sweet," Mac commented.

"Yeah," Gov grumbled, finishing the beer in his hand in one long pull and setting the glass on the bar, then sitting down. "They're a little too efficient at turning tables in the restaurant tonight."

Mac laughed without opening his mouth. "Just your luck. Probably scored some points with the Barbera, though. You're welcome, by the way. I opened a bottle for you."

"Duly noted. Ms. Reynolds seemed quite impressed. From the ten-seconds or so I got to spend with her," he replied with a derisive snort.

Mac nodded speculatively. "I thought that might be her."

Gov, about to take a sip from the second beer, froze. "You know her?" he astonished.

"Not personally. Well, I knew her as a kid when they used to spend summers up here."

Gov put the beer down. "They?"

"I know I've got a solid three decades on you, but tell me you've heard of Ronnie Reynolds."

"I have not."

Mac shook his head in disappointment. "You're breaking my heart, man. Singer, songwriter, activist back in the seventies and eighties? She passed away not long ago. That's got to be her granddaughter, all grown up. Looks just like her."

The name didn't even begin to ring a bell. "And you knew her?"

"Everybody knew everybody around here then. I'd just gotten sober, Ronnie wanted to get sober. So she bought a place up here to get away from L.A. for a while. She sang a little in the clubs—Crystal Bay, the CalNeva—to keep her toe in it, make some money. That's probably why it took her a couple of tries to get clean. She didn't have a support system or enter a program like I did. She had too many enablers for that, too much at stake for too many people. In the end it was the granddaughter who did the trick. Veronica wouldn't let her near the kid otherwise."

"Veronica?"

"Ronnie's daughter. Ronnie was married, albeit briefly, to Garry Reynolds, a big music producer in the sixties and seventies. I always got the impression that it was more of a merger than a marriage, but whatever it was, it produced a daughter, Veronica. He died in a plane crash years ago."

"What happened to the daughter?" Gov asked, oddly fascinated.

"She got caught in the growing up rich and famous trap. That's another reason Ronnie came up here. To get her daughter out of L.A., give her a shot at a normal life. But Veronica ended up pregnant anyway. Turned out to be the best thing that ever could have happened to either one of them, though. Gave them a common purpose, an incentive for Ronnie to get sober and a reason for Veronica to straighten up."

"So what happened to them?"

"Once Ronnie got sober she realized her days on stage were behind her. She had terrible stage fright. She'd have to be buzzed to perform in front of people. But she could write songs and record them in the privacy of her own studio sober as a judge. So she concentrated on that, helped her daughter raise the girl, did a lot of charity work. Stopped spending summers up here about fifteen years ago now, only came up every so often and then rarely. Veronica took over most of the philanthropy work after Laurel grew up and Ronnie's health started to deteriorate."

"Do they still have a place here?"

Mac shook his head. "Most of those quaint little houses are gone now, replaced by the multimillion dollar mansions that make up the lakefront side of Lakeshore between Country Club and Tahoe Boulevard."

"I wonder what she's doing here?" Gov asked himself as much as Mac.

"I couldn't tell you. Maybe feeling nostalgic or just passing through."

Gov was about to voice his vote for the former when his dinner arrived, ending the conversation.

"How'd I do?" Mac asked, as if he already knew the answer.

Gov looked down. "Bison. A little pricey, but an excellent choice."

"I figured you earned it today. Enjoy."

"Thanks. And thanks for the info. You're a wealth of information as usual. But just so you know, it's

Lauren," Gov informed him, unwrapping his napkin and silverware. At Mac's confused expression he clarified, "Ronnie Reynolds' granddaughter. Her name is Lauren, not Laurel."

Mac, who had been about to walk away, turned to face Gov again. "If that was Ronnie's granddaughter, and I'd bet my bottom dollar that it was, her name is Laurel. I think some of your more primal senses might have kicked into overdrive and compromised your hearing."

Gov knew what he'd heard, but he wasn't going to argue with Mac. "If you say so."

"Oh, I do," Mac maintained assuredly. "I've never heard of any songs written in Lauren Canyon, have you?" With raised eyebrows and a glimmer in his eye, he left Gov to his dinner.

Gov could only watch him walk away, speechless for the second time that night.

Christmas in Tahoe is available digitally and in paperback at online retailers everywhere.
Direct links at marthaosullivan.com